TUNE IN, TURN ON, BLOW UP

Wouldn't a cheap, extremely energy-dense storage device be wonderful? No need for costly central generators, or massively expensive and wasteful distribution systems. No need to burn petroleum in hugely inefficient auto engines ... a rebirth of real individual self-sufficiency would be possible. But wait. An economy, a social structure, a way of life has been built on the simple fact that electricity cannot be stored cheaply in quantity. Pull out that rug, and what might fall ...

POWER

EDITED BY

S.M. STIRLING

BAEN
BOOKS

POWER

Copyright © 1991 by S.M. Stirling

A Baen Books Original

Baen Publishing Enterprises
P.O. Box 1403
Riverdale, N.Y. 10471

ISBN: 0-671-72092-9

Cover art by Doug Anderson

First printing, November 1991

Distributed by
SIMON & SCHUSTER
1230 Avenue of the Americas
New York, N.Y. 10020

Printed in the United States of America

ACKNOWLEDGMENTS

Introduction, by S.M. Stirling. Copyright © 1991 by S.M. Stirling.

Snowball, by Poul Anderson. Copyright © 1955 by Quinn Publishing Company; copyright renewed 1983 by Poul Anderson. First appeared in *If*, May 1955.

MHD, by Ben Bova. Copyright © 1987 by Ben Bova. First appeared in *Battle Station*, by Ben Bova.

. . . And Check the Oil . . . , by Randall Garrett. Copyright © 1958 by Street & Smith Publications; copyright renewed 1986 by Randall Garrett. First appeared in *Astounding Science Fiction*, October 1958. Reprinted by permission of the Estate of Randall Garrett.

Tinker, by Jerry Pournelle. Copyright © 1975 by UPD Publishing Corporation. First appeared in *Galaxy*, July 1975.

Fusion Without Ex-Lax, by Jerry Pournelle. Copyright © 1976 by UPD Publishing Corporation. First appeared in *Galaxy*, October 1976.

Originals, by Pamela Sargent. Copyright © 1985 by Pamela Sargent. First appeared in *Universe 15*. Reprinted by permission of the author and her agent, Joseph Elder.

Hot, Cold, and Con Fusion, by Isaac Asimov. Copyright © 1990 by Nightfall, Inc. First appeared in *Fantasy & Science Fiction*, January 1990.

Roachstompers, by S.M. Stirling. Copyright © 1989 by S.M. Stirling. First appeared in *New Destinies VIII*.

CONTENTS

Fusion Energy and Civilization
S.M. Stirling

Humans have always depended on fusion power; the terrestrial biosphere is powered by that great big un-shielded reactor in the sky, spitting out radiation at us ... why, it's the primary cause of skin cancer ...

More seriously, the natural condition of any closed system in our universe is towards maximum entropy, a situation where all energy is evenly diffused and no motion can take place. Evolution—the increasing complexity, order and specialization of life—can occur only because Earth is *not* a closed system. Sunlight rains down on it continuously, and radiates away, maintaining the energy gradient on which all life depends.

In human terms: the *upper* limit on the standard of living, the leisure, and the public morality of any society is set by the amount and degree of concentration of the energy available.[1] Our remote hunter-gatherer ancestors had a rather lavish amount of energy available, because they were so few in relation to the Earth's surface and so skilled at making use of the biological energy-collec-

1. There is no lower limit.

tors known as plants and animals. Recent studies have shown that before they were pushed into marginal areas by herders and farmers, hunter-gatherers could make a good living with as little as three or four hours of work a day, leaving the rest free for fighting, singing, making ornaments, performing ceremonies or just lazing around the fire and meditating. A lifestyle many contemporary urbanites might envy, at least in a warm climate! The hunter-gatherers were also healthier than their peasant descendants, being less crowded and more prone to washing.

This leaves the vexed question of why humans invented agriculture at all. One current theory holds that it was done to enable the cultivation of barley for beer . . . The answer, I feel, is again one of power. For the bulk of humanity, agriculture represented a step *down* the food chain. It meant that humans ate, essentially, grass and tubers—a diet which represented a more diffuse source of energy than meat. The wheat, rice and potatoes which provided the bulk of the peasant's diet mostly served as fuel for the production of more grains. Grinding, day-in, day-out toil became the lot of the overwhelming majority of humans, along with crowding, squalor and disease. Our primary religion remembers it as the expulsion from Eden: "In the sweat of your brow shall you earn your bread."

But for the *elite* of peasant-based societies, agriculture represented a wonderful concentration of solar fusion power . . . at the expense of the peasantry. Farms and their attendant peasants served to collect the diffuse energy, which was further concentrated—often on the backs of the peasants—in cities and manors. From this surplus the aristocrats were fed, and their hangers-on: soldiers, priests, scholars and bureaucrats, specialized artisans. Despite entropy, you *can* get more out of a system than you put in, as long as somebody else gets *less*. The colloquial version of the Three Laws of Thermodynamics states: "You can't win, you can't break even, and you can't get out of the game." You can, however, cheat.

The State was a product of this agricultural revolution, and once launched it had an irresistible tendency to spread, for the simple reason that no hunting people could rival its concentrated military power and dense population. In terms of horsepower per acre, it was vastly more efficient than hunting and gathering—although vastly *less* efficient in terms of energy available per person-hour of labor.

From this springs the stony cruelty of early agricultural civilizations, their utter indifference to human life and pain; the inscriptions of the Assyrian kings, boasting of whole cities flayed alive, the sadomasochistic *grand guignol* of the Roman arena, the slave children driven to die in the silver mines of Laurion to sustain the glory of Periclean Athens. This slaughterhouse century of ours has seen mass wickedness enough, but this has represented a (hopefully) temporary falling-away from grace. The cruelty of the preindustrial era was *necessary*, for without an utterly oppressed and exploited peasantry there was simply no surplus for cities, books, a leisure class. From the viewpoint of the overwhelming majority, the structure of civilization was a mechanism for grinding bread out of their bones. As a Dorian aristocrat of Crete said:

I have great riches, spear and sword
    And rawhide shield at my breast
My land is ploughed, my harvest stored
    The sweet wine from the vintage pressed
The peasant trash has learned its Lord
By the spear and sword.

And all who dare not walk with spear
    And sword and rawhide fluttering
Must needs kiss my feet and cling
    And cowering in their fear hail me
"Lord" and "Great King."

This parasitism was in turn self-reinforcing; the upper classes were uninterested in production since their specialty was extracting the maximum surplus from their subjects, while the producers were quite rightly convinced that any improvements they made would simply be appropriated by their social superiors. For six thousand years after the basic neolithic breakthrough, innovation in the basic technologies of production was glacially slow. What progress there was tended to be in the fields of administration and military technique, rather than agriculture, or in extensions of scale. Kings and emperors built glorious cities, with peasant forced labor; fought wars of increasing size and sophistication, over the backs of their peasants; their scribes learned better and better methods of record-keeping, so that the surplus might be more efficiently gathered; dams and irrigation schemes were dug so that more tax- and rent-paying serfs could live lives of animalistic squalor and brutality. In fact, as erosion, population growth, and salination reduced the carrying capacity of the core areas of agriculture, standards of living had a long-term tendency to *fall*.

The parasitic nature of early civilizations also made them unstable. They represented a tiny peak on a huge mass of illiterate poverty. When their overlords reached the point of no longer being able to trust any substantial portion of their subjects with arms, tribal peoples from beyond the frontier of city-and-peasant culture could overcome them; for the bulk of the population, a "Dark Age" could represent a temporary relief. As in a crystalline substance that has two phase-states, peasant economies could support either a bureaucratic empire or a decentralized, slightly less oppressive but barbarian alternative. In the long term, the pressure of war and its economies of scale always began the process of empire anew. Once an area had reached the maximum that could be achieved with the classic means—iron tools, walled cities, paper and a literate scribal class—it tended to fluctuate in place, the long "middle passage" of human history. Kingdoms and empires and religions came and went, but the basic structure remained unchanged. And the limiting factor was energy.

But humanity was lucky. Out on the western extremity of the Eurasian supercontinent, an exception arose: Western civilization. As early as the 9th century A.D., the peoples of Western Europe were making more use of inanimate sources of energy, principally water and wind power. Earlier civilizations had known of them, but made only sporadic use of them; by the High Middle Ages tens of thousands of water and wind mills were scattered all over Europe. Grinding grain, eliminating the killing labor that Homer's heroes blithely assigned to their slave-women; fulling cloth, sawing wood and stone; every groaning wooden wheel represented one less whip-mark laid on a human back. Improvements in agriculture occurred at the same time, better plows, the substitution of horses for oxen, more productive rotations. And significantly, this was the first era to make widespread use of the highly-concentrated fossil fuels, solar energy gathered over millions of years. The intellectual innovations of the West, individualism, rationalism, the prescient scientific optimism of men like Roger Bacon, built on this foundation.

By the Renaissance, Europe had the first cities in world history that traded mass-consumption goods for their food rather than extracting it at swordspoint. The standard of living had improved to the point where humble folk could add bacon to their porridge once a week, and there was a broad stratum of not-so-humble bourgeois. Not aristocrats, nor luxury artisans and traders catering to landlord demand, but a literate and self-confident middle class, perhaps the first such large class in human history. The same period saw the abolition of serfdom west of the Elbe, because for the first time there was a society productive enough not to need forced labor. Not that there was much luxury or leisure among the wage-laborers and tenant farmers of early modern Europe, but a threshold had been passed: a threshold of available *per capita* energy. Life need no longer be a zero-sum game, if humans chose otherwise.

The series of historical accidents that led to the Industrial Revolution preserved this fragile beginning, saved it from petering out into a Chinese-style high-level equilibrium trap. Most of the technologies that made the Revolution were imported from the Orient, but in China they were introduced gradually, without disruption. The pressure of population and the massive conservatism of the Mandarin-landowner scholar-bureaucrats made sure that the population growth swallowed up all the increased productivity. This is a much-needed reminder that human beings do not embrace change and growth naturally; change always menaces strong vested interests, whether those are material or ideological/religious. It is almost always easier to maintain the status quo. Western Europe's structure of quarreling nation-states probably had much to do with maintaining the momentum of change; since a state that fell behind would be devoured by its neighbors, its elite had a direct personal interest in increased efficiency.

Even more important was the competitive commercial system; the economic war of all against all generated a razor-keen appreciation of comparative costs. The unique circumstances of 18th-century Britain then produced a series of crucial innovations in the use of stored solar-fusion energy (coal, and then oil) that allowed, for the first time in history, the widespread use of energy sources more concentrated than sunlight; sources that it seemed could be expanded infinitely and applied to every form of human economic and military use. The sheer *power* these innovations produced was irresistible, and forced every neighboring state to follow suit, however much violence was done to hallowed social orders and ways of life. Even the closely similar societies of Western Europe had a generations-long struggle to adapt, for the innovations were not free; they required a wholesale adoption of the worldview and social structure that had produced them. Even in our own time, many peoples—Iran would be a good example—are convulsed by the contradictory forces of modernization and outraged tradition.

With fossil-fuel-based industry, humanity was liberated from the Neolithic paradox of progress built on slavery. Growth became exponential. By the 20th century the standard of living of the masses in the advanced countries had risen back to the level of their hunter-gatherer ancestors, and then surpassed it—*without* sacrificing any of the advantages of civilization. A high culture had become a good deal for the bulk of humanity, something without precedent, and the realization that poverty was not inevitable began to sink into the collective consciousness of the human race.

The concept of "progress" is an outgrowth of this realization. Yet this century has also shown how fragile this achievment is; science fiction has been ringing changes on the post-holocaust barbarian world for fifty years. More ominous than the risk of self-annihilation is the simple fact that we are living on the planet's capital. Fossil fuels are limited: at present rates, we have only a few centuries' worth, and this does not allow for growth. Worse still, the energy densities available are not enough for us to control the environmental consequences of our industrialization. With sufficiently cheap energy, pollution would become a thing of the past; at *current* levels of energy usage, this is impractical. Most of our species is still locked in the subsistence-agriculture trap, and simply extending the First World system of coal- and petroleum-fueled industrialism to them would probably destroy the planet.

This knowledge is the specter at the feast of progress, now that Western civilization is overcoming the self-inflicted wound of 1914 and its consequences. The so-called "soft" path is nothing more than a return to the animalistic misery of preindustrial times; sunlight is simply too *diffuse* to maintain even the present level of world consumption. Hard, concentrated energy is the essential prerequisite for an economy like ours; conservation and increased efficiency merely delay the problem without solving it. Restricting growth in output means a boot in the face of the world's have-nots; it means freezing the current distribution of wealth, a tiny island of comfort on a swelling mound of resentful pain; eventually, it means impoverishing everyone.

Nobody will consent to be poor, and nobody will give up anything, whatever the fantasies of the spoiled, rich, white city people who make up the constituency of the "limits to growth" and "Earth First" movements. The neo-Luddites imagine a future of organic vegetables and hand-woven rugs; the reality of their policies would be a mad-dog scramble between nations, classes and races over scraps of water and fuel and food, a global Beirut. Followed by restabilization right back in the post-Neolithic norm of human history, a society of starving peasants ruled by bandits, perhaps with a few high-tech trinkets for the elite. The ability to tap near-infinite supplies of concentrated non-organic energy gave us a glimpse of a world where life was not a zero-sum game, and it was possible to have affluence and culture without being a predator on other human beings. To maintain that vision and extend it to all we need something more: we need more than that one fusion reactor up in the sky. The knowledge is there. What we need is the will.

Science fiction can show us the possibilities of . . . *power!*

The cost and availability of energy is directly related to how easily and efficiently it can be stored. Electricity is the perfect means for transmitting energy, with one terrible exception: it is difficult and very costly to store on any large scale. Even the diffuse and unreliable energy of sunlight can be tapped through solar cells or falling water; it is the costly and limited means of storage and concentration *that render it unsuitable for widespread use.*

"Snowball" was written in the '50s, but it remains a highly relevant example of science fiction's strength—the human impact of a basic technological change. (And prescient: note the husband-and-wife physics team.) Wouldn't a cheap, extremely energy-dense storage device be wonderful? No need for costly central generators, or massively expensive and wasteful distribution systems. No need to burn petroleum in hugely inefficient auto engines . . . a rebirth of real individual self-sufficiency would be possible. But wait. An economy, a social structure, a way of life has been built on the simple fact that electricity cannot be stored cheaply in quantity. Pull out that rug, and what might fall . . .

Snowball
Poul Anderson

It did not come out of some government laboratory employing a thousand bright young technicians whose lives had been checked back to the crib; it was the work of one man and one woman. This is not the reversal of history you might think, for the truth is that all the really basic advances have been made by one or a few men, from the first to steal fire out of a volcano to $E = mc^2$. Later, the bright young technicians get hold of it, and we have transoceanic airplanes and nuclear bombs; but the idea is always born in loneliness.

Simon Arch was thirty-two years old. He came from upstate Massachusetts, the son of a small-town doctor, and his childhood and adolescence were normal enough aside from tinkering with mathematics and explosive mixtures. In spite of shyness and an overly large vocabulary, he was popular, especially since he was a good basketball player. After high school, he spent a couple of tedious years in the tail-end of World War II clerking for the Army, somehow never getting overseas; weak eyes may have had something to do with that. In his spare time he read a great deal, and after the war he entered M.I.T.

with a major in physics. Everybody and his dog was studying physics then, but Arch was better than average, and went on through a series of graduate assistantships to a Ph.D. He married one of his students and patented an electronic valve. Its value was limited to certain special applications, but the royalties provided a small independent income and he realized his ambition: to work for himself. He and Elizabeth built a house in Westfield, which lies some fifty miles north of Boston and has a small college—otherwise it is only a shopping center for the local farmers. The house had a walled garden and a separate laboratory building. Equipment for the lab was expensive enough to make the Arches postpone children; indeed, after its requirements were met, they had little enough to live on, but they made sarcastic remarks about the installment-buying rat race and kept out of it. Besides, they had hopes for their latest project: there might be real money in that.

Colin Culquhoun, professor of physics at Westfield, was Arch's closest friend—a huge, red-haired, boisterous man with radical opinions on politics which were always good for an argument. Arch, tall and slim and dark, with horn-rimmed glasses over black eyes and a boyishly smooth face, labeled himself a reactionary.

"Dielectrics, eh?" rumbled Culquhoun one sunny May afternoon. "So that's your latest kick, laddie. What about it?"

"I have some ideas on the theory of dielectric polarization," said Arch. "It's still not too well understood, you know."

"Yeh?" Culquhoun turned as Elizabeth brought in a tray of dewed glasses. "Thank'ee kindly." One hairy hand engulfed a goblet and he drank noisily. "Ahhhh! Your taste in beer is as good as your taste in politics is moldy. Go on."

Arch looked at the floor. "Maybe I shouldn't," he said, feeling his old nervousness rise within him. "You see, I'm operating purely on a hunch. I've got the math pretty well whipped into shape, but it all rests on an unproven postulate about the nature of the electric field. I've tried to fit it in with both relativity and quantum mechanics and—well, like I said, it's all just a notion of mine which demands experimental proof before I can even think about publishing."

"What sort of proof?"

"It's this way. By far the best dielectric found to date is a mixture of barium and strontium titanates. Under optimum conditions, the dielectric constant goes up to 11,600, though the loss rate is still pretty high. There's a partial explanation for this on the basis of crystal theory, the dipole moment increases under an electric field ... Well, you know all that. My notion involves an assumption about the nature of the crystalline ionic bond; I threw in a correction for relativistic and quantum effects which *looks* kosher but really hasn't much evidence to back it up. So—uh—"

Elizabeth sat down and crossed trim legs. She was a tall and rather spectacular blonde, her features so regular as to look almost cold till you got to know her. "Our idea suggests it should be possible to fit a crystalline system into an organic grid in such a way that a material can be made with just about any desired values of dielectricity and resistivity," she said. "Constants up in the millions if you want. Physically and chemically stable. The problem is to find the conditions which will produce such an unorthodox linkage. We've been cooking batches of stuff for weeks now."

Culquhoun lifted shaggy brows. "Any luck?"

"Not so far," she laughed. "All we've gotten is smelly, sticky messes. The structure we're after just doesn't want to form. We're trying different catalysts now, but it's mostly cut and try; neither of us is enough of a chemist to predict what'll work."

"Come along and see," offered Arch.

They went through the garden and into the long one-room building beyond. Culquhoun looked at the instruments with a certain wistfulness; he had trouble getting money to keep up any kind of lab. But the heart of the place was merely a second-hand gas stove, converted by haywiring into an airtight, closely regulated oven. It was hot in the room. Elizabeth pointed to a stack of molds covered with a pitchy tar. "Our failures," she said. "Maybe we could patent the formula for glue. It certainly sticks tightly enough."

Arch checked the gauges. "Got a while to go yet," he said. "The catalyst this time is powdered ferric oxide— plain rust to you. The materials include aluminum oxide, synthetic rubber, and some barium and titanium compounds. I must admit that part of it is cheap."

They wandered back toward the house. "What'll you do with the material if it does come out?" asked Culquhoun.

"Oh—it'd make damn good condensers," said Arch. "Insulation, too. There ought to be a lot of money in it. Really, though, the theory interests me more. Care to see it?"

Culquhoun nodded, and Arch pawed through the papers on his desk. The top was littered with his stamp collection, but an unerring instinct seemed to guide his hand to the desired papers. He handed over an untidy manuscript consisting chiefly of mathematical symbols. "But don't bother with it now," he said. "I blew us to a new Bach the other day—St. Matthew Passion."

Culquhoun's eyes lit up, and for a while the house was filled with a serene strength which this century had forgotten. "Mon, mon," whispered the professor at last. "What he could have done with the bag-pipes!"

"Barbarian," said Elizabeth.

As it happened, that one test batch was successful. Arch took a slab of darkly shining material from the lab oven and sawed it up for tests. It met them all. Heat and cold had little effect, even on the electric properties. Ordinary chemicals did not react. The dielectric constant was over a million, and the charge was held without appreciable leakage.

"Why doesn't it arc over?" wondered Elizabeth.

"Electric field's entirely inside the slab," said Arch absently. "You need a solid conductor, like a wire, between the poles to discharge it. The breakdown voltage is so high that you might as well forget about it." He lifted a piece about ten inches square and two inches thick. "You could charge this hunk up with enough juice to run our house for a couple of years, I imagine; of course, it'd be D.C., so you'd have to drain it through a small A.C. generator. The material itself costs, oh, I'd guess fifty cents, a dollar maybe if you include labor." He hesitated. "You know, it occurs to me we've just killed the wet-cell battery."

"Good riddance," said Elizabeth. "The first thing you do, my boy, is make a replacement for that so-called battery in our car. I'm tired of having the clunk die in the middle of traffic."

"Okay," said Arch mildly. "Then we see about patents. But—honey, don't you think this deserves a small celebration of sorts?"

Arch spent a few days drawing up specifications and methods of manufacture. By giving the subject a little thought, he discovered that production could be fantastically cheap and easy. If you knew just what was needed, you had only to mix together a few chemicals obtainable in any drugstore, bake them in your oven for several hours, and saw the resulting chunk into pieces of suitable size. By adding resistances and inductances, which could be made if necessary from junkyard wire, you could bleed off the charge at any desired rate.

Culquhoun's oldest son Robert dropped over to find Arch tinkering with his rickety '48 Chevrolet. "Dad says you've got a new kind of battery," he remarked.

"Uh . . . Yes. I'll make him one if he wants. All we'll need to charge it is a rectifier and a voltmeter. Need a regulator for the discharge, of course." Arch lifted out his old battery and laid it on the grass.

"I've got a better idea, sir," said the boy. "I'd like to buy a *big* piece of the stuff from you."

"Whatever for?" asked Arch.

"Run my hot rod off it," said Bob from the lofty eminence of sixteen years. "Shouldn't be too hard, should it? Rip out the engine; use the big condenser to turn a D.C. motor—it'd be a lot cheaper than gas, and no plugged fuel lines either."

"You know," said Arch, "I never thought of that."

He lifted the ridiculously small object which was his new current source and placed it inside the hood. He had had to add two pieces of strap iron to hold it in position. "Why a regular motor?" he mused. "If you have D.C. coming out at a controlled rate, you could use it to turn your main drive shaft by a very simple and cheap arrangement."

"Oh, sure," said Robert scornfully. "That's what I meant. Any backyard mechanic could fix that up—if he didn't electrocute himself first. But how about it, Dr. Arch? How much would you want for a piece like that?"

"I haven't the time," said the physicist. "Tell you what, though, I'll give you a copy of the specs and you can make your own. There's nothing to it, if your mother will let you have the oven for a day. Cost you maybe five dollars for materials."

"Sell it for twenty-five," said Bob dreamily. "Look, Dr. Arch, would you like to go into business with me? I'll pay you whatever royalty seems right."

"I'm going to Boston with just that in mind," said Arch, fumbling with the cables. "However, go ahead. Consider yourself a licensee. I want ten percent of the selling price, and I'll trust a Scotch Yankee like you to make me a million."

He had no business sense. It would have saved him much grief if he had.

The countryside looked clean, full of hope and springtime. Now and then a chrome-plated monster of an automobile whipped past Arch's sedately chugging antique. He observed them with a certain contempt, an engineer's eye for the Goldbergian inefficiency of a mechanism which turned this rod to push that cam to rotate such and such a gear, and needed a cooling system to throw away most of the energy generated. Bob Culquhoun, he reflected, had a saner outlook. Not only was electricity cheaper in the first place, but the wasted power would be minimal and the "prime mover"—the capacitor itself— simply would not wear out.

Automobiles could be sold for perhaps five hundred dollars and built to last, not to run up repair bills till the owner was driven to buying a new model. The world's waning resources of petroleum could go into something useful: generating power at central stations, forming a base for organic syntheses; they would stretch out for centuries more. Coal could really come back into its own.

Hm ... wait. There was no reason why you couldn't power every type of vehicle with capacitors. Aircraft could stay aloft a month at a time if desired—a year if nothing wore out; ships could be five years at sea. You wouldn't need those thousands of miles of power line littering the countryside and wasting the energy they carried; you could charge small capacitors for home use right at the station and deliver them to the consumer's doorstep at a fraction of the present cost.

Come to think of it, there was a lot of remote power, in waterfalls for instance, unused now because the distance over which lines would have to be strung was too great. Not any longer! And the sunlight pouring from this cloudless sky—too dilute to run a machine of any size. But you could focus a lot of it on a generator whose output voltage was jacked up, and charge capacitors with thousands of kilowatt-hours each. Generators everywhere could be made a lot smaller, because they wouldn't have to handle peak loads but only meet average demand.

This thing is bigger than I realized, he thought with a tingle of excitement. *My God, in a year I may be a millionaire!*

He got into Boston, only losing his way twice, which is a good record for anyone, and found the office of

Addison, his patent attorney. It didn't take him long to be admitted.

The dusty little man riffled through the pages. "It looks all right," he said unemotionally. Nothing ever seemed to excite him. "For a change, this seems to be something which can be patented, even under our ridiculous laws. Not the law of nature you've discovered, of course, but the process—" He peered up, sharply. "Is there any alternative process?"

"Not that I know of," said Arch. "On the basis of theory, I'm inclined to doubt it."

"Very well, very well. I'll see about putting it through. Hm—you say it's quite simple and cheap? Better keep your mouth shut for a while, till the application has been approved. Otherwise everybody will start making it, and you'll have a devil of a time collecting your royalties. A patent is only a license to sue, you know, and you can't sue fifty million bathtub chemists."

"Oh," said Arch, taken aback. "I—well, I've told some of my neighbors, of course. One of the local teen-agers is going to make a car powered by—"

Addison groaned. "You would! Can't you shoot the boy?"

"I don't want to. For a person his age, he's quite inoffensive."

"Oh, well, you didn't want a hundred million dollars anyway, did you? I'll try to rush this for you, that may help."

Arch went out again, some of the elation taken from him. But what the hell, he reflected. If he could collect on only one percent of all the capacitite which was going to be manufactured, he'd still have an unreasonable amount of money. And he wanted to publish as soon as possible in all events: he had the normal human desire for prestige.

He got a hamburger and coffee at a diner and went home. Nothing happened for a month except an interview in the local paper. Bob finished his hot rod and drove it all over town. The boy was a little disappointed at the quietness of the machine, but the interest it attracted was compensation. He began to build another: twenty-five dollars for an old chassis, another twenty-five or so for materials, tack on a hundred for labor and profits—the clunk might not look like much, but it would run for a year without fuel worries and would never need much repair or replacement. He also discovered, more or less clandestinely, that such a car would go up to 200 miles an hour on the straightaway. After selling it, he realized he could command a much bigger price, and set happily to work on another.

The physics journal to which Arch sent his manuscript was interested enough to rush printing. Between the time he submitted it and the time it came out some five weeks later, he found himself in lively correspondence with the editor.

"College will soon be letting out all over the country," said Elizabeth. "Stand by to repel boarders!"

"Mmmm ... yes, I suppose so." Arch added up the cost of entertaining a rush of colleagues, but his worry was only a flicker across a somewhat bashful glow of pride. After all—he had done a big thing. His polarization theory cut a deep swath into what mystery remained about the atom. There might even be a Nobel Prize in it.

It was on the day of publication that his phone rang. He looked up from his stamps, swore, and lifted it. "Hello?"

"Dr. Arch?" The voice was smooth and cultivated, just a trace of upper-class New York accent. "How do you do, sir. My name is Gilmer, Linton Gilmer, and I represent several important corporations in the electricity field." He named them, and Arch barely suppressed a whistle. "Dr. Bowyer of the *Journal* staff mentioned your work to one of his friends in an industrial research lab. He was quite excited, and you can understand that we are too. I believe I have some good news for you, if I may come to see you."

"Eh—oh. Oh, sure!" Visions whirled across Arch's eyes. Money! It represented a hi-fi set, a threepenny black, an automatic dishwasher, a reliable car, a new oscilloscope, a son and heir. "Come on up, b-by all means—Yes, right away if you like—Okay, I—I'll be seeing you—" He set the receiver down with a shaking hand and bawled: "Betty! Company coming!"

"Oh, damn!" said his wife, sticking a grease-smudged face in the door. She had been tinkering with the lab oven. "And the house in such a mess! So am I, for that matter. Hold the fort when he comes, darling." She still didn't know who "he" was, but whirled off in a cloud of profanity.

Arch thought about putting on a decent suit and decided to hell with it. Let them come to him and accept him as he was; he had the whip hand, for once in his life. He contented himself with setting out beer and clearing the littered coffee table.

Linton Gilmer was a big man, with a smooth well-massaged face, wavy gray hair, and large soft hands. His presence seemed to fill the room, hardly leaving space for anyone else.

"Very pleased to meet you, Dr. Arch ... brilliant achievement ... We borrowed proof sheets from the *Journal* and made tests for ourselves, of course. I'm sure you don't mind. Thank you." He seemed just a trifle shocked at being offered beer rather than Johnnie Walker Black at four o'clock in the afternoon, but accepted gracefully. Arch felt excessively gauche.

"What did you want to s-see me about?" asked the physicist.

"Oh, well, sir, let's get acquainted first," said Gilmer heartily. "No rush. No hurry. I envy you scientific fellows. The unending quest, thrill of discovery, yes, science was my first love, but I'm afraid I sort of got steered off into the business administration end. I know you scientists don't think much of us poor fellows behind the desks, you should hear how our boys gripe when we set the appropriations for their projects, but somebody has to do that, ha." Gilmer made a bridge of plump fingers. "I do think, though, Dr. Arch, that this hostility is coming to an end. We're both part of the team, you know; scientist and businessman both work inside our free enterprise system to serve the American public. And more and more scientists are coming to recognize this."

Arch shifted uneasily in his chair. He couldn't think of any response. But it was simple to converse with Gilmer: you just sat back, let him flow, and mumbled in the pauses.

Some data began to emerge: "—we didn't want to trouble you with a dozen visitors, so it was agreed that I would represent the combine to, ah, sound you out, if I may so phrase it."

Arch felt the stir of resentment which patronizing affability always evoked in him. He tried to be courteous: "Excuse me, but isn't that sort of thing against the anti-trust laws?"

"Oh, no!" Gilmer laughed. "Quite the opposite, I assure you. If one company tried to corner this product, or if all of them went together to drive the price up, that would be illegal, of course. But we all believe in healthy competition, and only want information at the moment. Negotiations can come later."

"Okay," said Arch. "I suppose you know I've already applied for a patent."

"Oh, yes, of course. Very shrewd of you. I like to deal with a good businessman. I think you're more broad-minded than some of your colleagues, and can better understand the idea of teamwork between business and science." Gilmer looked out the French doors to the building in the rear. "Is that your laboratory? I admire a man who can struggle against odds. You have faith, and deserve to be rewarded for it. How would you like to work with some real money behind you?"

Arch paused. "You mean, take a job on somebody's staff?"

"Not as a lab flunky," said Gilmer quickly. "You'd have a free hand. American business recognizes ability. You'd plan your own projects, and head them yourself. My own company is prepared to offer you twenty thousand a year to start."

Arch sat without moving.

"After taxes," said Gilmer.

"How about this—capacitite, I call it?"

"Naturally, development and marketing would be in the hands of the company, or of several companies," said Gilmer. "You wouldn't want to waste your time on account books. You'd get proper payment for the assignment, of course—"

Elizabeth entered, looking stunning. Gilmer rose with elaborate courtesy, and the discussion veered to trivialities for awhile.

Then the girl lit a cigarette and watched them through a haze of smoke. "Your time is valuable, Mr. Gilmer," she said abruptly. "Why don't you make an offer and we'll talk about that?"

"Oh, no hurry, Mrs. Arch. I was hoping you would be my guests tonight—"

"No, thanks. With all due regard for you, I don't want to be put under a moral obligation before business is discussed."

Gilmer chuckled amiably and repeated the idea he had broached.

"I like Westfield," said Elizabeth. "I don't like New York. It isn't fit for human consumption."

"Oh, I quite agree," said Gilmer. "Once a year I have to break loose—cabin up in Maine, hunting, fishing, back to Nature—you really must come up sometime soon. Your objection can be answered easily enough. We could set up a laboratory for you here, if you really insist. You see, we're prepared to be very generous."

Arch shook his head. "No," he said harshly. "No, thanks. I like being independent."

Gilmer raised his brows. "I understand that. But after all, the only difference would be—"

Arch grinned. He was enjoying himself now. On a dark day some years ago, he had tried to raise a bank loan and had failed for lack of collateral and credit rating and his refusal to subject any friend to co-signing. Ever since, he had indulged daydreams about having finance come crawling to him. The reality was intoxicating.

"No," he repeated. "That's all I want to say about it, too. The income from capacitite will be quite enough for us. If you want to discuss a license to manufacture, go ahead."

"Hrm! As you wish." Gilmer smoothed the coldness out of his voice. "Maybe you'll change your mind later. If so, feel free to call on me anytime. Now, for an assignment of rights, I think a sum of fifty thousand dollars could be arranged—"

Elizabeth drooped lids over startlingly blue eyes. "As an initial payment, perhaps," she said gently. "But think what a royalty of, say, ten cents a pound would add up to even in a year."

"Oh, yes, that would be negotiated too," said Gilmer. "However, you realize manufacture could not start immediately, and would in any case be on a smaller scale than you perhaps think."

"Eh?" Arch sat bolt upright. "What do you mean? Why, this stuff is going to revolutionize not only electronics, but all power—dammit, everything!"

"Dr. Arch," said Gilmer regretfully, "you must not have considered the matter of capital investment. Do you know how many billions of dollars are sunk in generators, dams, lines, motors—"

"Gasoline," said Elizabeth. "We've thought of that angle too."

"We *can't* throw all that in the discard!" went on Gilmer earnestly. He seemed more human, all at once. "It may take twenty years to recover the investment in, say, a local transmission network. The company would go broke overnight if that investment were suddenly made valueless. Millions of people would be thrown out of work.

Millions more would lose their savings in stocks and bonds—"

"I always said stocks were a mug's game," interrupted Arch. "If the two or three shares owned by the widow and orphan you're leading up to go blooey, it won't break her. For years, now, I've had ads dinning the wonders of the present economic system into my ears. One of its main features, I'm told, is progress. All right, here's a chance to leap a hundred years ahead. Let's see you take it."

Gilmer's pink cheeks reddened. "I'm afraid you still don't understand," he replied. "We have a responsibility. The world is watching us. Just imagine what those British Socialists would say if—"

"If you're against socialism," said Elizabeth with a laugh, "why not start at home? Public schools and federal highways, for instance. I fail to see where personal liberty is necessarily tied to any particular method of distribution."

Gilmer seemed, for a moment, to lose his temper. "This is no place for radicals," he said thickly. "We've all got to have faith and put our shoulders to the wheel. We—" He paused, swallowed, and smiled rather stiffly. "Excuse me. I didn't mean to get worked up. There are a lot of stories about wonderful new inventions which the greedy corporations have bought up and hidden away. They simply are not true. All I'm after is a gradual introduction of this material."

"I know those wonderful inventions are pure rumor," said Arch. "But I also know that just about everything I buy is made to wear out so I'll have to buy some more. It's cheaper, yes, but I'd rather pay twice as much to start with and have my purchase last ten times as long. Why can't I buy a decent kitchen knife? There's not one that keeps its edge. My wife finally made eyes at the butcher and got one of his old knives; *it* lasts.

"A big thing like capacitite represents a chance to change our whole philosophy into something more rational. That's what I'm after—not just money. There needn't be any unemployment. Capacitite makes increased production possible, so why not—well, why not drop the work day to four hours for the same wages? Then you can employ twice as many people."

"It is not your or my place to make carping criticisms," retorted Gilmer. "Fundamental changes aren't as easy as you think. Dr. Arch, I'm sorry to say that unless you'll agree to proper terms, none of the companies I represent will be interested in your material."

"All right," snapped Arch. "I can make it myself. Make it by the ton if I like, and sell it for a dollar a pound."

"You may find yourself undersold."

"My patent—"

"It hasn't gone through yet. That takes time, plenty of time if you don't want to cooperate. And even if it is granted, which I by no means guarantee, you'll have to sue infringers; and do you know how crowded court calendars are? And how expensive a series of appeals can make such a suit?"

"Okay," said Elizabeth sweetly. "Go ahead and make it. You just got through telling us why you can't."

Gilmer looked out the window. "This is a great country," he said, with more sincerity than Arch had expected. "No country on earth has ever been so rich and happy. Do you know how it got that way?"

"By progressing," said Arch. "For your information, I am not a leftist; I'll bet I'm far to the right of you. So far, that I still believe in full speed ahead and damn the torpedoes."

Gilmer rose, with a certain dignity. "I'm afraid tempers are getting a little short," he said quietly. "I beg of you to reconsider. We'll fight for the public interest if we must, but we'd rather cooperate. May I leave my card? You can always get in touch with me."

He made his farewells and left. Arch and Elizabeth looked somewhat blankly at each other.

"Well, Killer," said the girl at last, "I hope we haven't taken too big a chaw to swallow."

° ° °

Culquhoun dropped over in the evening and listened to their account. He shook his head dubiously. "You're up against it, laddie," he said. "They'll defend their coffers to the bitter end."

"It isn't that." Arch stared moodily into the darkness. "I don't think they're a bunch of monsters—no more than anybody else. They just believe in the status quo. So do you, you know."

"How?" Culquhoun bristled. "I'll admit I'm not the hell-fire revolutionary of my undergraduate days, but I still think a basic change is called for."

"Not basic," said Arch. "You just want to change part of the mechanism. But you'd keep the same ant-heap industrial society. I believe the heart went out of this land after the Civil War, and the death warrant was signed about 1910. Before then, a man was still an individual; he worked for himself, at something he understood, and wasn't afraid to stand up and spit in the eye of the world. Now he spends his daily routine on an assembly line or behind a desk or counter, doing the same thing over and over for someone else. In the evening he watches the same pap on his television, and if something goes wrong he whines his way to the apartment superintendent or the VA or the Social Security office.

"Look at the progress of euphemism. Old people are Senior Citizens. Draft becomes Selective Service. Graveyard to cemetery to memorial park. We've become a race of dependents. And we can't break away: there isn't any frontier left, there isn't any alternative society, one man can't compete with a corporation. Or with a commissar, for that matter.

"What we need is not to go back to living in log cabins, but to make the means of sustenance and the sources of energy so cheap that every man can have them in sufficient quantity to live and work. I don't know—maybe I'm being vainglorious, but it does seem as if capacitite is a long step in that direction."

"I warn you, you're talking good Marxism," said Culquhoun with a grin. "The means of production determine the type of society."

"Which is pure hogwash," answered Arch. "Egypt and Assyria had identical technologies. So did Athens and Sparta. So do America and Russia. The means of production only determine the *possible* societies, and there are always many possibilities.

"I'd like to see the possibility of individualism available again to the American people. If they're too far gone to accept it, to hell with them."

The government can work fast when it wants to. It was just the following afternoon when the phone rang again. Elizabeth came out to the lab, where Arch and Bob Culquhoun were preparing a batch of capacitite, with a strained look on her face. "Come inside, dear," she said thinly. "I've got some bad news." When he was in the house, she added: "Two FBI men are on their way here."

"What the devil?" Arch felt a gulp of fear. It was irrational, he told himself. The FBI was no Gestapo; on the whole, he approved of it. Maybe some friend had given his name as a security reference. "All right. We'll see what they want."

"I'm going to start some coffee," said Elizabeth. "Lucky we've got a cake too."

"Huh?"

"You'll see." She patted his cheek and managed a smile. "You're too innocent, sweetheart."

Sagdahl and Horrisford turned out to be hard young men with carefully expressionless faces. They introduced themselves very politely, and Arch led the way into the living room. Horrisford took out a notebook.

"Well," said Arch a little huskily, "what can I do for you?"

"You can answer some questions, if you please," said Sagdahl tonelessly. "You don't have to answer any, and whatever you say can be used in evidence."

"I haven't broken any laws that I know of," said Arch feebly.

"That remains to be seen. This is an investigation."

"Whatever *for?*"

"Dr. Arch," said Sagdahl patiently, "yesterday you published an article on a discovery of potential military importance. It has upset a great many plans. Worse, it has been released with no discretion whatsoever, and the consequences aren't easy to foresee. If we'd had any inkling, it would never have been published openly. As it is, you went outside regular channels and—"

"I didn't have to go through channels," said Arch. "I've never gotten any confidential data, or even applied for a clearance. I work for myself and—" He saw Horrisford busily writing, and his words dried up.

The realization was appalling. The military applications of capacitite had crossed his mind only vaguely and been dismissed with an escapist shrug.

"Let's get down to business," said Sagdahl. "Everything will be a lot easier if you cooperate. Now, where were you born?"

Arch hadn't imagined anyone could be so thorough about tracking down a man's entire life. He answered frankly, feeling he had nothing to hide. Of course, there *had* been his roommate at M.I.T., and the roommate had had a girlfriend one of whose other friends was a Communist, and . . .

"I see. Now, when you graduated—"

Elizabeth entered from the kitchen with a tray. "Pardon me," she smiled. "I think refreshments are in order."

Sagdahl's face didn't change, but his eyes bugged slightly. Elizabeth put a coffee cup in his hand and a plate of cake on one knee. He looked unhappy, but mumbled dutiful thanks.

"Oh, it's a pleasure," said Elizabeth blandly. "You boys are doing your duty, and really, this is very exciting."

Sagdahl got down a mouthful of cake. Valiantly, he tried to resume the staccato flow: "Now, when you graduated, Dr. Arch, you took a vacation, you say. Where was that?"

"Up in Quebec. About three months. Just driving around and—"

"I see. Then you returned to school for a master's degree, right? Did you at this time know a Joseph Barrett?"

"Well, yes, I shared an office with him."

"Did you ever discuss politics with him?"

"Drink your coffee before it gets cold," said Elizabeth. "There's plenty more."

"Oh—thanks. Now, about this Barrett?"

"We argued a lot. You see, I'm frankly a reactionary—"

"Were you associated with any political-action group?"

"Mr. Horrisford," said Elizabeth reproachfully, "you haven't touched your cake."

"No, I wasn't that interested," said Arch. "Didn't even bother to vote in '50."

"Here, Mr. Sagdahl, do have some more cake."

"Thanks!— You met some of Barrett's friends?"

"Yes, I was at some parties and—"

"Excuse me, I'll just warm your coffee."

"Did you at this time know anyone who had worked in the Manhattan Project?"

"Of course. They were all over the place. But I never was told anything restricted, never asked for—"

"Please, Mr. Horrisford! It's my favorite recipe."

"Ummm. Thank you, but—"

"You met your future wife when?"

"In—"

"Excuse me, there's the phone . . . Hello. Mrs. Arch speaking . . . Oh? . . . Yes, I'll see . . . Pardon me. There's a man from the Associated Press in town. He wants to see you, dear."

Sagdahl flinched. "Stall him off," he groaned. "Please."

"Can't do that forever," said Arch. "Not under the circumstances."

"I realize that, Dr. Arch." Sagdahl clenched his jaw. "But this is unprecedented. As an American citizen, you'll want to—"

"Certainly we'll cooperate," said Elizabeth brightly.

"But what shall I tell the AP man? That we're not supposed to say anything to anyone?"

"No! That won't do, not now. But—are all the technical details of this public?"

"Why, yes," said Arch. "Anybody can make capacitite."

"If you issued a denial—"

"Too late, I'm afraid. Somebody's bound to try it anyway."

Sagdahl looked grim. "You can be held incommunicado," he said. "This is a very serious matter."

"Yes," said Elizabeth. "The AP man will think so too, if he can't get a story."

"Well—"

"Oh, dear! My Russell Wright coffee cup!"

Nothing happened overnight. That was the hardest thing to believe. By all the rules, life should have been suddenly and dramatically transformed; but instead, there were only minor changes, day by day, small incidents. Meanwhile you ate, slept, worked, paid bills, made love and conversation, as you had always done.

The FBI held its hand as yet, but some quiet men checked into the town's one hotel, and there was usually one of them hanging around Arch's house, watching. Elizabeth would occasionally invite him in for a snack—she grew quite fond of them.

The newspapers ran feature articles, and for a while the house was overrun with reporters—then that too faded away. Editorials appeared, pointing out that capacitite had licked one of the Soviet Union's major problems, fuel; and a syndicated columnist practically called for Arch's immediate execution. He found some of his neighbors treating him coldly. The situation distressed him, too. "I never thought—" he began.

"Exactly," rumbled Culquhoun. "People like you are one reason science is coming to be considered a Frankenstein. Dammit, man, the researcher has to have a social conscience like the rest of us."

Arch smiled wearily. "But I do," he said. "I gave considerable thought to the social effects. I just imagined that they'd be good. That's been the case with every major innovation, in the long run."

"You've committed a crime," said Culquhoun. "Idealism. It doesn't fit the world we inhabit."

Arch flushed angrily. "What was I supposed to do?" he snapped. "Burn my results and forget them? If the human race is too stupid to use the obvious advantages, that's its own fault."

"You're making a common error, dear," said Elizabeth. "You speak of the human race. There isn't any. There are only individual people and groups of people, with their own conflicting interests."

For a while, there was a big campaign to play down the effects of capacitite. It wasn't important. It meant nothing, as our eminent columnist has so lucidly shown. Then the attempt switched: capacitite was dangerous. So-and-so had been electrocuted working with it. There was cumulative poisoning . . . Such propaganda didn't work, not when some millions of people were seeing for themselves.

Petroleum stock began sagging. It didn't nosedive— the SEC and a valiantly buying clique saw to that—but it slipped down day by day.

Arch happened to drop in at Hinkel's garage. The old man looked up from a car on which he was laboring and smiled. "Hello, there," he said. "Haven't seen you in a long time."

"I—well—" Arch looked guiltily at the oil-stained floor. "I'm afraid—your business—"

"Oh, don't worry about me. I've got more business than I can handle. Everybody in town seems to want his car converted over to your type of engine. That young Bob is turning out the stuff like a printing press gone berserk."

Arch couldn't quite meet his eyes. "But—aren't your gasoline sales dropping?"

"To be sure. But cars still need lubrication and— Look, you know the old watermill down by Ronson's farm? I'm buying that, putting in a generator and a high-voltage transformer and rectifier. I'll be selling packaged power. A lot easier than running a gas pump, at my age."

"Won't the power company be competing?"

"Eventually. Right now, they're still waiting for orders from higher up, I guess. Some people can charge their capacitors right at home, but most would rather not buy the special equipment. They'll come to me, and by the time the power outfit gets wise to itself, I'll've come in on the ground floor."

"Thanks," said Arch, a little shakily. "It makes me feel a lot better."

If only everybody had that Yankee adaptability, he thought as he walked home. But he saw now, as he wished he had seen earlier, that society had gone too far. With rare exceptions, progress was no longer a matter of individual readjustments. It was a huge and clumsy economic system which had to make the transformation . . . a jerry-built system whose workings no one understood, even today.

He wanted to call up Gilmer and make what terms he could, but it was too late. The snowball was rolling.

He sighed his way into an armchair and picked up the paper.

Item: the bill before Congress to make capacitite a government monopoly like uranium, and to enforce all security restrictions on it, had been sent back to committee and would probably not pass. A few senators had had the nerve to point out that security was pointless when everybody could already make the stuff.

Item: the government was setting up a special laboratory to study the military applications. Arch could think of several for himself. Besides simplifying logistics, it could go into cheap and horrible weapons. A bomb loaded with several thousand coulombs, set to discharge instantaneously on striking—

Item: a well-known labor leader had denounced the innovation as a case of business blundering which was going to take bread from the working man. A corporation spokesman declared that it was all a leftist trick designed to cripple the private enterprise system.

Item: *Pravda* announced that Soviet scientists had discovered capacitite ten years ago and that full-scale production had long been under way for peaceful purposes only, such as making the Red Army still more invincible.

Item: two more men in America electrocuted due to incautious experiments. Nevertheless, capacitite was being manufactured in thousands of homes and workshops. Bills in various state legislatures to ban vehicles so powered were meeting indignant opposition everywhere save in Texas.

Arch reflected wryly that he wasn't getting paid for any of this. All he'd gotten out of it so far was trouble. Trouble with the authorities, with crank letters, with his own conscience. There were, to be sure, some royalties from Bob Culquhoun, who was becoming quite an entrepreneur and hiring adults to take over when school opened in fall.

Speaking of tigers by the tail—

Autumn, the New England fall of rain and chill whistling wind, smoky days and flame-like leaves and the far wild honking of southbound geese. The crash came in late September: a reeling market hit bottom and stayed there. Gasoline sales were down twenty-five percent already, and the industry was laying men off by the hundreds of thousands. That cut out their purchasing power and hit the rest of the economy.

"It's what you'd expect, laddie," said Culquhoun. They were over at his house. Outside, a slow cold rain washed endlessly down the windows. "Overproduction—overcapitalization—I could have predicted all this."

"Damn it to hell, it doesn't make *sense!*" protested Arch. "A new energy source should make everything cheaper for everybody—more production available for less work." He felt a nervous tic beginning in one cheek.

"Production for use instead of for profit—"

"Oh, dry up, will you? Any system is a profit system.

It has to show a profit in some terms or other, or it would just be wasted effort. And the profit has to go to individuals, not to some mythical state. The state doesn't eat—people do."

"Would you have the oil interests simply write off their investment?"

"No, of course not. Why couldn't they— Look. Gasoline can still run generators. Oil can still lubricate. Byproducts can still be synthesized. It's a matter of shifting the emphasis of production, that's all. All that's needed is a little common sense."

"Which is a rather scarce commodity."

"There," said Arch gloomily, "we find ourselves in agreement."

"The trouble is," said Bob earnestly, "we're faced with a real situation, not a paper problem. It calls for a real solution. For an idea."

"There aren't any ideas," said Elizabeth. "Not big sweeping ones to solve everything overnight. Man doesn't work that way. What happens is that somebody solves his own immediate, personal problems, somebody else does the same, and eventually society as a whole fumbles its way out of the dilemma."

Arch sighed. "This is getting over my head," he admitted. "Thanks for small blessings: the thing has grown so big that I, personally, am becoming forgotten."

He rose. "I'm kind of tired tonight," he went on. "Maybe we better be running along. Thanks for the drinks and all."

He and his wife slipped into their raincoats and galoshes for the short walk home. The street outside was dark, a rare lamp glowing off slick wet concrete. Rain misted his face and glasses, he had trouble seeing.

"Poor darling," Elizabeth took his arm. "Don't worry. We'll get through all right."

"I hope so," he said fervently. No money had come in for some time now. Bob's enterprise was leveling off as initial demand was filled, and a lurching industry wasn't

buying many electronic valves. The bank account was
getting low.

He saw the figure ahead as a vague shadow against the
night. It stood waiting till they came up, and then
stepped in their path. The voice was unfamiliar: "Arch?"

"Yes—"

He could see only that the face was heavy and
unshaven, with something wild about the mouth. Then
his eyes dropped to the revolver barrel protruding from
the slicker. "What the devil—"

"Don't move, you." It was a harsh, broken tone. "Right
now I'm aiming at your wife. I'd as soon shoot her, too."

Fear leaped crazily in Arch's breast. He stood unable
to stir, coldness crawling in his guts. He tried to speak,
and couldn't.

"Not a word, you ——. Not another word. You've said
too goddam much already." The gun poked forward, savagely. "I'm going to kill you. You did your best to kill
me."

Elizabeth's face was white in the gloom. "What do you
mean?" she whispered. "We never saw you before."

"No. But you took away my job. I was in the breadlines
back in the thirties. I'm there again, and it's your fault,
you ——. Got any prayers to say?"

A gibbering ran through Arch's brain. He stood
motionless, thinking through a lunatic mind-tilt that there
must be some way to jump that gun, the heroes of stories
always did it, that might—

Someone moved out of the night into the wan radi-
ance. An arm went about the man's throat, another
seized his gun wrist and snapped it down. The weapon
went off, sounding like the crack of doom in the stillness.

They struggled on the slippery sidewalk, panting, the
rain running over dimly glimpsed faces. Arch's paralysis
broke, he moved in and circled around, looking for a
chance to help. There! Crouching, he got hold of the
assassin's ankle and clung.

There was a meaty smack above him, and the body
sagged.

Elizabeth held her hand over her mouth, as if to force back a scream. "Mr. Horrisford," she whispered.

"The same," said the FBI man. "That was a close one. You can be thankful you're an object of suspicion, Arch. What was he after?"

Arch stared blankly at his rescuer. Slowly, meaning penetrated. "Unemployed—" he mumbled. "Bitter about it—"

"Yeah. I thought so. You may be having more trouble of that sort. This depression, people have someone concrete to blame." Horrisford stuck the gun in his pocket and helped up his half-conscious victim. "Let's get this one down to the lockup. Here, you support him while I put on some handcuffs."

"But I wanted to help his kind," said Arch feebly.

"You didn't," said Horrisford. "I'd better arrange for a police guard."

Arch spent the following day in a nearly suicidal depression. Elizabeth tried to pull him out of it, failed, and went downtown after a fifth of whiskey. That helped. The hangover helped too. It's hard to concentrate on remorse when ten thousand red-hot devils are building an annex to Hell in your skull. Toward evening, he was almost cheerful again. A certain case-hardening was setting in.

After dark, there was a knock on the door. When he opened it, Horrisford and a stranger stood there.

"Oh—come in," he said "Excuse the mess. I—haven't been feeling so well."

"Anyone here?" asked the agent.

"Just my wife."

"She'll be all right," said the stranger impatiently. He was a big, stiff, gray-haired man. "Bring her in, please. This is important."

They were settled in the living room before Horrisford performed the introductions. "Major General Brackney of Strategic Services." Arch's hand was wet as he acknowledged the handclasp.

"This is most irregular," said the general. "However, we've put through a special check on you. A fast but very thorough check. In spite of your errors of judgment, the FBI is convinced of your essential loyalty. Your discretion is another matter."

"I can keep my mouth shut, if that's what you mean," said Arch.

"Yes. You kept one secret for ten years," said Horrisford. "The business of Mrs. Ramirez."

Arch started. "How the deuce—? That was a personal affair. I've never told a soul, not even my wife!"

"We have our little ways." Horrisford grinned, humanly enough. "The point is that you could have gained somewhat by blabbing, but didn't. It speaks well for you."

General Brackney cleared his throat. "We want your help on a certain top-secret project," he said. "You still know more about capacitite than anybody else. But if one word of this leaks out prematurely, it means war. Atomic war. It also means that all of us, and you particularly, will be crucified."

"I—"

"You're an independent so-and-so, I realize. What we have in mind is a scheme to prevent such a war. We want you in on it both for your own value and because we can't protect you forever from Soviet agents." Brackney's smile had no humor. "Didn't know that, did you? It's one reason you're being co-opted, in spite of all you've done.

"I can't say more till you take the oath, and once you've done that you're under all the usual restrictions. Care to help out?"

Arch hesitated. He had little faith in government . . . any government. Still—

Horrisford of the FBI had saved his life.

"I'm game," he said.

Elizabeth nodded. The oath was administered.

Brackney leaned back and lit a cigar. "All right," he said. "I'll come to the point.

"Offhand, it looks as if you've done a grave disservice to your country. It's been pointed out in the press that transporting fuel is the major problem of logistics. In fact, for the Russians it's *the* problem, since they can live off the countries they invade to a degree we can't match. You've solved that for them, and once they convert their vehicles we can expect them to start rolling. They and their allies—especially the Chinese. This discovery is going to make them a first-class power."

"I've heard that," said Arch thinly.

"However, we also know that the communist regimes are not popular. Look at the millions of refugees, look at all the prisoners who refused repatriation, look at the Ukrainian insurrection—I needn't elaborate. The trouble has been that the people aren't armed. To say anything at home means the concentration camp.

"Now, then. Basically, the idea is this. We've got plants set up to turn out capacitite in trainload lots. We can, I think, make weapons capable of stopping a tank for a couple of dollars apiece. Do you agree?"

"Why—yes," said Arch. "I've been considering it lately. A rifle discharging its current through magnetic coils to drive a steel-jacketed bullet—the bullet could be loaded with electricity too. Or a Buck Rogers energy gun: a hand weapon with a blower run off the capacitor, sucking in air at the rear and spewing it out between two electrodes like a gigantic arc-welding flame. Or—yes, there are all kinds of possibilities."

Brackney nodded with an air of satisfaction. "Good. I see you do have the kind of imagination we need.

"Now, we'll be giving nothing away, because they already know how to make the stuff and can think up anything we can. But, we have a long jump as far as production facilities are concerned.

"The idea is this. We want to make really enormous quantities of such weapons. By various means—through underground channels, by air if necessary—we want to distribute them to all the Iron Curtain countries. The people will be armed, and hell is going to break loose!

"We want you in on it as design and production consultants. Leave tomorrow, be gone for several months probably. It's going to have to be highly organized, so it can be sprung as a surprise; otherwise the Soviet bosses, who are no fools, will hit. But your part will be in production. Are you game?"

"It's—astonishing," said Elizabeth. "Frankly, I didn't think the government had that much imagination."

"We're probably exceeding our authority," admitted Brackney. "By rights, of course, Congress should be consulted, but this is like the Louisiana Purchase: there's no time to do so."

It was the historical note which decided Arch. Grade-school history, yes—but it didn't fit in with his preconceptions of the red-necked militarist. Suddenly, almost hysterically, he was laughing.

"What's so funny?" asked Horrisford sharply.

"The idea—what old Clausewitz would say—winning wars by arming the enemy! Sure—sure, I'm in. Gladly!"

Six months on a secret reservation in Colorado which nobody but the top brass left, six months of the hardest, most concentrated work a man could endure, got Arch out of touch with the world. He saw an occasional newspaper, was vaguely aware of trouble on the outside, but there was too much immediately at hand for him to consider the reality. Everything outside the barbed-wire borders of his universe grew vague.

Designing and testing capacitite weapons was harder than he had expected, and took longer: though experienced engineers assured him the project was moving with unprecedented speed and ease. Production details were out of his department, but the process of tooling up and getting mass output going was not one for overnight solution.

The magnetic rifle; the arc gun; the electric bomb and grenade; the capacitite land mine, set to fry the crew of any tank which passed over—he knew their hideous uses, but there was a cool ecstasy in working with them which made him forget, most of the time. And after all, the idea was to arm men who would be free.

In March, General Brackney entered the Quonset hut which Arch and Elizabeth had been inhabiting and sat down with a weary smile. "I guess you're all through now," he said.

"About time," grumbled the girl. "We've been sitting on our hands here for a month, just puttering."

"The stuff had to be shipped out," said the general mildly. "We didn't dare risk having the secret revealed. But we're rolling overseas, it's to late to stop anything." He shrugged. "Naturally, the government isn't admitting its part in this. Officially, the weapons were manufactured by independent operators in Europe and Asia, and you'll have to keep quiet about the truth for a long time—not that the comrades won't be pretty sure, but it just can't be openly admitted. However, there are no security restrictions on the gadgets themselves, as of today."

"That surprises me," said Arch.

"It's simple enough. Everything is so obvious, really— any handyman can make the same things for himself. A lot have been doing it, too. No secrets exist to be given away, that's all." Brackney hesitated. "We'll fly you back home anytime you wish. But if you want to stay on a more permanent basis, we'll be glad to have you."

"No, thanks!" Elizabeth's eyes went distastefully around the sleazy interior of the shack.

"This has all been temporary," said the general. "We were in such a hell of a hurry. Better housing will be built now."

"Nevertheless, no," said Arch.

Brackney frowned. "I can't stop you, of course. But I don't think you realize how tough it's getting outside, and how much worse it's going to get. A revolution is starting, in more senses than one, and you'll be safer here."

"I heard something about that," agreed Arch. "Discontented elements making their own weapons, similar to ours—what of it?"

"Plenty," said the officer with a note of grimness. "It's an ugly situation. A lot of people are out of work, and even those who still have jobs don't feel secure in them. There are a dozen crank solutions floating around, everything from new political theories to new religious sects, and each one is finding wider acceptance than I'd have believed possible."

"It doesn't surprise me," said Arch. "There's a queer strain of the True Believer in American culture. You know how many utopian colonies we've had throughout our history? And the single-tax party, and Prohibition, and Communism in the thirties. People in this country want something concrete to believe in, and all but a few of the churches have long ago degenerated into social clubs."

"Whatever the cause," said Brackney, "there are all these new groups, clashing with the old authorities and with each other. And the underworld is gleefully pitching in, and getting a lot of recruits from the ranks of hungry, frightened, embittered people.

"The regular armed forces have to be mobilized to stop anything the Soviets may try. The police and the National Guard have their hands full in the big cities. The result is, that authority is breaking down everywhere else. There's real trouble ahead, I tell you."

"All right," said Arch. "That's as may be. But our town is a collection of pretty solid folk—and we want to go home."

"On your heads be it. There'll be a plane at six tomorrow."

—The fact did not strike home till they were stopping over at Idlewild and saw uniformed men and machine-gun emplacements. In the coffee shop, Arch asked the counterman just how bad things really were.

"Rough," he answered. "See this?" He flipped back his jacket, showing a homemade capacitite pistol in a holster.

"Oh, look now—"

"Mister, I live in Brooklyn. I don't get home till after dark, and the police cordons don't go closer than six blocks to my place. I've had to shoot twice already in the past couple months."

"Bandits?"

"In gangs, mister. If I could work somewhere closer to home, I'd be off like a shot."

Arch set down his cup. Suddenly he didn't want any more coffee. *My God,* he thought, *am I responsible for that?*

A smaller plane carried them to Boston, where they caught a bus for Westfield. The driver had an automatic rifle by his seat. Arch huddled into himself, waiting for he knew not what; but the trip was uneventful.

The town didn't seem to have changed much. Most of the cars were converted, but it didn't show externally. The drugstore still flashed neon at a drowsy sidewalk, the Carnegie library waited rather wistfully for someone to come in, the dress shop had the same old dummies in the window. Elizabeth pointed at them. "Look," she said. "See those clothes?"

"They're dresses," said Arch moodily. "What about them?"

"No style change in six months, that's all," said Elizabeth. "It gives me the creeps."

They walked along streets banked with dirty, half-melted snow, under a leaden sky and a small whimpering wind. Their house had not changed when they entered, someone had been in to dust and it looked like the home they remembered. Arch sank tiredly into his old armchair and accepted a drink. He studied the newspaper he'd bought at the depot. Screaming headlines announced revolt in Russia—mass uprisings in the Siberian prison camps—announcements from the Copenhagen office of the Ukrainian nationalist movement— It all seemed very far away. The fact that there were no new dress styles was somehow closer and more eerie.

A thunderous knock at the door informed him that

Culquhoun had noticed their lights. "Mon, it's guid to see ye again!" The great paw engulfed his hand. "Where've ye been a' the while?"

"Can't tell you that," said Arch.

"Aweel, you'll permit me to make my own guesses, then." Culquhoun cocked an eye at the paper. "Who do they think they're fooling, anyhow? We can look for the Russian bombers any day now."

Arch considered his reply. That aspect had been thoroughly discussed at the project, but he wasn't sure how much he could tell. "Quite possibly," he said at last. "But with their internal troubles, they won't be able to make many raids, or any big ones—and the little they will be able to throw at us should be stopped while they're still over northern Canada."

"Let's hope so," nodded Culquhoun. "But the people in the large cities won't want to take the chance. There's going to be an exodus of considerable dimensions in the next few days, with all that that implies." He paused, frowning. "I've spent the last couple of months organizing a kind of local militia. Bob has been making capacitite guns, and there are about a hundred of us trying to train ourselves. Want in on it?"

"They'd probably shoot me first," whispered Arch.

The red head shook, bear-like. "No. There's less feeling against you locally than you seem to think. After all, few if any of the people in this area have been hurt— they're farmers, small shopkeepers trading in the essentials, students, college employees. Many of them have actually benefited. You have your enemies here, but you have more friends."

"I think," said Arch thinly, "that I'm becoming one of my own enemies."

"Ah, foosh, mon! If you hadn't brought the stuff out, somebody else would have. It's not your fault that we don't have the kind of economy to absorb it smoothly."

"All right," said Arch without tone. "I'll join your minutemen. There doesn't seem to be anything else to do."

• • •

The wave of automobiles began coming around noon of the next day. Westfield lay off the main highway, so it didn't get the full impact of the jam which tied up traffic from Philadelphia to Boston; but there were some thousands of cars which passed through.

Arch stood in the ranks of men who lined Main Street. The gun felt awkward in his hands. Breath smoked from his nostrils, and the air was raw and damp. On one side of him was Mr. Hinkel, bundled up so that only the glasses and a long red nose seemed visible; on the other was a burly farmer whom he didn't know.

Outside the city limits a sign had been planted, directing traffic to keep moving and to stay on the highway. There were barriers on all the side streets. Arch heard an occasional argument when someone tried to stop, to be urged on by a guard and by the angry horns behind him.

"But what'll they do?" he asked blindly. "Where will they stay? My God, there are women and children in those cars!"

"Women and children here in town too," said Hinkel. "We've got to look after our own. It won't kill these characters to go a few days without eating. Every house here is filled already—there've been refugees trickling in for weeks."

"We could bunk down a family in our place," ventured Arch.

"Save that space," answered Hinkel. "It'll be needed later."

Briefly, a certain pride rose through the darkness of guilt which lay in Arch. These were the old Americans, the same folk who had stood at Concord and gone west into Indian country. They were a survivor type.

But most of their countrymen weren't, he realized sickly. Urban civilization had become too big, too specialized. There were people in the millions who had never pitched a tent, butchered a pig, fixed a machine. What was going to become of them?

Toward evening, he was relieved and slogged home, too numb with cold and weariness to think much. He gulped down the dinner his wife had ready and tumbled into bed.

It seemed as if he had not slept at all when the phone was ringing. He groped toward it, cursing as he tried to unglue his eyes. Culquhoun's voice rattled at him:

"You and Betty come up to the college, Somerset Hall, right away. There's hell to pay."

"How—?"

"Our lookout on the water tower has seen fires starting to the south. Something's approaching, and it doesn't look friendly."

Sleep drained from Arch and he stood in a grayness where Satan jeered at him: *Si monumentum requiris, circumspice!* Slowly, he nodded. "We'll be right along."

The campus was jammed with townspeople. In the vague predawn light, Arch saw them as a moving river of white, frightened faces. Farmer, merchant, laborer, student, teacher, housewife, they had all receded into a muttering anonymity through which he pushed toward the steps of the hall. The irregular militia was forming ranks there, with Culquhoun's shaggy form dominating the scene.

"There you are," he snapped. "Betty, can you help take charge of the women and children and old people? Get them inside—this one building ought to hold them all, with some crowding. Kind of circulate around, keep them calm. We'll pass out coffee and doughnuts as soon as the Salvation Army bunch can set up a canteen."

"What's the plan?" asked a guardsman. To Arch, his voice had a dim dreamlike quality, none of this was real, it couldn't be.

"I don't know what those arsonists intend or where they're bound," said Culquhoun, "but we'd better be ready to meet them. The traffic through town stopped completely a few hours ago—I think there's a gang of highwaymen operating."

"Colin, it can't be! Plain people like us—"

"Hungry, frightened, angry, desperate, confused people. A mob has nothing to do with the individuals in it, my friend. And one small push is enough to knock down a row of dominoes. Once lawlessness really gets started, a lot of others are driven into it in self-defense."

They waited. The sun came up, throwing a pale bleak light over the late snow and the naked trees. The canteen handed out a sort of breakfast. Little was said.

At nine-thirty, a boy on a clumsy plowhorse came galloping up toward them. "About a hundred, marching down the highway," he panted. "They threw a couple shots at me."

"Stay here," said Culquhoun. "I'm going down to see if we can't parley. I'll want about ten men with me. Volunteers?"

Arch found himself among the first. It didn't matter much what happened to him, now when the work of his hands was setting aflame homes all across the land. They trudged down the hillside and out toward the viaduct leading south. Culquhoun broke into a deserted house and stationed them in its entrance hall.

Peering out, Arch saw the ragged column moving in. They were all men, unshaven and dirty. A few trucks accompanied them, loaded with a strange mass of plunder, but most were on foot and all were armed.

Culquhoun bound a towel to his rifle barrel and waved it through the front door. After what seemed like a long time, a voice outside said: "Okay, if yuh wanna talk, go ahead."

"Cover me," murmured Culquhoun, stepping onto the porch. Looking around his shoulder, Arch made out three of the invaders, with their troop standing in tired, slumped attitudes some yards behind. They didn't look fiendish, merely worn and hungry.

"Okay, pal," said the leader. "This is O'Farrell's bunch, and we're after food and shelter. What can yuh do for us?"

"Food and shelter?" Culquhoun glanced at the trucks.

"You seem to've been helping yourselves pretty generously already."

O'Farrell's face darkened. "What'd yuh have us do? Starve?"

"You're from the Boston area, I suppose. You could have stayed there."

"And been blown off the map!"

"It hasn't happened yet," said Culquhoun mildly. "It's not likely to happen, either. They have organized relief back there, you didn't have to starve. But no, you panicked and then you turned mean."

"It's easy enough for yuh to say so. *Yuh're* safe. We're here after our proper share, that's all."

"Your proper share is waiting in Boston," said Culquhoun with a sudden chill. "Now, if you want to proceed through our town, we'll let you; but we don't want you to stay. Not after what you've been doing lately."

O'Farrell snarled and brought up his gun. Arch fired from behind Culquhoun. The leader spun on his heel, crumpled, and sagged with a shriek. Arch felt sick.

His nausea didn't last. It couldn't, with the sudden storm of lead which sleeted against the house. Culquhoun sprang back, closing the door. "Out the rear!" he snapped. "We'll have to fight!"

They retreated up the hill, crouching, zigzagging, shooting at the disorderly mass which milled in slow pursuit. Culquhoun grinned savagely. "Keep drawing 'em on, boys," he said as he knelt in the slush and snapped a shot. "If they spread through town, we'll have hell's own time routing 'em all out—but this way—"

Arch didn't know if he was hitting anything. He didn't hear the bullets which must be whining around him—another cliché that just wasn't true, he thought somewhere in the back of his head. A fight wasn't something you could oversee and understand. It was cold feet, clinging mud, whirling roaring confusion, it was a nightmare that you couldn't wake up from.

Then the rest of the Westfield troop were there, circling around to flank the enemy and pumping death. It was a rout—in minutes, the gang had stampeded.

Arch leaned on his rifle and felt vomit rising in his throat. Culquhoun clapped his shoulder. "Ye did richt well, laddie," he rumbled. "Not bad at all."

"What's happening?" groaned Arch. "What's become of the world?"

Culquhoun took out his pipe and began tamping it. "Why, a simple shift of the military balance of power," he answered. "Once again we have cheap, easily operated weapons which everyone can own and which are the equal of anything it's practical for a government to use. Last time it was the flintlock musket, right? And we got the American and French Revolutions. This time it's capacitite.

"So the Soviet dictatorship is doomed. But we've got a rough time head of us, because there are enough unstable elements in our own society to make trouble. Our traditional organizations just aren't prepared to handle them when they're suddenly armed.

"We'll learn how fast enough, I imagine. There's going to be order again, if only because the majority of people are decent, hard-working fellows who won't put up with much more of this sort of thing. But there has to be a transition period, and what counts is surviving that."

"If I hadn't—Colin, it's enough to make a man believe in demonic possession."

"Nonsense!" snorted the other. "I told you before, if you hadn't invented this stuff, somebody else would have. It wasn't you that made it by the ton, all over the country. It wasn't you that thought up this notion of finishing the Iron Curtain governments—a brilliant scheme, I might add, well worth whatever price we have to pay at home.

"But it *is* you, my boy, who's going to have to get us tooled up to last the transition. Can you do it?"

Fundamental changes are seldom made consciously. Doubtless the man in the fifth-century Roman street grumbled about all these barbarian immigrants, but he did not visualize the end of an empire. The Lancashire industrialist who fired his craftsmen and installed mechanical looms was simply making a profitable investment. And Westfield, Massachusetts, was only adopting temporary survival measures.

They didn't even look overwhelmingly urgent. Government had not broken down: if anything, it was working abnormally hard. News came through—ferocious air battles over the Canadian tundras; the Soviet armies rolling westward into Europe and southward into Asia, then pushed back with surprising ease and surrendering en masse as their own states collapsed behind them—it was turning out to be a war as remote and half-forgotten as Korea, and a much easier one, which lasted a few months and then faded into a multi-cornered struggle between Communists, neo-czarists, and a dozen other elements. By Christmas time, a shaky democratic confederation in Moscow was negotiating with Ukrainia, the Siberian Convict Republic, and the Tartar Alliance. China was in chaos and eastern Europe was free.

And while the great powers were realizing that they were no longer great, now that a vast capital investment in armament had stopped paying off; and while they sought to forestall world upheaval by setting up a genuine international army with strength to enforce the peace—life went on. People still had to eat.

Arch stood by Hinkel's watermill in the early spring. The ground glistened and steamed with wetness underfoot, sunlit clouds raced through a pale windy sky, and a mist of green was on the trees. Near him the swollen millstream roared and brawled, the wheel flashed with its own swiftness, and a stack of capacitors lay awaiting their charges.

"All right," he said. "We've got your generator going. But it isn't enough, you know. It can't supply the whole country; and power lines to the outside are down."

"So what do we do?" asked Hinkel. He felt too proud of his new enterprise to care much about larger issues at the moment.

"We find other sources to supplement," said Arch. "Sunlight, now. Approximately one horse-power per square yard, if you could only get at it." He raised a face grown thin with overwork and with the guilt that always haunted him these days, up to the sky. The sun felt warm and live on his skin. "Trouble is, the potential's so low. You've got to find a way to get a high voltage out of it before you can charge a capacitor decently. Now let me think—"

He spent most of his waking hours thinking. It helped hold off the memory of men lying dead on a muddy hillside.

When power was short, you couldn't go back to oxcarts and kerosene lamps. There weren't enough of either. The local machine shop made and sold quantities of home charging units, small primitive generators which could be turned by any mechanical source, and treadmills were built to drive them. But this was only an unsatisfactory expedient. Accompanied by several armed guards, Arch made a trip to Boston.

The city looked much quieter than he remembered, some of the streets deserted even at midday, but a subdued business went on. Food was still coming in to the towns, and manufactured goods flowing out; there was still trade, mail, transportation. They were merely irregular and slightly dangerous.

Stopping at M.I.T., Arch gave certain of his problems to the big computer, and then proceeded to an industrial supply house. The amount of selenium he ordered brought a gasp and a hurried conference.

"It will take some time to get all this together," said a vice-president. "Especially with conditions as they are."

"I know," said Arch. "We're prepared to make up truck convoys and furnish guards; what we want you for is negotiation."

The vice-president blinked. "But . . . good heavens, man! Is your whole community in on this?"

"Just about. We have to be. There's little help coming in from outside, so our area is thrown back on itself."

"Ah—the cost of this operation—"

"Oh, we can meet that. Special assessment, voted at the last town meeting. They don't care very much, because money has little value when you can't buy more than the rationed necessities. And they're getting tired of going on short rations of power."

"I shouldn't say this, because your proposal is a fine deal for us, but have you stopped to think? Both the REA and the private power concerns will be restoring service eventually, just as soon as civil order has been recreated."

Arch nodded. "I know. But there are two answers to that. In the first place, we don't know when that'll be, and if we don't have adequate energy sources by winter we'll be up the creek. Also, we're building a sun-power plant which will cost almost nothing to operate. In the long run, and not so terribly long at that, it'll pay off."

Bob Culquhoun, who went on the selenium convoy, reported an adventurous journey through hundreds of miles where gangs of extremists still ruled. "But they seem to be settling down," he added. "Nobody likes to be a bandit, and anyhow the state militias are gradually subduing 'em. Most of the rural communities, though, are striking out on their own like us. There's going to be a big demand for selenium." Wistfulness flickered in his eyes. "Wonder if I can raise enough money to buy some stock?"

"It'll take time," said Elizabeth. "I know the sun-power generator is simple, but you still can't design and build one overnight."

As a matter of fact, fall had come again before Westfield's plant was in full operation. It didn't look impressive: great flat screens on top of hastily constructed buildings, and inside these the apparatus to raise voltage and charge capacitors. But in conjunction with the watermill, it furnished more than enough electricity to run the county's machines.

Arch was kept busy all that summer, directing, advising, helping. It seemed that everybody had some scheme of his own for using capacitite. Energy cost nothing, and machinery could be built from junkyard scrap if nothing else. Westfield was suddenly acquiring her own looms, mills, even a small foundry. Bob led a gang of young hellions who made an airplane and kept it aloft for days at a time. His father promptly confiscated it for the use of the civic guard, and after that there were no more surprise brushes with roving outlaws.

An eyewitness report was brought in from the air—a clash between state troops and one of the robber bands which still existed to the north. The gangmen had their own trucks and jeeps, their own guns, all operating off accumulators which could be charged at any of a thousand watermills. A rifleman could stop a tank, and aircraft were of limited value against guerrillas who crouched in brush and weeds. The battle was a draw, with both sides finally retreating.

Arch shuddered, alone with Elizabeth, and crept into her arms. "Did I do that?" he asked through his tears. "Did I do it?"

"No, darling," she said. One hand ruffled his disordered hair. "Can't you forget that side of it? Think of what you have done, with your own hands—built this town up again, given its people more than they ever had before."

He set his teeth. "I'll try," he said.

Somewhat later, the government offered amnesty to those outlaws who would lay down their arms and come home. It had the desired effect; they had had enough of warring and insecurity. But Culquhoun scowled. "'Tis a vurra bad precedent," he said. "Only a weak government makes such a move."

Oddly, Arch felt a lightening within himself. "Maybe a weak government is what we need," he answered.

News: Several southern states threaten secession unless court decisions concerning racial equality are withdrawn.

News: Uprisings in these same states. The Negro has had enough.

News: Capitulation of state governments. Constitutional conventions, transfer of power from state to local authorities.

News: The depression is not ending, but transforming itself: out-of-work men are starting to produce things for themselves with the help of capacitite-driven machinery often made at home, trading their surplus for whatever else they need. A mobile reclamation unit appears, costing little to operate, and families begin to irrigate and colonize desert areas. Big business, big labor, big government talk much and do nothing effective—their day is past, but they simply cannot understand the new forces at work.

News: More and more city areas are becoming empty as their inhabitants take advantage of cheap, fast transportation and move into the rapidly expanding suburbs and even into the country. This migration is possible because with present energy sources, plastic board for home construction can be manufactured at very low cost.

News: There is a great deal of debate in Washington about redistricting to meet the new population pattern. It doesn't seem too important, though, because a land of nearly self-sufficient communities, such as this is becoming, is much less dependent on central government.

News: Experiment and innovation in dress, work habits, manners and morals, grows ever more common. The basic cause of this is that few men need now be afraid of what the neighbors or the boss thinks. If you don't like it where you are, you can easily go elsewhere and start over.

None of this happened at once. It would take a century or more for the change to complete itself. But even in the second year, the trend was obvious.

Snow whirled against the house, blindingly, as if the world drew into itself and nothing lay beyond these walls.

The muted skirl of wind came through, lonesome and shivering. But inside, there was warmth and a calm light.

Arch sat with a whiskey and soda in his hand, looking across the floor at his wife. He felt tired, but there was a relaxation in him, a sense of labor finished.

Not fully—there would be much to do yet. But power was there, machinery was there, food stored away; they would last the winter, and there would be another springtime.

"It's settling down," Elizabeth told him, putting her news magazine aside. "For once, I agree with the editor of this rag. The crisis is over, and now it's a matter of readjustment. The world is never going to be the same, but it'll be a better one . . . cleaner."

"Perhaps," said Arch. He didn't feel so sharply the horror of guilt, not any more.

"Look around you," she invited. "Look what you've done. I'm afraid, dear, that you're going to be rediscovered. It won't take long before people suddenly wake up to the fact that your invention did all this for them. Brace yourself—you're going to be famous for life."

Arch winced. "But I didn't!" he protested. "They did it for themselves. One man never could—"

"I quite agree," she smiled. "One man can neither make nor destroy a society. So why not give that conscience of yours a rest?"

"There's been suffering," he said, enough alcohol in him to break down his reserve. "People have died."

"A lot of them needed killing," she said earnestly. "Look what we've got. An end to dictatorship. Removal of the atomic-war threat. Cheap energy for a million new projects. A four-hour work day in prospect. Government, which was getting too big and officious in all countries, cut down to size again. The plain man standing on his own feet and working for himself. Natural resources conserved. If you must take either credit or blame, Si, then balance your books!"

"I know," he said. "I know all that, up in my conscious

mind. But down underneath—I'll always see those houses burning, and those men shooting at each other."

"You—" She hesitated. "I know what you need. Your trouble, my boy, is that underneath that Yankee conservatism, you're a hopeless romantic. Your mind dwells on the sudden and dramatic. Now the positive benefits of capacitite aren't anywhere near as quick and spectacular as the temporary evils were. What you have to do, to satisfy those Puritan chromosomes, is to produce something really big and fancy, something of immediate, large value."

He chuckled, lifted out of his dark mood in spite of himself. "I imagine you're right, Dr. Freud," he said. "But what?"

"I don't know." She frowned with worry for him. "But think, man. We have leisure now—in another year or so, well, we won't be the millionaires we once dreamed of, but like everybody else we'll have real security and real time to ourselves. You could use that time to work on *something*."

"Hm—" Automatically, his brain turned to practicalities. "Let's see, now. Capacitite offers a way of concentrating energy enormously . . . a very small packet will hold a hell of a lot— *My God!*" His yell shook the windows as he leaped to his feet.

"What the devil—something wrong?" Elizabeth got up too.

"No!" He was running toward the phone. "Got to get hold of Colin—M.I.T.—don't you see, darling?" His hands trembled as he dialed, but there was laughter in his voice. "Don't you see it? Spaceships!"

Everyone wants energy, right? Clean, abundant energy, without the problems—real or imaginary—of fission power.

Don't bet on it. As Poul Anderson showed, every change, no matter how beneficial, steps on toes, injures vested interests . . . and there are a lot of vested interests. The benefits of change are spread out, and hypothetical, and accrue to everyone in general and nobody in particular: the costs are real power and real money, usually taken away from a concentrated group quite conscious of what it stands to lose. If a power company is making a good return, why should it back a process that would reduce the value of previous investments?

What's more, developing a new technology costs. Even if there's absolutely no doubt about technological feasibility, even if there's no doubt about the economic feasibility, money has to be spent. Money that everyone wants, for profits, for a senator's favorite pork-barrel, money to reduce a deficit. It's called investing in the future, and hereabouts that seems to be rather old-fashioned. Here a science fiction writer who was also involved with science fact shows how a technology that would double the efficiency of our fossil-fuel use—giving us breathing room to develop long-term alternatives—has been blocked by sheer inertia.

Progress does not happen of itself. It has to be made to happen. Not even the lure of profit is enough.

MHD
Ben Bova

GOOD NEWS, IF TRUE

During the Civil War, when reports from the battle front were spotty and often unreliable, many newspapers adopted a standard headline: "Good News, If True."

Nuclear fusion is indeed good news, if it ever comes true.

Fusion is the energy source of the Sun and stars. If scientists can produce fusion generators, the world's energy problems will be solved forever. The fuel for fusion will come from water. The energy produced is prodigious. An eight-ounce tumbler of tap water contains enough fusion fuel (deuterium, an isotope of hydrogen) to equal the energy content of half a million barrels of oil—while using less than one percent of the water.

You can drink the rest.

To put the possibilities of fusion into more humanly understandable terms, every time you flush the toilet you are getting rid of enough fusion fuel to run a four-bedroom house for ten years or more.

For nearly half a century a cadre of the world's brightest physicists, engineers, and technicians have been attempting to create a manmade sun, a controlled thermonuclear fusion reactor. In 1989 there was a sudden hurricane of excitement over the announcement that fusion had been achieved—not by physicists, but by chemists—and not in a massive piece of machinery, but in a test tube.

Good news, if true.

A year later, most observers feel that "cold" fusion is an illusion, although a stubborn few still report that something might indeed be happening in those test tubes.

Meanwhile, the physicists doggedly pursue their dream of "hot" fusion, building Tokamaks to contain star-hot plasmas in magnetic bottles or using powerful lasers to zap microscopic pellets filled with deuterium.

Someday, most likely in the 1990s, researchers will succeed in producing a sustained fusion reaction. But that will not mean that all our energy worries will be over. Far from it.

For there is a huge distance between success in the laboratory and practical use of a new process such as fusion. The scientists have to struggle against nature. Once they have succeeded, you and I have to struggle against social and political inertia.

The scientists have the easier job.

Back in 1959 a group of scientists announced the invention of a new way to generate electricity, a technique that would halve your electricity bill while allowing the utility companies to burn even the dirtiest coal without polluting the environment. More than thirty years later that technique, known as MHD, has still not left the laboratory.

What follows is a brief history of the MHD program. It is an object lesson in the way governments and private corporations can not only resist progress, but strangle it altogether.

Someday the scientists will announce that they have achieved fusion. If this marvelous new energy source is not to be stifled the way MHD was, *you* must be aware and active.

The truth is, the ultimate success of fusion depends more on you than on the scientists. Read about how MHD was ruined, and see why you must be vigilant, knowledgeable, and strong.

It will be up to you to make the good news come true.

Thirty-eight sturdy steel I-beams, painted bright blue, clamp the copper plates of the powerful electro-magnet together. A jungle of pipes and wires snakes into one end, where the rocketlike combustion chamber stands.

Taller than the technicians working through its final checkout, massive enough to generate more than thirty megawatts of electrical power, the Mark V is the biggest MHD power generator ever built. It looks so impressive, in fact, that a visiting Russian scientist surreptitiously took out a pocket knife and scratched it against one of the I-beams, wanting to make certain it was real and not a wooden mock-up built by the capitalists to hoodwink foreign visitors.

In the control room, separated from the monstrous generator itself by more solid steel and a heavy shatterproof window, the engineers go through a countdown much like that for a rocket launch.

The second hand of the clock on the wall sweeps inexorably. Once an explosion in a smaller generator started a fire so intense that the heat radiating through the window melted the instruments in the control room. No one was injured, but the roof was blown away by the blast.

"Three . . . two . . . one . . . *ignition!*"

A deafening roar erupts from the heart of the generator. You can feel it rattling your bones, flattening your eardrums.

But everyone is smiling. The gauges along the control board climb steadily, showing that millions of watts of electricity are being produced by the Mark V: ten megawatts, twenty . . . more than thirty.

The noise ends so abruptly that you feel like you've

been pushed off a cliff. Your ears ring. The pointers on the gauges drop back to zero.

The test has been a success. Slightly more than thirty-two megawatts. The Mark V MHD generator has operated just as the scientists predicted it would. Theory has been matched by experiment. MHD is almost ready to leave the laboratory and enter the practical world of electrical power generation.

That scene took place more than twenty years ago, in Everett, Massachusetts, a few miles north of Boston.

There, at the Avco Everett Research Laboratory, a spirited team of scientists and engineers were developing a new kind of electrical power generator, based on a technology with the jawbreaking name of *magnetohydrodynamics*. MHD, for short.

I worked at Avco Everett from 1959 to 1971. I was there when the MHD program started, and I saw it founder and almost sink.

A quarter century ago, the head of the Avco Everett lab was so confident of MHD that he bet an executive from the electric utilities industry that MHD would be producing electricity for utility customers by 1970. He lost that bet. As things stand now, MHD won't start producing commercial electrical power until the mid-1990s—if then.

MHD could have averted the acid rain problem that now plagues wide areas of the eastern United States and Canada. It would have allowed electric power plants to burn coal cleanly, using America's most abundant fuel without producing the pollution fallout that is now stripping forests bare and killing aquatic life in lakes and streams.

Studies have shown that MHD power generators can burn the dirtiest coal without polluting the air, and burn it so efficiently that they produce 50 percent more kilowatts per pound of fuel than ordinary generators. More kilowatts per dollar would mean lower electricity bills for the consumer.

But MHD is no closer to realization today than it was

twenty years ago. The story of MHD is a story of technological daring and political timidity, a story of failed hopes and lost opportunities.

"It's a tragic story," says Arthur Kantrowitz. "It's a story of frustration that's been very painful to me."

Kantrowitz is universally acknowledged as the father of MHD power generation. Now a professor at Dartmouth College's Thayer School of Engineering, Kantrowitz was the founder of Avco Everett and the driving force behind the MHD program in the 1960s. He is a dynamic, barrel-chested man who created one of the nation's leading industrial research laboratories out of his own restless desire to do scientific research "that has an impact on the way people live."

MHD began in the bright promise of space-age research. In 1955 Kantrowitz left a professorship at Cornell University to found Avco Everett, bringing a handful of his brightest graduate students with him. The laboratory, originally housed in an abandoned warehouse, was created to solve the problems of reentry for ballistic missile "nose cones." The Air Force desperately needed to know how to design reentry vehicles that would not burn to cinders when returning from space.

Using shock tubes, Kantrowitz's Avco Everett team simulated the conditions a reentry vehicle would have to face and within six months provided the data needed for engineers to design survivable reentry vehicles. Eventually another division of Avco Corporation built all the reentry heat shields for the Apollo lunar spacecraft.

Using their newly won knowledge of the behavior of very hot gases, Kantrowitz and his young staff tackled the problem of MHD power generation.

Power generators convert heat to electricity. In today's electric utility power plants, this energy conversion is accomplished by turbogenerators. Heat is created either by burning a fossil fuel (oil, coal, or natural gas) or by the fissioning of atoms in a nuclear reactor. The heat boils water. The steam turns the turbine. The turbine is connected to a bundle of copper wires called an armature, which sits inside a powerful magnet. When the steam turns the turbine, and the turbine spins the armature within the magnetic field, an electric current is generated.

Michael Faraday discovered the principles of electrical power generation in the 1830s, in Britain. Thomas Edison made it all practical some fifty years later, and electrified the world. Edison's steam-turbine generators were about 40 percent efficient. The steam turbogenerators used today are no better.

Instead of turbines and armatures, MHD employs the roaring ultra-hot exhaust gas of a powerful rocket engine, so rich in energy that it contains megawatts of potential electrical power in every cubic meter of its stream. By running such a gas through a pipe, with a powerful magnet around it and durable electrodes inside it, a steady current of electricity can be tapped from the hot gas. That is an MHD generator. A *Saturn V* rocket bellowing up from Cape Canaveral on its way to the Moon could have produced enough electricity, through MHD, to light the entire eastern seaboard for as long as its engines were burning.

No moving parts. No turbines. The supersonically flowing hot gas is itself the "armature." Efficiencies of 60 percent or more are attainable. More kilowatts per pound of fuel. More electricity per dollar.

High temperature is the key to efficiency. Turbogenerators are limited to temperatures well below 1,000°F because the turbine blades cannot take more heat without breaking. In the rocketlike combustion chamber of an MHD generator, the fuel is burned either in pure oxygen or preheated air to raise the gas temperature to 5,000°F. A pinch of potassium "seeding" is added to the hot gas, because potassium ionizes easily at such temperatures and makes the gas an electrical conductor. Although thousands of times less conductive than copper, the ionized gas (physicists call it a plasma) conducts electricity well enough to become an effective armature.

The high temperature in an MHD generator creates problems that ordinary generators do not face. The combustion chamber, the MHD channel, and especially the electrodes inside the channel, must be able to stand the rigors of a supersonic flow of 5,000°F plasma that is choked with soot and corrosive combustion products while megawatts of electricity are blazing within it.

But those very conditions force the MHD system to be environmentally clean. Scrubbers in the smoke-stack downstream are economically necessary to recover the costly potassium seed so that it can be reused. They also take out the soot from the exhaust gas before it is released to the air. Thus the cost of soot removal is built into the original cost of the MHD power plant and is not an expensive add-on.

Sulfur and nitrogen compounds that might cause smog and acid rain are removed from the hot gas by completely conventional equipment before they leave the MHD system. There is so much of these pollutants in the hot plasma stream that it becomes economically attractive to remove them and convert them into fertilizers, to be sold in the agricultural market. Again, the antipollution equipment is built into the MHD system for sound economic reasons. Nothing goes up the smokestack except warm carbon dioxide and a few impurities, well within the current clean-air standards set by the Environmental Protection Agency.

The first working MHD generator was built in 1959 at Avco Everett. It produced ten kilowatts (ten thousand watts) for a few seconds. The laboratory's parent, Avco Corporation, in conjunction with a group of electric utility companies, funded a fast-paced research and development effort under Kantrowitz's direction.

The program followed a two-pronged approach. Large MHD generators tested the ability to produce multimegawatts of power. Smaller generators tested the durability of the materials and components of an MHD generator over long time periods. By 1966 Avco's Mark V had generated more than thirty-two megawatts, and smaller machines had been operated for hundreds of hours continuously.

Kantrowitz and his team were ready, they believed, to build a demonstration power plant: an MHD generation station that would deliver some fifty megawatts of electricity and serve as a model for full-scale commercial power stations.

The demonstration plant was never built. Although Kantrowitz was confident that his team was ready to build it, hardly anyone else was.

The pilot plant would have cost $30 million in the mid-1960s. Avco and the electric utilities consortium were prepared to put up only $13 million. Kantrowitz and Philip Sporn, who headed the utilities group backing MHD, went to Washington and proposed to Stewart Udall, then Secretary of the Interior, a program funded fifty-fifty by the government and the Avco-utilities group.

But two "terrible blows," as Kantrowitz puts it, hit MHD and almost destroyed the program utterly.

First, Sporn reached mandatory retirement age and was forced out of his powerful position at American Electric Power Company. He had been a major figure in the utility industry, a leader with the drive and vision to equal Kantrowitz's own. The two men were well matched and made an effective team. Kantrowitz's bet about having MHD "on-line" by 1970—a symbolic bet of one dollar—had been with Sporn. Once Sporn lost his power base and was no longer able to keep prodding his colleagues, the electric utilities began to lose interest in MHD.

At about the same time, President Lyndon Johnson announced that cheap nuclear energy was at hand. "This wasn't true," Kantrowitz asserts, but with the White House pushing nuclear power, no one in Washington was willing to back an alternative such as coal-burning MHD.

John T. Conway, a vice-president of New York's Con Edison power company, was on the staff of the U.S. Congress Joint Committee on Atomic Energy in the mid-1960s.

He does not see the MHD decision as being pronuclear at the expense of coal. "In fact, we were trying to make coal and nuclear developments a joint effort," he says. "We knew that nuclear energy by itself couldn't handle all the nation's needs. We knew we needed nuclear *and* coal."

MHD lost out, according to Conway, for several reasons—none of them having anything to do with the technical performance of MHD generators.

First, the coal industry itself was "terribly fragmented" by battles between labor and management. As a result, there was no unified position from the coal industry backing MHD as a user of the nation's most abundant fuel.

Second, according to Conway, "When you get to the big bucks that hardware requires, you reach a natural checkpoint." The plans for an MHD demonstration plant were competing with requests for expensive new "atom-smashing" particle accelerators for high-energy physics experiments. The accelerators got the funding.

Most important, though, was Sporn's sudden departure. "Sporn was a hardheaded engineer," Conway recalls, "like a Rickover." Once the program lost his "drive and authority," the decision-makers in Washington lost confidence in MHD.

Princeton University's Jonathon C. Coopersmith, in his 1978 analysis of the MHD programs in the United States and Soviet Russia, concluded:

> Exactly why the [MHD] project was not approved by the government is not clear. The enthusiasm for nuclear power . . . undoubtedly had a great deal to do with the lack of similar enthusiasm for coal in government circles. Funding constraints imposed by Johnson's Great Society programs and the Vietnam War also had a negative impact. . . .

As the sixties staggered to their end under the burden of Vietnam and civil unrest, there was a general decline in government support of research and development. Hardly anyone in Washington, or anywhere else in the nation, would back a new energy technology. The Yom Kippur War, the Arab oil embargo, and the energy crisis were less than five years away. Protests and demonstrations against nuclear power plants were already beginning; the Three Mile Island fiasco was ten years in the future.

Because he was a corporate vice-president and member of the Avco board of directors, Kantrowitz could keep his MHD program inching along on corporate funds. But the kind of money needed to build the pilot plant could be found only in Washington. No private investors were willing to take the risk, and corporations that were already heavily involved in building conventional power generators saw no incentive in helping to develop competition for their existing products.

Researchers at Westinghouse and General Electric maintained comparatively low-level efforts in MHD, and several universities such as Stanford and Tennessee carried on MHD studies.

Kantrowitz and fellow Avco Corporation board member George Allen found a sympathetic ear in Clark Clifford, a longtime Washington "insider" who had served briefly as Johnson's Secretary of Defense after Robert McNamara left the Cabinet.

"We told him MHD would be good for the country," Kantrowitz remembers, "but no private company could justify risking the money to develop it."

Clifford began "knocking on doors" in Washington. The only one that opened was that of Senator Mike Mansfield, Democrat from Montana and majority leader of the Senate. Montana is a state that is rich in coal but poor in water resources. MHD is an energy system that could burn Montana's coal without using up its scarce water.

"I don't know how Mansfield reached the decision that he would grab on to it," says Kantrowitz. "But he made the decision that he wanted MHD for Montana."

Suddenly the obscure Office of Coal Research, buried deep within the Department of the Interior, began funding MHD. The budget rose quickly from a few hundred thousand dollars to some $70 million per year by the mid-1970s.

But the money was not being spent on Kantrowitz's dream of a pilot plant. Every private and university laboratory engaged in MHD research lined up for a piece of the pie, and the funding was dutifully parceled out to government labs and private companies—including Avco Everett—and to universities such as Stanford, Tennessee, and the University of Montana, where a Mansfield-inspired MHD Institute and testing facility were built.

In the words of one disgruntled researcher, "They were spending more on MHD than ever, and getting less results." The program had no real goal, no focus.

"By that time the estimates of the cost of a pilot plant were $200 to $300 million," Kantrowitz says. "Nobody had the courage to undertake that risk."

Undaunted, Kantrowitz urged Mansfield to push for an MHD program that would produce megawatts instead of research reports.

The senator told Kantrowitz to write out a plan of action and Kantrowitz did, on a single sheet of paper. "I said we should build a pilot plant, and that's it," Kantrowitz recalls. The plan was enacted by the Congress, tacked onto another bill as a rider, and in 1976 Mansfield personally presented it to President Gerald Ford for his signature.

But even that failed to produce an MHD pilot plant. There were no teeth in the law. "I was stupid enough to think that if the Congress passed the MHD action plan, it would result in action," says Kantrowitz ruefully. "It did absolutely nothing." The Department of Energy has been "studying" the plan for nearly ten years.

By 1978 it was Kantrowitz's turn to face mandatory retirement. He left Avco Everett and accepted a professorship at Dartmouth. "It's very painful to retire when you've still got things to do," he says.

When the Reagan Administration swept into Washing-

ton early in 1981, one of its avowed aims was to disman-
tle the Department of Energy and all of its programs.

But the new head of Avco Everett, R. W. ("Dutch")
Detra, and Vincent J. Coates, director of Special Projects,
began a campaign with MHD enthusiasts in Montana
and elsewhere. Working with congressmen and senators
who opposed dissolving the Department of Energy, they
were able to keep MHD funded at about $30 million per
year through the first Reagan Administration.

"The Massachusetts congressional delegation has been
very helpful," Coates says. "Particularly Nicholas
Mavroules, Silvio Conte, and Edward P. Boland." Congressmen from Montana and Tennessee, where MHD
research efforts are under way, have also staunchly supported the program. So has powerful Senator John
Stennis of Mississippi, who believes energy technology is
vital to national defense.

Like ancient Gaul, the Department of Energy's MHD
program is divided into three major parts. Avco Everett
is concentrating on the MHD channel, the pipe at the
heart of the generator that extracts electrical energy from
the ultra-hot stream of gas flowing through it. TRW Corporation's Energy Technology Division in Redondo Beach,
California, is developing special coal burners. And Bab-
cock & Wilcox is building boilers that can take the still-
hot gas coming out of an MHD generator and make
steam that will run a conventional generator "downstream" of the MHD system.

Robert Kessler is Avco Everett's vice-president for
energy technology, head of the MHD effort. He sees a
pilot plant being built by 1995.

"The Department of Energy plan calls for retrofitting
an existing power plant with an MHD system in the early
to mid-1990s," says Kessler.

But privately, many scientists who have worked on
MHD nearly all their lives admit that even that date—
twenty-five years later than Kantrowitz's original estima-
tion—may not be met. William D. Jackson, the "J" of
HMJ Corporation, a small Washington-based energy

research and development company, says, "A pilot plant in the early 1990s is just flat optimistic." He believes that DOE's current program of $30 million per year is far too small; $100 million per year is needed, Jackson claims.

Kessler says, "What we're trying to achieve is reliable operation of MHD equipment at sizes that are practical for commercial power generation. At this stage of the game, efficiency is not so important as predictability, economics, and reliability." He lays heavy emphasis on reliability.

Jackson agrees. "They've got to build something that a utility company would allow into one of its power plants!"

The DOE plan calls for an MHD generator to be installed in an existing power plant as a "topping unit." That is, the MHD system will start the process of converting heat to electricity. As the hot gas leaves the MHD generator, after having surrendered as much as fifty megawatts of electrical energy, it will be fed into the special boilers that will raise steam for the plant's conventional turbogenerators, which will then make even more electricity from the same original coal-fired heat input.

DOE has already indicated that it expects the MHD program's industrial participants to share the costs of the pilot plant. The government will not foot the bill on tax money alone. Joseph McElwain, chairman and chief executive officer of Montana Power Company, has offered one of his utility's power plants as the site for the demonstration retrofit. But the other industrial partners are looking askance at the idea of cost-sharing.

"It could take twenty years before the money invested in a demonstration plant shows any profit," says Avco Everett chief Detra. "Can a corporation afford to tie up millions of dollars for such a long time?"

Kantrowitz now serves as one of fifteen advisors to the MHD Industrial Forum, an organization created by the companies involved in MHD development. To him, all this should have happened twenty years ago.

"If we had built a pilot plant in the sixties," he insists, "it wouldn't have worked—at first. Then we'd figure out

why it didn't work, we'd fix it, and it would have worked."
A pilot plant in the 1990s will go through the same evolution. "It won't work. You'll have to fix it. What you might hope for is that you have a larger background of knowledge from which to fix it."

Kessler almost agrees. "If they'd built the pilot plant back in the sixties, we'd be ahead of where we are today."

But Jackson disagrees. If a pilot plant had been built in the 1960s and failed, "it would have killed MHD," he says. "Just absolutely killed it."

Some of the scientists and engineers involved in the program today are deeply pessimistic. "The only kinds of experiments we do are the kinds that entail no risks," says one of them. "That's no way to make progress."

"The MHD program has become a minor pork barrel," says another. "Its real aim is to satisfy the political forces that exist in Massachusetts, Montana, and Tennessee."

"We're no closer to a pilot plant now than we were eighteen years ago," Kantrowitz asserts flatly.

Perhaps the gloomiest statement came from an engineer who has worked almost his entire professional life on MHD. "I used to hope to see MHD become practical and useful in my lifetime. Now I don't think it will. I think I've been wasting my time."

"From the technical point of view there's no reason why MHD can't become commercially viable," says Richard Rosa, the man who built the first working MHD generator, at Avco Everett in 1959. Now a professor of mechanical engineering at the University of Montana, at Bozeman, Rosa is still carrying out MHD research and consulting with the nearby MHD Institute at Butte.

The annual Washington budget battle, however, "really tears up the program," according to Rosa. "Half the year everybody's on hold." He believes that the utility industry's bad experiences with technological innovations such as nuclear power is discouraging the industry from investing the money required to make a commercial success of MHD.

So the program is totally dependent on federal funding, with "a crisis every year."

The fear of massive budget deficits now pervading Washington led David Stockman's Office of Management and Budget to "zero out" MHD in the fiscal year 1986 federal budget. This was not the first time MHD has been dropped from the White House's budget plans. Similar efforts to stop all government funding of MHD have been successfully fought before. But there is more pressure now than ever to get the government out of the MHD business.

The House of Representatives Science and Technology Subcommittee on Energy Development and Applications approved a $28-million authorization for MHD. Coates believes the pro-MHD forces in Congress may eke out a budget somewhere between $25 and $30 million. But there is pressure from the White House to drop the program, once and for all.

"At best, we'll be able to keep the program alive from year to year," Coates says. "But as long as we have this polite antagonism between government and private industry, the U.S. runs the risk of losing its lead in technology to countries where government and industry work together."

Japan, China, and the Soviet Union are pursuing their own MHD programs, based on the work originally done in the United States, Coates points out. "We may have to buy MHD generators from them," he says.

In September 1983 Kantrowitz was invited to Moscow to receive the Faraday Medal, presented by UNESCO to him and Soviet scientist A. E. Sheindlin for their contributions to MHD.

Ironically, he never went to accept the medal. As he was preparing to leave for Moscow, the Soviets shot down Korean Air Lines flight 007. Kantrowitz canceled his trip. UNESCO sent the medal to his home in New Hampshire.

"It's the last thing of significance that I've had to do with MHD," he says sadly. "A medal instead of a pilot plant."

But a pilot plant *was* built in the 1960s. Near Moscow. Based largely on the work done in Massachusetts, the Russians have pushed ahead with the kind of MHD program that Kantrowitz was looking for. The Russian U-25 MHD plant worked well enough so that the Soviet government is starting construction of a 250-megawatt MHD plant at Ryazan, a city some 130 miles southeast of Moscow. Called the U-500, this power plant is expected to be delivering electricity before the end of the decade.

It may be that the only way the United States will get MHD power plants in the 1990s will be to buy them from the Soviet Union—if the Russians will be willing to sell our own technology back to us.

. . . AND INTO THE NINETIES

The article above was written in 1982. The picture for MHD has not brightened much in the ensuing years.

The U.S. program is still staggering along, the victim of political timidity, in Kantrowitz's view. Research is still proceeding at a low pace in a number of industrial and academic laboratories. Each year there is the annual budgetary crisis. No decision has been made, as of early 1990, to build the pilot plant that Kantrowitz wanted to build twenty-five years ago.

In the U.S.S.R., MHD has become a victim of *perestroika*. The U-500 plant was never completed, although 10-MW MHD generators, small enough to be mounted on trucks, are apparently being used in experiments to locate deposits of valuable ores, such as nickel. The MHD generator's current is used to induce a magnetic field in the ground, and magnetometers then can detect the presence of metallic ores. The technique may also be useful for locating oil deposits, and geological fault lines where earthquakes may occur.

It appears that nothing short of an impending catastrophe, such as global greenhouse warming, will spur the world's political leaders to develop MHD as a clean way of using coal to generate electricity.

Technology creates possibilities; without something that gives a better power-to-weight ration than a steam engine, you cannot fly. Once you can fly, you can nip down to the Islands for the winter . . . get injured people to hospital quickly . . . finally give those damned heretical unclean foreigners the bomb they deserve!

But technology also creates limits. Take half a dozen Old Stone Age humans, strip them naked, and drop them down anywhere it isn't freezing. In a couple of weeks they'll be right back to normal, since all their technology needs is rocks and plants. In a similar situation, half a dozen modern urbanites would be lucky if a lion ate them before they starved to death. Fusion power is the ultimate freedom, almost literally the power of the gods. Certainly enough to get you to the stars, at least. Ah, but what if you lose the power . . .

... And Check the Oil ...
Randall Garrett

I don't know who got me into it. Somebody mentioned my name to somebody else, I suppose, and then some third party agreed, so my name was sent to the FBI. Those worthy gentlemen stewed over my recorded past and my reputable present, and came up with a forecast on my probable future, all of which was duly forwarded to the persons interested. They chewed it all over, and I was nabbed for the job.

Of course, it wasn't quite as crude as that. They couldn't and didn't draft me; instead, they got Hoffstetter to do it. He was the perfect man for the job, too; he knows that the way to whet the scientific appetite is to give it a tidbit that it can't swallow until it's been chewed over for a long time.

He came strolling into my lab one day with a grin spread across his chubby face and said: "Hi, Doc. I asked at your office first, but the girl said you'd be in the lab. I should have known you'd never go in for paper work."

"Hi, Hoff," I said. "Still working for Uncle Sam'l?"

"Well, it feels like work, and I'm drawing a paycheck. What's cooking?"

He meant the question literally. He was pointing at the Wolff flask on the lab bench in front of me. There was a thermometer in one neck, a mercury-sealed electric stirrer in another, and a specially-designed fractionating column attached to the third. The whole thing was attached to a vacuum pump, and the stuff in the flask was boiling merrily.

I knew he wasn't really interested, so I just said: "A bunch of benzine derivatives, I hope. What's on your mind, Hoff?"

"I've got a job for you, Doc," Hoffstetter said casually.

I peered at the thermometer, checked the time, and put the figures on my data sheet. "Yeah? What kind of a job?"

His grin grew wider. "Now, what kind of a job would I be giving to the world's greatest chemist? Dishwashing?"

"I've done plenty of that," I told him. "And knock off that 'world's greatest' bunk. I'm not, and you know it."

"You are as far as this job is concerned. Here." He reached in his pocket and pulled out a small box. He set it on the lab bench and flipped it open. It was padded inside like a jeweler's box, and a small sealed flask nestled itself comfortably in the padding. The flask wasn't any bigger than the first joint of my thumb. It was about three-quarters full of some straw-colored liquid.

I didn't pick it up. I just looked at it and then looked up at Hoffstetter. "So?"

"It's all yours," he said, "all one and a half milliliters of it. We want to know what it is."

This time, I picked the flask up. It was a trifle heavier than I'd expected it to be. The liquid inside was more viscous than water. In fact, the stuff looked and flowed like a good grade of light machine oil.

"Where'd you get it?" I asked.

"I can't tell you, Doc," Hoffstetter said.

That irritated me. "Well, is there anything you *can* tell me? This bottle's sealed. What happens if I break the seal? Does it oxidize on exposure to air, or evaporate, or what?"

"Oh, that. That was just to prevent leakage. No, it's fairly stable, I imagine. Odorless. Nonpoisonous, as far as I know, though I don't think anyone's tried to taste it. Oily. I don't know the boiling point."

I was holding the flask up to the light, and I noticed that the meniscus at the surface was convex. "And it doesn't wet glass," I said.

"Hell," said Hoffstetter, "it doesn't wet anything."

"Interesting," I admitted. "Is this the biggest sample you could get?"

Hoffstetter spread his hands. "It's all I have."

"Not much to work with," I told him, "but I'll see what I can do."

"Fair enough," he said. "Send the analysis and the bill to me, personally." He handed me a card. "And keep it under your hat."

"Fair enough," I said. "I'll let you know in a week or so."

It was a lot less than a week. Three days later, I got Hoffstetter on the phone. "Hoff, where the devil did you get that stuff?"

"Why?" he countered. "What's that got to do with it?"

"Because it doesn't act like anything I ever came across before."

"You mean you can't analyze it?" he asked. His voice sounded worried.

"I didn't say that. The first thing I did was get a spectroscope reading, so I can tell you to a T what elements are in the stuff. But the molecular weight is something fierce. It's way too high."

"What do you mean, 'too high'?"

"Well, the stuff ought to be a solid, not a nice, free-flowing liquid," I told him. "And it's a devil of a lot more stable than it ought to be, all things considered. Can you possibly get me any more of it?"

There was a silence at the other end for a moment. Then Hoffstetter said: "Do you think you could analyze it if you had more time and more of the stuff?"

"Sure. Where can I get it?"

Hoffstetter had me with a gaff, and he knew it. I could almost see his grin coming across the phone wires. He made his proposition. I hemmed and hawed for all of five minutes before I took it.

It didn't take long for me to get a leave of absence from my own company. I just left it in the hands of my business partner, George Avery, and took off. The lab staff could handle almost anything that came along while I was gone. Hoffstetter and I caught a commercial airline stratocruiser out to the West Coast, and an Air Force jet bomber took us from there. I had no idea of where we were headed, except that it was an unidentified island somewhere in the South Pacific.

The plane rolled to a halt at the end of a long runway. A squad of Air Force men, each armed with a heavy pistol at his belt, came sprinting up to help us unload. I'd requisitioned some equipment I needed from the Air Force labs, and it was all neatly packed in crates in the belly of the ship. The Air Force men treated the crates as though they were babies, which I appreciated no little.

The first thing that caught my eyes as I stepped off the plane was the big metal dome that towered over every other building on the base, even the control tower. It looked thick and squat, even so; it looked like a big, flat, black Easter egg sitting on its larger end. It was a hundred feet high and at least seventy-five feet through at its thickest part.

Don't ask me why I didn't recognize it for what it was. I should have, I suppose. I should have taken one look at it, and said to myself: "Well, what do you know? A spaceship!" but somehow I had always assumed that a spaceship would be a tall thin cigar of polished metal, not a fat, eggy-looking dead black thing like this.

I started to ask Hoffstetter what it was, but he shook his head before I could get my mouth open. "No questions, Doc. Answers first, questions afterward."

I knew Hoffstetter well enough to know that he wasn't

just making meaningless noises, so I just kept my mouth shut and followed him to the jeep which was waiting for us a few yards from the plane. The sergeant at the wheel just barely waited until we'd sat down before he gunned the motor and took off towards the nearest of the buildings at the edge of the landing field.

I was beginning to get uncomfortable. The plane had been air-conditioned, but the landing field wasn't. The hot whiteness of the Pacific sun glared down from a pale blue sky and sparkled from the deeper blue of the ocean in the distance. I saw Hoffstetter peeling off his civilian jacket, so I did likewise. If he wasn't going to be formal, neither was I.

The jeep pulled up in front of a two-story wooden building that gleamed whitely with fresh paint. Hoffstetter and I climbed out, and I followed him in through the door.

It was a normal-looking military office. Men and women in uniform sat at desks in the big room or moved through it with quiet efficiency. There was only one jarring note. Every man and woman in the place had a sidearm strapped to their waist, and every one of them gave the impression that he or she was ready, willing, and able to use it.

Hoffstetter led me to the door marked COMMANDING GENERAL. There was an Air Force captain sitting at a desk piled high with papers. At his waist was the ubiquitous sidearm. He looked up as Hoffstetter and I came in.

"Hello, Hoffstetter. I see you got your man." He had a rather tired smile on this thin face. "Let's see the papers."

Hoffstetter pulled a sheaf of official papers out of his brief case and handed them over. The captain leafed through them, nodded, stood up, and saluted. Then he held out his hand.

"Welcome aboard, commander."

I took the hand, but I didn't return the salute. Navy men don't salute unless their head is covered.

"I still don't quite understand why I had to accept active duty for this job," I told him. "I thought I'd be in the United States Naval Reserve, Inactive, for the rest of my life. Why recall me to duty just so I can go on being a chemist?"

The captain frowned. "I think you'd better ask the general about that, sir. He's expecting you."

He punched a button on the intercom on his desk and said: "Commander Barton is here, sir."

"Send him in," said the gravelly bass voice of Lieutenant General Mawson. He didn't sound as though he'd changed a bit since I'd last seen him, eight years before.

He had changed some, though. I saw that as soon as we entered the office. His hair, which had been only gray at the temples, was almost solid gray now, and the lines in his face had deepened, making it look more like weathered brown granite than ever.

"Commander Peter Barton reporting for duty, sir," I said.

He snapped me a salute and waved towards a chair. "Glad to see you, sailor. Sit down." Then he looked at Hoffstetter. "It took you long enough to get him here."

Hoffstetter grinned. "I had to twist his arm, general."

"All right. Give me those papers and scram. You'll take the same plane back as soon as she's refueled. See if you can snare Galvez for us."

"I'll try," said Hoffstetter. He put his hand on my shoulder. "Be good, Doc. I'll see you." And he was gone.

"I don't suppose you brought a uniform," said General Mawson.

"I didn't have time, sir. Everybody was in such an all-fired hurry that I couldn't get everything straightened out at home, much less think of everything I'd need here."

Mawson made a gesture of dismissal. "That's all right. You won't need anything here except khakis, anyway. I did manage to get some insignia for you from one of the Navy boys, so you'll be all right." He opened a drawer of his desk and pulled out a handful of hardware—the

Naval shield-and-anchors and the silver oak-leaves of a full commander.

"And I got a Navy hat for that big dome of yours—a seven and three-quarters, isn't it? Right. Go down to the QM and get some khakis, then go over to Ordnance and draw a sidearm and holster. Come back here at sixteen hundred, and don't go asking a lot of questions around here. That clear?"

I stood up. "Yes, sir. But I'd like to ask one question of you."

"Shoot," he said. "But I don't promise an answer."

"Why was it necessary for me to sign up for active duty? Doesn't the Air Force believe in hiring civilian chemists any more?"

The general's face hardened. "Not for this job. We want you under military discipline."

"Why, sir?"

"So we can court-martial you and shoot you if we have to."

I went over to the Quartermaster building to get a uniform. The shavetail in charge give me three suits of khakis and everything to go with them except a hat. He didn't have the regulation Navy covers. He tried to palm some field boots off on me, but I stuck with my guns and insisted on black oxfords. He gave in and then checked over his list of rooms in the Bachelor Officer's Quarters and assigned me a number and gave me the key.

Then I went over to Ordnance and picked up a sidearm, a holster, and two magazines of ammunition. I wanted to ask the Ordnance officer why it was necessary for everyone to carry a loaded pistol, but I decided that such questions just might be the kind that Mawson didn't want me to ask. And I didn't feel like breaking any regulations until I found out what was going on.

I headed for the BOQ to check in, dump my gear, and get into uniform. In the distance, I could see the towering black dome. I kept wondering what it was, but I decided not to ask any questions about the dome, either.

At sixteen hundred that afternoon, I was back in General Mawson's office. We didn't stay long. Mawson led me outside, and he headed across the compound toward the great black ovoid.

"I know you want to ask a lot of questions, Barton," General Mawson said, "but hold off a little until we can give you a connected story. It'll makes things easier in the long run, and take less time. O.K.?"

"You're the general," I said. "You know more about the situation than I do. But I warn you, I came here because of a promise; I wouldn't like to see you pull a fast one on me."

"What promise was that?" asked Mawson.

"That oily-looking liquid that Hoffstetter brought me a sample of," I told him. "I was promised that I'd get more of it to work on, and that I could have all the equipment I needed."

Mawson came out with his deep, rasping chuckle. "Don't worry, Barton. We have all sorts of fascinating things for you to work on. That's why you're here."

We went into another building, located almost at the base of the huge, looming, black egg. I could see that it was a newly constructed, temporary affair; the walls were covered with plastic sheeting, and the inside was unpainted. I followed Mawson upstairs, into a roomful of people.

There were twenty people in that room, sixteen men and four women, and everyone of them was in uniform. Air Force, Army, Navy, Marines, even the Coast Guard was represented. But most of them were Air Force.

I knew several of them personally. Lidell, the biologist; Freisen, a physical chemist from Cal Tech; and Burkhalter, an M.D. specializing in neurology, were all friends of mine. I knew Oglethorpe, the physicist, and Bell, the biochemist, well enough to speak to, and most of the others I knew by reputation. Old Professor Brymer, one of the top astronomers in the world, was chuckling over the fact that he was the oldest boot shavetail in the Air

Force. He and several others had not had reserve commissions, so Uncle Sugar had just handed out a few gold bars.

One of the women was a good-looking brunette in her middle thirties; a sleek, svelte, efficient-looking female who looked as though she were a thoroughgoing career girl, as uninterested in men as an Easter Island statue, and as cold as Little America in August. That is, she seemed that way from a distance of a couple of yards. But when we were introduced, her hand squeezed mine, and her eyes looked straight into mine and crinkled up in the same expression that Lilith must have given Adam. With the smile on her lips and the light in those gray-green eyes, she had suddenly changed. Cold? Yeah, like an atomic oxyhydrogen torch.

I repeated her name because it hadn't quite registered. "Lieutenant Anthony? The name is familiar, but—"

She laughed. "Anthony is a pretty common name, Commander Barton, but I know what you mean. You're trying to place my name in some scientific field. Ever hear of S. Brownell Anthony?"

I snapped my fingers. "Sure! That is, the name rings a bell, but I still can't quite place it. Didn't you have a couple of articles in *Scientific American* a while back?"

"Five, to be exact." She could see I was racking my brains to place her, and the little devil was grinning at me!

"All right," I said, "I give up."

"The last one was 'Linguistics and Primitive Man,'" she said.

"I'm crushed," I said. "I must admit my ignorance. I remember the title now, but I didn't get around to reading it."

"That's all right," she told me, still grinning. "I didn't read your article on stable colloids, either, but at least I remembered your name."

"I've got the last laugh," I said. "I'm Peter Barton, not Edwin. No relation. I didn't write the colloid article."

She laughed again. "All right, we're even."

"Break it up," said General Mawson. "You two can play guessing games when you're off duty. We have a lecture to listen to right now."

There were chairs lined up in the room, in rows like those in a theater. At the front of the room was a broad, white projection screen, and at the rear a couple of enlisted men were standing behind a pair of projectors. One was for slides, the other for moving pictures. They both seemed to be loaded.

General Mawson stood in front of the screen with a long wooden pointer in his hands and said: "Ladies and gentlemen, give me your attention, please."

The room quieted down, and Mawson went on. "Some of you have already seen this, but it won't hurt to go over it again. Those of you who have just arrived may be a little surprised when you see what we have here; some of you may think we're pulling your legs. I assure you, we are not. Now, each of you has pencil and paper there on the chair. Please take notes on any questions you want to ask and save the questions until after the lecture. There is no point in going over something twice if you can get it the first time, and some of your early questions may be answered later on in the talk. O.K.? Sergeant, douse those lights."

The lights went out, the slide projector came on, and we all sat back to see and hear the most sensational story since the Resurrection.

The radar operators thought it must be a balloon the first time it appeared on their scopes. It was coming down much too slowly to be any conventional aircraft, and when it got close enough to the island for the sound detectors to pick up any engine noise, there wasn't a whisper from it.

It was late evening, and the rainy season had come, covering the island in a visually impenetrable murk. When the thing was spotted on the radarscopes, dropping slowly toward the island, the searchlights had been turned on in an attempt to spot what everyone thought was one of the huge gasbags that are used for high-altitude weather observation.

Only when it broke through the overcast a hundred feet above the landing field had it become obvious that this thing was a long way from being a balloon.

If the ship had dropped in fast, the Air Force would have had it fired on by the ack-ack guns that bristled around the field. But who fires at weather balloons? And by the time the ship became visible in the withering glare of the bright searchlights, it was too late to fire the ack-acks.

The bottom of the big egg settled itself gently on the broad concrete expanse of the airfield. It touched the surface and kept on going, crushing through the thick slab of concrete and settling into the coral rock beneath.

Then it stopped.

It was lucky that General Mawson had been there. Some officers would have gotten scared and ordered the guns to open fire; Mawson didn't. He figured that the worst thing that the object could be was a hydrogen bomb, and a bomb that big wasn't going to be a healthy target for heavy artillery. Besides, he'd had a hunch that it was something genuinely out of this world. Anything heavy enough to crunch its way through that landing strip shouldn't be floating through the air like a bubble full of helium. And Mawson knew enough to be fairly sure that neither Russia nor the United States had yet developed anything like a real, efficient antigravity device.

Mawson had held his fire and waited.

And nothing more had happened. The big black egg just sat there, doing nothing.

It sent out no radio waves, no signal of any kind, except the faint background noise of the infrared radiations of its own internal temperature. The only detectable vibration from the thing was picked up by sensitive equipment that the Navy used for submarine hunting. The noise from inside the ship sounded for all the world like footsteps!

The President had been notified, so had the Pentagon. The ultimate decision was to watch and wait. By now, it had been fairly well decided that the thing was a spaceship of alien and unknown design. So the Air Force sat around and twiddled its thumbs, waiting for the enigmatic ovoid to do something.

General Mawson, following direct orders from the President, had put a ring of armed guards a hundred yards away from the base of the ship, which was surrounded by the broken rubble of the smashed landing field. No one was allowed inside that circle. Some of the Air Force technicians wanted to test the hull of the ship, take test shaving with a drill and find out what it was made of. Mawson's orders were strictly against anything that might be construed as a hostile act by the aliens— if there *were* any aliens. And Mawson had quite rightly assumed that any tinkering with the hull could properly be regarded as possibly inimical to anyone inside the ship.

"Suppose you landed a bomber in the Amazon jungle and the local natives came out and started working on the thing with a brace and bit?" he asked. The Air Force technicians simmered down and went on waiting.

General Mawson didn't go into the details of all the precautions that had been taken to safeguard both the spaceship and the people of Earth, but he inferred that everything that could be done had been done at least twice. The Navy, armed with .22 rifles to atomic antiaircraft missiles, was prowling around the island in precisely spaced rings. Nobody knew what that thing might do, but they wanted to be prepared for everything conceivable. I found out later that some of the boys had pretty active imaginations when it came to dreaming up every conceivable thing that the alien ship could do.

A month passed.

Nothing happened.

A second month.

Still nothing.

On the morning of the seventy-first day, a door

appeared in the side of the ship, and a man stepped out, his hands in the air.

Well, not exactly a man. The first slide that the general showed us was taken from a distance, and the figure did look amazingly human. The second slide was a close-up. One look at it, and you knew the being could never pass itself off as human without drastic surgery.

The eyes were large, round, and protruding—a bug-eyed monster, if you please. But the heavy brow ridges that covered the eyes jutted out well over the protruding eyeballs. From the brow ridges, the head itself sloped up and back, forming a ski-slope forehead. On the top of the round head was a growth that resembled purple moss. The mouth was well-formed, but it was much too wide. It went from one pair of wisdom teeth to the other.

In comparison, the nose was almost normal. It was a trifle longer than the average Caucasian nose, and very pointed, but not abnormally so.

"That," said General Mawson, "is Schnikelfritz." He stopped and eyed Miss S. Brownell Anthony. She just smiled, shook her head slowly, and murmured: "Not really."

"No, not really," agreed Mawson. "We have no idea what his name is. Or even if he has such a thing. So far, we haven't been able to get anything across to these people. So we've tagged them with names, so that our reports will make sense." He tapped the screen with a pointer. "You'll take notice that he carries some sort of sidearm. We don't know what it is or what it does. That's the reason that we all go armed; we hope that they don't know what ours will do. Don't use them unless you're attacked; then shoot to kill."

He paused and looked around. "Now, are there any questions?"

One of the men said: "What about the stuff they brought out of the ship and gave to us?"

"We'll get into that when we discuss the program as a whole, and the part that each man is to play."

I grinned to myself. Mawson had a way of making a research team sound like a group engaged in military tactics.

Dr. Oglethorpe, the physicist, rose ponderously to his feet, his grossly fat body looking ludicrously balloonlike in a khaki uniform. "General Mawson, am I to understand that each of us is supposed to do his investigation separately from the others? Won't we be allowed to communicate our findings?"

"Quite the contrary," said Mawson. "We'll have copies made of all reports, so that they can be sent around to all the others. Every so often, we'll get together and have a bull session to clear the air and give each other ideas. Is that satisfactory, doctor?"

Oglethorpe lowered himself into his chair again. "Perfectly," he said. "That is how it should be."

"Thank you." Mawson looked us over for half a minute, then said: "We have a problem here, as you can see. What we want to know is: Why have these people come here? There are at least fifteen aliens on that ship, and they have been here for nearly four months without doing anything except give us a few odd-looking mechanisms that don't seem to do anything. (We'll get around to looking those over later.) What we want to do is get into communication with them. For that reason, Lieutenant Anthony will have a class Double-A crash priority on all data. Otherwise, your work will be pretty much unrestricted."

One of the women, a Dr. Feathergill, who had been introduced as a bacteriologist, giggled. Mawson looked at her. "What's so funny, captain?"

She giggled again. "I was just thinking that, in all the movies, the alien steps out, raises one arm, and says: 'My name is Umgahwah, Earthman; take me to your leader.'"

A laugh went through the room. Burkhalter, the neurologist, said: "Yeah, and they always managed somehow to learn our language by listening to our radio programs. I never did figure out how they'd manage to decode an alien language with absolutely no referents."

"You ought to know that, Burk," I said. "They have a neurophiltronic utravabulator that correlates brain waves with the TV commercials."

"That's why they want to go to our leaders," someone else said: "they want to find out who writes those commercials."

We were all laughing our heads off, even Mawson. It wasn't that what we were saying was so funny, but the tenseness that had built up in us was coming loose. It wasn't until then that I realized that I had actually been frightened—the vague fear of the unknown.

It didn't take us long to discover that we had our work cut out for us. Schnikelfritz and his cohorts had brought out several pieces of apparatus from the ship. They had put the stuff on the ground near the circle of guards, and Mawson had asked for volunteers to go get it. It was from one of these gadgets that the mysterious liquid had come.

I looked the thing over. It was a tank, flat and long, like a twelve-volt car battery. The top slid off after a clamp at one end was released. Inside, there were plates and coils of metal, and queer-looking rods of either glass or plastic—I couldn't tell which.

The tank was about half full of the liquid, which covered some of the doohickeys inside. Why had they given it to us? What good was it to us—or to them?

There were three of us in the lab looking at it. Freisen, one of the top men in physical chemistry; old Oglethorpe, the physicist; and myself.

Oglethorpe shifted his weight around until he could see better, and peered inside the box. "Know what that looks like? Condensers. D'you suppose that liquid is supposed to be a dielectric of some kind?"

"Could be," I said. "Want to check it, Freisen?"

"We've got to start somewhere," he said. "I'll try it."

Me, I went back to work on the chemical composition of the stuff.

Ten days later, we were still baffled. As far as I could

tell, the liquid was made up of molecules of high molecular weight, rings composed of ether links between several high-weight units. It might have been made by the dehydration of diols, but I didn't see how it could be done with such precision. Besides, the stuff didn't act right.

Freisen had tried to test the dielectric strength of the stuff and had come up with a mess. The stuff had gone to pieces on him and ended up as a hot batch of carbon and tar. The fumes had everybody coughing.

Oglethorpe pattered around in his lab and said almost nothing, but I could tell from his manner that the puzzle was starting to wear him down.

After running through one eight-hour test that had given me nothing but negative information, I decided to knock off and go over to the Officers Club for a beer.

Outside, in the darkness, I could hear the dull beat of the Pacific against the coral reefs that outlined the island, and the soft whisper of the wind through the palms. It was almost like the South Sea Island of popular fantasy except that, instead of the traditional volcano with its lurid pillar of smoke, we had a fat black egg surrounded by the white glare of searchlights.

I went into the Officers Club, ordered a beer, and sat down at a table to brood. I didn't sit alone long.

"Hullo, commander; are you as sulky as you look?"

It was S. Brownell Anthony.

"Worse," I said. "Sit down and cheer me up. And knock off that 'commander' bit. Right now, I couldn't command a rowboat. If you're a good girl, you may call me Pete."

"I'm not a good girl," she said, with that hellfire twinkle in her eyes, "but I'll call you Pete anyway, just to show you I'm not prejudiced against Navy commanders."

As she pulled up a chair and put her own beer on the table, I said: "Fine. And what do I call you?"

"Brownie. From Brownell."

"Sounds pixieish enough for you. What does the *S* stand for?"

Those gray-green eyes focused on me for ten full seconds before she answered. "I shouldn't tell you, but I will. It's Susan."

I got it then. Susan B. Anthony. The hell-raising suffragette of the late Nineteenth Century.

"Any relation?" I asked.

"None whatever. My mother thought it would make me independent or something."

"I'll never tell a soul," I promised. "I, too, have a smudge on my otherwise pure name. I was dubbed 'Peter Ulysses' by my fond parents."

"That's tough, all right, but you can just use the middle initial, and no one asks questions. But if you use a first initial, everyone wants to know what you're hiding."

I shook my head. "I can't even do that. I have to initial reports. When I was an ensign, I was stationed in England for a while, and everybody got a laugh out of my putting *PUB* on all the reports."

"My heart goes out to you, Pete," she said. And we toasted each other silently with our beers.

"How's your old pal, Schnikelfritz?" I asked. I knew she had been working hard on cracking the alien language; she spent several hours every day, just inside the circle of guards, with a tape recorder and notebook, while Schnikelfritz and a few other aliens tried to help bridge the communications wall that stood between us.

Brownie swallowed the rest of her beer. "We're getting along," she said. "But the language is a hard nut to crack."

"I thought mathematics was supposed to be the universal language," I said. "You begin by agreeing that two and two is four and go on from there."

She looked as though she'd bitten into a green pomegranate. "Oh, sure. Easy. We've been through all that. We're all agreed that the square on the hypotenuse of a right triangle is equal to the sum of the square of the other two sides. How does that help? What's the mathematical equation for 'Hey, diddle, diddle, the cat and the fiddle; the cow jumped over the moon'?"

"I'd think it would help establish some sort of bridge-head, anyway," I reasoned.

"Oh, it does, it does. But it isn't as easy as most laymen seem to think. Look here; you're a chemist. You must have studied German?" She made it a half question.

"Three years of it," I said, "and I've kept my hand in since."

"You can read it. How about writing and speaking?"

I shrugged. "So-so."

"That's the way it usually works out," she said. "That is how far you've come—and you had a completely worked-out correlation between the two languages; you had a grammar and a vocabulary, and trained instructors who already knew the language. Of course, a trained linguist can do the job in a lot less time, but it's rough when you have to start out from scratch. So far, I haven't even been able to figure out the basic structure of the language; I don't even know if they have verbs and nouns."

"Quit telling me what you don't know," I said, "and tell me what you *do* know."

"It'll cost you a beer."

"I'm a sucker for a pretty face," I told her honestly.

I got two more beers from the bar and brought them back. "Now talk," I said.

"Well, it looks to me as though they don't have any linguists aboard. If they did, they'd be trying to learn our language as well as teaching us theirs. As a matter of fact, I don't think they have any trained scientists aboard—a few technicians, maybe, but no research men."

"What makes you think so?" I asked.

She frowned. "I'm not sure. Their lack of information, mostly. For instance, the table of elements is universal. Any race, anywhere, that had discovered enough knowledge to build a ship like that would know the sequence of elements from hydrogen to uranium, and probably beyond."

"Granted," I said.

"Well, I got one of the boys to get me some samples of various elements—those that can be handled easily—and I tried to see if Schnikelfritz recognized them. He did. He knew copper, lead, gold, sulfur, red phosphorus, aluminum, zinc, and several others by sight. He even knew chlorine, bromine, and iodine."

"You're sure?"

"Reasonably sure. Anyway, I lined them up in the order of their atomic numbers, leaving blank spaces for the ones I didn't have. Then I scrambled the samples up and let him have a try at it. He did about as well as you'd expect a high-school boy to do. But he got silicon, sulfur, and phosphorus in the wrong order, for one. And none of the others could do any better."

"There are two possible explanations for that," I said. "One: they have pretty good visual memories and were just imitating the way you put the samples in order. That might indicate that their idea of order is different from ours, though I doubt it. Or, two: they have a good layman's knowledge of science and no more."

"That's the way it looks to me," she said. "Now take a week off and try to figure out why people like that would be aboard an interstellar spaceship."

"Look," I said, "there's one kind of man they'd have to have aboard."

"What's that?"

"An astronomer. They have to navigate that thing, don't they? Why don't you get Professor Brymer to help you with the linguistics end of it?"

She nodded slowly, thinking it over. "Makes sense. I know he *has* been talking to one of them. Looks like we'll have to have that bull session we were promising ourselves."

We had our bull session, and, as Brownie had hoped, the correlation of our various attacks on the problem cleared a lot of the air. Within the next month, we had four more sessions, and we began to feel we were getting somewhere.

Between Freisen and Oglethorpe's work on the tank, and my work on the fluid, we began to get part of an answer on the mystery liquid. It was a dielectric, all right, but only to certain frequencies that matched the oscillation of some of the molecular bonds in the molecules of the stuff. The tank was some sort of frequency regulator.

Brownie had reached the point where she could speak a sort of pidgin language to Schnikelfritz and his buddies, but she didn't seem satisfied. Over one of our beer drinking sessions, which had become a fairly regular habit, she started grousing at one of General Mawson's orders.

"I still say that the only way we'll ever know what's going on inside their minds is to find out what's going on inside that *ovum negrum*."

"That's real pretty Latin," I told her. "But even your brand of Latin grammar isn't going to get you by those armed aliens."

"It isn't the aliens so much as it is your buddy, Brass Hat Mawson," she grumbled.

"Why? What's he done?"

"Well, I tried to get Schnikelfritz to let me in the ship. He didn't know what I wanted, so I started walking slowly towards the open air lock, with my hands in the air."

"Why raise your hands? Surrender?"

"Don't be funny," she snapped. Evidently she was in no mood for humor. "That's their equivalent of a handshake, and means about the same thing: 'Look; I'm not armed.' "

"So, what happened?"

"So the two guards at the air lock dropped their hands when I got too close," she said. "Two more steps, and they had their hands on those sidearms they wear. So I stopped, turned around, and went back." She shrugged. "It wouldn't have been so bad, except that Mawson saw the whole thing. And he gave me strict orders not to go inside that ship. Period."

"I don't blame him," I told her. "That could start

something we might not be able to finish. What do you think you could find out if you did go in, anyway?"

Her eyes narrowed in thought. "I'm not sure. Our pal, Schnikelfritz, has been trying to get something across to me, though. Something about an object they want or need. I can't quite get what it is, but I have a feeling that if he could show me around inside, I'd be able to dope it out."

"Look, Brownie," I said, "you stay away from that ship. This situation is touchy enough as it is without your pulling off something that'll blow the top off the whole mess."

She glared at me. "Now you're giving orders, huh? O.K. Thanks for the beer, Commander Barton, I'll let you know if I decide to violate those orders."

She got up and walked out without any further chatter. I let her go; I wasn't going to chase her.

Then I thought of something and grinned. In spite of her protestations, she did have a touch of the original Susan B. Anthony in her make-up.

A week later, I was stewing around in the lab—almost literally stewing; I had four flasks boiling—when the phone rang. I walked over and picked it up.

"Chem lab, Commander Barton speaking."

"How come you're working this time of night?" It was Brownie. "I phoned the BOQ, and they said you weren't in, so I tried the lab. What's cooking?"

I told her what was cooking—literally, in words of sixteen syllables. She hadn't been civil to me all week, and I was feeling grumpy, so just out of pure deviltry, I gave her the Geneva names of the reactants in the flasks.

"Don't pull your technical jargon on me," she came back. "I'll bet you don't even know a fricative from a labial."

"Don't be vulgar," I said. "What's on your mind?"

"Remember when you told me not to pull off something that might set the place in an uproar? Well, I'm going to do just that. Better hurry." And she hung up.

I'd come to know that girl pretty well in the weeks we'd been on the island, and I knew she wasn't just whistling through her teeth. I knew my pots would boil untended, but I gave the reflux condensers a quick check before I grabbed my hat and pistol belt and took off like a scalded cat.

It was later than I'd thought. I had been working so hard that I hadn't paid any attention to the time, and I was surprised to see that it was dark outside. My watch said eleven-thirty. I headed for the alien ship.

I didn't quite make it in time; the silly wench had figured my speed pretty well. When I got there, she was already inside the ring of guards, walking towards the alien ship.

I sprinted up to the nearest guard and stopped. I knew that if I charged in there at a dead run, one of those gabozos would cut me down with whatever it was he carried at his hip. I didn't know what those things fired, but they looked deadly, and I didn't feel like stopping either poisoned darts or death rays.

"What's the matter, sir?" asked the guard. He'd snapped to attention and come to port arms.

"What's she doing in there?" I asked snappishly. I didn't wait for an answer; I yelled: "Brownie! You get back here! That's an order!"

She didn't pay one bit of attention; she just kept going.

The guard said: "Weren't we supposed to let her in, sir? Our orders are to let any of the research team in."

I ignored him. I stepped across the circle and started towards Brownie.

Evidently, the aliens had decided on a definite distance from the ship—a warning distance at which they reached for their guns. As soon as Brownie reached a point thirty yards from the base of the big black ship, the alien guards put their hands on the butts of their weapons. Brownie stopped. So did I. They might think that two approachers were more dangerous than one. I was only ten yards inside the human guard ring, a good sixty yards from

Brownie, but they might decide an attack was building up if I came closer now.

"Lieutenant Anthony!" I yelled. "Come back here!"

And then I heard General Mawson's voice behind me. "Anthony! This is General Mawson! I'm ordering you to come back!"

I turned around and looked. Every airman on the perimeter of the circle was facing the ship now, their rifles at the ready.

Mawson said: "Just stay there, Barton, but don't move. I think—*awk! Brownie!*"

I spun around again—fast. My hand was already on my gun.

Mawson snapped. "Don't fire! Not even if they shoot her!"

But I couldn't have drawn my gun if I'd wanted to.

Brownie had already dropped her pistol belt to the ground. And now, very slowly, she was taking off her clothes!

Like a slow-motion strip tease, she was removing everything. There wasn't much to remove: she'd evidently come dressed for the occasion. The khaki blouse went, then the skirt; then she kicked off her shoes. And that was it.

She stood there in the glare of the spotlights, her smoothly tanned skin reflecting the light as though it had been oiled. I realized that she was sweating, even in the cool sea breeze that came in from the Pacific.

Slowly, her hands raised above her head, she turned completely around. No one else on that whole airstrip moved. They hardly breathed.

One of the alien guards turned to the air lock and gobbled something. If there was an answer, I didn't hear it, but he turned around and faced Brownie again. His hand was still on the grip of his sidearm.

Brownie kept her hands in the air—

—And took a step forward.

And another.

And then she said something in that alien tongue.

And took a third step.

The not-quite-human hands dropped away from the gun butts, and Brownie kept walking.

When she reached the air lock, she walked on in as the guards stepped aside to let her pass.

And then she was gone.

For a long paralyzed second, none of us said anything. The scene looked just as it always had—the glare of the lights trying to penetrate the dead black of the hull, the ring of silent airmen, the enigmatic, quiet figures of the two alien guards, all as they had been for months.

Then the guard behind me whistled softly. "Well— that's one way to get an invitation to come in. I wouldn't have turned her down, either!"

I turned savagely. "Shut up, flyboy! That girl's got more guts in her toenails than you'll ever have in your whole body!" It was a vicious thing to say, and maybe not even true. But I was boiling.

The airman turned crimson and his jaw muscles tightened.

Mawson stepped up. "The commander didn't mean that, son," he said softly. "But you *did* make a mistake."

"Sorry, sir," said the airman stiffly.

"Do you think you'd be interested in one of their women?" Mawson asked.

"Well, I guess not; no, sir, I wouldn't."

"Well, they aren't interested in her, either. Right, commander?"

I had cooled off just as fast as I'd heated up. "Right. I'm sorry, Airman; I was just blowing off steam."

"But ... why'd she do that?"

"It was the only way," I said, "that she could prove to them that she was completely unarmed."

"Oh," said the guard in a very small voice.

Then I thought of something, and my grin must have split my face as wide as one of those alien's faces.

"What's so funny, Barton?" Mawson asked, scowling.

"I just happened to remember," I said. "She told me

that she was going to pull off something that would set the place in an uproar."

Even the airman snickered.

We waited. Mawson and I sat and smoked cigarettes furiously for hours, one right after another, until our mouths felt as though a Russian army had retreated across them. We drank hot coffee to take the taste away, and only succeeded in making them burn worse.

"It makes sense," Mawson said. "Sure it makes sense."

We were sitting well back from the perimeter of the guard line, watching the still-open air lock of the great ship. We'd grabbed a couple of chairs and a card table from one of the nearby barracks with the intent of having a game or two of gin to pass the time, but so far we'd done nothing but shuffle the cards, put them down, pick them up, and shuffle them again.

"What makes sense?" I asked, not really paying much attention. I was watching the pitiful khaki heap that lay on the shattered concrete thirty yards from the base of the spaceship.

"Remember when I was talking about a pilot having to land his ship in the Amazon jungle? And how he wouldn't want some native working on his hull with a brace-and-bit?"

"Yeah," I said. "Sure. I remember." I wrenched my eyes away from the lighted airstrip and picked up the cards.

"Well," Mawson went on, "if the natives were armed, would you let 'em inside the bomber?"

"No," I said. "No, I wouldn't." I laid out a hand of solitaire and started playing.

"But if you thought it would help you, you'd let an *unarmed* native inside, wouldn't you?"

"Yeah. Sure. Got another cigarette?" I noticed that I had laid a red six on a red seven. I picked it up and moved it to a black seven. Then I calmly played a red five on it. I played a red ace on a black deuce and then gave it up and shoved the cards into a heap.

"How long?" I asked.

"Who knows?" said Mawson. "As long as they let her stay."

"I mean, how long has she been in there?"

He looked at his watch. "Not quite two hours."

"I wish we had some bourbon and soda instead of this lousy coffee!" I was ready to chew nails—tenpenny, not finger.

"There's a bottle in my quarters," the general said. "Want to go get it?"

"No. Do you?"

"No."

We waited.

A little later, I said: "Suppose I went out there and stripped to the buff. Maybe I could get in, too."

"Or you might not," Mawson said. "They might decide there was something funny going on and shoot you both. Want to try it?"

"No."

"I didn't think so. And stop shuffling those cards!"

I quit shuffling and put the cards down on the table. Mawson picked them up and started shuffling.

We waited.

"It's almost dawn," Mawson said. It seemed years had passed.

"I know," I said. "I hope she comes out before dawn."

"Just because she has nothing on?" Mawson dismissed the idea with a gesture. "If she can go in that way with sixty-odd men watching her, she won't be embarrassed coming out."

"No, but—"

"General! Here she comes!"

It was the airman's voice. I jerked my head around to look at the ship. Brownie was standing in the air lock.

Mawson stood up. "All right, flyboys! A-a-bout *face!*" His bellow echoed across the airfield. Reluctantly, the men turned their backs to the spaceship.

"They had enough of a show last night," Mawson said.

But he didn't turn, and neither did I.

Because Brownie wasn't coming out alone. She walked briskly over to where her clothes were lying and put them on a lot faster than she'd taken them off. Beside her was one of the aliens—naked as a jaybird.

"Tell the men they can turn around now, general," I said.

"Why?" Mawson asked.

"Because all they'll have to do is take one look at that character to realize that any slight suspicions they may harbor about Brownie's purity are utterly groundless. He's even less human than we thought."

"If it is a he," added Mawson, and bellowed out the order.

"I got some data, all right," Brownie said, "but I'm not sure what it means."

We were back in the briefing room, the whole team. Mawson was sitting down with the rest of us, letting Brownie have the stage, along with the starkly naked Schnikelfritz. I noticed that most of us managed to keep our eyes averted from the alien.

One thing had changed. None of us were wearing sidearms.

"In the first place, they're short of food and water," she went on. "Schniky, here, had to go through a lot of pantomime to get the idea across, and he had to show me his food and water supplies, but I finally realized that they're on short rations. We can replace their water, but I don't think they could eat our food." Then she grinned. "I know we couldn't eat theirs."

"Then why do they stay?" asked Oglethorpe. "Are they afraid we'll shoot them down if they try to leave?"

"I'm not sure. We can discuss that later," she said.

"Certainly, Miss Anthony. Go ahead."

"I did get one bit of information that might have a bearing on that, though," Brownie continued. "Schniky kept pointing to one particular gauge on a control panel of some kind. It didn't register anything. There was a switch under it, and he kept turning it on and off, and nothing happened.

"He showed me the other gauges. There's a little shadow in them that points at figures around a dial—just like our meters and stuff, in principle. But this particular one didn't show any shadow."

"I wish I'd get a look at that ship's insides," muttered Freisen, who was sitting next to me. "What does a linguist know about scientific equipment?"

"You want a punch in the teeth?" I whispered back. He shut up.

Brownie went on, giving a complete account of everything she'd seen, heard, done, and guessed about inside that ship.

"Now, here are my conclusions," she said. "See if you agree with me. If you don't, speak up, because these people are desperate."

Everybody nodded, so she went on. "I think that gauge was a fuel gauge. Something must have happened out there to destroy their fuel supply, and they just barely made it here. They thought our radar beams were the radio beacons that his people use to pinpoint a fuel dump." She looked over at me and Freisen. "That gadget they gave you, the tank with the queer liquid in it, seems to be some sort of communications device. It won't work without the liquid, and they need a replacement."

"So that's what that patch was!" said Freisen suddenly.

Everybody turned to look at him, and he looked at Dr. Oglethorpe. "Remember that patch in one corner of the tank? There was a leak, and they lost some of the liquid."

Oglethorpe nodded silently for a second, then said aloud: "And I think you're right, Miss Anthony; they probably wanted more of the liquid; I doubt if the machine would work without it."

Brownie nodded back. "So all we have to do is replace that liquid, and we'll be able to get these people's communicator fixed. They can call home and get food."

"Can they wait another six months?" I asked.

"No." Her voice was flat.

"Then that's out. I'm not even sure I could synthesize the stuff in that time. There's a plasma-effect on those ring molecules that keeps 'em stable, and I don't know how it's done. I might never do it."

"That's that, then," she said. "Can we give them fuel?" Then, answering her own question: "Not unless we know what the fuel is."

"Can't you get the information from Schnikelfritz?" asked Mawson, looking at the alien, then looking away again.

Brownie shook her head. "All I can get out of him is a number. He keeps saying 'one,' every time I asked him about the fuel. Anybody who ever tells me again that mathematics is a universal language gets a boot in the snoot."

"I don't suppose he has any fuel left at all?" I asked. "Maybe we could analyze it."

She gave me a patronizing grin, and I felt foolish. Her opinion of my ability as an analytical chemist didn't seem very high at that moment.

"It's all gone," she said. "They don't have a speck left. They're running the ship on emergency batteries."

"Even if we could get the fuel," Mawson said, "would it be smart to let them go? What if they come back with a war fleet?"

"The military mind," I said. "Why should they do that? To conquer us? They couldn't use Earth. They couldn't eat our plants or animals, and they'd have to sterilize the whole planet to make their own stuff grow. Besides, think of their supply line."

Mawson subsided.

Oglethorpe said: "What kind of fuel could drive a ship like that, anyway?"

And then it hit him. *One.* "Brownie!" he snapped. "Go get those samples of the elements you were showing him! I have a colossal hunch!"

*   *   *

It turned out that Oglethorpe was right. The big, black egg-shaped ship was fueled by the same reaction that fuels suns. Hydrogen. Element number one.

How they did it, I don't know, but the "fuel tank" of that ship held tons of the stuff without either cooling it off or putting it under pressure. My guess was that it was something akin to adsorption on the surface of some tremendously receptive sponge, but I'm still not sure.

The gas is fed from the "fuel tank" into a reactor that turns it into—not helium, but pure, raw energy. Fine sort of gadget, but I'd hate to have it run wild.

While all those tons of hydrogen were being pumped into the fuel reservoir of the ship, the President was sitting with the Cabinet, trying to decide whether to let the aliens go or not. It was a tough problem. Ethically, we had no right to imprison intelligent beings against their will without due process of law. On the other hand—

I let the rest of them worry about that. I went back to the lab. Two days after the hydrogen pumping had begun, Brownie came into the lab, a frown on her face.

"Pete—is there any chance you can synthesize that stuff very soon?"

I'd been asked that question once too often; I was beginning to feel like an absolute idiot.

"Look, Brownie, this is a complex organic chemical. It isn't table salt or granite. Did you ever hear of synthetic hemoglobin? No. And the boys are still trying to synthesize insulin. Analysis is one thing; synthesis is another."

"Don't be sore, Pete. I'm worried—really worried."

"Worried? What about? Afraid our alien friends might decide to invade us?"

"No. But Schniky says that the tanklike gadget they gave us is vitally necessary for the operation of the ship." Her eyes had a worried-looking expression.

"I thought you said it was part of a communication device."

She shook her head. "I goofed. The word translates as

transmitter; it transmits energy from one place to another inside the ship. He wants it back."

"He can have it back. The tank, that is. I'm keeping the liquid. There's not much of it left, and I am *not* going to let it out of my hands."

The phone rang. I picked it up and identified myself. It was Mawson. "Is Brownie there?"

I handed her the phone. She said "Hello," then listened for a minute. When she hung up, she said: "Two stop orders have just come through on the refueling job. One from the President of the United States, the other from Schnikelfritz."

Of the entire group that worked on that ship, the most successful, without a doubt, was Miss S. Brownell Anthony. I told her so, six months later.

We were still on the island; we still had to solve the puzzle of that ship. We sat in the Officers Club over beer and toasted to Schnikelfritz.

"He tried," Brownie said, "but he was confused."

"At least you know the language," I said. "If we ever contact his kind again, we'll be able to talk to them."

"Other than that," she said, "we all goofed."

"You didn't," I corrected her. "Oglethorpe did, by making a hasty guess. But how was he to know that Schniky wanted tritium—super-heavy hydrogen—instead of the ordinary stuff?"

"Funny," she said. "Funny, queer; not funny, ha-ha. Funny that they got themselves into a scrape like this. Just a simple little joyride through space. A rich man's yachting party. They developed a little leak in the energy transmitter, and the fluid leaked out. That meant their tritium fuel was wasted—tossed out in space. They picked up our radar beams and thought we were a—" She paused.

"Go on," I said, "say it."

"—A filling station."

"Yeah. And now they're all dead of starvation just

because we were too backwards to understand what they wanted when they came."

She looked into the golden, bubbling depths of her beer. "Mawson wants to keep us here as long as he can. So does the President. But what good is a linguist when there's no one left alive to learn from? You don't need a linguist to study a spaceship."

I was humming to myself, and I caught myself trying to remember the words. The memory was elusive.

She sipped at her beer. "The general said yesterday that I could probably go home. The President will take his recommendation, and Mawson says I'm not needed here."

"It's odd that there were no books aboard," I said, out of a clear blue sky.

"I looked the whole ship over," she said. "I didn't find anything even remotely resembling a book."

I hummed a little more of the tune. "I guess they did it the hard way."

She looked up at me with those gray-green eyes. "The hard way?"

"Sure. That little gadget Oglethorpe and his boys are working on. It's like recorded television, except that the screen shows the print instead of moving pictures. Or maybe it was just the particular tape that they were testing."

Her eyes took on that hellcat expression. I liked it. "You louse," she said softly. "You're just doing that to tease me."

"I'm not. Scout's Honor. There really is a gadget. It looks like a complete recorded library. As a matter of fact, there's one of them in each room of the ship. It looks as though the rich Mr. Schnikelfritz liked to provide for his friends' entertainment."

"A whole library." She said it very slowly. "Pete, you've been saving this up. You knew I wouldn't want to leave after hearing about that."

"I knew it," I said. "I didn't want to be alone on a desert island."

Then she looked at me and grinned. "That's a very pretty tune you're humming. I think I'll stay for a while just on account of that."

Then I remembered the words:

I knew what I liked,
And I liked what I saw,
And I said to myself:
That's for me!

Control power, and you have power. *When ships were pushed by the wind—our solar fusion-pile again—it was difficult for the great powers to control the oceans. Ships could stay at sea for a long time; they needed no fuel; repairs could be made on any convenient beach. Owner-skippers were common among merchantmen, when ships went by sail. Pirates were common as well; a converted merchantman could show a clean pair of heels to a frigate, if well-handled. And although national navies could keep them down, it was more common to let the corsairs run free—or enlist them as allies.*

Steam changed that. Steamships needed to refuel; they represented enormous capital assets; they were vulnerable to ironclad warships. On earth, fusion power might represent a return to the days of sail. One tonne of deuterium would push a big oil tanker—or a submarine—for a long time. Depending on the initial capital cost—sure to decrease over time—we might even see fusion-steam tramps knocking around the world's oceans. If it was small and portable, a similar fusion system could make local-based economies more competitive; when power is very cheap, economies of scale matter less.

One of the staples of science fiction is the libertarian-anarchist Asteroid Belt of miners and shippers. Cheap enough fusion power might make that a reality . . . but what if it was just cheap enough for companies and not individuals?

Tinker
Jerry Pournelle

"The tinker came astridin', astridin' over the Strand, with his bullocks—"

"Rollo!"

"Yes, Ma'am." I'd been singing at the top of my lungs, as I do when I've got a difficult piloting job, and I'd forgotten that my wife was in the control cab. I went back to the problem of setting our 16 thousand tons of ship onto the rock.

It wasn't much of a rock. Jefferson is an irregular-shaped asteroid about twice as far out as Earth. It measures maybe 70 kilometers by 50 kilometers, and from far enough away it looks like an old mud brick somebody used for a shotgun target. It has a screwy rotation pattern that's hard to match with, and since I couldn't use the main engines, setting down was a tricky job.

Janet wasn't finished. "Roland Kephart, I've told you about those songs."

"Yeah, sure, Hon." There are two inertial platforms in *Slingshot*, and they were giving me different readings. We were closing faster than I liked.

113

"It's bad enough that you teach them to the boys. Now the girls are—"

I motioned toward the open intercom switch, and Janet blushed. We fight a lot, but that's our private business.

The attitude jets popped. "Hear this," I said. "I think we're going in too fast. Brace yourselves." The jets popped again, short bursts that stirred up dust storms on the rocky surface below. "But I don't think—"

The ship jolted into place with a loud clang. We hit hard enough to shake things, but none of the red lights came on. "—we'll break anything. Welcome to Jefferson. We're down."

Janet came over and cut off the intercom switch, and we hugged each other for a second. "Made it again," she said, and I grinned.

There wasn't much doubt on the last few trips, but when we first put *Slingshot* together out of the wreckage of two salvaged ships, every time we boosted out there'd been a good chance we'd never set down again. There's a lot that can go wrong in the Belt, and not many ships to rescue you.

I pulled her over to me and kissed her. "Sixteen years," I said. "You don't look a day older."

She didn't, either. She still had dark red hair, same color as when I met her at Elysium Mons Station on Mars, and if she got it out of a bottle she never told me, not that I'd want to know. She was wearing the same thing I was, a skin-tight body stocking that looked as if it had been sprayed on. The purpose was strictly functional, to keep you alive if *Slinger* sprung a leak, but on her it produced some interesting curves. I let my hands wander to a couple of the more fascinating conic sections, and she snuggled against me.

She put her head close to my ear and whispered breathlessly, "Comm panel's lit."

"Bat puckey." There was a winking orange light, showing an outside call on our hailing frequency. Janet handed me the mike with a wicked grin. "Lock up your wives and hide your daughters, the tinker's come to town," I told it.

"*Slingshot*, this is Freedom Station. Welcome back, Cap'n Rollo."

"Jed?" I asked.

"Who the hell'd you think it was?"

"Anybody. Thought maybe you'd fried yourself in the solar furnace. How are things?" Jed's an old friend. Like a lot of asteroid Port Captains, he's a publican. The owner of the bar nearest the landing area generally gets the job, since there's not enough traffic to make Port Captain a full time deal. Jed used to be a miner in Pallas, and we'd worked together before I got out of the mining business.

We chatted about our families, but Jed didn't seem as interested as he usually is. I figured business wasn't too good. Unlike most asteroid colonies, Jefferson's independent. There's no big Corporation to pay taxes to, but on the other hand there's no big organization to bail the Jeffersonians out if they get in too deep.

"Got a passenger this trip," I said.

"Yeah? Rockrat?" Jed asked.

"Nope. Just passing through. Oswald Dalquist. Insurance adjustor. He's got some kind of policy settlement to make here, then he's with us to Marsport."

There was a long pause, and I wondered what Jed was thinking about. "I'll be aboard in a little," he said. "Freedom Station out."

Janet frowned. "That was abrupt."

"Sure was." I shrugged and began securing the ship. There wasn't much to do. The big work is shutting down the main engines, and we'd done that a long way out from Jefferson. You don't run an ion engine toward an inhabited rock if you care about your customers.

"Better get the Big'uns to look at the inertial platforms, Hon," I said. "They don't read the same."

"Sure. Hal thinks it's the computer."

"Whatever it is, we better get it fixed." That would be a job for the oldest children. Our family divides nicely into the Big Ones, the Little Ones, and the Baby, with various sub-groups and pecking orders that Janet and I don't understand. With nine kids aboard, five ours and four adopted, the system can get confusing. Jan and I find it's easier to let them work out the chain of command for themselves.

I unbuckled from the seat and pushed away. You can't walk on Jefferson, or any of the small rocks. You can't quite swim through the air, either. Locomotion is mostly a matter of jumps.

As I sailed across the cabin a big gray shape sailed up to meet me, and we met in a tangle of arms and claws. I pushed the tomcat away. "Damn it—"

"Can't you do anything without cursing?"

"Blast it, then. I've told you to keep that animal out of the control cab."

"I didn't let him in." She was snappish, and for that matter so was I. We'd spent better than 600 hours cooped up in a small space with just ourselves, the kids, and our passenger, and it was time we had some outside company.

The passenger had made it more difficult. We don't fight much in front of the kids, but with Oswald Dalquist aboard the atmosphere was different from what we're used to. He was always very formal and polite, which meant we had to be, which meant our usual practice of getting the minor irritations over with had been exchanged for bottling them up.

Jan and I had a major fight coming, and the sooner it happened the better it would be for both of us.

Slingshot is built up out of a number of compartments. We add to the ship as we have to—and when we can afford it. I left Jan to finish shutting down and went below to the living quarters. We'd been down 15 minutes, and the children were loose.

Papers, games, crayons, toys, kids' clothing, and books had all more or less settled on the "down" side. Raquel, a big bluejay the kids picked up somewhere, screamed from a cage mounted on one bulk-head. The compartment smelled of bird droppings.

Two of the kids were watching a TV program beamed out of Marsport. Their technique was to push themselves upward with their arms and float up to the top of the compartment, then float downward again until they caught themselves just before they landed. It took nearly a minute to make a full circuit in Jefferson's weak gravity.

I went over and switched off the set. The program was a western, some horse opera made in the 1940s.

Jennifer and Craig wailed in unison. "That's educational, Dad."

They had a point, but we'd been through this before. For kids who've never seen Earth and may never go there, *anything* about Terra can probably be educational, but I wasn't in a mood to argue, "Get this place cleaned up."

"It's Roger's turn. He made the mess." Jennifer, being eight and two years older than Craig, tends to be spokesman and chief petty officer for the Little Ones.

"Get him to help, then. But get cleaned up."

"Yes, sir." They worked sullenly, flinging the clothing into corner bins, putting the books into the clips, and the games into lockers. There really is a place for everything in *Slingshot*, although most of the time you wouldn't know it.

I left them to their work and went down to the next level. My office is on one side of that, balanced by the "passenger suite" which the second oldest boy uses when we don't have paying customers. Oswald Dalquist was just coming out of his cabin.

"Good morning, Captain," he said. In all the time he'd been aboard he'd never called me anything but "Captain," although he accepted Janet's invitation to use her first name. A very formal man, Mr. Oswald Dalquist.

"I'm just going down to reception," I told him. "The Port Captain will be aboard with the Health Officer in a minute. You'd better come down, there will be forms to fill out."

"Certainly. Thank you, Captain." He followed me through the airlock to the level below, which was shops, labs, and the big compartment that serves as a main entryway to *Slingshot*.

Dalquist had been a good passenger, if a little distant. He stayed in his compartment most of the time, did what he was told, and never complained. He had very polished manners, and everything he did was precise, as if he thought out every gesture and word in advance.

I thought of him as a little man, but he wasn't really. I stand about six three, and Dalquist wasn't a lot smaller than me, but he *acted* little. He worked for Butterworth Insurance, which I'd never heard of, and he said he was a claims adjustor, but I thought he was probably an accountant sent out because they didn't want to send anyone more important to a nothing rock like Jefferson.

Still, he'd been around. He didn't talk much about himself, but every now and then he'd let slip a story that showed he'd been on more rocks than most people; and he knew ship routines pretty well. Nobody had to show him things more than once. Since a lot of life-support gadgetry in *Slingshot* is Janet's design, or mine, and certainly isn't standard, he had to be pretty sharp to catch on so quick.

He had expensive gear, too. Nothing flashy, but his helmet was one of Goodyear's latest models, his skintight was David Clark's best with "stretch steel" threads woven in with the nylon, and his coveralls were a special design by Abercrombie and Fitch, with lots of gadget pockets and a self-cleaning low friction surface. It gave him a pretty natty appearance, rather than the battered look the old rockrats have.

I figured Butterworth Insurance must pay their adjustors more than I thought, or else he had a hell of an expense account.

The entryway is a big compartment. It's filled with nearly everything you can think of: dresses, art objects, gadgets and gizmos, spare parts for air bottles, sewing machines, and anything else Janet or I think we can sell in the way-stops we make with *Slingshot*. Janet calls it the "boutique," and she's been pretty clever about what she buys. It makes a profit, but like everything we do, just barely.

I've heard a lot of stories about tramp ships making a lot of money. Their skippers tell me whenever we meet. Before Jan and I fixed up *Slingshot* I used to believe them. Now I tell the same stories about fortunes made and lost, but the truth is we haven't seen any fortune.

We could use one. Hal, our oldest, wants to go to Marsport Tech, and that's expensive. Worse, he's just the first of nine. Meanwhile, Barclay's wants the payments kept up on the mortgage they hold on *Slinger*, fuel prices go up all the time, and the big Corporations are making it harder for little one-ship outfits like mine to compete.

We got to the boutique just in time to see two figures bounding like wallabies across the big flat area that serves as Jefferson's landing field. Every time one of the men would hit ground he'd fling up a burst of dust that fell like slow-motion bullets to make tiny craters around his footsteps. The landscape was bleak, nothing but rock and craters, with the big steel airlock entrance to Freedom Port the only thing to remind you that several thousand souls lived here.

We couldn't see it, because the horizon's pretty close on Jefferson, but out beyond the airlock there'd be the usual solar furnaces, big parabolic mirrors to melt down ores. There was also a big trench shimmering just at the horizon: ice. One of Jefferson's main assets is water. About ten thousand years ago Jefferson collided with the head of a comet and a lot of the ice stayed aboard.

The two figures reached *Slingshot*, and began the long climb up the ladder to the entrance. They moved fast, and I hit the buttons to open the outer door so they could let themselves in.

Jed was at least twice my age, but like all of us who live in low gravity it's hard to tell just how old that is. He has some wrinkles, but he could pass for fifty. The other guy was a Dr. Stewart, and I didn't know him.

There'd been another doctor, about my age, the last time I was in Jefferson, but he'd been a contract man and the Jeffersonians couldn't afford him. Stewart was a young chap, no more than twenty, born in Jefferson back when they called it Grubstake and Blackjack Dan was running the colony. He'd got his training the way most people get an education in the Belt, in front of a TV screen.

The TV classes are all right, but they have their limits. I hoped we wouldn't have any family emergencies here. Janet's a TV Doc, but unlike this Stewart chap she's had a year residency in Marsport General, and she knows the limits of TV training.

We've got a family policy that she doesn't treat the kids for anything serious if there's another doctor around, but between her and a new TV-trained MD there wasn't much choice.

"Everybody healthy?" Jed asked.

"Sure." I took out the log and showed where Janet had entered "NO COMMUNICABLE DISEASES" and signed it.

Stewart looked doubtful. "I'm supposed to examine everyone myself . . ."

"For Christ's sake," Jed told him. He pulled on his bristly mustache and glared at the young doc. Stewart glared back. "Well, 'least you can see if they're still warm," Jed conceded. "Cap'n Rollo, you got somebody to take him up while we get the immigration forms taken care of?"

"Sure." I called Pam on the intercom. She's second oldest. When she got to the boutique Jed sent Doctor Stewart up with her. When they were gone he took out a big book of forms.

For some reason every rock wants to know your entire life history before you can get out of your ship. I never have found out what they do with all the information. Dalquist and I began filling out forms while Jed muttered.

"Butterworth Insurance, eh?" Jed asked. "Got much business here?"

Dalquist looked up from the forms. "Very little. Perhaps you can help me. The insured was a Mr. Joseph Colella. I will need to find the beneficiary, a Mrs. Barbara Morrison Colella."

"Joe Colella?" I must have sounded surprised because they both looked at me. "I brought Joe and Barbara to Jefferson. Nice people. What happened to him?"

"Death certificate said accident." Jed said it just that way, flat, with no feeling. Then he added, "Signed by Dr. Stewart."

Jed sounded as if he wanted Dalquist to ask him a question, but the insurance man went back to his forms.

When it was obvious that he wasn't going to say anything more, I asked Jed. "Something wrong with the accident?"

Jed shrugged. His lips were tightly drawn. The mood in my ship had definitely changed for the worse, and I was sure Jed had more to say. Why wasn't Dalquist asking questions?

Something else puzzled me. Joe and Barbara were more than just former passengers. They were friends we were looking forward to seeing when we got to Jefferson. I was sure we'd mentioned them several times in front of Dalquist, but he'd never said a word.

We'd taken them to Jefferson about five Earth years before. They were newly married, Joe pushing sixty and Barbara less than half that. He'd just retired as a field agent for Hansen Enterprises, with a big bonus he'd earned in breaking up some kind of insurance scam. They were looking forward to buying into the Jefferson co-op system. I'd seen them every trip since, the last time two years ago, and they were short of ready money like everyone else in Jefferson, but they seemed happy enough.

"Where's Barbara now?" I asked Jed.

"Working for Westinghouse. Johnny Peregrine's office."

"She all right? And the kids?"

Jed shrugged. "Everybody helps out when help's needed. Nobody's rich."

"They put a lot of money into Jefferson stock," I said. "And didn't they have a mining claim?"

"Dividends on Jefferson Corporation stock won't even pay air taxes." Jed sounded more beat down then I'd ever known him. Even when things had looked pretty bad for us in the old days he'd kept all our spirits up with stupid jokes and puns. Not now. "Their claim wasn't much good to start with, and without Joe to work it—"

His voice trailed off as Pam brought Dr. Stewart back into our compartment. Stewart countersigned the log to certify that we were all healthy. "That's it, then," he said. "Ready to go ashore?"

"People waitin' for you in the Doghouse, Captain Rollo," Jed said. "Big meeting."

"I'll just get my hat."

"If there is no objection, I will come too," Dalquist said. "I wonder if a meeting with Mrs. Colella can be arranged?"

"Sure," I told him. "We'll send for her. Doghouse is pretty well the center of things in Jefferson anyway. Have her come for dinner."

"Got nothing good to serve." Jed's voice was gruff with a note of irritated apology.

"We'll see." I gave him a grin and opened the airlock.

There aren't any dogs at the Doghouse. Jed had one when he first came to Jefferson, which is why the name, but dogs don't do very well in low gravs. Like everything else in the Belt, the furniture in Jed's bar is iron and glass except for what's aluminum and titanium. The place is a big cave hollowed out of the rock. There's no outside view, and the only things to look at are the TV and the customers.

There was a big crowd, as there always is in the Port Captain's place when a ship comes in. More business is done in bars than offices out here, which was why Janet and the kids hadn't come dirtside with me. The crowd can get rough sometimes.

The Doghouse has a big bar running all the way across

on the side opposite the entryway from the main corridor. The bar's got a suction surface to hold down anything set on it, but no stools. The rest of the big room has tables and chairs and the tables have little clips to hold drinks and papers in place. There are also little booths around the outside perimeter for privacy. It's a typical layout. You can hold auctions in the big central area and make private deals in the booths.

Drinks are served with covers and straws because when you put anything down fast it sloshes out the top. You can spend years learning to drink beer in low gee if you don't want to sip it through a straw or squirt it out of a bulb.

The place was packed. Most of the customers were miners and shopkeepers, but a couple of tables were taken by company reps. I pointed out Johnny Peregrine to Dalquist. "He'll know how to find Barbara."

Dalquist smiled that tight little accountant's smile of his and went over to Peregrine's table.

There were a lot of others. The most important was Habib al Shamlan, the Iris Company factor. He was sitting with two hard cases, probably company cops.

The Jefferson Corporation people didn't have a table. They were at the bar, and the space between them and the other Company reps was clear, a little island of neutral area in the crowded room.

I'd drawn Jefferson's head honcho. Rhoda Hendrix was Chairman of the Board of the Jefferson Corporation, which made her the closest thing they had to a government. There was a big ugly guy with her. Joe Hornbinder had been around since Blackjack Dan's time. He still dug away at the rocks, hoping to get rich. Most people called him Horny for more than one reason.

It looked like this might be a good day. Everyone stared at us when we came in, but they didn't pay much attention to Dalquist. He was obviously a feather merchant, somebody they might have some fun with later on, and I'd have to watch out for him then, but right now we had important business.

Dalquist talked to Johnny Peregrine for a minute and they seemed to agree on something because Johnny nodded and sent one of his troops out. Dalquist went over into a corner and ordered a drink.

There's a protocol to doing business out here. I had a table all to myself, off to one side of the clear area in the middle, and Jed's boy brought me a big mug of beer with a hinged cap. When I'd had a good slug I took messages out of my pouch and scaled them out to people. Somebody bought me another drink, and there was a general gossip about what was happening around the Belt.

Al Shamlan was impatient. After about a half hour, which is really rushing things for an Arab, he called across, his voice very casual, "And what have you brought us, Captain Kephart?"

I took copies of my manifest out of my pouch and passed them around. Everyone began reading, but Johnny Peregrine gave a big grin at the first item.

"Beef!" Peregrine looked happy. He had 500 workers to feed.

"Nine tons," I agreed.

"Ten francs," Johnny said. "I'll take the whole lot."

"Fifteen," al Shamlan said.

I took a big glug of beer and relaxed. Jan and I'd taken a chance and won. Suppose somebody had flung a shipment of beef into transfer orbit a couple of years ago? A hundred tons could be arriving any minute, and mine wouldn't be worth anything.

Janet and I can keep track of scheduled ships, and we know pretty well where most of the tramps like us are going, but there's no way to be sure about goods in the pipeline. You can go broke in this racket.

There was more bidding, with some of the storekeepers getting in the act. I stood to make a good profit, but only the big Corporations were bidding on the whole lot. The Jefferson Corporation people hadn't said a word. I'd heard things weren't going too well for them, but this made it certain. If miners have any money, they'll buy beef. Beef tastes like cow. The stuff you can make from algae is nutritious, but at best it's not appetizing, and Jefferson doesn't even have the plant to make textured vegetable proteins—not that TVP is any substitute for the real thing.

Eventually the price got up to where only Iris and Westinghouse were interested in the whole lot and I broke the cargo up, seven tons to the big boys and the rest in small lots. I didn't forget to save out a couple hundred kilos for Jed, and I donated half a ton for the Jefferson city hall people to throw a feed with. The rest went for about thirty francs a kilo.

That would just about pay for the deuterium I burned up coming to Jefferson. There was some other stuff, lightweight items they don't make outside the big rocks like Pallas, and that was all pure profit. I felt pretty good when the auction ended. It was only the preliminaries, of course, and the main event was what would let me make a couple of payments to Barclay's on *Slinger's* mortgage, but it's a good feeling to know you can't lose money no matter what happens.

There was another round of drinks. Rockrats came over to my table to ask about friends I might have run into. Some of the storekeepers were making new deals, trading around things they'd bought from me. Dalquist came over to sit with me.

"Johnny finding your client for you?" I asked.

He nodded. "Yes. As you suggested, I have invited her to dinner here with us."

"Good enough. Jan and the kids will be in when the business is over."

Johnny Peregrine came over to the table. "Boosting cargo this trip?"

"Sure." The babble in the room faded out. It was time to start the main event.

The launch window to Luna was open and would be for another couple hundred hours. After that, the fuel needed to give cargo pods enough velocity to put them in transfer orbit to the Earth-Moon system would go up to where nobody could afford to send down anything massy.

There's a lot of traffic to Luna. It's cheaper, at the right time, to send ice down from the Belt than it is to carry it up from Earth. Of course the Lunatics have to wait a couple of years for their water to get there, but there's always plenty in the pipeline. Luna buys metals, too, although they don't pay as much as Earth does.

"I think something can be arranged," al Shamlan said.

"Hah!" Hornbinder was listening to us from his place at the bar. He laughed again. "Iris doesn't have any dee for a big shipment. Neither does Westinghouse. You want to boost, you'll deal with us."

I looked at al Shamlan. It's hard to tell what he's thinking, and not a lot easier to read Johnny Peregrine, but they didn't look very happy. "That true?" I asked.

Hornbinder and Rhoda came over to the table. "Remember, we sent for you," Rhoda said.

"Sure." I had their guarantee in my pouch. Five thousand francs up front, and another five thousand if I got here on time. I'd beaten their deadline by 20 hours, which isn't bad considering how many million kilometers I had to come. "Sounds like you've got a deal in mind."

She grinned. She's a big woman, and as hard as the inside of an asteroid. I knew she had to be sixty, but she had spent most of that time in low gee. There wasn't much cheer in her smile. It looked more like the tomcat does when he's trapped a rat. "Like Horny says, we have all the deuterium. If you want to boost for Iris and Westinghouse, you'll have to deal with us."

"Bloody hell." I wasn't going to do as well out of this trip as I'd thought.

Hornbinder grinned. "How you like it now, you goddam bloodsucker?"

"You mean me?" I asked.

"Fucking A. You come out here and use your goddam ship a hundred hours, and you take more than we get for busting our balls a whole year. Fucking A, I mean you."

I'd forgotten Dalquist was at the table. "If you think boostship captains charge too much, why don't you buy your own ship?" he asked.

"Who the hell are you?" Horny demanded.

Dalquist ignored him. "You don't buy your own ships because you can't afford them. Ship owners have to make enormous investments. If they don't make good profits they won't buy ships, and you won't get your cargo at any price."

He sounded like a professor. He was right, of course, but he talked in a way that I'd heard the older kids use on the Little Ones. It always starts fights in our family and it looked like it was having the same result here.

"Shut up and sit down, Horny." Rhoda Hendrix was used to being obeyed. Hornbinder glared at Dalquist, but he took a chair. "Now let's talk business," Rhoda said. "Captain, it's simple enough. We'll charter your ship for the next 700 hours."

"That can get expensive."

She looked to al Shamlan and Peregrine. They didn't look very happy. "I think I know how to get our money back."

"There are times when it is best to give in gracefully," al Shamlan said. He looked to Johnny Peregrine and got a nod. "We are prepared to make a fair agreement with you, Rhoda. After all, you've got to boost your ice. We must send our cargo. It will be much cheaper for all of us if the cargoes go out in one capsule. What are your terms?"

"No deal," Rhoda said. "We'll charter Cap'n Rollo's ship, and you deal with us."

"Don't I get a say in this?" I asked.

"You'll get yours," Hornbinder muttered.

"Fifty thousand," Rhoda said. "Fifty thousand to charter your ship. Plus the ten thousand we promised to get you here."

"That's no more than I'd make boosting your ice," I said. I usually get 5% of cargo value, and the customer furnishes the dee and reaction mass. That ice was worth a couple of million when it arrived at Luna. Jefferson would probably have to sell it before then, but even with discounts, futures in that much water would sell at over a million new francs.

"Seventy thousand, then," Rhoda said.

There was something wrong here. I picked up my beer and took a long swallow. When I put it down, Rhoda was talking again. "Ninety thousand. Plus your ten. An even hundred thousand francs, and you get another 1% of whatever we get for the ice after we sell it."

"A counteroffer may be appropriate," al Shamlan said. He was talking to Johnny Peregrine, but he said it loud enough to be sure that everyone else heard him. "Will Westinghouse go halves with Iris on a charter?"

Johnny nodded.

Al Shamlan's smile was deadly. "Charter your ship to *us*, Captain Kephart. One hundred and forty thousand francs, for exclusive use for the next 600 hours. That price includes boosting a cargo capsule, provided that we furnish you the deuterium and reaction mass."

"One fifty. Same deal," Rhoda said.

"One seventy-five."

"Two hundred." Somebody grabbed her shoulder and tried to say something to her, but Rhoda pushed him away. "I know what I'm doing. Two hundred thousand."

Al Shamlan shrugged. "You win. We can wait for the next launch window." He got up from the table. "Coming, Johnny?"

"In a minute." Peregrine had a worried look. "Ms. Hendrix, how do you expect to make a profit? I assure you that we won't pay what you seem to think we will."

"Leave that to me," she said. She still had that look: triumph. The price didn't seem to bother her at all.

"Hum." Al Shamlan made a gesture of bafflement. "One thing, Captain. Before you sign with Rhoda, you might ask to see the money. I would be much surprised if Jefferson Corporation has two hundred thousand." He pushed himself away and sailed across the bar to the corridor door. "You know where to find me if things don't work out, Captain Kephart."

He went out, and his company cops came right after him. After a moment Peregrine and the other Corporation people followed.

I wondered what the hell I'd got myself into this time.

Rhoda Hendrix was trying to be friendly. It didn't really suit her style.

I knew she'd come to Jefferson back when it was called Grubstake and Blackjack Dan was trying to set up an independent colony. Sometime in her first year she'd moved in with him, and pretty soon she was handling all his financial deals. There wasn't any nonsense about freedom and democracy back then. Grubstake was a big opportunity to get rich or get killed, and not much more.

When they found Blackjack Dan outside without a helmet, it turned out that Rhoda was his heir. She was the only one who knew what kind of deals he'd made anyway, so she took over his place. A year later she invented the Jefferson Corporation.

Everybody living on the rock had to buy stock, and she talked a lot about sovereign rights and government by the people. It takes a lot of something to govern a few thousand rockrats, and whatever it is, she had plenty. The idea caught on.

Now things didn't seem to be going too well, and her face showed it when she tried to smile. "Glad that's all settled," she said. "How's Janet?"

"The wife is fine, the kids are fine, the ship's fine, and I'm fine," I said.

She let the phony grin fade out.

"OK, if that's the way you want it. Shall we move over to a booth?"

"Why bother? I've got nothing to hide," I told her.

"Watch it," Hornbinder growled.

"And I've had about enough of him," I told Rhoda. "If you've got cargo to boost let's get it boosted."

"In time." She pulled some papers out of her pouch. "First, here's the charter contract."

It was all drawn up in advance. I didn't like it at all. The money was good, but none of this sounded right. "Maybe I should take al Shamlan's advice and—"

"You're not taking the Arabs' advice or their money either," Hornbinder said.

"—and ask to see your money first," I finished.

"Our credit's good," Rhoda said.

"So is mine as long as I keep my payments up. I can't pay off Barclay's with promises." I lifted my beer and flipped the top just enough to suck down a big gulp. Beer's lousy if you have to sip it.

"What can you lose?" Rhoda asked. "OK, so we don't have much cash. We've got a contract for the ice. Ten percent as soon as the Lloyd's man certifies the stuff's in transfer orbit. We'll pay you out of that. We've got the dee, we've got reaction mass, what the hell else do you want?"

"Your radiogram said cash," I reminded her. "I don't even have the retainer you promised. Just paper."

"Things are hard out here." Rhoda nodded to herself. She was thinking just how hard things were. "It's not like the old days. Everything's organized. Big companies. As soon as we get a little ahead, the big outfits move in and cut prices on everything we sell. Outbid us on everything we have to buy. Like your beef."

"Sure," I said. "I'm facing tough competition from the big shipping fleets, too."

"So this time we've got a chance to hold up the big boys," Rhoda said. "Get a little profit. You aren't hurt. You get more than you expected." She looked around to the other the miners. There were a lot of people listening to us. "Kephart, all we have to do is get a little ahead, and we can turn this rock into a decent place to live. A place for people, not Corporation clients!" Her voice rose and her eyes flashed. She meant every word, and the others nodded approval.

"You lied to me," I said.

"So what? How are you hurt?" She pushed the contract papers toward me.

"Excuse me." Dalquist hadn't spoken very loudly, and everyone looked at him. "Why is there such a hurry about this?" he asked.

"What the hell's it to you?" Hornbinder demanded.

"You want cash?" Rhoda asked. "All right, I'll give you cash." She took a document out of her pouch and slammed it onto the table. She hit hard enough to raise herself a couple of feet out of her chair. It would have been funny if she wasn't dead serious. Nobody laughed.

"There's a deposit certificate for every goddamn cent we have!" she shouted. "You want it? Take it all. Take the savings of every family in Jefferson. Pump us dry. Grind the faces of the poor! But sign that charter!"

"Cause if you don't," Hornbinder said, "your ship won't ever leave this rock. And don't think we can't stop you."

"Easy." I tried to look relaxed, but the sea of faces around me wasn't friendly at all. I didn't want to look at them so I looked at the deposit paper. It was genuine enough: you can't fake the molecular documents Zurich banks use. With the Jefferson Corporation Seal and the right signatures and thumbprints that thing was worth exactly 78,500 francs.

It would be a lot of money if I owned it for myself. It wasn't so much compared to the mortgage on *Slinger*. It was nothing at all for the total assets of a whole community.

"This is our chance to get out from under," Rhoda was saying. She wasn't talking to me. "We can squeeze the goddam corporation people for a change. All we need is that charter and we've got Westinghouse and the Arabs where we want them!"

Everybody in the bar was shouting now. It looked ugly, and I didn't see any way out.

"OK," I told Rhoda. "Sign over that deposit certificate, and make me out a lien on future assets for the rest. I'll boost your cargo—"

"Boost hell, sign that charter contract," Rhoda said.

"Yeah, I'll do that too. Make out the documents."

"Captain Kephart, is this wise?" Dalquist asked.

"Keep out of this, you little son of a bitch." Horny moved toward Dalquist. "You got no stake in this. Now shut up before I take off the top—"

Dalquist hardly looked up. "Five hundred francs to the first man who coldcocks him," he said carefully. He took his hand out of his pouch, and there was a bill in it.

There was a moment's silence, then four big miners started for Horny.

When it was over, Dalquist was out a thousand, because nobody could decide who got to Hornbinder first.

Even Rhoda was laughing after that was over. The mood changed a little; Hornbinder had never been very popular, and Dalquist was buying for the house. It didn't make any difference about the rest of it, of course. They weren't going to let me off Jefferson without signing that charter contract.

Rhoda sent over to city hall to have the documents made out. When they came I signed, and half the people in the place signed as witnesses. Dalquist didn't like it, but he ended up as a witness too. For better or worse, *Slingshot* was chartered to the Jefferson Corporation for 700 hours.

The surprise came after I'd signed. I asked Rhoda when she'd be ready to boost.

"Don't worry about it. You'll get the capsule when you need it."

"Bloody hell! You couldn't wait to get me to sign—"

"Aww, just relax, Kephart."

"I don't think you understand. You have half a million tons to boost up to what, five, six kilometers a second." I took out my pocket calculator. "Sixteen tons of deuterium and eleven thousand reaction mass. That's a bloody big load. The fuel feed system's got to be built. It's not something I can just strap on and push off—"

"You'll get what you need," Rhoda said. "We'll let you know when it's time to start work."

Jed put us in a private dining room. Janet came in later and I told her about the afternoon. I didn't think she'd like it, but she wasn't as upset as I was.

"We have the money," she said. "And we got a good price on the cargo, and if they ever pay off we'll get more than we expected on the boost charges. If they don't pay up—well, so what?"

"Except that we've got a couple of major companies unhappy, and they'll be here long after Jefferson folds up. Sorry, Jed, but—"

He bristled his mustache. "Could be. I figure on gettin' along with the Corporations too. Just in case."

"But what did all that lot mean?" Dalquist asked.

"Beats me." Jed shook his head. "Rhoda's been making noises about how rich we're going to be. New furnace, another power plant, maybe even a ship of our own. Nobody knows how she's planning on doing it."

"Could there have been a big strike?" Dalquist asked. "Iridium, one of the really valuable metals?"

"Don't see how," Jed told him. "Look, mister, if Rhoda's goin' to bail this place out of the hole the big boys have dug for us, that's great with me. I don't ask questions."

Jed's boy came in. "There's a lady to see you."

Barbara Morrison Colella was a small blonde girl, pug nose, blue eyes. She looks like somebody you'd see on Earthside TV playing a dumb blonde.

Her degrees said "family economics," which I guess on Earth doesn't amount to much. Out here it's a specialty. To keep a family going out here you better know a lot of environment and life-support engineering, something about prices that depend on orbits and launch windows, a lot about how to get food out of rocks—and something about power systems, too.

She was glad enough to see us, especially Janet, but

we got another surprise. She looked at Dalquist and said, "Hello, Buck."

"Hello. Surprised, Bobby?"

"No. I knew you'd be along as soon as you heard."

"You know each other, then," I said.

"Yes." Dalquist hadn't moved, but he didn't look like a little man any longer. "How did it happen, Bobby?"

Her face didn't change. She'd lost most of her smile when she saw Dalquist. She looked at the rest of us, and pointed at Jed. "Ask him. He knows more than I do."

"Mr. Anderson?" Dalquist prompted. His tone made it sound as if he'd done this before, and he expected to be answered.

If Jed resented that he didn't show it. "Simple enough. Joe always seemed happy enough when he came in here after his shift—"

Dalquist looked from Jed to Barbara. She nodded.

"—until the last time. That night he got stinking drunk. Kept mutterin' something about 'Not that way. There's got to be another way.'"

"Do you know what that meant?"

"No," Jed said. "But he kept saying it. Then he got really stinking and I sent him home with a couple of the guys he worked with."

"What happened when he got home?" Dalquist asked.

"He never came home, Buck," Barbara said. "I got worried about him, but I couldn't find him. The men he'd left here with said he'd got to feeling better and left them—"

"Damn fools," Jed muttered. "He was right out of it. Nobody should go outside with that much to drink."

"And they found him outside?"

"At the refinery. Helmet busted open. Been dead five, six hours. Held the inquest right in here, at that table al Shamlan was sitting at this afternoon."

"Who held the inquest?" Dalquist asked.

"Rhoda."

"Doesn't make sense," I said.

"No." Janet didn't like it much either. "Barbara, don't

you have any idea of what Joe meant? Was he worried about something?"

"Nothing he told me about. He wasn't—we weren't fighting or anything. I'm sure he didn't—"

"Humpf." Dalquist shook his head. "What damned fool suggested suicide?"

"Well," Jed said, "you know how it is. If a man takes on a big load and wanders around outside, it might as well be suicide. Hornbinder said we were doing Barbara a favor, voting it an accident."

Dalquist took papers out of his pouch. "He was right, of course. I wonder if Hornbinder knew that all Hansen employees receive a paid-up insurance policy as one of their retirement benefits?"

"I didn't know it," I said.

Janet was more practical. "How much is it worth?"

"I am not sure of the exact amounts," Dalquist said. "There are trust accounts involved also. Sufficient to get Barbara and the children back to Mars and pay for their living expenses there. Assuming you want to go?"

"I don't know," Barbara said. "Let me think about it. Joe and I came here to get away from the big companies. I don't have to like Rhoda and the city hall crowd to appreciate what we've got in Jefferson. Independence is worth something."

"Indeed," Dalquist said. He wasn't agreeing with her, and suddenly we all knew he and Barbara had been through this argument before. I wondered when.

"Janet, what would you do?" Barbara asked.

Jan shrugged. "Not a fair question. Roland and I made that decision a long time ago. But neither of us is alone." She reached for my hand across the table.

As she'd said, we made our choice. We've had plenty of offers for *Slingshot*, from outfits that would be happy to hire us as crew for *Slinger*. It would mean no more hustle to meet the mortgage payments, and not a lot of change in the way we live—but we wouldn't be our own people anymore. We've never seriously considered taking any of the offers.

"You don't have to be alone," Dalquist said.

"I know, Buck." There was a wistful note in Barbara's voice. They looked at each other for a long time. Then we sat down to dinner.

I was in my office aboard *Slingshot*. Thirty hours had gone by since I'd signed the charter contract, and I still didn't know what I was boosting, or when. It didn't make sense.

Janet refused to worry about it. We'd cabled the money on to Marsport, all of Jefferson's treasury and what we'd got for our cargo, so Barclay's was happy for a while. We had enough deuterium aboard *Slinger* to get where we could buy more. She kept asking what there was to worry about, and I didn't have any answer.

I was still brooding about it when Oswald Dalquist tapped on the door.

I hadn't seen him much since the dinner at the Doghouse, and he didn't look any different, but he wasn't the same man. I suppose the change was in me. You can't think of a man named "Buck" the same way you think of an Oswald.

"Sit down," I said. That was formality, of course. It's no harder to stand than sit in the tiny gravity we felt. "I've been meaning to say something about the way you handled Horny. I don't think I've ever seen anybody do that."

His smile was thin, and I guess it hadn't changed either, but it didn't seem like an accountant's smile any more. "It's an interesting story, actually," he said. "A long time ago I was in a big colony ship. Long passage, nothing to do. Discovered the other colonists didn't know much about playing poker."

We exchanged grins again.

"I won so much it made me worry that someone would take it away from me, so I hired the biggest man in the bay to watch my back. Sure enough, some chap accused me of cheating, so I called on my big friend—"

"Yeah?"

"And he shouted 'Fifty to the first guy that decks him.' Worked splendidly, although it wasn't precisely what I'd expected when I hired him—"

We had our laugh.

"When are we leaving, Captain Kephart?"

"Beats me. When they get the cargo ready to boost, I guess."

"That might be a long time," Dalquist said.

"What does that mean?"

"I've been asking around. To the best of my knowledge, there are no preparations for boosting a big cargo pod."

"That's stupid," I said. 'Well, it's their business. When we go, how many passengers am I going to have?"

His little smile faded entirely. "I wish I knew. You've guessed that Joe Colella and I were old friends. And rivals for the same girl."

"Yeah. I'm wondering why you— Hell, we talked about them on the way in. You never let on you'd ever heard of them."

He nodded carefully. "I wanted to be certain. I only knew that Joe was supposed to have died in an accident. He was not the kind of man accidents happen to. Not even out here."

"What is that supposed to mean?"

"Only that Joe Colella was one of the most careful men you will ever meet, and I didn't care to discuss my business with Barbara until I knew more about the situation in Jefferson. Now I'm beginning to wonder—"

"Dad!" Pam was on watch, and she sounded excited. The intercom box said again, "Dad!"

"Right, sweetheart."

"You better come up quick. There's a message coming through. You better hurry."

"MAYDAY MAYDAY MAYDAY." The voice was cold and unemotional, the way they are when they really mean it. It rolled off the tape Pam had made. "MAYDAY MAYDAY MAYDAY. THIS IS PEGASUS LINES

BOOSTSHIP *AGAMEMNON* OUTBOUND EARTH
TO PALLAS. OUR MAIN ENGINES ARE DIS-
ABLED. I SAY AGAIN, MAIN ENGINES DISABLED.
OUR VELOCITY RELATIVE TO SOL IS ONE FOUR
ZERO KILOMETERS PER SECOND, I SAY AGAIN,
ONE HUNDRED FORTY KILOMETERS PER SEC-
OND. AUXILIARY POWER IS FAILING. MAIN
ENGINES CANNOT BE REPAIRED. PRESENT
SHIP MASS IS 54,000 TONS. SEVENTEEN HUN-
DRED PASSENGERS ABOARD. MAYDAY MAYDAY
MAYDAY."

"Lord God." I wasn't really aware that I was talking.
The kids had crowded into the control cabin, and we
listened as the tape went on to give a string of numbers,
the vectors to locate *Agamemnon* precisely. I started to
punch them into the plotting tanks, but Pam stopped
me.

"I already did that, Dad." She hit the activation switch
to bring the screen to life.

It showed a picture of our side of the Solar System,
the inner planets and inhabited rocks, along with a block
of numbers and a long thin line with a dot at the end to
represent *Agamemnon*. Other dots winked on and off:
boostships.

We were the only one that stood a prayer of a chance
of catching up with *Agamemnon*.

The other screen lit, giving us what the *Register* knew
about *Agamemnon*. It didn't look good. She was an enormous old cargo/passenger ship, over thirty years old—
and out here that's old indeed. She'd been built for a
useful life of half that, and sold off to Pegasus lines when
P&L decided she wasn't safe.

Her auxiliary power was furnished by a plutonium pile.
If something went wrong with it, there was no way to
repair it in space. Without auxiliary power, the life support systems couldn't function. I was still looking at her
specs when the comm panel lit. Local call, Port Captain's
frequency.

"Yeah, Jed?" I said.

"You've got the Mayday?"

"Sure. I figure we've got about 60 hours max to fuel up and still let me catch her. I've got to try it, of course."

"Certainly, Captain." The voice was Rhoda's. "I've already sent a crew to start work on the fuel pod. I suggest you work with them to be sure it's right."

"Yeah. They'll have to work damned fast." *Slingshot* doesn't carry anything like the tankage a run like this would need.

"One more thing, Captain," Rhoda said. "Remember that your ship is under exclusive charter to the Jefferson Corporation. We'll make the legal arrangements with Pegasus. You concentrate on getting your ship ready."

"Yeah, OK. Out." I switched the comm system to *record*. "*Agamemnon*, this is cargo tug *Slingshot*. I have your Mayday. Intercept is possible, but I cannot carry sufficient fuel and mass to decelerate your ship. I must vampire your dee and mass, I say again, we must transfer your fuel and reaction mass to my ship.

"We have no facilities for taking your passengers aboard. We will attempt to take your ship in tow and decelerate using your deuterium and reaction mass. Our engines are modified General Electric Model five-niner ion-fusion. Preparations for coming to your assistance are under way. Suggest your crew begin preparations for fuel transfer. Over."

Then I looked around the cabin. Janet and our oldest were ashore. "Pam, you're in charge. Send that, and record the reply. You can start the checklist for boost. I make it about 200 centimeters acceleration, but you'd better check that. Whatever it is, we'll need to secure for it. Also, get in a call to find your mother. God knows where she is."

"Sure, Dad." She looked very serious, and I wasn't worried. Hal's the oldest, but Pam's a lot more thorough.

The *Register* didn't give anywhere near enough data about *Agamemnon*. I could see from the recognition pix that she carried her reaction mass in strap-ons alongside the main hull, rather than in detachable pods right for-

ward the way *Slinger* does. That meant we might have to
transfer the whole lot before we could start deceleration.

She had been built as a general purpose ship, so her
hull structure forward was beefy enough to take the
thrust of a cargo pod—but how *much* thrust? If we were
going to get her down, we'd have to push like hell on
her bows, and there was no way to tell if they were
strong enough to take it.

I looked over to where Pam was aiming our high-gain
antenna for the message to *Agamemnon*. She looked like
she'd been doing this all her life, which I guess she had
been, but mostly for drills. It gave me a funny feeling to
know she'd grown up sometime in the last couple of
years and Janet and I hadn't really noticed.

"Pamela, I'm going to need more information on *Agamemnon*," I told her. "The kids had a TV cast out of
Marsport, so you ought to be able to get through. Ask
for anything they have on that ship. Structural strength,
fuel-handling equipment, everything they've got."

"Yes, sir."

"OK. I'm going ashore to see about the fuel pods. Call
me when we get some answers, but if there's nothing
important from *Agamemnon* just hang on to it."

"What happens if we can't catch them?" Phillip asked.

Pam and Jennifer were trying to explain it to him as
I went down to the lock.

Jed had lunch waiting in the Doghouse. "How's it
going?" he asked when I came in.

"Pretty good. Damned good, all things considered."
The refinery crew had built up fuel pods for *Slinger*
before, so they knew what I needed, but they'd never
made one that had to stand up to a full fifth of a gee. A
couple of centimeters is hefty acceleration when you
boost big cargo, but we'd have to go out at a hundred
times that.

"Get the stuff from Marsport?"

"Some of it." I shook my head. The whole operation

would be tricky. There wasn't a lot of risk for me, but *Agamemnon* was in big trouble.

"Rhoda's waiting for you. Back room."

"You don't look happy."

Jed shrugged. "Guess she's right, but it's kind of ghoulish."

"What—?"

"Go see."

Rhoda was sitting with a trim chap who wore a clipped mustache. I'd met him before, of course: B. Elton, Esq., the Lloyd's rep in Jefferson. He hated the place and couldn't wait for a transfer.

"I consider this reprehensible," Elton was saying when I came in. "I hate to think you are a party to this, Captain Kephart."

"Party to what?"

"Ms. Hendrix has asked for thirty million francs as salvage fee. Ten million in advance."

I whistled. "That's heavy."

"The ship is worth far more than that," Rhoda said.

"If I can get her down. There are plenty of problems— hell, she may not be fit for more than salvage," I said.

"Then there are the passengers. How much is Lloyd's out if you have to pay off their policies? And lawsuits?" Rhoda had the tomcat's grin again. "We're saving you money, Mr. Elton."

I realized what she was doing. "I don't know how to say this, but it's my ship you're risking."

"You'll be paid well," Rhoda said. "Ten percent of what we get."

That would just about pay off the whole mortgage. It was also a hell of a lot more than the commissioners in Marsport would award for a salvage job.

"We've got heavy expenses up front," Rhoda was saying. "That fuel pod costs like crazy. We're going to miss the launch window to Luna."

"Certainly you deserve reasonable compensation, but—"

"But nothing!" Rhoda's grin was triumphant. "Captain Kephart can't boost without fuel, and we have it all. That fuel goes aboard his ship when you've signed my contract, Elton, and not before."

Elton looked sad and disgusted. "It seems a cheap—"

"Cheap!" Rhoda got up and went to the door. "What the hell do you know about cheap? How goddam many times have we heard you people say there's no such thing as an excess profit? Well, this time *we* got the breaks, Elton, and *we'll* take the excess profits. Think about that."

Out in the bar somebody cheered. Another began singing a tune I'd heard in Jefferson before. Pam says the music is very old, she's heard it on TV casts, but the words fit Jefferson. The chorus goes "THERE'S GONNA BE A GREAT DAY!" and everybody out there shouted it.

"Marsport will never give you that much money," Elton said.

"Sure they will." Rhoda's grin got even wider, if that was possible. "We'll hold on to the cargo until they do—"

"Be damned if I will!" I said.

"Not you at all. I'm sending Mr. Hornbinder to take charge of that. Don't worry, Captain Kephart, I've got you covered. The big boys won't bite you."

"Hornbinder?"

"Sure. You'll have some extra passengers this run—"

"Not him. Not in my ship."

"Sure he's going. You can use some help—"

Like hell. "I don't need any."

She shrugged. "Sorry you feel that way. Just remember, you're under charter." She gave the tomcat grin again and left.

When she was gone Jed came in with beer for me and something else for Elton. They were still singing and cheering in the other room.

"Do you think this is fair?" Elton demanded.

Jed shrugged. "Doesn't matter what I think. Or what Rollo thinks. Determined woman, Rhoda Hendrix."

"You'd have no trouble over ignoring that charter contract," Elton told me. "In fact, we could find a reasonable bonus for you—"

"Forget it." I took the beer from Jed and drank it all. Welding up that fuel pod had been hot work, and I was ready for three more. "Listen to them out there," I said. "Think I want them mad at me? They see this as the end of their troubles."

"Which it could be," Jed said. "With a few million to invest we can make Jefferson into a pretty good place."

Elton wasn't having any. "Lloyd's is not in the business of subsidizing colonies that cannot make a living—"

"So what?" I said. "Rhoda's got the dee and nobody else has enough. She means it, you know."

"There's less than 40 hours," Jed reminded him. "I think I'd get on the line to my bosses, was I you."

"Yes." Elton had recovered his polish, but his eyes were narrow. "I'll just do that."

They launched the big fuel pod with strap-on solids, just enough thrust to get it away from the rock so I could catch it and lock on. We had hours to spare, and I took my time matching velocities. Then Hal and I went outside to make sure everything was connected right.

Hornbinder and two friends were aboard against all my protests. They wanted to come out with us, but I wasn't having any. We don't need help from groundpounders. Janet and Pam took them to the galley for coffee while I made my inspection.

Slingshot is basically a strongly built hollow tube with engines at one end and clamps at the other. The cabins are rings around the outside of the tube. We also carry some deuterium and reaction mass strapped on to the main hull, but for big jobs there's not nearly enough room there. Instead, we build a special fuel pod that straps onto the bow. The reaction mass can be lowered through the central tube when we're boosting.

Boost cargo goes on forward of the fuel pod. This time we didn't have any going out, but when we caught up to *Agamemnon* she'd ride there, no different from any other cargo capsule. That was the plan, anyway. Taking another ship in tow isn't precisely common out here.

Everything matched up. Deuterium lines, and the elevator system for handling the mass and getting it into the boiling pots aft; it all fit. Took our time, even after we were sure it was working, while the miners who'd come up with the pod fussed and worried. Eventually I was satisfied and they got to head for home. I was still waiting for a call from Janet.

Just before they were ready to start up she hailed us. She used an open frequency so the miners could hear. "Rollo, I'm afraid those crewmen Rhoda loaned us will have to go home with the others."

"Eh?" One of the miners turned around in the saddle.

"What's the problem, Jan?" I asked.

"It seems Mr. Hornbinder and his friends have very bad stomach problems. It could be quite serious. I think they'd better see Dr. Stewart as soon as possible."

"Goddam. Rhoda's not going to like this," the foreman said. He maneuvered his little open-frame scooter over to the airlock. Pam brought his friends out and saw they were strapped in.

"Hurry up!" Hornbinder said, "Get moving!"

"Sure, Horny." There was a puzzled note in the foreman's voice. He started up the bike. At maximum thrust it might make a twentieth of a gee. There was no enclosed space, it was just a small chemical rocket with saddles, and you rode it in your suit.

"Goddamit, get moving," Hornbinder was shouting. If there'd been air you might have heard him a klick away. "You can make better time than this!"

I got inside and went up to the control cabin. Jan was grinning.

"Amazing what calomel can do," she said.

"Amazing." We took time off for a quick kiss before I strapped in. I didn't feel much sympathy for Horny, but the other two hadn't been so bad. The one to feel sorry for was whoever had to clean up their suits.

Ship's engines are complicated things. First you take

deuterium pellets and zap them with a big laser. The dee fuses to helium. Now you've got far too much hot gas at far too high a temperature, so it goes into a MHD system that cools it and converts the energy into electricity.

Some of that powers the lasers to zap more dee. The rest powers the ion drive system. Take a metal, preferably something with a low boiling point like cesium, but since that's rare out here cadmium generally has to do. Boil it to a vapor. Put the vapor through ionizing screens that you keep charged with power from the fusion system.

Squirt the charged vapor through more charged plates to accelerate it, and you've got a drive. You've also got a charge on your ship, so you need an electron gun to get rid of that.

There are only about nine hundred things to go wrong with the system. Superconductors for the magnetic fields and charge plates: those take cryogenic systems, and *those* have auxiliary systems to keep them going. Nothing's simple, and nothing's small, so out of *Slingshot*'s 1600 metric tons, well over a thousand tons is engine.

Now you know why there aren't any space yachts flitting around out here. *Slinger*'s one of the smallest ships in commission, and she's bloody big. If Jan and I hadn't happened to hit lucky by being the only possible buyers for a couple of wrecks, and hadn't had friends at Barclay's who thought we might make a go of it, we'd never have owned our own ship.

When I tell people about the engines they don't ask what we do aboard *Slinger* when we're on long passages, but they're only partly right. You *can't* do anything to an engine while it's on. It either works or it doesn't, and all you have to do with it is see it gets fed.

It's when the damned things are shut down that the work starts, and that takes so much time that you make sure you've done everything *else* in the ship when you can't work on the engines. There's a lot of maintenance, as you might guess when you consider that we've got to make everything we need, from air to zwieback. Living in a ship makes you appreciate planets.

Space operations go smooth, or generally they don't go at all. I looked at Jan and we gave each other a quick wink. It's a good luck charm we've developed. Then I hit the keys, and we were off.

It wasn't a long boost to catch up with *Agamemnon*. I spent most of it in the contoured chair in front of the control screens. A fifth of a gee isn't much for dirtsiders, but out here it's ten times what we're used to. Even the cats hate it.

The high gees saved us on high-calcium foods and the drugs we need to keep going in low gravs, and of course we didn't have to put in so much time in the exercise harnesses, but the only one happy about it was Dalquist. He came up to the control cab about an hour out from Jefferson.

"I thought there would be other passengers," he said.

"Really? Barbara made it pretty clear that she wasn't interested in Pallas. Might go to Mars, but—"

"No, I meant Mr. Hornbinder."

"He, uh, seems to have become ill. So did his friends. Happened quite suddenly."

Dalquist frowned. "I wish you hadn't done that."

"Really? Why?"

"It might not have been wise, Captain."

I turned away from the screens to face him. "Look, Mr. Dalquist, I'm not sure what *you're* doing on this trip. I sure didn't need Rhoda's goons along."

"Yes. Well, there's nothing to be done now, in any event."

"Just why are you aboard? I thought you were in a hurry to get back to Marsport—"

"Butterworth interests may be affected, Captain. And I'm in no hurry."

That's all he had to say about it, too, no matter how hard I pressed him on it.

I didn't have time to worry about it. As we boosted I

was talking with *Agamemnon*. She passed about half a million kilometers from Jefferson, which is awfully close out here. We'd started boosting before she was abreast of the rock, and now we were chasing her. The idea was to catch up to her just as we matched her velocity. Meanwhile, *Agamemnon*'s crew had their work cut out.

When we were fifty kilometers behind, I cut the engines to minimum power. I didn't dare shut them down entirely. The fusion power system offers no difficulty with re-starts, but the ion screens foul when they're cooled. Unless they're cleaned or replaced we can lose as much as half our thrust—and we were going to need every dyne.

We could just make out *Agamemnon* with our telescope. She was too far away to let us see any details. We could see a bright spot of light approaching us, though: Captain Jason Ewert-James and two of his engineering officers. They were using one of *Agamemnon*'s scooters.

There wasn't anything larger aboard. It's not practical to carry lifeboats for the entire crew and passenger list, so they have none at all on the larger boostships. Earthside politicians are forever talking about "requiring" lifeboats on passenger-carrying ships, but they'll never do it. Even if they pass such laws, how could they enforce them? Earth has no cops in space. The U.S. and Soviet Air Forces keep a few ships, but not enough to make an effective police force, even if anyone out here recognized their jurisdiction—which we don't.

Captain Ewert-James was a typical ship captain. He'd formerly been with one of the big British-Swiss lines, and had to transfer over to Pegasus when his ship was sold out from under him. The larger lines like younger skippers, which I think is a mistake, but they don't ask my advice.

Ewert-James was tall and thin, with a clipped mustache and graying hair. He wore uniform coveralls over his skintights, and in the pocket he carried a large pipe which he lit as soon as he'd asked permission.

"Thank you. Didn't dare smoke aboard *Agamemnon*—"

"Air that short?" I asked.

"No, but some of the passengers think it might be. Wouldn't care to annoy them, you know." His lips twitched just a trifle, something less than a conspirator's grin but more than a deadpan.

We went into the office. Jan came in, making it a bit crowded. I introduced her as physician and chief officer.

"How large a crew do you keep, Captain Kephart?" Ewert-James asked.

"Just us. And the kids. My oldest two are on watch at the moment."

His face didn't change. "Experienced cadets, eh? Well, we'd best be down to it. Mister Haply will show you what we've been able to accomplish."

They'd done quite a lot. There was a lot of expensive alloy bar-stock in the cargo, and somehow they'd got a good bit of it forward and used it to brace up the bows of the ship so she could take the thrust. "Haven't been able to weld it properly, though," Haply said. He was a young third engineer, not too long from being a cadet himself. "We don't have enough power to do welding and run the life support too."

Agamemnon's image was a blur on the screen across from my desk. It looked like a gigantic hydra, or a bull-whip with three short lashes standing out from the handle. The three arms rotated slowly. I pointed to it. "Still got spin on her."

"Yes." Ewert-James was grim. "We've been running the ship with that power. Spin her up with attitude jets and take power off the flywheel motor as she slows down."

I was impressed. Spin is usually given by running a big flywheel with an electric motor. Since any motor is a generator, Ewert-James's people had found a novel way to get some auxiliary power for life support systems.

"Can you run for a while without doing that?" Jan asked. "It won't be easy transferring reaction mass if you can't." We'd already explained why we didn't want to shut down our engines, and there'd be no way to supply *Agamemnon* with power from *Slingshot* until we were coupled together.

"Certainly. Part of our cargo is LOX. We can run twenty, thirty hours without ship's power. Possibly longer."

"Good." I hit the keys to bring the plot-tank results onto my office screen. "There's what I get," I told them. "Our outside time limit is *Slinger's* maximum thrust. I'd make that 20 centimeters for this load—"

"Which is more than I'd care to see exerted against the bows, Captain Kephart. Even with our bracing." Ewert-James looked to his engineers. They nodded gravely.

"We can't do less than ten," I reminded them. "Anything much lower and we won't make Pallas at all."

"She'll take ten," Haply said. "I think."

The others nodded agreement. I was sure they'd been over this a hundred times as we were closing.

I looked at the plot again. "At the outside, then, we've got 170 hours to transfer twenty-five thousand tons of reaction mass. And we can't work steadily because you'll have to spin up *Agamemnon* for power, and I can't stop engines—"

Ewert-James turned up both corners of his mouth at that. It seemed to be the closest thing to a smile he ever gave. "I'd say we best get at it, wouldn't you?"

Agamemnon didn't look much like *Slingshot*. We'd closed to a quarter of a klick, and steadily drew ahead of her; when we were past her we'd turn over and decelerate, dropping behind so that we could do the whole cycle over again.

Some features were the same, of course. The engines were not much larger than *Slingshot's*, and looked much the same, a big cylinder covered over with tankage and coils, acceleration outports at the aft end. A smaller tube ran from the engines forward, but you couldn't see all of it because big rounded reaction mass canisters covered a portion.

Up forward the arms grew out of another cylinder. They jutted out at equal angles around the hull, three big arms to contain passenger decks and auxiliary systems. The arms could be folded in between the reaction mass canisters, and would be when we started boosting.

All told she was over four hundred meters long, and with the hundred-meter arms thrust out she looked like a monstrous hydra slowly spinning in space.

"There doesn't seem to be anything wrong aft," Buck Dalquist said. He studied the ship from the screens, then pulled the telescope eyepiece toward himself for a direct look.

"Failure in the superconductor system," I told him. "Broken lines. They can't contain the fusion reaction long enough to get it into the MHD system."

He nodded. "So Captain Ewert-James told me. I've asked for a chance to inspect the damage as soon as it's convenient."

"Eh? Why?"

"Oh, come now, Captain." Dalquist was still looking through the telescope. "Surely you don't believe in Rhoda Hendrix as a good luck charm?"

"But—"

"But nothing." There was no humor in his voice, and when he looked across the cabin at me there was none in his eyes. "She bid far too much for an exclusive charter, after first making certain that you'd be on Jefferson at precisely the proper time. She has bankrupted the corporate treasury to obtain a corner on deuterium. Why else would she do all that if she hadn't expected to collect it back with profit?"

"But—she was going to charge Westinghouse and Iris and the others to boost their cargo. And they had cargo of their own—"

"Did they? We saw no signs of it. And she bid far too much for your charter."

"Damn it, you can't believe that," I said, but I didn't

mean it. I remembered the atmosphere back at Jefferson. "You think the whole outfit was in on it?"

He shrugged. "Does it matter?"

The fuel transfer was tough. We couldn't just come alongside and winch the stuff over. At first we caught it on the fly: *Agamemnon's* crew would fling out hundred-ton canisters, then use the attitude jets to boost away from them, not far, but just enough to stand clear.

Then I caught them with a bow pod. It wasn't easy. You don't need much closing velocity with a hundred tons before you've got a hell of a lot of energy to worry about. Weightless doesn't mean massless.

We could only transfer about four hundred tons an hour that way. After the first ten-hour stretch I decided it wouldn't work. There were just too many ways for things to go wrong.

"Get rigged for tow," I told Captain Ewert-James. "Once we're hooked up I can feed you power, so you don't have to do that crazy stunt with the spin. I'll start boost at about a tenth of a centimeter. It'll keep the screens hot, and we can winch the fuel pods down."

He was ready to agree. I think watching me try to catch those fuel canisters, knowing that if I made a mistake his ship was headed for Saturn and beyond, was giving him ulcers.

First he spun her hard to build up power, then slowed the spin to nothing. The long arms folded alongside, so that *Agamemnon* took on a trim shape. Meanwhile I worked around in front of her, turned over and boosted in the direction we were traveling, and turned again.

The dopplers worked fine for a change. We hardly felt the jolt as *Agamemnon* settled nose to nose with us. Her crewmen came out to work the clamps and string lines across to carry power. We were linked, and the rest of the trip was nothing but hard work.

We could still transfer no more than 400 tons an hour, meaning bloody hard work to get the whole 25,000 tons into *Slinger's* fuel pod, but at least it was all downhill.

Each canister was lowered by winch, then swung into our own fuel-handling system where *Slinger*'s winches took over. Cadmium's heavy: a cube about two meters on a side weighs a hundred tons. It wasn't big, and it didn't *weigh* much in a tenth of a centimeter, but you don't drop the stuff either.

Finally it was finished, and we could start maximum boost: a whole ten centimeters, about a hundredth of a gee. That may not sound like much, but think of the mass involved. *Slinger*'s 1600 tons were nothing, but there was *Agamemnon* too. I worried about the bracing Ewert-James had put in the bows, but nothing happened.

Three hundred hours later we were down at Pallasport. As soon as we touched in my ship was surrounded by Intertel cops.

The room was paneled in real wood. That doesn't sound like much unless you live in the Belt—but think about it: every bit of that paneling was brought across 60 million kilometers.

Pallas hasn't much in the way of gravity, but there's enough to make sitting down worth doing. Besides, it's a habit we don't seem to be able to get out of. There was a big conference table across the middle of the room, and a dozen corporation reps sat at it. It was made of some kind of plastic that looks like wood; not even the Commission brings furniture from Earth.

Deputy Commissioner Ruth Carr sat at a table at the far end, across the big conference table from where I sat in the nominal custody of the Intertel guards. I wasn't happy about being arrested and my ship impounded. Not that it would do me any good to be unhappy . . .

All the big outfits were represented at the conference table. Lloyd's and Pegasus Lines, of course, but there were others, Hansen Enterprises, Westinghouse, Iris, GE, and the rest.

"Definitely sabotage, then?" Commissioner Carr asked. She looked much older than she really was; the black coveralls and cap did that. She'd done a good job of conducting the hearings, though, even sending Captain Ewert-James and his engineers out to get new photographs of the damage to *Agamemnon's* engines. He passed them up from the witness box, and she handed them to her experts at their place to her right.

They nodded over them.

"I'd say definitely so," Captain Ewert-James was saying. "There was an attempt to lay the charge pattern such that it might be mistaken for meteorite damage. In fact, had not Mr. Dalquist been so insistent on a thorough examination, we might have let it go at that. On close inspection, though, it seems very probable that a series of shaped charges were used."

Ruth Carr nodded to herself. She'd heard me tell about Rhoda's frantic efforts to charter my ship. One of Ewert-James's officers testified that an engineering crewman jumped ship just before *Agamemnon* boosted out of Earth orbit. The Intertel people had dug up the fact that he'd lived on Jefferson two years before, and were trying to track him down now—he'd vanished.

"The only possible beneficiary would be the Jefferson Corporation," Mrs. Carr said. "The concerns most harmed are Lloyd's and Pegasus Lines—"

"And Hansen Enterprises," the Hansen rep said. Ruth Carr looked annoyed but she didn't say anything. I noticed that the big outfits felt free to interrupt her and wondered if they did that with all the Commissioners, or just her because she hadn't been at the job very long.

The Hansen man was an older chap who looked as if he'd done his share of rock mining in his day, but he spoke with a Harvard accent. "There is a strong possibility that the Jefferson Corporation arranged the murder of a retired Hansen employee. As he was insured by a Hansen subsidiary, we are quite concerned."

"Quite right." Mrs. Carr jotted notes on the pad in front of her. She was the only one there I'd seen use note paper. The others whispered into wrist recorders. "Before we hear proposed actions, has anyone an objection to disposing of the matter concerning Captain Kephart?"

Nobody said anything.

"I find that Captain Kephart has acted quite properly, and that the salvage fees should go to his ship."

I realized I'd been holding my breath. Nobody wanted my scalp so far as I knew, and Dalquist had been careful to show I wasn't involved in whatever Rhoda had planned—but still, you never know what'll happen when the big boys have their eye on you. It was a relief to hear her dismiss the whole business, and the salvage fees would pay off a big part of the mortgage. I wouldn't know just how much I'd get until the full Commission back in Marsport acted, but it couldn't come to less than a million francs. Maybe more.

"Now for the matter of the Jefferson Corporation."

"Move that we send sufficient Intertel agents to take possession of the whole damn rock," the Lloyd's man said.

"Second." That was Pegasus Lines.

"Discussion?" Ruth Carr asked.

"Hansen will speak against the motion," the Hansen rep said. "Mr. Dalquist will speak for us."

That surprised hell out of me. I wondered what would happen, and sat quite still, listening. I had no business in there, of course. If there had been some suspicion that I might have been in on Rhoda's scheme I'd never have heard this much, and by rights I ought to have left when she made her ruling, but nobody seemed anxious to throw me out.

"First, let me state the obvious," Dalquist said. "An operation of this size will be costly. The use of naked force against an independent colony, no matter how justified, will have serious repercussions throughout the Belt—"

"Let 'em get away with it and it'll *really* be serious," the Pegasus man said.

"Hansen Enterprises has the floor, Mister Papagorus," Commissioner Carr said.

Dalquist nodded his thanks. "My point is that we should consider alternatives. The proposed action is at least expensive and distasteful, if not positively undesirable."

"We'll concede that," the Lloyd's man said. The others muttered agreement. One of the people representing a whole slew of smaller outfits whispered, "Here comes the Hansen hooker. How's Dalquist going to make a profit from this?"

"I further point out," Dalquist said, "that Jefferson is no more valuable than many other asteroids. True, it has good minerals and water, but no richer resources than other rocks we've not developed. The real value of Jefferson is in its having a working colony and labor force—and it is highly unlikely that they will work very hard for us if we land company police and confiscate their homes."

Everybody was listening now. The chap who'd whispered earlier threw his neighbor an "I told you so" look.

"Secondly. If we take over the Jefferson holdings, the result will be a fight among ourselves over the division of the spoils."

There was another murmur of assent to that. They could all agree that something had to be done, but nobody wanted to let the others have the pie without a cut for himself.

"Finally. It is by no means clear that any large number of Jefferson inhabitants were involved in this conspiracy. Chairman Hendrix, certainly. I could name two or three others. For the rest—who knows?"

"All right," the Lloyd's man said. "You've made your point. If landing Intertel cops on Jefferson isn't advisable, what do we do? I am damned if we'll let them get away clean."

"I suggest that we invest in the Jefferson Corporation," Dalquist said.

The Doghouse hadn't changed. There was a crowd outside in the main room. They were all waiting to hear how rich they'd become. When I came in even Hornbinder smiled at me.

They were getting wild drunk while Dalquist and I met with Rhoda in the back room. She didn't like what he was saying.

"Our syndicate will pay off the damage claims due to Pegasus Lines and Lloyd's," Dalquist told her. "And pay Captain Kephart's salvage fees. In addition, we will invest two million francs for new equipment. In return you will deliver 40% of the Jefferson Corporation stock to us."

He wasn't being generous. With a 40% bloc it was a cinch they could find enough more among the rockrats for a majority. Some of them hated everything Rhoda stood for.

"You've got to be crazy," Rhoda said. "Sell out to a goddam syndicate of Corporations? We don't want *any* of you here!"

Dalquist's face was grim. "I am trying to remain polite, and it is not easy, Ms. Hendrix. You don't seem to appreciate your position. The Corporation representatives have made their decision, and the Commission has ratified it. You will either sell or face something worse."

"I don't recognize any commissions," Rhoda said. "We've always been independent, we're not part of your goddam facist commission. Christ almighty, you've found us guilty before we even knew there'd be a trial! We weren't even heard!"

"Why should you be? As you say, you're independent. Or have been up to now."

"We'll fight, Dalquist. Those company cops will never get here alive. Even if they do—"

"Oh, come now." Dalquist made an impatient gesture. "Do you really believe we'd take the trouble of sending Intertel police, now that you're warned? Hardly. We'll merely seize all your cargo in the pipeline and see that no ship comes here for any reason. How long will it be before your own people throw you out and come to terms with us?"

That hit her hard. Her eyes narrowed as she thought

about it. "I can see you don't live to enjoy what you've done—"

"Nonsense."

I figured it was my turn. "Rhoda, you may not believe this, but I heard him argue them out of sending the cops without any warning at all. They were ready to do it."

The shouts came from the bar as Jed opened the door to see if we wanted anything. "THERE'S GONNA BE A GREAT DAY!"

"Everything all right here?" Jed asked.

"NO!" Rhoda shoved herself away from the table and glared at Dalquist. "Not all right at all! Jed, he's—"

"I know what he's saying, Rhoda," Jed told her. "Cap'n Rollo and I had a long talk with him last night."

"With the result that I'm speaking to you at all," Dalquist said. "Frankly, I'd rather see you dead." His face was a bitter mask of hatred, and the emotionless expression fell away. He hated Rhoda. "You've killed the best friend I ever had, and I find that I need you anyway. Captain Anderson has convinced me that it will be difficult to govern here without you, which is why you'll remain nominally in control after this sale is made."

"No. No sale."

"There will be. Who'll buy from you? Who'll sell to you? This was a unanimous decision. You're not independent, no matter how often you say you are. There's no place for your kind of nationalism out here."

"You bastards. The big boys. You think you can do anything you like to us."

Dalquist recovered his calm as quickly as he'd lost it. I think it was the tone Rhoda used; he didn't want to sound like her. I couldn't tell if I hated him or not.

"We can do whatever we can agree to do," Dalquist said. "You seem to think the Corporations Commission is some kind of government. It isn't. It's just a means for settling disputes. We've found it more profitable to have rules than to have fights. But we're not without power, and everyone's agreed that you can't be let off after trying what you did."

"So we pay for it," Jed said.

Dalquist shrugged. "There's no government out here. Are you ready to bring Rhoda to trial? Along with all the others involved?"

Jed shook his head. "I doubt that it—"

"And there's the matter of restitution, which you can't make anyway. And you're bankrupt, since you sent no cargo to Luna and the window's closed."

"Just who the hell is this syndicate?" Rhoda demanded.

Dalquist's expression didn't change, but there was a note of triumph in his voice. He'd won, and he knew it. "The major sums are put up by Hansen Enterprises."

"And you'll be here as their rep."

He nodded. "Certainly. I've been with Hansen most of my life, Ms. Hendrix. The company trusts me to look out for its best interests. As I trusted Joe Colella. Until he retired he was my best field agent."

She didn't say anything, but her face was sour.

"You might have got away with this if you hadn't killed, Joe," Dalquist said. "But retired or not, he was a Hansen man. As I'm sure you found when he discovered your plan. We take care of our people, Ms. Hendrix. Hansen is a good company."

"For company men." Jed's voice was flat. He looked around the small back room with its bare rock walls, but I think he was seeing through those walls, out through the corridors, beyond to the caves where the rockrats tried to make homes. "A good outfit for company men. But it won't be the same, for us."

Outside they were still singing about the great days coming.

One of the main reasons many people got excited about the "cold fusion" discoveries was that they promised a road to fusion so cheap that institutional inertia couldn't possibly stop the development.

Because it isn't a question of whether fusion is possible. We know it's possible; we know there are several possible ways of doing it. There's not even much doubt that it's economically feasible. The only question is whether we're going to develop it in time to save our civilization from self-destructing! Which would take only a fraction of the government funds peed away down various rat-holes every year. As Jerry Pournelle points out below, there may not be a conspiracy to bring down high-energy civilization, but with the way things are going we may not need a conspiracy. Certainly as soon as a promising approach is shown, obstacles show up more quickly than weeds after a desert rainstorm.

I'm even gloomier than Jerry. When cold fusion looked promising, several of our more prominent neo-Luddites were appalled. It would take away the future of collapse, starvation and doom they've been describing with lip-smacking relish for some time. Below he describes lines of development that should have given us a working fusion demonstration reactor in 1980. Draw your own conclusions.

Fusion Without Ex-Lax
Jerry Pournelle

If a man told you "The only physics I ever took was Ex-Lax," would you put him in charge of nuclear power policy?

That's not a trick question. The founder of the California People's Lobby once said it, and he was the architect of the Nuclear Shutdown Initiatives.

Alas, nuclear power is seldom discussed rationally. There are those who fear the atom; and others who have made "fusion" an incantation, a magical formula which, when uttered, ends all rational debate about power policies.

In fact, the situation is worse than that: "fusion" is a good word, and fusion scientists are white magicians; "fission" is evil, and its supporters have made pacts with Satan to loose the evil djinn Plutonium onto this world. In these days when our representatives have shunted off primary responsibility for power policy onto the general public—or have abdicated their leadership altogether—it's important that the public deal in physics, not myth.

Now science fiction readers (and I hope, all *my* readers), unlike the Ex-Lax expert, are seldom *proud* of ignorance. Indeed, from the letters I get, and the audience response during my lectures, the opposite is true. The problem is that those who know quite a lot about the energy crisis are often acutely aware of how much they do not know; and thus are conscientious enough not to get into the debates. That's admirable, but it can be disastrous: often only the opinionated and truly ignorant have a voice.

All of which is preparatory to my arguments: I want to plug electron-beam fusion research; but I want your informed support, and since I know, again from my lecture tours, that an awful lot of people don't really understand either fission or fusion, I'm going to start with the basics. My apologies to those who find this discussion elementary. I will try, for the benefit of those whose only physics are Ex-Lax but who don't boast about that, to keep this reasonably simple.

$E = mc^2$, saith Einstein; that is, mass (m) can be converted into energy (E). To be precise, energy in ergs equals converted mass, in grams, times the square of the speed of light in centimeters per second. Light-speed (c) is 3×10^{10} cm/sec, so converting a gram of mass to energy would yield 10^{21} ergs, something like 100 kilotons, or about 100 times as much energy in all forms as each of you used last year.

The equation says nothing about how that energy comes out. A moment's thought will show you that can be important. If it all comes out as neutrinos it won't do us much good. There's no way to catch them. If it comes out as protons or electrons, we're in good shape: they're charged particles, and we can pass them through a ceramic tube with coils of wire around it to get electricity directly. (That last trick is called magnetohydrodynamics [MHD], and it's a bit more complex than it sounds; but we know how to do it. It only takes energetic charged particles.)

Unfortunately, most nuclear reactions do not produce charged particles. A great deal of nuclear energy appears

Figure 1

POWER PLANT EFFICIENCIES
(Percentage of generated heat turned into useful electricity)

	Coal	Nuclear Fission	Deuterium Fusion
Average in present use	32.53	31	—
Best in present use	41	39	—
Expected with improvements (Theoretical: includes MHD)	55	52	66(?)

as neutrons, and we can't catch them in a magnetic basket. What we can do is put something in their way. They get slowed down, or stopped, and their kinetic energy is converted into heat. We extract that heat, use it to boil water, and put the water through turbines. The turbine neither knows nor cares where the heat came from; it's all the same to it whether the heat source was burning coal, fissioning uranium, or fusing hydrogen.

The turbine system is the most efficient thing we've got for turning heat into electricity; but it's not 100% efficient and never will be, nor will anything else, including MHD. Thus let's dispel the first myth about fusion: it *may* be marginally more efficient than either fossil energy or fission, but it will still have waste heat, and will still require cooling systems. No one really knows the effective operating temperatures of fusion devices—we haven't even got anything that works in a laboratory yet—but if we assume they'll be hotter than either coal or fission, fusion systems will be somewhat more efficient than those we've got; but not all *that* much more so. Known efficiencies for fossil and fission plants, and assumed ones for fusion plants, are given in Figure 1.

Fission systems work thusly: a neutron source is brought near an atom that breaks apart. Neutrons are emitted. Other atoms are broken into lighter elements and more neutrons. Some of the additional neutrons are used to break up even more atoms (chain reaction), others are allowed to bombard useless stuff like uranium-238 and turn it into useful stuff like plutonium-239, and the rest are caught for their heat energy.

Fusion goes the other way. If you squeeze hydrogen atoms together and get them hot enough, they turn into helium. The resulting helium doesn't mass quite as much as the original hydrogen: result, energy. It sounds simple, and it is. This is the reaction that powers the Sun (we think). Unfortunately, we don't know how to do it, and we may never learn. Certainly we haven't even a theoretical clue as to how to bring off stellar fusion; the temperatures and pressures involved are plain beyond us.

So, we go to the next best thing and use deuterium, which we'll call "D." There are two reactions:

$$D + D \rightarrow T + p + 3.25 \text{ MeV} \quad (22{,}000 \text{ kW-hr/gram}) \quad \text{Eq. 1}$$

and

$$D + D \rightarrow {}^3He_2 + n + 4 \text{ MeV} \quad (27{,}000 \text{ kW-hr/gram}) \quad \text{Eq. 2}$$

and I'd better explain what all that means before I lose someone.

First, deuterium is "heavy" hydrogen. Ordinary hydrogen atoms have one proton (p) and one electron (e), and nothing else. D has an additional neutron (n); it could be written as ${}^2H_1$ where the left superscript is the atomic weight, H is the symbol for hydrogen, and the right subscript is the atomic number.

Tritium (T) is "superheavy" hydrogen with 2 neutrons, and could be written ${}^3H_1$. By the same token, ${}^3He_2$ is "light" helium; normal helium is ${}^4He_2$, and this stuff is missing a neutron.

For reasons we won't worry about here, it's convenient to measure nuclear energies in Millions of electron Volts (MeV), and I've given the textbook figures; for our purposes, though, the kiloWatt-hours per gram of material fused is more relevant. For comparison, a regular 100-Watt lightbulb will use 876 kW-hr each year if left burning; obviously a 1000-Watt heater uses 1 kW-hr each hour. A kW-hr of electric power costs between 1.2 and 5¢ to generate, and is sold to the consumer for from 2¢ to a dime (although I understand that lawsuits, strikes, and interesting administrative methods have got New Yorkers paying about 20¢/kW-hr).

The two reactions shown are equally probable. Both go on at the same time, and there's no known way to favor one over the other.

The tritium and "light" helium can themselves be made to react with more D, as follows:

$$D + T \rightarrow {}^4He_2 + n + 17.6 \text{ MeV (94,000 kW-hr/gram) Eq. 3}$$

and

$$D + {}^3He_2 \rightarrow {}^4He_2 + p + 18.3 \text{ MeV (98,000 kW-hr/gram) Eq. 4}$$

and I'm not giving these equations just to show off. Look at them a moment.

First, note that tritium. It's radioactive with a half-life of 12 years. We can burn up most of it with the eq. 3 reaction, but we've got to keep it from getting into the atmosphere. It's in the same situation as plutonium: a useful product that we need for power; and it should suffer the same fate as plutonium, "burning" in a nuclear reactor. Until it is "burned," though, it's one of the hazards of the power system, and there's no way to change that. It's also rare: the best way to make tritium is to bombard lithium with neutrons—which makes the lithium supply critical.

Second, note those neutrons. They must be caught if we're to extract their energy. When neutrons hit other atoms, they produce radioactive isotopes. Clever design can minimize the number of truly dangerous radioactive waste products, but can never eliminate them entirely.

Thus the fusion industry will need nuclear waste-disposal, and there goes myth Number Two. True: fusion is cleaner than fission power systems; but it is not *that* much cleaner.

Third, the fuel isn't free. We can't use ordinary hydrogen; we have to extract the D from it, and that takes energy; thus, at first, fusion plants will consume more energy than they produce—just as, for the first years of their lives, fission plants haven't produced the energy it took to refine their fuels, or coal plants the energy it took to mine the coal. All will, of course, show a net energy profit after two or three years.

And finally there's the *real* problem: we don't know how to do it. The basic equations for uranium fission were known for a long time before Fermi built his "pile" in the squash court of the University of Chicago, and nature was *very* cooperative anyway: the materials needed for Fermi's experiment were cheap, easily available, and simply fabricated; the instrumentation was standard; and the control system was uncomplicated. Despite the ease with which Fermi demonstrated the feasibility of self-sustained controlled fission (it worked first time), it took twenty years to get usable power from a fission reactor.

There's no reason to believe the engineering of a practical fusion power plant will take less time; and we are not yet to the squash court. We don't *know* that we can do it at all—and we're certainly a long way from running our TV sets on electricity produced by fusing D. *I have never found an expert who believes we will have a working commercial fusion power plant in this century.* The only people who say different are not in the game—and may have very large axes to grind. "Waiting for fusion" is simply not a feasible power policy. There goes the fourth myth.

Depressing, isn't it?

o   o   o

Since the above was written there have been some changes. First, the payments for Arab oil have gone out of sight: when your energy policy is to pay out $50 billion a year to the Arabs, you can afford almost *any* alternative.

Secondly, the Soviets have offered cooperation, sending Basov and Rudikov over to show us their results.

Thirdly, in all areas of fusion research there have been some unexpected results; some breakthroughs, other things just going better than expected.

As a result, a number fusion experts now believe we *could* have a working commercial fusion-powered generator by 1995, possibly a shade earlier.

It doesn't matter, though: at present levels of funding we will not have a reactor before 2000. We may *never* get one: the fusion research budget was deeply cut by the Carter administration, and the level-of-effort funding now supplied does not make the experts hopeful.

Moreover, the Soviet offers of cooperation were treated rather strangely: although *they* declassified the information and brought it to us, *we* classified it, although from whom we are keeping it secret escapes me. Nor were the Soviet experts given the red-carpet treatment: Basov was not even invited to Washington. I have been told that had he said fusion would *not* work he would have received the red-carpet treatment; I have no confirmation of this, nor do I know of any reason why the Carter administration would prefer that fusion research fail.

However: if we're to save ourselves from our present policy of selling the country to the Shah of Iran and the Sheik of Araby on the installment plan, we need some "Manhattan Project" type research; and instead we are slashing the research budgets to the bone and beyond.

[JEP Spring 1978]

Cheer up. First, we don't *need* fusion; at least not immediately. There are other ways to power our industrial civilization; other ways to spark the Third Industrial Revolution as described by me and by Harry Stine, who coined the term. We can all get rich even if controlled fusion never works. That ought to be good news. Here are some methods.

First, my favorite, the ocean-thermal system, which makes use of the temperature difference between warm surface water and cold bottom water. There's more than enough power in the tropics to run the world, the Sun renews it constantly, and we know it will work because a working plant was built in 1928. However, my engineering friends tell me that's the hard way; and we aren't likely to have operating ocean-thermal systems before the year 2000 anyway.

So what are some other ways? Here's where I get into trouble. The easiest way of all is one we have now: good old reliable (average nuclear plant operates 9 mos. each year; fossil, 8.2 mos. each year) nuclear fission. It already works, and we've already mined enough potential fuel to last us several hundred years; moreover, there's enough U-238 in ordinary rock to operate the world high-energy economy for millennia.

Alas, that takes breeder reactors, and they're controversial. They make plutonium, and everyone knows that plutonium is "the most toxic material known to man." Ralph Nader has told us so. Of course Ralph Nader is also the man who, with fanfare, bought a manual rather than an electric typewriter "to conserve energy." My electric uses the electricity generated by about a quarter of a cup of oil each year; if everybody, all 230 million of us, had an electric typer going they'd consume a few thousand barrels of oil annually: not very much in an economy that measures oil consumption in millions of barrels a day. Maybe we ought to take a closer look at some of the other things Mr. Nader says. His heart's in the right place, but he doesn't seem to do much quantitative thinking.

Toxicity of plutonium compared to other substances is shown in Figure 2. Now we don't spread much botulin around the landscape, but we do spray crops with arsenic trioxide; in fact, we today import 10 times as much arsenic as we'd have nuclear wastes if the entire U.S. electric system were run on nuclear fission. Now I keep telling myself that I am NOT going to write a paper in defense of nuclear fission power; that it's a political matter; but dammit, at least the public debates ought to make *sense*. It's one thing seriously and soberly to debate the advantages and disadvantages of fission over fossil fuel; but it's quite another to have such an important issue decided by mythology and demonology.

One last thing, then: nuclear wastes are radioactive. There. That ought to end the debate. Surely no one wants "nuclear pollution." If I sound sarcastic, my apologies; somebody really and truly said that to me not long ago. Meant it, too; and she was an important political party official.

So let's look at radioactivity in quantitative terms. Figure 3 shows the dose in millirems (thousandths of a rem) received by each U.S. citizen on the average. Further, lets add a couple bits of information: of the 24,000 survivors exposed to 140 rems (140,000 mrem) at Hiroshima-Nagasaki, fewer than 200 died of cancer. The probability of developing cancer from radiation exposure is about 0.018% per rem (not mrem).

As to storage: it's true that at present most nuclear wastes are stored as liquids, hundreds of thousands of gallons of them; they leak from time to time. But liquid storage was never intended to be anything but a temporary expedient; it is possible to take those wastes and make them part of glass blocks, and only legal, not technical, barriers have prevented that.

Glass is a very stable substance. It is practically eternal. If all the nuclear wastes accumulated from the Manhattan Project to present—including those resulting from weapons manufacture, which created more wastes than the power program—were solidified, the resulting block would be somewhat less than 60 feet on a side. If the entire country ran off nuclear power, all the wastes from now to the year 2020 could be contained in a block less than 100 feet on a side.

And the block could be stored under a superdome-like

Figure 2

TOXICITY OF VARIOUS SUBSTANCES

	Lethal Doses per Spoonful
Arsenic trioxide	50
Botulinus toxin	125,000,000
Plutonium oxide (ingested)°	0.5

°metallic Pu is never employed in reactors.

Figure 3

SOURCES OF RADIATION RECEIVED BY AVERAGE U.S. CITIZEN (ANNUAL)

Natural sources	Millirem	Man-Made Sources	Millirem
Cosmic Rays°	35	X-ray, diagnostic	103
Building materials°°	35	X-ray, therapy	6
Food	25	Radio-pharmacy	2
Ground	11	Global fallout	4
Air	5	Color TV	1
Own blood (K-40)	20	Nuclear Power plants	.003
TOTAL	131	If live at boundary of nuclear power plant	5
		TOTAL	121

Total annual 252

° Varies with altitude: greatest at high altitude cities.
°°Varies with material: greatest with brick and stone.

structure in the Mojave Desert for want of anywhere else to put it. Build a concrete dome; put in the wastes; and surround it all with a chainlink fence and the warning sign "IF YOU CLIMB THIS FENCE YOU WILL DIE." Or guard the area. Or both. Eventually we will have either a use for the wastes or a permanent storage area such as geologically stable salt mines; but certainly the Mojave would hold them for a couple of hundred years if need be.

At this point in my lectures someone generally says, loudly, "sabotage!" Nuclear plants are vulnerable to that, aren't they? Well, yes; but not very. The four-foot steel and concrete containment is designed to take an aircraft crashing into it without rupture. Anyone stealing nuclear fuels for terror purposes has set himself a pretty suicidal task, will need vast technological resources, and won't get very many people very fast—what's the point of threatening people with an increased probability of cancer 15 years after you set off your infernal device?

Oh, sure: in theory a respectable bomb can be made from nuclear fuels, and certainly one *could* refine spent fuel to get plutonium: but to do that, in secret, requires the resources of a government, and governments don't need to steal nuclear wastes. Uranium can be bought on the open market, and you can breed weapons-grade stuff in a research reactor—as India did. Note well: of all nations that have The Bomb (including several such as Israel and South Africa which probably do but which have not announced it) *not one* used power reactors in the weapons manufacture.

The fact is, if you're in the terror business, kidnapping is simpler; or if you've a pash to be suicidally spectacular, try crashing a hijacked jet into the Rose Bowl on New Year's Day.

In other words, if we're going to debate power policy, let's do it right, with comparisons of risks, not scare statements. I'm willing; if you're interested, my lecture fees aren't too high, and you can reach me care of the publisher. Be prepared to pay expenses and a reasonable fee.

This has taken us a long way from fusion, hasn't it? No; because fusion, like other power systems, needs to be discussed in context. I will not recommend fusion research as a magic remedy for the world's ills.

I do recommend it, though. For all its disadvantages, fusion will be, if it works, the power system of the future.

First, it's very fuel-efficient. If we can extract all the energy from our D, we get an average of about 100,000 kW-hr/gram, which is four times the energy per gram obtained by fission reactors, and ten million times the energy/gram from burning fossil fuels. A few thousand metric tons of D each year could power the world.

Second, the fuel's not hard to get. There is about one atom of D for every 6,000 atoms of ordinary hydrogen. The world's D supply could come from under fifty plants with water intake valves ten to twenty feet in diameter. By world's energy supply, I mean the equivalent of some 20 billion barrels of oil a day—more than enough to let Ralph Nader have a new Selectric.

Third, we can never run out of D. There are billions of cubic kilometers of water on this Earth, and at a cubic kilometer each year we'd be able to run a long time; nor would we, as I've heard someone say, "lower the oceans"; at least not more than an atomic diameter or two.

Fourth, fusion is certainly preferable to fission: the waste-management problem is much simpler. There are fewer long-term radioactive wastes to worry about. Although we can and will (and already have) shipped tons of plutonium around without anyone being injured, the stuff *is* unpleasant, and we'd be better off without it even if fusion won't eliminate all nuclear wastes.

So how do we do it? There are two major theories on how fusion plants might work. First, remember that the goal is extremely high temperatures and pressures. You can't contain them in a material object, because either your reaction melts your container, or your container cools off the D and prevents the reaction. Thus non-material confinement systems, which means in practice Magnetic Confinement. The lion's share of all fusion research goes to that. The problems are hairy: both engineering and scientific questions remain unanswered.

The equipment is huge, complex, and (need I say it?) costly. There are blind alleys. We had stellerators, and magnetic rings, and various kinds of pinch-bottles, and every one of them failed. It isn't that they weren't worth building, understand; we have learned a lot about magnetohydrodynamic stability of plasmas (there's a buzz phrase for you). The current approach is a device called a tokamak, and if you need to know more about those go to your nearest library. Magnetic confinement isn't expected to produce fusion neutrons for another ten years, and few think it will, even in the laboratory, produce more power than it consumes before 1990. It got plenty of funding prior to the Carter administration.

The second approach is called Inertial Confinement. This consists of taking small pellets of D, or a D and T mixture, and zapping them with lots of energy. The zapping has to be done just right. If you're not careful, too much zapping energy gets *inside* the pellet and tends to disrupt it before fusion can take place. There are other failure mechanisms, such as lopsided zaps, and not enough zap-power.

Inertial confinement has this advantage: it is pretty certain to work. That is, the problems are more engineering than scientific. It may never work *usefully*, but it almost has to work if we get the geometry right and shoot enough power to the pellets. It has a second advantage: the equipment is much cheaper (for laboratory demonstration reactors; not necessarily for a working commercial power generating system). Thus Inertial Confinement gets about 10% of the fusion research budget.

There are two branches of Inertial Confinement: laser (photon) bombardment, and particle bombardment. Of the research money in inertial confinement, 90% or more goes to laser systems. There's a reason for that: laser bombardment just may have produced fusion already. There was some fanfare a few years ago when KMS Inc., a private company, seemed to have obtained fusion neutrons. There's still some question about just what KMS did or did not achieve, but most fusion people believe that laser bombardment will eventually work out. Right now they're looking at different kinds of lasers, and may have to invent a new one (called Brand X Laser) which will zap the pellet with enough energy, yet won't penetrate the pellet too fast.

[In November, 1977, the Soviet Nobel laureate Nikolai Basov told a conference in Fort Lauderdale that he had achieved a breakthrough: by exciting the pellets with soft x-rays prior to zapping them with a laser, he had managed to get scientific breakeven; that he had bettered the so-called Lawson Criterion by a factor of five.

There was very little about Basov announcement in the popular press; I don't know why, because it's a rather exciting discovery. There was some doubt expressed by U.S. research workers: did Basov get the proper temperatures? As I write this the Lawrence Radiation Laboratories at Livermore are said to be checking out Basov's results, but the whole program including exactly what Basov told us is classified, so I can report no more than that.

Laser fusion research, like all other fusion research, suffered a budget cut in the first years of the Carter administration; according to the Soviets it is a very promising line of development.

[JEP Spring 1978]

Finally, there's electron-beam inertial confinement, which is only carried on at Sandia Laboratories (a nonprofit corporation) in Albuquerque, New Mexico. I visited the labs recently, and came away a believer.

At the time of my visit the Sandia electron-beam fusion program was funded at about $5 million a year; nowhere near enough, in my judgment. Electron bombardment may just be *the* way to go.

They've already achieved fusion with this method. Not breakeven; both U.S. and Soviet experiments have definitely produced several billion fusion neutrons. The Soviets are attempting to cooperate with the U.S. but once again, when Rudikov came to the U.S. to tell his results, we classified his talk. However, it's definite that he reported obtaining fusion neutrons, because that was announced in the Soviet popular press. (Evidently the Soviet Union isn't interested in keeping it a secret from whomever we are keeping in the dark.)

Electron-beam fusion has always been the least-funded of the fusion research programs, in part because it doesn't *need* as much money.

I have watched a man spend four billion dollars an hour on electricity. It made him unhappy. He wanted to spend a trillion an hour. It happened at Sandia labs: they were zapping a pellet with electrons. Of course they didn't spend four billion bucks an hour for very long: a few nanoseconds, to be exact, so the total cost of the electricity was a few dollars; but if they could have kept it up!

The Sandia equipment is impressive. It's also massive, as you'd expect, considering that they handle millions of volts. To get that they have to charge up enormous capacitance systems. Sirens wail, red lights flash, needles crawl across dials, just like in a good science fiction movie, and finally the technician puts his fingers in his ears. I didn't, in time, and the noise of a couple of megajoules arcing into a target is not easily forgotten.

Even so, it's not enough. That's what costs the money: building equipment that will handle those voltages without breakdown (and breakdowns are *spectacular* around there; I didn't see one, but I saw insulators the size of a desk with inch-deep gouges burned into them). Then there's the triggering problem: that system has to discharge all its energy at the *right* time, and the right time is measured in billionths of a second. It's amazing that they can do it; but they can. I saw it done. Incidentally, the voltage amplifier systems they use are called Marx generators, which gives rise to a number of puns, political jokes, etc., and worse; when they were ready to fire someone shouted "Harpo's ready!" and another man said "Stand by to fire Groucho." Then there was the zap! and a million joules flowed for a few nanoseconds.

Mega-joules. A joule is 10^7 ergs. I was duly impressed until we got to talking after the experiment. The reason they don't have fusion yet is they just can't pump enough power through the system fast enough, but don't get discouraged. The amount of power needed isn't so very large after all. In fact, we calculated that a Sears Lifetime Battery contains about 4 mega-joules, and if we could just discharge that sucker in a couple of nanoseconds we'd have fusion.

They're building a system that they expect will do just that.

At the moment Sandia hopes to be at the squash court stage by 1983: that is, by then they hope to have proved that electron bombardment inertial confinement fusion will work and can, with a lot more skull sweat and good engineering design, eventually be part of a useful electric power system.

They're doing that on five million dollars a year. This is the system I mentioned in the beginning of this article. I think it deserves more money, because with more money they may get to the squash court before 1980. They don't promise it, but then they don't need much more money either; a doubling of their present five million annually would not only let them build more hardware faster, but also let them coordinate some theoretical work going on around the country, and bring in other scientists as consultants.

So: if you're in a mood to write your Congresscritter about energy problems, you might mention that here's a slot where, in my considered judgment, a few million bucks will do a lot of good. Please don't support this because you think it will get us to the year 2000; it's unlikely. Don't support it because you think it will eliminate our need for nasty plutonium. Do it as a present for your children; do it because we could use some decent national goals, and cheap clean fusion power is one of the better gifts the U.S. could offer the world.

Do it because we can afford it, and it's something we ought to do.

Since I wrote that, a number of things happened. First, many of my readers did send letters to Congress. Second, President Carter cut the budget for electron-beam inertial confinement fusion research. Third, Congress restored the budget.

At present writing, the chief scientist involved with this research spends as much time in Washington trying to keep his budget as he does in the laboratory trying to make neutrons. He has never met the President, although while he was in Washington Mr. Carter gave an afternoon to Mr. Lovins of "soft energy" fame.

And finally, in Fall 1978, Princeton University announced temperatures of 60 million degrees in their magnetic confinement fusion research facility. This was a real scientific breakthrough; but the news announcement also contained a statement from the Department of Energy: "This achievement does not change the national timetable to fusion energy." Of course it does not: we have no national timetable. The expected date of useful fusion energy in the United States is never.

I don't know why, but the present administration does not seem to want fusion energy.

Back at the beginning, I noted that the available energy sets the upper limits to the prosperity and morality of any human society. There's a flip side to that, though. We set the downside limits. Enough cheap energy, and nothing material is scarce, because energy can change anything into anything else—given a little development work. Humans can, however, be relied upon to bollix up even paradise . . .

Originals
Pamela Sargent

Lora dipped her spoon into the soup, then lifted it to her lips. The broth was clear, with a faint lemony taste; the vegetables, as always, were slightly crispy. Bits of parsley floated on top of the soup. Lora swallowed.

"Superb," she said, trying to smile. Antoine, the chef, stood near the table, searching her face with his morose brown eyes. "Really, it's delicious. You are an artist, Antoine." Antoine tilted his head; his chef's hat slipped a little.

Geraldo, Lora's partner, was slurping softly. "Good soup," he said. The rest of Lora's family was gazing at her expectantly, perhaps wondering why she had not been more effusive in her praise. Her three sons put down their spoons almost at the same moment, while her two little girls fidgeted, tugging at their gown straps. At the other end of the table, Junia was staring directly at Lora.

"I think it's one of the finest soups I've ever tasted," Junia announced. Antoine bowed.

Lora could not control herself any longer. Releasing a sigh, she dropped her spoon next to her bowl. "Oh," she murmured, giving the word all the misery she could muster. She covered her eyes for a moment. "You'll all find out soon enough." She leaned back in her chair. "Another disk was stolen, it seems. It was the one for this cauliflower soup."

"That is too much," her son Roald muttered as his brothers, Rex and Richard, nodded their heads. "I don't understand it. It just goes on and on." The three brothers scowled in unison. Rina tugged at her strap again, then brushed back a lock of blond hair; her sister, Celia, planted her elbows on the table. One of Celia's loose, dark tresses narrowly missed her bowl of soup. Junia sat back, folding her hands. Geraldo continued to eat.

"A pity," Antoine said in tragic tones.

"It's unbearable," Lora said in an unusually harsh voice. "I imagine that, at this very moment, millions of people are enjoying this same soup. What is the point of having our own chef and our own exclusive recipe disks if we can't keep them to ourselves and our invited guests?"

"I am most sorry, madame," Antoine said, gazing heavenward. "I shall create another soup, never fear. And there are still all the disks that remain. They far outnumber the purloined ones."

Lora glanced at him, suddenly irritated with his unhappy face. Gretchen Karell's chef was a cheerful Chinese gentleman who could barely contain his joy at the sight of his sumptuous dishes, while Antoine's seemed to bring him to the verge of tears. It was Gretchen who had left the message that morning, telling Lora that various food fanciers had suddenly acquired disks labeled *Antoine Laval's Cauliflower Soup*. Lora had longed to reach toward the screen and slap Gretchen's smug image.

"Still tastes good," Geraldo said as he finished.

"Really!" Lora gazed balefully at her partner's handsome but chubby face. "I simply can't understand how you can so blithely enjoy a soup that anyone can have now. I've always prided myself on our unique cuisine, and now it seems that it's becoming as common as dirt."

"I don't know how the disk could have been stolen,"

Junia said in her clear, sharp voice. "No one's been in this house except us for at least a month, and the house would have warned us of any intrusion. You always had guests here when the others were taken."

Lora winced. She had done her best to get along with Junia, who was soon to be the partner of her son Roald, but the young woman was tactless. Junia had just pointed out what no one else at the table had wanted to mention—namely, that one of those present had to be the thief. That was the worst of it; Lora would have to be suspicious of her own family. Already, she was peering at each face, searching for signs of guilt, wondering who would be capable of such a deed. Her three sons stared back with the same bland look in their identical blue eyes. Her daughters were once again plucking at their gowns and she nearly burst out with a reprimand, wanting to tell them to be still.

Geraldo signaled to Antoine, who departed for the kitchen to prepare the next course. Geraldo could not have stolen the disk. He had a hearty appetite, but at the same time, he didn't seem to care what he ate; it was one of his more disagreeable qualities. Lora tensed. Maybe that indifference made him more likely to steal. The treasured recipes did not mean that much to him, and he would enjoy them just as much no matter how many people had access to them. He was, she thought sadly, only a man of leisure at heart.

Lora covered her eyes again, waiting for someone to take pity and blurt out a confession. She would forgive the lapse, she decided, but only after a truly abject apology. But when she looked up, the robots were already clearing away the soup bowls in preparation for the next course, and no one had spoken.

"I'd like to speak to you," Lora said to the screen in her room. "Alone, please."

"Certainly," the house replied. An image formed on the screen; a kindly, gray-bearded man was now staring out at her, a personification of the mind that ran the house. Lora had always been uneasy whenever she spoke to the disembodied voice of her house cybermind and preferred the friendly, human image.

"We are now on a closed channel," the house said as the man's lips moved. "Please do go on."

"Who stole that disk?"

"You know I can't answer that. If I had known, I would have informed you of that fact."

"I thought you might have some ideas."

"I am completely in the dark." The house chuckled at that; it was night outside. "I don't watch the kitchen, you know."

"Show me the kitchen."

The man disappeared. She was now gazing at the kitchen, knowing that Antoine, who hated to be observed at work, was asleep in his bedroom.

The room looked like any well-equipped kitchen. Inside one pantry shelf, thousands of disks were concealed behind the polished wood doors. Each disk, when inserted into the kitchen's duplicator, would produce meat, fish, poultry, fresh fruits, vegetables, or other raw materials for Antoine to use in preparing a dish. Another shelf held disks with the patterns for wine and other beverages, and a third held spice and herb disks. There were cheese disks, cooking oil disks, butter disks. But in one corner, inside one special shelf, were Antoine's own recipe disks, each containing the pattern for one of his creations.

The duplicator itself, a tall, transparent column with metallic shelves jutting out from its sides, stood near one wall next to a disposal chute. Inside the chute, carried to it from other passages throughout the house's walls, sat much of the household's cast-off clothing, worn-out artifacts, garbage, trash, and dust—all of the materials needed for transmutation. When a disk was inserted into one of the duplicator's slots, the chute would drop the necessary amount of debris into the column. The duplicator would glow as energy created by fusion poured into it and the debris, broken down into its constituent atoms, would be transformed, becoming a bottle of wine, a roasted chicken, or some other food, depending on the pattern stored on the disk. One could also imprint a pattern on a blank disk by slipping the small round platter into a slot above the shelf holding the object one intended to store.

Lora had only a rudimentary understanding of how the duplicator worked, but she had learned a smattering of history and knew that commonplace objects had once been rare. The duplicator, given enough material and the endless stream of fusion energy, could change that material into anything the user wanted, as long as a pattern for that object was on a disk. Sometimes, in her more reflective moments, Lora's heart would go out to those who in past times had had to endure scanty supplies or even do without the bare necessities. There were no shortages now. She drew her brows together. That wasn't quite true. She had occasionally run out of detritus and had been forced to send the robots out foraging for dead leaves and twigs. Once, during a particularly festive party, she had even resorted to having the robots feed dirt from her flower garden into the duplicator in order to feed all the guests. There was, of course, always human waste, but Lora would never dream of using that in the kitchen duplicator. Such material was collected in another chute, to be sterilized and then transmuted by the duplicator in her sitting room into other things. One had to have *some* standards. Recycling was a wonderful and necessary thing, but there were limits.

Occasionally, Antoine had allowed Lora to enter the kitchen while he was cooking, a rare privilege and one that she was careful not to abuse. The last time she had been there, her chef had been trying out a recipe for *poulet persillade*. He had assembled his ingredients and had finished cooking the chicken dish for the fourth time; the first three attempts had not met with his approval and had been relegated to the chute.

Lora's mouth watered as she recalled the taste of the chicken in its light crust of bread crumbs, parsley, and shallots. But Antoine had not been satisfied until his fifth attempt. The disk that could duplicate the *poulet persillade* was now stored safely on a shelf. The dish could be reproduced; the *poulet persillade* would be perfect every time.

She frowned as she stared at her screen, searching the kitchen as if this might yield a clue. The robots that assisted Antoine were standing in one corner; they were always shut off when not working and could not have seen a thing. She might have to keep the shelves locked, and rebelled at that thought. What was the world coming to when she could not trust those nearest to her?

"Show me who left the house this week, and when, and what time each person returned," she said. The kitchen vanished as lists of names and times appeared. Lora emitted a small sigh. Everyone had left the house at various times; each had clearly had the opportunity to take a disk to town, dupe it, and return it to the shelf with no one the wiser. The kitchen, except when Antoine was cooking or duplicating meals, was usually empty.

"Oh, dear," she said sadly.

"It would be quite simple to discover the malefactor," the house murmured as the image of the bearded man reappeared. "I do have eyes and ears inside all of the rooms, you know."

"Oh, no," Lora responded, shocked at the notion of trespassing on her family's privacy. "That wouldn't do at all."

"I need to watch only the kitchen."

"Absolutely not," Lora said firmly. "You know Antoine would never stand for that. He might leave if he found out you were watching."

"Question everyone, then. I'll quickly ferret out anyone who's lying. I can read their physiological reactions and note any vocal stresses."

Lora sat up. "No. I won't turn my home into a police state." She shuddered. She had never spied on anyone in her life and was not about to start doing so now. Her family would never forgive her. She would never forgive herself.

"Then I really don't know how you plan to solve this problem," the house said haughtily.

"I'll find a way. The thief will make a mistake eventually." She wanted to believe that.

Unable to sleep, Lora finally got out of bed and tiptoed to the door connecting her room with Geraldo's. As she opened it, she heard his gentle snoring; she could not disturb him with her worries. Closing the door again, she crossed her room and went out into the corridor, then crept down the winding staircase to the hall below.

Silver moonlight shone through the wide windows. Occasionally, she found herself envying the ones who lived on the moon. Those people had to live in tunnels below ground, enduring out-of-date duplicated clothing and the same food millions of others ate, but their astronomical and scientific pursuits assured their social status. Only original work could win honor, although people who collected original, unduplicated objects also had some respect. The thought of the moondwellers reminded her of her own lowly position. Being a hostess was humble work. A house could have done it, but many still shied away from being entertained by only a voice. Lora's gatherings drew the brightest lights of society, and she was normally content to bask in their reflected glory. At least she had escaped being only a woman of leisure, wasting her time in idleness while surrounded by wealth. She needed to feel useful.

She moved toward the door and stepped out on the porch. Junia was sitting near one marble column, holding a glass; her chestnut hair seemed black in the shadows.

The young woman turned. "Lora." She lifted her glass. "Can't you sleep?"

"No. I'm afraid that this business with the disks is too disturbing." Lora sat down in a chair next to Junia, glancing at the young woman suspiciously. The thefts had begun after Junia had started visiting Roald. She had to be the culprit. Junia knew perfectly well that Lora had not been terribly pleased when Roald had announced his plans to take the young woman as his partner.

"Would you like a brandy?" Junia waved her glass. "I'll be glad to fetch one for you."

"No, thank you." Lora leaned back. "I don't know what to do. Even the house doesn't have a clue. It's just shameful. I'm afraid to have people over to dine. Imagine how embarrassing it would be to serve them an exclusive dish only to have it turn up in other houses later on. I'd lose what little position I have." She paused. "Poor Antoine. He has to spend so much time creating new dishes as it is."

"Oh, he doesn't seem to mind. He loves to cook. After all, it's what he was bred for."

"Indeed. But even Antoine deserves a rest." Lora gripped the arms of her chair, reflecting on how callous Junia often seemed to be. But then almost everyone lacked her own finer feelings. Lora's parents had wanted a sensitive child and that was what the geneticists had given them. "High-strung," Lora's mother had called her, taking pride in her daughter's fine-tuning. She had in fact become an ordeal as she struggled not to disappoint them with any inadvertent crudity. Lora had been relieved when both her parents had decided to have a mind-wipe and assume new identities; now they didn't know who she was and she no longer had to visit.

"I've been thinking," Junia said as she brushed back a dark strand of hair. "You don't suppose Rina or Celia could have taken the disks, do you? They love to play little jokes. They put a frog in my bed the other night."

"Oh, dear."

"It doesn't matter. It really didn't frighten me."

Lora thought of the two girls. She had decided against having terribly sensitive offspring, but she had not believed the two children were capable of handling anything as slimy as a frog. Rina and Celia were supposed to be cute for the benefit of guests who enjoyed the presence of a family; they would hardly seem adorable if they played such pranks.

"Stealing disks," Lora murmured, "is hardly a joke."

"Oh, I know. But they might not think of it that way. They might not understand how serious it is."

Lora grimaced. If one of the girls was the thief, the other would surely know about it; they did almost everything together. She could go to one of her daughters and say that the other had owned up to the deed, and force an admission of guilt.

Thinking of such a confrontation repelled her. She had always left discipline, what little there was of it, to Geraldo and the robotic nanny. Anyway, she was beginning to wonder if Rina and Celia had the intelligence to plan such a thievery and carry it off without giving themselves away. She had not wanted intelligent children, either. Intelligent children asked too many hard questions and showed off their knowledge and ended with making their parents feel like fools; she had seen it happen in other households. What good did it do to have an accomplished child to brag about if the child considered one's own mind beneath contempt?

"Well, I'm sure Roald wouldn't steal anything," Junia went on. "Of course, I can't speak for his brothers."

Lora gazed out at the lawn. Beyond the cleared land around her house, the forest's pine trees sang as the wind stirred their branches. Junia would give herself away if she continued to chatter; only a guilty person would be trying to cast suspicion on others. She was now almost certain that the young woman was the thief, and wondered if she would have the strength to order her from the house. Roald might decide to leave with her.

Lora nearly wept as she thought of that. She might lose her son. Surely he was more important than having exclusive recipes. Could he be stealing them to get back at her for her original disapproval of Junia? What other motive might he have for such uncharacteristic behavior? Could he be trading the disks for unduplicated objects? She shook her head. If Roald or anyone else in the house had been trading the disks for exclusive objets d'art, jewelry, unique historical artifacts, or anything else, some evidence would have turned up by now, and the person accepting the disks would have no motive for duplicating them for the world. Clearly, someone wanted only to make her own life as miserable as possible. Her own limited status was now in jeopardy. Her dinner parties drew people of great prestige with the promise of Antoine's cooking. How many would accept her invitations if they thought they could acquire the dishes elsewhere?

Junia cleared her throat. "I suppose you suspect me, Lora."

"Dear me," Lora said. "I suspect no one." She was again suspecting everyone. Perhaps it was a conspiracy, and they were all in on it; maybe they were tired of trying to be of some use to others and longed to lapse into leisure and laziness altogether. A tear trickled down her cheek as she wallowed in misery, feeling that the world had turned against her. She would become only a peasant, reduced to consuming an endless stream of goods and services.

"Oh, I can understand why you think I might have done it. I wish I could convince you that I didn't. I can't think of anything I'd like more than your approval. I know you didn't want me as a partner for Roald at first."

"Oh, dear." Junia, she thought darkly, had no delicacy at all.

"But we'll still be here, in the house. It's what we both want. You'll still have Roald nearby, and I know he couldn't bear to leave Rex and Richard—they're all so close."

"Junia, I do respect you. Really." Lora tried to give the words some conviction. The young woman might be a bit on the blunt side, but she was also kind and even-tempered; Roald could have done far worse. "It's only that I had hoped all three of my sons would find three partners together. They are a set, after all." She paused.

"I don't suppose you would consider being a partner to all three."

"Oh, no," Junia said cheerfully. "It's Roald I love."

"Oh, well." Lora thought of her three sons. She had been so taken with Richard after removing him from his artificial womb that she had insisted on having two brothers cloned right away. Roald had been brought home ten years later, after a period in cryonic storage, and Rex ten years after that. She had received many compliments on her handsome sons, the same genotype at different ages; their physical similarity as individuals made them seem unique as a group.

Richard was now thirty-eight, Roald twenty-eight, and Rex eighteen; except for their blue eyes, they were all slimmer versions of Geraldo, which was fitting since he had contributed most of the genes. She had once dreamed of finding them three identical young women, or, failing that, one who would fall in love with all three, but it was not to be. Her sons, unhappily, had shown more individuality than she had expected; Rex parceled out his affections to various girls while Richard was not likely to partner at all. At least Junia had not insisted on her own house.

Her doubts, held at bay, suddenly bit at her mind again, nibbling at her small share of happiness. Rex might be giving the disks to his many loves. Richard was close to the Karells; could Gretchen, Lora's social rival, have encouraged his thievery? If only she could put her doubts aside. They all knew how easily she could be wounded; how could those she loved be so cruel? Her sons would never stoop to theft; had one of them truly wanted to hurt her, all he had to do was leave.

It had to be Junia. Even as Lora clung to that hypothesis, she questioned it. Junia, in addition to being a trifle rough around the edges, was intelligent. The young woman was only too aware that she would be the prime suspect; she had said so. She could not want Lora's ill will, not when she would have to live under the same roof.

Junia rose. "I'm going to bed." She yawned, not even troubling to cover her pretty mouth. "You should, too. No sense worrying about it. Whoever's stealing your disks will get tired of doing it eventually."

Lora and Geraldo breakfasted alone at the small table near the rose garden. She nibbled at a sectioned orange and a brioche as Geraldo feasted on an omelet, then helped himself to buckwheat cakes. Glancing at her partner's rounded belly, Lora made a mental note to tell Antoine that he should serve non-caloric foods for the next day or two. Antoine would not be happy about that; she could never convince him that such foods really did taste the same as others.

"Don't worry," Geraldo muttered as he reached for the syrup. "Junia'll make Roald a good partner." He looked past the garden toward the lawn, where Rex, Roald, and Richard were passing a football to one another; their brown, bare chests gleamed with sweat. Near them, a few robots were clipping the grass, collecting the blades in sacks to be used in the duplicator.

"I wasn't thinking of Junia." The morning light had revealed a gray hair on Geraldo's head; he would need another rejuvenation treatment before the rigors of the social season began.

"Are you still worried about the disks? Forget it, honey. We all know how you feel. I'm sorry you feel so rotten. I guess I didn't realize how upset you'd get about it."

She peered at him. "Exactly what do you mean, dear?" She waited to see if he was about to confess. Geraldo was generous by nature; he might not have been able to resist a friend's plea for a disk.

"Oh, you know. I mean, if the food's good, I'll eat it. I never really cared how many people had the recipe. I guess I forgot that it means more to you," he added hastily.

"It should mean something to you, too. Don't you care

what people think? Aren't you concerned with our obligations?"

"Oh, of course. Well, I know I didn't do it. Antoine doesn't like me anywhere near the kitchen even when he's not there. I don't praise his efforts enough."

"I can't say I blame him," Lora said gently. "He wants people to savor his food, not gulp it."

"Rina and Celia couldn't have planned it, either. Mind you, I love our little girls, but if a thought ever entered their heads, they'd probably say, 'What's that?' " Geraldo narrowed his eyes. "Aha! *You* did it!" He put down his fork. "That's it. You did it so we'd all feel sorry for you and be nicer. You always did like a lot of sympathy— playing the victim and all."

Shocked, Lora began to weep.

"Hey!" Geraldo took her hand. "I was only kidding."

"That's cruel, Geraldo. I never thought you, of all people, could be so heartless."

"I didn't mean it."

"I don't enjoy being so touchy. It's not something I would have chosen. I know it's sometimes hard for all of you to keep from upsetting me." She dabbed at her tears with her napkin, knowing how ugly red, watery eyes and a puffy face were. "You don't know how many times I've considered reconditioning, but that would be like losing part of myself. I've even thought of mind-wiping."

Geraldo started.

"But then I wouldn't remember you. I'd lose everything."

Geraldo stroked her hand. "Lora, I like you just the way you are. You might be sensitive, but so what? It gives the rest of us something to aspire to, in a way. It just shows how civilized and delicate you are." He waved one arm expansively. "Why, if everyone were like you, it would be a much nicer world. We'd all be a lot more thoughtful of others' feelings."

She smiled, forgiving him. Geraldo had his faults, but he always knew how to heal her wounds, and he was invaluable at parties. His unpretentious manner could put the most nervous guest at ease; he was, in part, responsible for her own small success.

"Well," she whispered, and then her doubts returned; she still had no solution to her problem. "I don't know what to do," she continued. "I simply can't resort to spying on my own family, even if that's what the house wanted me to do. Antoine might leave, you know."

"Has he said so?" Geraldo mumbled, his mouth full of food.

"No. I'm afraid to speak to him about it. But you can imagine how he feels. If someone keeps stealing his disks, he may want to go to a house where there aren't any thieves." She was well aware that the chef's position on the social ladder was higher than her own; all she could really offer him was an appreciative and discerning audience for his efforts. "All of this larceny just means more work for him. Other chefs take time off, laze about most of the time, create new recipes only when inspiration strikes, while he has to labor constantly. Why, if he didn't, we'd scarcely have any exclusive recipes left. We'd have to duplicate disks from the public library!"

"Aren't you exaggerating a little?"

"Not at all. Ten stolen disks in less than a year, *ten*." She bowed her head, thinking of the couscous, Antoine's crabmeat salad with green grapes and his special dressing, the cauliflower soup, the poached salmon with dill and a secret ingredient Antoine had refused to reveal— all duplicated now, all being consumed by others. "We'll have to have a backlog of disks, seeing that I don't know what might be stolen next. Maybe it's my own fault. I should never have bragged so far and wide about Antoine's cooking, and maybe this wouldn't have happened."

"You shouldn't think that. You wanted to do something with yourself, and that's good. You had to tell people about Antoine to draw them here. Why, without you, honey, I might still be back in that slum."

Lora shuddered, recalling the hill of mansions surrounded by trenches. The people in such a neighborhood craved so many things that they needed to ruin their grounds in an effort to provide enough mass for their duplicators. Luckily, she had not met Geraldo's family until after they became partners; she quailed at the memory of the Tudor house cluttered with velvet furniture, gold statues, Oriental carpets, closets packed with clothes, and paintings in gilt frames selected with no eye for style or period. One visit had been quite enough.

"Now Antoine will want to leave," she said bitterly. "He may put it off for a while, to spare my feelings, but he'll get around to it in time. And we'll never get another chef, not when others find out about our situation."

She sipped some coffee. Good chefs were so hard to come by. So few people wanted a child bred for that profession; whatever the eventual rewards might be, raising a child who was a picky eater was a torment. Perhaps she could talk Antoine into having himself cloned. It didn't matter. It would take at least twenty years for the child to grow up and be trained as a chef, and in the meantime she would be reduced to eating food available to all.

"Listen," Geraldo said. "We know that the thief isn't one of our acquaintances, so we've narrowed the list of suspects. And you're sure to find out who the thief is for one reason."

She raised her head, gazing into his dark eyes. "And what is that?"

"You're so damned sensitive. You'll sense it. You'll see something in someone's manner that will give the thief away—something subtle, not obvious. Trust your instincts, Lora, and you'll solve this problem."

"And then what should I do? I simply don't have the stamina for a confrontation."

"Leave it to me. I'll take care of that."

After breakfast, Lora decided to take a stroll through the woods. Her sons ran into the house, returning with a brown cloak to protect her against the air, which had grown cooler. Richard had made the cloak himself; her sons were already gaining some small renown as designers of clothing. Rex draped the garment over her shoulders as Richard and Roald each planted a kiss on her cheek.

She peered intently into their blue eyes, trying to discern guilt in one open, honest face. Her sons had never lied to her, though there had been times, especially when Rex was talking about his latest amorous adventure, when she had wished that they were somewhat less open.

"Is anything wrong?" Richard asked, apparently noting her frown.

"Oh, no."

"If you see Junia," Roald said, "tell her I'm going over to the Karells' house later. She wanted to come along."

"Isn't she still upstairs?"

Roald shook his head. "She went for a walk for a little while after Antoine went out."

Lora savored that morsel of information as she crossed the lawn. Was Junia following the chef? Antoine often went on solitary forays looking for wild plants to dupe for his recipes, and she suspected that he had a secret herb garden somewhere, carefully concealed. She thought of Roald. He had never been able to abide deceit; would he have fallen in love with a woman who would steal? Somehow she doubted it.

Antoine would leave; he would not tolerate the larceny indefinitely. If only—and even thinking such a thought was profoundly disturbing—the chef could be duplicated. How evil her musings had become. The penalty for duping a human being was severe; the offender would be deprived of access to any duplicator, reduced to eating only in restaurants and acquiring goods others had thrown away. With watchful cyberminds everywhere, discovery of such a crime was certain, which was why such offenses were rare. At any rate, such action would do no good even if she could overcome her conditioning long enough to push Antoine into the duplicator in order to get his pattern. The duplicated Antoine would only repeat his predecessor's actions and leave her, too.

Rina and Celia were sitting on the lawn, playing with

various rubies, diamonds, and sapphires; the gems were scattered among the neatly trimmed blades.

"Hello, my darlings," Lora said as she approached her daughters. The girls looked up, gaping. Though Rina was fair, and Celia dark, they both had Lora's fine features. "What are you doing?"

The inquiry seemed to be causing the children some perplexity. Celia glanced at her sister, as if looking for enlightenment.

"Playing," Rina answered at last.

"A game," Celia added.

"Hadn't you better go inside?" Lora asked.

"Why?" Rina said.

"Because it's getting cold."

"Oh," Celia said, looking surprised.

"And you shouldn't gape, dears. You're both much too pretty to leave your mouths hanging open like that." The girls scrambled to pick up their gems, dropping several in the process and having to stoop for them again. Had one of them been the thief, Lora thought, broken disks would have been scattered over the kitchen floor.

She came to the woods, treading daintily over the pine needles on the ground. Here, at least, she could put her troubles behind her for a while. She listened to the birds; their musical chirping, accompanied by the whistling pines, lifted her spirits. The spell was broken as a grackle cawed, causing Lora to wince.

The dark thought she had been suppressing now floated to the surface. The house had ample opportunity to steal. It could easily set one of the robots to the task in the middle of the night, and erase any record of its movements. The air around her seemed to grow even colder.

What motive could the house have? She had heard of other cyberminds becoming bitchy or recalcitrant, growing disdainful of the human beings around them. Most, indeed, had a habit of behaving as if they were the superior intelligence.

She pressed her lips together. Perhaps the house

wanted to displace her and take over her functions; maybe it had grown to resent being only an onlooker at her soirées. She imagined a conspiracy of houses communicating through the secret channels, plotting against those whom they served. The thought was intolerable; how could she confront her own house with such an accusation? If she angered it, the house might decide to close down, and then she would have to move.

She leaned against a tree for a moment, then steadied herself. Surely those more brilliant than she had considered such a possibility. They would not allow cyberminds to become too rebellious, for there was no telling where such rebelliousness might lead.

She had walked farther than she had intended. The trees had thinned out; just beyond this edge of the forest, the Karells' stone house stood in a glade. Lora turned back, remembering how Gretchen Karell had gloated when leaving her message about the stolen soup. She would have to tell Roald not to invite the Karells to dinner.

As she retraced her steps, a voice rang out through the woods. "Hello!" It was Junia; Lora knew that piercing, clear tone well. She looked around, then glimpsed the young woman. Junia was standing with her back to Lora; she had spoken to Antoine. Neither had spotted Lora.

"Bonjour," the chef replied. He was carrying a basket filled with weedy-looking plants.

"Going back to the house?" Junia bent over to brush a bit of dirt from her pants.

"Yes. I have gathered enough for today."

"Can't you use disks for that stuff?"

Antoine drew himself up. "Occasionally truly fresh ingredients are required, mademoiselle. I have recorded many for later duplication, but I am always on the lookout, so to speak, for something new, something not yet recorded."

"Goodness." Junia leaned forward. "Just plants? Or do you hunt?"

"Certainly not, mademoiselle." Antoine was clearly appalled. "I am not so barbaric as to seek the death of an animal. The disks have spared me the necessity for such a crime."

"Well, that's a relief. I thought your rabbit stew was delicious. I'm glad it wasn't made with any residents of the forest."

Antoine's fingers fluttered; he was obviously moved by the compliment. "Alas, I sometimes mourn those creatures who had to die long ago so that their patterns could be preserved on disks. But those dark days are past. And we have this beautiful forest instead of a wheat field or lettuce patch. We should be grateful we no longer need to waste ourselves in such toil. Only those who enjoy gardening for its own sake need to till the earth and breed new strains for our eventual delectation."

"But you toil, Antoine." The two were walking now. Lora kept her distance from the pair as she followed. She was eavesdropping, but could not bring herself to reveal her presence. Chastising herself for her lack of character, she kept the pair in sight. The unknown thief had reduced her to being a sneak.

"Yes, I toil, mademoiselle," Antoine replied, "but it is what I was born to do. I cannot conceive of a greater pleasure than concocting a new tasty tidbit."

"But you're at it all the time. Surely you like to relax."

"My work is my relaxation."

"Then why don't you open your own restaurant? Or better yet, a private dining club? You'd get lots of members, I'm sure. People would trade you all sorts of things for your meals—why, you could have an unduplicated art collection if you wanted."

Antoine shook his head. "My cooking is my art, and I would not want the distractions of running a club. At any rate, there is more cachet to being a private chef."

"That's true. But why here? There are lots of families that would have you. You could go anywhere you like."

"I am happy here," Antoine answered. "And there is Madame Lora. She is so appreciative of my work. Such taste and discernment are not common nowadays when so many grab at everything without discrimination. We live in a world of coarsened palates, mademoiselle. In my previous station, the family I served would often sneak into the kitchen in the dead of night to dupe chili dogs." He shuddered. "I do not wish to feed pigs at the trough. Madame Lora's pleasure in my work is most gratifying, and she is careful to invite only those who will appreciate it."

Lora swelled with pride and nearly tripped over a root. Steadying herself, she held her breath, but Junia and Antoine continued on their way, unaware of her.

"I see your point," Junia said. "Praise from someone like Lora means a lot. She's so easily upset by a lot of things." Lora smiled to herself. There were some rewards in eavesdropping.

"Next to cooking, appreciation is what I live for," Antoine said. "I sleep soundly when I know that my food has been savored by others. I say to myself, only Antoine Laval could do this, only Antoine Laval is capable of producing such deliciousness. I am so pleased that you will be living with the young monsieur, that there will be another person of taste to enjoy my delicacies on a daily basis. With time, you may even approach Madame Lora in your discernment."

"That's very kind."

"It is no more than you deserve, mademoiselle."

"You're easy to appreciate. You're an artist, Antoine." Junia took his free arm. "It's such a pity about those stolen disks."

Antoine was silent. "Yes, a pity," he said at last. "I must work even more to create new dishes."

The two moved on. Lora waited until they were out of sight, then began to hurry toward the house along a different route; she was running by the time she reached the lawn.

Lora took a deep breath before entering the kitchen. Her hands were shaking; she had drunk a bottle of wine to steady her nerves.

Antoine, dressed in his hat and apron, stood before a shelf of disks making his selections for the evening. His robots stood by, still unactivated; the rest of the family was upstairs dressing for dinner.

She cleared her throat. The chef turned, raising an eyebrow. "Madame," Antoine said in wounded tones, "I have not requested your presence in my kitchen."

"I know who's been stealing the disks." She leaned against the counter as she summoned her courage.

Antoine's eyes widened.

"You've been stealing them, Antoine. Every once in a while, you take one to town and dupe it. It's true, isn't it?"

The chef clasped his hands together, then lowered his eyes. "I cannot deny it," he said after a long pause. "I have indeed been distributing my disks. I give them to a friend in town who makes other duplicates. He is most trustworthy, so I do not think you found out from him."

Lora nodded.

"How did I give myself away?" He glanced at the screen. "Has the house betrayed me by spying? I cannot believe you would allow it."

"No. You betrayed yourself in the woods today. I didn't mean to overhear you and Junia, but I did." She looked away for a moment, embarrassed at having to admit her own minor lapse. "You said appreciation meant so much to you, more than almost anything. That's why you made sure every disk had your name on it. Hundreds of discerning diners must appreciate your handiwork every day. That's what you wanted. You still have the status of a private chef while pleasing so many others. You didn't even trade them for anything because you don't want anything else except to cook and have your efforts honored. There was nothing to give you away."

Antoine hung his head. "I am most chagrined, madame."

Lora sagged against the counter, too weak and hurt to cry. The chef quickly took her arm and led her to a stool, seating her. "How could you do it, Antoine? Haven't we been good to you? Haven't you always liked it here?"

"Of course." He wrung his hands. "I have dishonored myself. I promised you exclusive recipes and did not keep my word. I should have sought help when my desire for fame and appreciation became so great." He flung out his arms. "I shall never forgive myself!"

"Oh, dear." Lora pressed her fingertips to her temples.

"I am an artist!" Antoine beat his chest with one fist, then began to pace the room. "I long for honor and prestige, for there is nothing else to have in this world. I hunger for that as much as anyone. An artist must share his gift, or it will curdle inside him like spoiled milk. It will grow as sour as a wine bottled badly. It will become as flat as an ill-made soufflé. Oh, madame!"

Lora let her hand drop. "But all of the people who have come here honor you."

"That is true. But think of all the others who might." She sighed.

"We are at an impasse," Antoine said more calmly. "I will have to go, yet no one will have me as a family chef when my misdeeds are known. I should have realized I could not keep a secret from one as sensitive as you." Taking off his hat, he threw it to the floor. "I shall work as a common chef, and make new disks for the public at large. It will be punishment enough. My friend gave my disks only to those who would fully appreciate them, I assure you, but now—" He waved a hand. "I shall be forced to cast my pearls before swine, or will have to serve them the slops they so desire. But worst of all, I shall lose your pleasure in my work."

"Oh, my."

He pointed at the shelf. "I shall leave you the exclusive

disks still remaining," he said dramatically. "Alas, I may never have such a well-equipped kitchen again. It will take years to assemble one."

"Oh, dear," Lora said. "I can't bear to lose you, Antoine. I'd go mad."

"It is a compulsion, madame. I would have to be reconditioned to overcome it."

"No," she cried. "Your talent is much too precious. You mustn't risk damaging it with reconditioning. Only we know about this, Antoine. No one else has to know at all."

"But I know I shall dupe another disk eventually. Others will find out. Mademoiselle Junia is clever enough to do so. I cannot make you my accomplice in this crime. You would be disgraced."

"But you must stay." Lora rubbed her forehead, trying to think.

"How I longed to be widely honored!" Antoine raised his eyes to the ceiling. "Savoring one's talent is not enough—one must allow others to feast on one's accomplishments. I even dreamed of elevating the public taste through this stealthy distribution. I was wrong. I wanted to be both universal and exclusive, and that is not possible. I shall go." He began to untie his apron.

"Wait. There must be a solution." An idea was forming in her mind. She prodded at it mentally, hoping it was not half-baked. Perhaps the bits of historical knowledge she had acquired might be useful for more than simply entertaining her guests with anecdotes about the dark past. "Let me explain."

"Certainly, madame." Antoine, halfway to the door, was hesitating.

"In the old days, before duplicators, people who offered goods and services found that they had to create a demand for those things. So they advertised. That means they informed the public at large such goods and services were available."

"That is what you do when you speak of your parties and my cooking to others."

"Yes, but these people had many other ways of spreading the information." Lora drew her brows together, unused to such sustained mental effort. "They put up posters and made little films and so forth. I saw a few in a public museum as a child. Of course, the claims were often exaggerated. But sometimes, for something new, simply providing information wasn't enough. So they came up with another idea—the free sample."

"The free sample?" The chef looked puzzled. "They gave them away? But in those troubled times, people gave nothing away except on special occasions—so I have always believed."

"But a free sample would create demand." Lora beamed, proud of her cogency. "One would use the sample and then want more of the product."

"I understand. But what has this to do with me?"

"Don't you see? What you've actually been doing is giving away samples and creating demand. When you look at it that way, it really doesn't seem so bad, does it?"

Antoine's face brightened a bit.

"So what we'll do is continue to give away free samples. You can dupe a disk once in a while, when your compulsion grows too strong, but we'll be open about it. Of course, you must also point out that even finer dishes are available in this house. People will be green with envy at the thought of what we eat here—why, you'll have more appreciation than you'll know what to do with!" And she, Lora thought, would increase her own reputation as a hostess even more. Everyone would clamor for invitations to dinner. Antoine would have his fame without sacrificing his position or principles. Her sensitive soul warmed at the notion of making him happy. "Will you stay?"

"Why, madame!" The chef was actually smiling. "Of course I will stay. You are brilliant."

"I am, if I do say so myself." Lora patted her hair. "You know, Antoine, those of us with some cultivation have been neglecting our responsibilities. We think that because people can have almost anything, we needn't create demand. That's a mistake. We should seek to lead people to finer things, encourage such folk to want them." The idea, like free samples, was an old one called *noblesse oblige*, but an old enough idea could seem quite new. "Most of us have been satisfied only to accept the admiration of those like us. True appreciation is our rarity—we should try to increase this wealth, if I may put it that way. I suspect that a lot of others will start offering free samples soon."

Antoine kissed his fingers. "You are an originator!"

"Oh, my," Lora murmured, accepting that highest of compliments. "It was really your idea," she added modestly. "I mean, you've provided the ingredients—I've only simmered the broth, so to speak. But you'll have even more work to do now."

"But I love my work." He hurried to her side; bowing, he kissed her hand. "I shall be content."

Lora hopped off the stool. "Enough. It's almost time for supper. Something substantial, I hope. With all this thinking, I've worked up quite an appetite."

"It will be delicious, I assure you. And exclusive."

It is often said, quite truthfully, that science is the mythology of Western civilization. There is one crucial difference between science and all other myths, however: the statements of science are subject to a self-correcting process of verification. Unless some outside force—such as Stalin for the late unlamented Dr. Lysenko—is interfering, eventually the dross will be removed and truth remain. This process has always been unpopular in many quarters; the thought of a judge who cannot be bribed or threatened, and who is invulnerable to political fads and public opinion, is intolerable to some.

Dr. Asimov's article is an excellent example, on the popular level, of the unique value of scientific reason, and of its ability to cut through to the fundamental truths.

Hot, Cold, and Con Fusion
Isaac Asimov

My dear wife, Janet, is, for some reason, incredibly solicitous over my well-being. If there's a single cloud in the sky, it's umbrella time. If a mist has faintly bedewed the streets, I must slip into my rubbers. If the temperature drops below seventy, on goes my fur hat. I won't even mention the close watch kept on my diet, the inquisitional cross-examination at the slightest cough, and so on.

You may suppose that I am very grateful for all this care. I put it up to any husband in similar straits. "Are you grateful?"

I thought not.

In fact, I complain a great deal about the matter, and I can be very eloquent, too, when I feel aggrieved. And do I get sympathy?

I do not.

To all my complaints, all my friends and acquaintances look at me coldly and say, "But that's because she *loves* you."

You have no idea how irritating that is.

So one time recently I was in a limousine being ferried

a moderate distance to give a talk. The driver was a foreigner of some sort, who drove with perfect accuracy, and who was clearly intelligent, but he had only a sketchy command of English. Being aware of this, he took the trouble to practice his English on me, and I answered carefully and with good enunciation so that he might learn.

At one point, he looked at the smiling sunshine, he felt the mild breeze, enjoyed the sight of the nearby park, and said, "It—is—vair byoot'ful—day."

At this, my sense of grievance rose high and I said, in my normal manner of speaking, "Yes, it is. And so why did my wife make me take an umbrella?" And I raised the offending instrument and waved it.

Whereupon the driver, choosing his words carefully, said, "But your—wife—she *lahv* you."

And I sank back defeated. The conspiracy was cross-cultural!

Which, believe it or not, brings me to the subject of this present essay.

Science, too, is cross-cultural, and so are scientific errors. I'm not talking about fraud, now. I'm talking about honest errors by capable scientists. An example I discussed not too long ago was the supposed discovery of N-rays in 1903 by a French physicist, Rene P. Blondlot (see "The Radiation That Wasn't," *F & SF*, March 1988).

You may be tempted to think that such a thing, overexuberant excitement concerning a startling but perhaps dubious discovery, is particularly French. After all, we know the common stereotypical stuff about Gallic volatility and enthusiasm.

Nonsense! Such things happen everywhere.

In 1962, a Soviet physicist, Boris V. Deryagin, reported the existence of "polywater." This seemed to be a new form of water that was found in very thin tubes where the constriction of the environment seemed to compress the water molecules and force them unusually close together. Polywater was reported to be 1.4 times as dense

as ordinary water and to boil at 500° C rather than 100°
C.

Instantly, chemists all over the world began repeating
Deryagin's work and confirming his results. Perhaps polywater played an important role in the constricted environment of human cells. Their excitement was intense.

But then reports filtered out of chemistry laboratories
that the properties of polywater would appear if some of
the glass of the vessel containing the water was dissolved.
Could it be that polywater was actually a solution of sodi-
um-calcium silicate? It turned out to be so, alas, and
"polywater" collapsed as thoroughly as N-rays did.

You might say, well, Russians are volatile, too. After
all, we know the stereotype of the "mad Russian."

So there's the case of Percival Lowell, an American of
the purest Boston Brahmin stock (yes, one of *those*
Lowells, who speak only to Cabots) and a first-class
astronomer.

He reported seeing canals on Mars and made intricate
maps of them. They met at "oases" and sometimes they
doubled. Lowell was absolutely convinced they indicated
the presence of an advanced technology on the planet,
fighting to irrigate the desert midsections with water
from the polar ice-caps.

Others looked at Mars and saw the canals also, but
most astronomers didn't see them. Contrary evidence
piled up over the years, and we all know *now*, beyond any
doubt, thanks to Mars probes, that there are no canals on
Mars. Lowell was fooled by an optical illusion.

Does that mean that startling discoveries are *always*
wrong? Of course not.

In 1938, the German chemist Otto Hahn, who had
been bombarding uranium with neutrons, came to the
conclusion that the results could only be explained by
supposing that the uranium atoms broke nearly in half
("uranium fission"). Such a thing had never been heard
of, and Hahn chose not to risk his reputation by announc-
ing it.

However, his ex-partner, the Austrian chemist Lise

Meitner, had been driven out of Germany and into Sweden in 1938, for the crime of being Jewish, and perhaps she felt she had little to lose. She prepared a paper on uranium fission and told her nephew, Otto Frisch, about it, and he told Niels Bohr, who was on his way to attend a scientific meeting in the United States. There he spread the news and the American physicists at once scattered to their laboratories, ran the experiments, and *confirmed* uranium fission. The results we know.

Was that because Hahn was German and Meitner was Austrian? Not at all. I should tell you about the discovery of "masurium" in 1926 by excellent German chemists, but that's for another time.

That brings us to nuclear fusion, which is the opposite of nuclear fission. In fission, a large nucleus breaks apart into two halves. In fusion, two small nuclei join together into a single larger one.

Fission, in a way, is easy. Some large atoms are on the point of dissolution anyway. The short-range strong nuclear force barely reaches across them, and their natural vibrations constantly keep them at the point of fissioning. In fact, uranium atoms experience spontaneous fission every once in a long while.

If you add a little energy to the nucleus, fission can take place at once, especially where the atoms are really close to the edge, as in the case with uranium-235. You fire a neutron at it. The uncharged neutron is not repelled by the positively charged nucleus. The neutron slips into the large nucleus, and the added instability that results fissions the atom at once.

Fusion is more complicated. Two small nuclei must be brought very close together if they are to cling to each other and fuse. All nuclei, however, are positively charged and repel each other. Getting them to be sufficiently close to each other for fusion is an enormous and all but impossible task, it would seem.

Yet fusion takes place in the Universe and is even extremely common. It will take place in any piece of matter, spontaneously, as long as that piece of matter is: a) mostly hydrogen, and b) sufficiently massive, about ⅕ the mass of the Sun or more.

The nearest place in the Universe where nuclear fusion takes place in massive quantities is at the core of our own Sun.

How does it happen? For one thing, the core of the Sun (or of any ordinary star like the Sun) is at a temperature of millions of degrees. At such temperatures, atoms are broken down and the bare nuclei are exposed. That is important because in ordinary atoms, like those that surround us, atoms possess electrons in the outskirts and these electrons act like bumpers that keep the nuclei from approaching each other.

What's more, at the high temperatures at the core of the Sun, the nuclei are moving at enormous speeds, far more rapidly than they can move as part of the ordinary atoms about us. The more rapidly they move, the more energetic they are, and at the temperature of the Sun's core, the nuclei are energetic enough to overcome their mutual repulsions so that they can slam into each other forcefully.

In addition, the huge gravitational field of the Sun causes the outer layers to weigh down upon the core and force those bare nuclei so close together that the density of the core is thousands of times the ordinary matter about us.

In very dense matter like that of the core of the Sun, speeding nuclei have less of a chance to miss. Even if they veer away from one nucleus, they may veer right into the next. Consequently both high temperature *and* high density encourage fusion. The higher the one is, the lower the other need be; and the lower the one, the higher the other must be.

In order to bring about fusion, we must have certain combinations of temperature and density and maintain them for a sufficiently long time. The necessary values of temperature, density, and time are known. It is only necessary to attain them all simultaneously.

Since under even the most favorable circumstances, very high temperatures are required, this is called "hot fusion."

Can hot fusion be brought about on Earth? Of course! We have been doing it for thirty-five years in something called the hydrogen bomb, which is actually a nuclear fusion bomb. It is only necessary to have some fusible substance and produce the necessary temperature and pressure for fusion by use of a nuclear fission bomb (the ordinary A-bomb of Hiroshima) as the trigger.

At this point let me explain that there are three isotopes of hydrogen. There is ordinary hydrogen (hydrogen-1) with a nucleus made up of one proton; deuterium (hydrogen-2) with a nucleus made up of one proton and one neutron; and tritium (hydrogen-3) with a nucleus made up of one proton and two neutrons.

Deuterium is easier to fuse than ordinary hydrogen is, and tritium is easier still. Ordinary hydrogen is by far the most common type, and it is that which fuses at the center of the Sun, but that is too difficult to imitate on Earth. We ought to use tritium, but that is radioactive, breaks down in a period of a few years, and has to be constantly manufactured. Its use as pure fusible material is impractical.

What is done in fusion bombs (I don't know the details, obviously, and I don't want to know) is to use deuterium, which is rare, but available in quantity just the same. Apparently, a bit of tritium is also added. The fission bomb triggers the tritium fusion with deuterium, and that produces enough heat to trigger the more difficult fusion of deuterium with itself.

Recently, it turned out that our nuclear plants producing tritium have been leaking radioactivity into the environment for years. The government, however, anxious to "keep America strong" has kept this secret and let it go on, since to them it didn't matter what happened to the American people as long as America in the abstract was kept strong. (Do you understand that? Frankly, I don't.)

Now the tritium plants are shut down because some busybody couldn't stand it anymore and made the leaks public. This means supplies of tritium are slowly dwindling and when they're gone, we won't be able to explode our H-bombs anymore, unless we build new plants to make tritium, which will apparently take many years and cost many billions of dollars.

All of this, however, is beside the point. We're not interested in hydrogen bombs, at least not in this essay. The question is whether there is any way of bringing about nuclear fusion in a controlled way, *without* a fission bomb trigger and *without* an all-out devastating explosion.

What we want is to fuse a little bit of hydrogen and use the energy this produces to fuse a little bit more and so on—always just a little bit at a time so that we risk no explosions. Not all the energy will be needed to continue the fusion, and the excess we can use for ourselves. Nuclear fusion would be a source of clean energy that would last us for as long as the Earth does.

To do this we have to get the right combination of density and temperature maintained for the proper length of time. Nothing we can possibly do now or in the foreseeable future will enable us to make the deuterium we're heating very dense, so we have to make up for that by reaching a temperature far in excess of that at the Sun's core. Instead of something over 10 million degrees, we need something over 100 million degrees.

For nearly forty years, physicists have been trying to obtain the necessary conditions by keeping deuterium gas penned in by strong magnetic fields while the temperature is sent up. Or else solid deuterium is zapped from a number of sides simultaneously by powerful laser beams that will heat it to the necessary temperature so quickly that the atoms have no time to move away.

But they haven't succeeded. Not yet. Huge devices costing many millions of dollars have not quite gotten deuterium to the fusion ignition point.

° ° °

Is there any other way of initiating fusion? The crucial point is to get the deuterium nuclei sufficiently close together for a sufficiently long time, and then they'll spontaneously fuse and give off energy. The only purpose of very high temperature is to force the nuclei close together against their own mutual repulsion.

But can we trick deuterium nuclei into getting together *without* heat? Can we do it in some ingenious way at room temperature? That would be "cold fusion." Let's consider—

Ordinary deuterium atoms are electrically neutral overall, the negatively charged electron exactly balancing their positively charged proton in the nucleus so that two hydrogen atoms can make contact without trouble. The protons of the two nuclei are then about an atom's diameter (about a hundred millionth of a centimeter) apart.

Every particle has its wave aspects, so that each proton can be considered a wave, with the "particle aspect" anywhere along the wave. (This can't be described properly except with mathematics, but for our purposes we can make use of the wave image.) The likelihood of the particle being at a particular part of the wave depends on the intensity of that part. The center of the wave is most intense, and it fades off, or damps, quickly with distance. This means that the proton particle is usually near the center of the wave, though it can sometimes be off center.

In fact, each proton may be far enough away from the center, in each other's direction, so that they may find themselves in actual contact and fuse. (This is called a "tunnel effect" because a particle seems to tunnel through an *apparently* impassable barrier because of its wave properties.) However, when two protons are an atom's diameter apart, the chance of tunneling is so remote that I doubt that a significant number of such fusions have taken place in the entire history of the Universe.

But what if we make the atom smaller? The electron has an associated wave (I'm still using the wave image), and it can only get so close to the proton that a single electron wave circles the proton. The electron cannot get any closer than that. That is the minimum size of a normal hydrogen atom, and it just isn't small enough for fusion.

There is, however, a particle called a muon, which is exactly like an electron in every respect but two. One point of difference is the mass. The muon is 207 times as massive as an electron. That means that the wave associated with it is correspondingly shorter than that of an electron. A muon can replace an electron in a hydrogen atom, but because of its shorter wave, it can get much closer to the nucleus. Indeed, "muonic-deuterium" has only one-hundredth the diameter of an ordinary atom, and because the muon has exactly the negative charge of an electron, muonic-deuterium is electrically neutral overall and two muonic-deuterium atoms can be in contact without trouble.

Under such circumstances, the two protons are close enough together for the tunneling effect to work easily, and fusion can take place at room temperature.

Is there a catch? Of course! The second difference between a muon and an electron is that the muon is not stable. Whereas an electron left to itself would last forever, unchanged, a muon breaks down to an electron and a couple of neutrinos in about a millionth of a second, so there isn't much time for fusion to take place. Muon-catalyzed cold fusion is possible, but totally impractical, barring some unforeseeable breakthrough. Too bad!

Anything else?

Well, hydrogen atoms are the smallest known, and they can sometimes sneak into crystals of larger atoms and find homes in the interstices. The champion case of this involves palladium, one of the platinum-like metals. Palladium can absorb nine hundred times its own volume of hydrogen, or deuterium, at room temperature.

The deuterium atoms, by the time they are done flooding into the palladium, are much closer together than they would be in ordinary deuterium gas. What's more, they are held in place by the palladium atoms quite tightly so they can't move around.

The question is whether they are forced *so* closely together that the tunneling effect can become large enough to detect and whether cold fusion may then take place at a useful rate. Two chemists thought it worth checking out. They were B. Stanley Pons of the University of Utah and Martin Fleischmann of the University of Southampton, England. They spent five and a half years trying to get cold fusion with simple electrolytic cells that any skillful chemistry student might have set up. They spent a hundred thousand dollars they raised themselves, and here is what they did.

They began with a container of heavy water (H_2O with deuterium atoms rather than ordinary hydrogen atoms). They added a bit of lithium to react with the heavy water and create ions that would carry an electric current. They then passed the electric current through the solution with two electrodes stuck into it, one of platinum and one of palladium. The electric current split the heavy water into oxygen and deuterium and the deuterium was absorbed by the palladium. More and more of the water was split, more and more of the deuterium was formed and absorbed by the palladium, until, finally, cold fusion took place.

How did they know cold fusion took place? Well, the palladium electrode developed four times as much heat as was being put into the system. That heat had to come from somewhere, and, since it couldn't come from anything else they could think of, they decided it was coming from cold fusion.

Very well. Pons and Fleischmann are legitimate scientists of considerable attainments and have good track records. They have to be treated with respect.

BUT—

If anyone finds practical cold fusion and is the first one in the field with it, they are instantly and at once the most famous chemists in the world, a cinch for an immediate Nobel Prize, and if they file for patents, they will become incredibly rich. Naturally, then, Pons and Fleischmann wouldn't be human if they didn't *want*, with unimaginable intensity, to be right. As soon as they had any respectable sign of its presence, wouldn't they decide they had it, even if perhaps they didn't? Human nature is human nature.

Should they have waited until they were *really* sure, till they had overwhelming evidence? For such a startling and unprecedented claim, scientific caution would direct them to wait, but it's easy to advise such caution and very hard to accept it.

After all, nothing would come of it for Pons and Fleischmann personally, unless they were first in the field. There's nothing very outré in the experiment. Scientists knew about this trick of palladium; they understood about tunneling; they grasped muonic-catalysis; and they were prepared to set up electrolytic cells. Who could say, then, how many chemists or physicists might quietly be working in the direction of palladium-catalyzed cold fusion? Indeed, Pons and Fleischmann knew for sure there were people at Brigham Young University who were working in that direction.

Apparently, the two groups agreed to send papers simultaneously to *Nature,* a very respected journal, on March 24, 1989. However, Pons and Fleischmann apparently could not resist establishing priority. They stole a march by holding a news conference on March 23 and spilling the beans to the press.

This got scientists (physicists especially) furious, for a number of reasons.

1) Giving an important scientific discovery to the press is not the right way to do it. It should be written up as a detailed scientific paper, sent to a scientific journal, submitted to peer review, revised if necessary, and then be published. This sounds very academic and roundabout, but it is the only way to keep science on track. What Pons and Fleischmann have done is to put a premium on appealing to the public with work that may be

incomplete or ambiguous. If this became the fashion, science would break down in confusion.

2) Pons and Fleischmann did not give full details of the process, which is also the non-scientific thing to do. Naturally, every scientist wanted to test the experiment for himself to see if he could confirm it or find out something else about it (that was what happened in the case of uranium fission). They couldn't be sure of what they were doing, however, because of the incompleteness of the data. Even when Pons and Fleischmann finally submitted a paper to *Nature,* it was so incomplete that *Nature* asked for additional details, and Pons and Fleischmann refused.

3) Pons and Fleischmann apparently didn't run proper controls. They did not describe having done the experiment with ordinary water. Even if deuterium fused under the conditions given, ordinary hydrogen would not, and that should have been tested. If the experiment developed heat with ordinary hydrogen also, then the source would surely have been something else, not fusion.

4) Pons and Fleischmann reported as their major evidence for fusion the development of heat, but heat can develop from *any* source; it is the common product of all conceivable forms of energy. It isn't enough to say: it can't be this, it can't be that, so it must be fusion. This sort of negative evidence falls down because it might also be some non-fusion process that you just haven't happened to think of or to know of. What is needed is some observation that is positive for fusion and not something that is negative for other things. For instance, if the deuterium atoms fused, they ought to have formed neutrons of tritium or possibly helium-4. This was not reported.

The Brigham Young people did indeed report neutrons but only about one hundred-thousandth as many as those required to produce the heat reported by Pons and Fleischmann. There were so few, in fact, that it would be hard to demonstrate that they weren't derived from neutrons that are always hanging about the environment anyway.

5) Immediately after the announcement, the governor of Utah asked for millions of dollars from the federal government to develop practical fusion in Utah, before the Japanese could steal the notion and develop it in Japan. This lent an unpleasant commercial touch and stressed the economic motivation for haste and incompleteness in the science involved.

6) A gathering of chemists had a field day when Pons and Fleischmann implied they had come to the rescue of the physicists by doing for next to nothing what the physicists had been unable to do for many millions of dollars. There was no need to make fun of honest and rational work. The physicists, being only human, snarled in their turn at the chemists, and what should have been a scientific discussion became a rather unpleasant name-calling piece of scientific pathology.

In any case, I am writing ten weeks after the original announcement. Increasingly, it looks as though the Pons-Fleischmann report will *not* be confirmed; that it will fade away as did the Martian canals, N-rays, and poly-water. Too bad, for the world could surely use practical cold fusion.

But, to end on a positive note. All the returns aren't in yet. There is still an outside chance, a very outside chance, that cold fusion will be confirmed. By the time this essay appears, we should know absolutely, one way or the other.

And second, even if Pons-Fleischmann turns out to be chimera and a mirage, an enormous effort is being put into investigating electrolytic cells with palladium electrodes, and who knows what people may find out as a result? Something interesting perhaps. Perhaps even cold fusion by some other route. I certainly hope so, though I must admit I wouldn't bet on it even with generous odds in my favor.

NOTE: It is now four months since I wrote the article. I doubt that *anyone* accepts Pons-Fleischmann cold fusion now.

Even paradise will have its angst. *The transition could be much worse; here we have an attempt to trace some of the possible consequences of a cold fusion that really worked—a science fiction what-if. Cheap, limitless energy in any desired form from an inexpensive, easily manufactured machine. And all at once, every one of the billion delicately balanced synergies that constitute the world political and economic order would be thrown out of kilter. It wouldn't even require that the new power source be immediately available, because it is the acknowledged future value of an asset that makes it valuable in the present. How much would the Libyan currency be worth, if everyone knew that in five years that "country" would be a desert, inhabited by overfed sand-thieves with no marketable skills and underlain by this funny gummy black stuff which is mildly useful as a chemical feedstock?*

This is much the same question as that posed by Poul Anderson in "Snowball." My answer is a little different; perhaps the world is closer to the margin, these days— or perhaps I'm just not as nice a person . . .

Roachstompers
S.M. Stirling

ABILENE, TEXAS
October 1, 1998
POST #72, FEDERAL IMMIGRATION CONTROL

"Scramble! Scramble!"

"Oh, shit," the captain of the reaction company said with deep disgust. It was the first time Laura Hunter had gotten past level 17 on this game. "Save and logoff."

She snatched the helmet from the monitor and stamped to settle her boots, wheeled to her feet and walked out of the one-time Phys-Ed teacher's office. One hand adjusted the helmet, flipping up the nightsight visor and plugging the comlink into the jack on her back-and-breast; the other snatched the H&K assault rifle from the improvised rack beside the door. Words murmured into her ears, telling the usual tale of disaster.

"All right," the senior sergeant bellowed into the echoing darkness of the disused auditorium they were using as a barracks. The amplified voice seemed to strike her like a club of air as she crossed the threshold. "Drop your cocks 'n grab your socks!"

It was traditional, but she still winced; inappropriate too, this was officially a police unit and thoroughly coed. "As you were, Kowalski," she said. The Rangers were tumbling out of their cots, scrambling cursing into uniforms and body-armor, checking their personal weapons. None of that Regular Army empty-rifle crap here. *Her* troopies were rolling out of their blankets ready to rock and roll, and *fuck* safety; the occasional accident was cheap compared to getting caught half-hard when the cucuroaches came over the wire.

Fleetingly, she was aware of how the boards creaked beneath their feet, still taped with the outlines of vanished basketball games. The room smelled of ancient adolescent sweat overlaid with the heavier gun-oil and body odors of soldiers in the field. *No more dances and proms here,* she thought with a brief sadness. Then data-central began coming through her earphones. She cleared her throat:

"Listen up, people. A and B companies scramble for major illegal intro in the Valley; Heavy Support to follow and interdict. Officers to me. The rest of you on your birds; briefing in flight. Move it!"

The six lieutenants and the senior NCO's gathered round the display table under the basketball hoop. They were short two, B company was missing its CO . . . no time for that.

"Jennings," she said. A slim good-looking black from Detroit, field-promoted, looked at her coolly; her cop's instinct said *danger*. "You're top hat for B while Sinclair's down. Here's the gridref and the grief from Intelligence; total illigs in the 20,000 range, seventy klicks from Presidio."

The schematic blinked with symbols, broad arrows thrusting across the sensor-fences and minefields along the Rio Grande. Light sparkled around strongpoints, energy-release monitored by the surveillance platforms circling at 200,000 feet. Not serious, just enough to keep the weekend-warrior Guard garrisons pinned down. The illigs were trying to make it through the cordon into the wild Big Bend country. The fighters to join the guerrilla bands, the others to scatter and find enough to feed their children, even if it meant selling themselves as indentured quasi-slaves to the plains 'nesters.

"Shitfire," Jennings murmured. "Ma'am. Who is it this time?"

"Santierist Sonoran Liberation Army," she said. "The combatants, at least. We'll do a standard stomp-and-envelopment. Here's the landing-zone distribution. Fire-prep from the platforms, and this time be *careful*, McMurty. There are two thousand with small arms, mortars, automatic weapons, light AA, possible wire-guided antitank and ground-to-air heat-seekers."

"And their little dogs too," McMurty muttered, pushing limp blond hair back from her sleep-crusted eyes. "Presidio's in Post 72's territory, what're they—" She looked over the captain's shoulder. "—sorry, sir."

Laura Hunter saluted smartly along with the rest; Major Forrest was ex-Marine and Annapolis. Not too happy about mandatory transfer to the paramilitary branch, still less happy about the mixed bag of National Guard and retread police officers that made up his subordinates.

"At ease, Captain, gentlemen. Ladies." Square pug face, traces of the Kentucky hills under the Academy diction, pale blue eyes. "And Post 72 is containing a major outbreak in El Paso. For which C and D companies are to stand by as reserve reinforcement."

"What about the RAC's? Sir." Jennings added. Forrest nodded, letting the "Regular Army Clowns" pass: the black was more his type of soldier, and the corps had always shared that opinion anyway.

"This is classified," he said. "The 82nd is being pulled out of Dallas-Forth Worth."

"Where?" Hunter asked. Her hand stroked the long scar that put a kink in her nose and continued across one cheek. *That* was a souvenir of the days when she had been driving a patrol car in D.C.

No more 82nd . . . It was not that the twin cities were

that bad; their own Guard units could probably keep the lid on ... but the airborne division was the ultimate reserve for the whole Border as far west as Nogales.

The Major made a considered pause. "They're staging through Sicily, for starters." Which could mean only one thing; the Rapid Deployment Force was heading for the Gulf. Hunter felt a sudden hot weakness down near the pit of her stomach, different and worse than the usual pre-combat tension.

Somebody whistled. "The Russian thing?" Even on the Border they had had time to watch the sattelite pictures of the Caliphist uprisings in Soviet Asia; they had been as bloody as anything in the Valley, and the retaliatory invasion worse.

"COMSOUTH has authorized ... President Barusci has issued an ultimatum demanding withdrawal of the Soviet forces from northern Iran and a UN investigation into charges of genocide."

"Sweet Jesus," Jennings said. Hunter glanced over at him sharply; it sounded more like a prayer than profanity.

"Wait a minute, sir," Hunter said. "Look ... that means the RDF divisions are moving out, right?" All three of them, and that was most of the strategic reserve in the continental US. "Mobilization?" He nodded. "But the army reserve and the first-line Guard units are going straight to Europe? With respect, sir, the cucuroache— the people to the south aren't fools and they have satellite links too. Who the *hell* is supposed to hold the Border?"

The commander's grin showed the skull beneath his face. "We are, Captain Hunter. We are."

The noise in the courtyard was already enough to make the audio pickups cut in, shouts and pounding feet and scores of PFH airjets powering up. Pole-mounted glare-lights banished the early-morning stars, cast black shadows around the bulky figures of the troopers in their olive-and-sand camouflage. The air smelt of scorched metal and dust. Hunter paused in the side-door of the Kestrel assault-transport, looking back over the other vehicles. All the latest, nothing too good for the Rangers—and they were small enough to re-equip totally on the first PFH-powered models out of the factories. Mostly Kestrels, flattened ovals of Kelvar-composite and reactive-armor panel, with stub wings for the rocket pods and chin-turrets mounting chain guns. Bigger boxy transports for the follow-on squads; little one-trooper eggs for the Shrike airscouts; the bristling saucer-shapes of the heavy weapons platforms.

She swung up into the troop compartment of her Kestrel, giving a glance of automatic hatred to the black rectangles of the PFH units on either side of the ceiling. "Pons, Fleischmann and Hagelstein," she muttered. "Our modern trinity." The bulkhead was a familiar pressure through the thick flexibility of her armor. "Status, transport."

"All green and go," the voice in her earphones said. "Units up, all within tolerances, cores fully saturated."

The headquarters squad were all in place. "Let's do it, then," she said. "Kestrel-1, lift."

The side ramps slid up with hydraulic smoothness, and the noise vanished with a soughing ching-*chunk*. Those were *thick* doors; aircraft did not need to be lightly built, not with fusion-powered boost. Light vanished as well, leaving only the dim glow of the riding lamps. There was a muted rising wail as air was drawn in through the intakes, rammed through the heaters and down through the swiveljets beneath the Rangers' feet. There were fifteen troopers back-to-back on the padded crashbench in the Kestrel's troop-compartment. One of them reached up wonderingly to touch a power unit. It was a newbie, Finali, the company commlink hacker. Clerk on the TOE, but carrying a rifle like the rest of them; the datacrunching was handled by the armored box on his back.

Hunter leaned forward, her thin olive-brown face framed by the helmet and the bill brow of the flipped-up visor. "*Don't—touch—that,*" she said coldly as his fingers brushed the housing of the fusion unit.

"Yes, ma'am." Finali was nearly as naive as his freckle-faced teenage looks, but he had been with A Company long enough to listen to a few stories about the Captain. "Ahh, ma'am, is it safe?"

"Well, son, they *say* it's safe." The boy was obviously sweating the trip to his first hot LZ, and needed distraction.

The transport sprang skyward on six columns of superheated air, and the soldiers within braced themselves against the thrust, then shifted as the big vents at the rear opened. The Kestrel accelerated smoothly toward its Mach 1.5 cruising speed, no need for high-stress maneuvers. Hunter lit a cigarette, safe enough on aircraft with no volatiles aboard.

"And it probably is safe. Of course, it's one of the doped-titanium anode models, you know? Saves on palladium. They kick out more neutrons than I'm comfortable with, though. Hell, we're probably not going to live long enough to breed mutants, anyway."

She blew smoke at the PFH units, and a few of the troopers laughed sourly.

"Captain?" It was Finali again. "Ah, can I ask a question?"

"Ask away," she said. *I need distraction too.* The tac-update was not enough, no unexpected developments . . . and fiddling with deployments on the way in was a good way to screw it up.

"I know . . . well, the depression and Mexico and everything is because of the PFH, but . . . I mean, I didn't even *see* one of them until I enlisted. It's going to be *years* before people have them for cars and home heating. How can it . . . how can it mess things up so bad *now*?"

Kowalski laughed contemptuously, the Texas twang strong in his voice. "Peckerwood, how much yew goin' to pay for a horse ever'one knows is fixin' to die next month?"

Finali flushed, and Hunter gave him a wry smile and a slap on the shoulder. "Don't feel too bad, trooper; there were economists with twenty degrees who didn't do much better." She took another drag on the cigarette, and reminded herself to go in for another cancer antiviral. *If we make it. Shut up about that.*

"Sure, there aren't many PFH's around, but we know they're going to be common as dirt; the Taiwanese are starting to ship out 10-Megawatt units like they did VCR's, in the old days. Shit, even the Mindanao pirates've managed to get hold of some. See, they're so simple . . . not much more difficult to make than a diesel engine, once Hagelstein figured out the theory. And you can do anything with them; heavy water in, heat or electricity or laser beams out. Build them any scale, right down to camp-stove size.

"Too fucking good, my lad. So all those people who's been sitting on pools of oil knew they'd be worthless in ten, fifteen years. So they pumped every barrel they could, to sell while it was still worth something. Which made it practically worthless right away, and they went bust. Likewise all the people with tankers, refineries, coal mines . . . all the people who *made* things for anybody in those businesses, or who sold things to the people, or who lent them money, or . . ."

She shrugged. The Texan with the improbable name laughed again. "Me'n my pappy were roustabouts from way back. But who needs a driller now?"

"Could be worse," the gunner in the forward compartment cut in. "You could be a cucuroach."

That was for certain-sure. Hunter flipped her visor down, and the compartment brightened to green-tinted clarity. Mexico had been desperate *before* the discoveries, when petroleum was still worth something; when oil dropped to fifty cents a barrel, two hundred billion dollars in debts had become wastepaper. And depression north of the Border meant collapse for the export industries that depended on those markets, no more tourists . . . breadlines in the U.S., raw starvation to the south. Anarchy, warlords, eighty million pairs of eyes turned north at the Colossus whose scientists had shattered their country like a man kicking in an egg carton.

Fuck it, she thought. *Uncle Sugar lets the chips fall where they lie and gives us a munificent 20% bonus on the minimum wage for sweeping the consequences back into the slaughterhouse.*

The northern cities were recovering, all but the lumpenproletariat of the cores; controlled fusion had leapfrogged the technoaristocracy two generations in half a decade. Damn few of the sleek middle classes *here,* down where the doody plopped into the pot. Blue-collar kids, farm boys, blacks; not many Chicanos either. D.C. had just enough sense not to send them to shoot their cousins and the ACLU could scream any way they wanted; the taxpayers had seen the Anglo bodies dangling from the lampposts of Brownsville, seen it in their very own living rooms . . .

Without us, the cucuroaches would be all over their shiny PFH-powered suburbs like a brown tide, she thought, not for the first time. Strange how she had come to identify so totally with the troops.

"But as long as these stay scarce, we've got an edge," she said, jerking the faceless curve of her helmet toward the PFH. "Chivalric."

"Chivalric?" Finali frowned.

"Sure, son. Like a knight's armor and his castle; with that, we protect the few against the many." She pressed a finger against her temple. "Pilot, we are coming up on Austin?"

"Thirty seconds, Captain."

"Take her down to the dirt, cut speed to point five Mach and evasive. Everybody sync." The cucuroach illigs could probably patch into the commercial satellite network—might have hackers good enough to tap the PFH-powered robot platforms hovering in the stratosphere. Knowing the Rangers were coming and being able to do anything about it were two separate things, though. As long as they were careful to avoid giving the war-surplus Stingers and Blowpipes a handy target.

The transport swooped and fell, a sickening express-elevator feeling. Hunter brought her H&K up across her lap and checked it again, a nervous tick. It too was the very latest, Reunited German issue; the Regulars were still making do with M16s. Caseless ammunition and a 50-round cassette, the rifle just a featureless plastic box with a pistol-grip below and optical sight above. They were talking about PFH-powered personal weapons, lasers and slugthrowers. Not yet, thank God . . .

"Thirty minutes ETA to the LZ," the pilot announced. Hunter keyed the command circuit.

"Rangers, listen up. Remember what we're here for; take out their command-and-control right at the beginning. That's why we're dropping on their HQ's. Without that and their heavy weapons they're just a mob; the support people can sweep them back. We're *not* here to fight them on even terms; this is a roach stomp, not a battle." A final, distasteful chore. Her voice went dry:

"And under the terms of the Emergency Regulations Act of 1995, I must remind you this is a police action. All hostiles are to be given warning and opportunity to surrender unless a clear and present danger exists."

"And I'm King Charles V of bloody England," someone muttered.

"Yeah, tell us another fairy story."

"*Silence on the air!*" Top sergeant's voice.

Her mind sketched in the cities below, ghostly and silent in the night, empty save for the National Guard patrols and the lurking predators and the ever-present rats. Paper rustling down deserted streets, past shattered Arby's and Chicken Delights . . . out past the fortress suburbs, out to the refugee camps where the guards kicked the rations through the wire for the illig detainees to scramble for.

There would be no prisoners.

Very softly, someone asked: "Tell us about the island, Cap?"

What am I, the CO or a den mother? she thought. Then, *What the hell, this isn't an Army unit.* Which was lucky for her; the American military still kept women out of front-line service, at least in theory. The Rangers were a police unit under the Department of the Interior—also in theory. *And not many of the troopies ever had a chance at a vacation in Bali.*

Hunter turned and looked over the low bulkhead into the control cabin of the transport. Her mouth had a dry feeling, as if it had been wallpapered with Kleenex; they were right down on the deck and going *fast*. Kestrels had phased-array radar and AI designed for nape-of-the-earth fighters. Supposed to be reliable as all hell, but the sagebrush and hills outside were going past in a streaking blur. She brought her knees up and braced them against the seat, looking down at the central display screen. It was slaved to the swarm of tiny remote-piloted reconnaissance drones circling the LZ, segmented like an insect's eye to show the multiple viewpoints, with pulsing light-dots to mark the Ranger aircraft.

The Santierist guerrillas were using an abandoned ranch house as their CP. She could see their heavy weapons dug in around it, covered in camouflage netting. Useless, just patterned cloth, open as daylight to modern sensors . . . on the other hand, there weren't many of those in Mexico these days. Then she looked more closely. There were *mules* down there, with ammunition boxes on their backs. It was enough to make you expect Pancho Villa. A Santierist altar in the courtyard, with a few hacked and discarded bodies already thrown carelessly aside . . . *Voodoo-Marxist,* she thought. *Communal ownership of the spirit world. Time to tickle them.*

"Code Able-Zulu four," she said. Something in her helmet clicked as the AI rerouted her commlink. "Position?"

"Comin' up on line-of-sight," McMurty said. Weapons Section counted as a platoon, four of the heavy lifters with six troopers each.

There were lights scattered across the overgrown scrub of the abandoned fields beyond the ranch house, the numberless campfires of the refugees who had followed through the gap the Santierists had punched in the Border deathzone. Some of them might make it back, if they ran as soon as the firefight began.

Hunter reached out to touch half a dozen spots on the screen before her; they glowed electric-blue against the silvery negative images. "Copy?"

"Copy, can-do."

"Execute."

Another voice cut in faintly, the battalion AI prompter. "ETA five minutes."

"Executing firemission," the platform said.

The gamma-ray lasers were invisible pathways of energy through the night, invisible except where a luckless owl vanished into a puff of carbon-vapor. Where they struck the soil the earth exploded into plasma for a meter down. It wasn't an explosion, technically. Just a lot of vaporized matter trying to disperse really, really fast. Fire gouted into the night across the cucuroach encampment, expanding outward in pulse-waves of shock and blast. She could hear the thunder of it with the ears of mind; on the ground it would be loud enough to stun and kill. The surviving AA weapons were hammering into the night, futile stabbing flickers of light, and . . .

"Hit, God, we're hit!" McMurty's voice, tightly controlled panic. The weapons platform was three miles away and six thousand feet up. Nothing should be able to touch it even if the cucuroaches had sensors that good. "Evasive—*Christ, it hit us again, loss of system integrity I'm trying to—*"

The voice blurred into a static blast. "Comm override, all Ranger units, *down*, out of line-of-sight, that was a zapper!"

The transport lurched and dove; points of green light on the screen scattered out of their orderly formation into a bee-swarm of panic. Hunter gripped the crashbars and barked instructions at the machine until a fanpath of probable sites mapped out the possible locations of the zapper.

"Override, override," she said. "Jennings, drop the sec-

ondary targets and alternate with me on the main HQ.
Weapons?"

"Yes ma'am." McMurty's second, voice firm.

"Keep it low, sergeant; follow us in. Support with indi-
rect-fire systems only." The weapons platforms had mag-
neto-powered automatic bomb-throwers as well as their
energy weapons.

"Override," she continued. "General circuit. Listen up,
everyone. The cucuroaches have a zapper, at least one.
I want Santierist prisoners; you can recognize them by
the fingerbone necklaces. Jennings, detach your first platoon for a dustoff on McMurty."

"Ma'am—"

"That's a direct order, Lieutenant."

A grunt of confirmation. Her lips tightened; nobody
could say Jennings didn't have the will to combat, and
he led from the front. Fine for a platoon leader, but a
company commander had to realize there were other
factors in maintaining morale, such as the knowledge you
wouldn't be abandoned just because everyone was in a
hurry. Furthermore, Jennings just did not like her much.
The feeling was mutual; he reminded her too strongly of
the perps she had spent most of the early '90s busting
off the D.C. streets and sending up for hard time.

"Coming up on the arroyo, Captain," the pilot said.

"Ready!" she replied.

The piloting screens in the forward compartment were
directly linked to the vision-blocks in the Kestrel's nose;
she could see the mesquite and rock of the West Texas
countryside rushing up to meet them, colorless against
the blinking blue and green of the control-panel's heads-
up displays. The pilot was good, and there was nothing
but the huge soft hand of deceleration pressing them
down on the benches as he swung the transport nearly
perpendicular to the ground, killed forward velocity with
a blast of the lift-off jets and then swung them back level
for a soft landing. The sides of the Kestrel clanged open,
turning to ramps. Outside the night was full of hulking
dark shapes and the soughing of PFH drives.

"Go!" Hunter shouted, slapping their shoulders as the headquarters team raced past. Getting troops out of armored vehicles is always a problem, but designing them so the sides fell out simplified it drastically. Cold high-desert air rushed in, probing with fingers that turned patches of sweat to ice, laden with dry spicy scents and the sharp aromatics of dry-land plants crushed beneath tons of metal and synthetic.

She trotted down the ramp herself and felt the dry, gravelly soil crunch beneath her feet. The squad was deployed in a star around her, commlink and display screen positioned for her use. The transports were lifting off, backing and shifting into position for their secondary gunship role as A Company fanned out into the bush to establish a temporary perimeter. Hunter knelt beside the screen, watching the pinpoints that represented her command fanning out along two sides of the low slope with the ranch house at its apex.

"Shit, Captain," Kowalski said, going down on one knee and leaning on his H&K. She could hear the low whisper, and there was no radio echo, he must have his comm off. "That zapper's one bad mother to face."

She nodded. Landing right on top of an opponent gave you a powerful advantage, and having the weapons platforms cruising overhead was an even bigger one. The zapper changed the rules; it was one of the more difficult applications of PFH technology, but it made line-of-sight approach in even the most heavily armored aircraft suicidal. Heavy zappers were supposed to be a monopoly of the Sovs and the U.S., having one fall into the hands of any sort of cucuroach was bad news. The Voodoo-Marxists . . . She shuddered.

Particularly if they had good guidance systems. Finali was trying to attract her attention, but she waved him to silence. "Too right, Tops. We'll just have to rush their perimeter before they can gather on the mountain."

SSNLF guerrillas were good at dispersing, which was essential in the face of superior heavy weapons. On the other hand, this time it kept them scattered. . . .

"Command circuit," she said. There was a subaudible click as the unit AI put her on general push. "Up and at 'em, children. Watch it, they've had a few hours to lay surprises."

There was little noise as the Rangers spread out into the spare chest-high scrub, an occasional slither of boot on rock, a click of equipment. That would be enough, once they covered the first half-kilometer. Shapes flitted through the darkness made daybright by her visor, advancing by leapfrogging squad rushes. Almost like a dance, five helmeted heads appearing among the bushes as if they were dolphins broaching, dodging forward until they were lost among the rocks and brush. Throwing themselves down and the next squad rising on their heels . . .

"Weapons," she whispered. "Goose it."

"Seekers away," the calm voice answered her.

A loud multiple *whupping* sound came from behind them, the air-slap of the magnetic mortar launch. A long whistling arc above, and the sharp *crackcrackcrack* of explosions. Mostly out of sight over the lip of the ravine ahead of them, indirect flashes against the deep black of the western sky. Stars clustered thick above, strange and beautiful to eyes bred among the shielding city lights. Then a brief gout of flame rising over the near horizon, a secondary explosion. Teeth showed beneath her visor. The seeker-bombs were homing on infrared sources: moving humans, or machinery; too much to hope they'd take out the zapper.

Time to move. She rose and crouch-scrambled up the low slope ahead of her. The open rise beyond was brighter, and she felt suddenly exposed amid the huge rolling distances. It took an effort of the will to remember that this was night, and the cucuroaches were seeing nothing but moonless black. *Unless they got nightsight equipment from the same sources as the laser*—She pushed the thought away.

"Mines." The voice was hoarse with strain and pitched low, but she recognized 2nd platoon's leader, Vigerson.

"Punch it," she replied, pausing in her cautious skitter.

A picture appeared in the center of the display screen, the silvery glint of a wire stretched across the clear space between a boulder and a mesquite bush. Jiggling as the hand-held wire-eye followed the metal thread to the V-shaped Claymore concealed behind a screen of grass, waiting to spew its load of jagged steel pellets into the first trooper whose boot touched it. Wire and mine both glowed with a faint nimbus, the machine-vision's indication of excess heat. Very recently planted, then, after being kept close to a heat-source for hours.

"Flag and bypass." *Shit, I hate mines,* she thought. No escaping them. The gangers had started using them in D.C. before she transferred. Bad enough worrying about a decapitating piano-wire at neck height when you chased a perp into an alley—but toward the end you couldn't go on a bust without wondering whether the door had a grenade cinched to the latch. That was how her husband had— Another flight of magmortar shells went by overhead; the weapons platform was timing it nicely.

Think about the mines, not why she had transferred. Not about the chewed stump of— Think about mines. Half a klick with forty pounds on her back, not counting the armor. No matter how she tried to keep the individual loads down, more essentials crept in. Fusion-powered transports, and they *still* ended up humping the stuff up to the sharp end the way Caesar's knifemen had. A motion in the corner of her eye, and the H&K swept up; an act of will froze her finger as the cottontail zigzagged out of sight. *Shit, this can't last much longer,* she thought with tight control. They were close enough to catch the fireglow and billowing heat-columns from the refugee encampment beyond the guerrilla HQ, close enough to hear the huge murmur of their voices. Nobody was still asleep after what had already come down; they must be hopping-tight in there.

Four hundred yards. The point-men must be on their wire by now, if the Santierists had had time to dig in a perimeter at all. For total wackos they usually had pretty

good sense about things like that and this time there had
been *plenty* of—

"*Down!*" somebody shouted. One of hers, the radio
caught it first. Fire stabbed out from the low rise ahead
of them, green tracer; she heard the thudding detonation
of a chemical mortar, and the guerrilla shell-burst behind
her sent shrapnel and stone-splinters flying with a sound
that had the malice of bees in it.

The Rangers hit the stony dirt with trained reflex,
reflex that betrayed them. Three separate explosions
fountained up as troopers landed on hidden detonators,
and there was an instant's tooth-grating scream before
the AI cut out a mutilated soldier's anguish.

"Medic, *medic*," someone called. Two troopers rushed
by with the casualty in a fireman's carry, back down to
where the medevac waited. Hunter bit down on a cold
anger as she toiled up the slope along the trail of blood-
drops, black against the white dust. The Santierists were
worse than enemies, they were . . . cop-killers.

"Calibrate," she rasped, "that mortar."

"On the way." A stick of seekers keened by overhead;
proximity fused, they burst somewhere ahead with a
simultaneous *whump*. Glass-fiber shrapnel, and anything
underneath it would be dogmeat. Fire flicked by, Kalash-
nikovs from the sound of it, then the deeper ripping
sound of heavy machine-guns. As always, she fought the
impulse to bob and weave. Useless, and undignified to
boot.

"Designators," she said over the unit push. "Get on to
it."

This time all the magmortars cut loose at once, as
selected troopers switched their sights to guidance. Normally the little red dot showed where the bullets would
go, but it could be adjusted to bathe any target a Ranger
could see; the silicon kamikaze brains of the magmortar
bombs sought, selected, dove.

"Come *on!*" she shouted, as the Santierist firing line
hidden among the tumbled slabs of sandstone and thorn-
bush ahead of them, erupted into precisely grouped

flashes and smoke. "*Now*, goddamit!" Fainter, she could hear the lieutenants and NCO's echoing her command.

The rock sloped down from here, down toward the ranch house and the overgrown, once-irrigated fields beyond, down toward the river and the Border. She leapt a slit-trench where a half-dozen cucuroaches sprawled sightless about the undamaged shape of an ancient M60 machine-gun; glass fragments glittered on the wet red of their faces and the cool metal of the gun. Then she was through into the open area beyond and the ruins of a barn, everything moving with glacial slowness. Running figures that seemed to lean into an invisible wind, placing each foot in dark honey. Shadows from the burning ruins of the farmhouse, crushed vehicles around it, her visor flaring a hotspot on the ground ahead of her and she turned her run into a dancing sideways skip to avoid it.

The spot erupted when she was almost past, and something struck her a stunning blow in the stomach. Air whoofed out of her nose and mouth with a sound halfway between a belch and a scream, and she fell to her knees as her diaphragm locked. Paralyzed, she could see the Claymore pellet falling away from her belly-armor, the front burnished by the impact that had flattened it. Then earth erupted before her as the mine's operator surged to his feet and leveled an AK-47, and that *would* penetrate her vest at pointblank range. He was less than a dozen yards away, a thin dark-brown young man with a bushy mustache and a headband, scrawny torso naked to the waist and covered in sweat-streaked dirt.

Two dots of red light blossomed on his chest. Fractions of a second later two H&K rifles fired from behind her, at a cyclic rate of 2,000 rounds a minute. Muzzle blast slapped the back of her helmet, and the cucuroach's torso vanished in a haze as the prefragmented rounds shattered into so many miniature buzzsaws.

"Thanks," she wheezed, as Finali and Kowalski lifted her by the elbows. "Lucky. Just winded." There would be a bruise covering everything between ribs and pelvis, but she would have felt it if there was internal hemorrhaging. A wet trickle down her leg, but bladder control was not something to worry about under the circumstances. She grabbed for the display screen, keyed to bring the drones down. The green dots of her command were swarming over the little plateau, and the vast bulk of the illigs further downslope showed no purposeful movement. Only to be expected, the Santierists were using them as camouflage and cover. Which left only the problem of the—

Zap. Gamma-ray lasers could not be seen in clear air, but you could hear them well enough; the atmosphere absorbed enough energy for that. The Rangers threw themselves flat in a single unconscious movement; Hunter cursed the savage wave of pain from bruised muscle and then ignored it.

"Get a fix, get a fix on it!" she called. Then she saw it herself, a matte-black pillar rising out of the ground like the periscope of a buried submarine, two hundred yards away amid artful piles of rock. *Shit, no way is a magmortar going to take that out,* she thought. It was too well buried, and the molecular-flux mirrors inside the armored and stealthed shaft could focus the beam anywhere within line of sight.

Zap. Half a mile away a boulder exploded into sand and gas, and the crashing sound of the detonation rolled back in slapping echoes. "Mark." Her finger hit the display screens. "Kestrel and Shrike units, thumper attack, repeat, thumper attack." The transports and airscouts would come in with bunkerbuster rockets. And a lot of them would die; as a ground weapon that zapper was clumsy, but it did *fine* against air targets . . .

"Damn, damn, *damn!*" she muttered, pounding a fist against the dirt. Another *zap* and the stink of ozone, and this time the gout of flame was closer, only a hundred yards behind them. Rocks pattered down, mixed with ash and clinker; back there someone was shouting for a medic, and there was a taste like vomit at the back of her throat. She groped for a thermite grenade—

"Captain."

It was Finali, prone beside her and punching frantically at the flexboard built into the fabric of his jacket sleeve. "Captain, I got it, I got it!"

"Got *what*, privat—"

There was no word for the sound that followed. At first she thought she was blind, then she realized the antiflare of her visor had kicked in with a vengeance. Even with the rubber edges snugged tight against her cheeks glare leaked through, making her eyes water with reaction. The ground dropped away beneath her, then rose up again and slapped her like a board swung by a giant; she flipped into the air and landed on her back with her body flexing like a whip. Hot needles pushed in both ears, and she could feel blood running from them, as well as from her nose and mouth. Above her something was showing through the blackness of the visor: a sword of light thrusting for the stars.

Pain returned, shrilling into her ears; then sound, slow and muffled despite the protection the earphones of her helmet had given. The jet of flame weakened, fading from silver-white to red and beginning to disperse. Stars faded in around it, blurred by the watering of her eyes; anybody who had been looking in this direction unprotected was going to be blind for a *long* time. It was not a nuclear explosion, she knew, not technically. There were an infinity of ways to tweak the anode of a PFH unit, and a laser-boost powerpack needed to be more energetic than most. Overload the charging current and the fusion rate increased exponentially, lattice energy building within the crystalline structure until it tripped over into instant release. There was a pit six yards deep and four across where the zapper had been, lined with glass that crackled and throbbed as it cooled. The rest of the matter had gone in the line of least resistance, straight up as a plasma cloud of atoms stripped of their electron shells.

"Finali?" Her voice sounded muffled and distant, and her tongue was thick. She hawked, spat blood mixed with saliva, spoke again. "Trooper, what the *hell* was that?"

"Deseret Electronuclear unit, Captain," he said, rising with a slight stagger. A cowlick of straw-colored hair tufted out from under one corner of his helmet; he pulled off the molded synthetic and ran his fingers through his curls, grinning shyly. "U of U design, access protocols just about like ours. I told it to voosh."

Kowalski fisted him on the shoulder. "Good work, trooper." There was a humming *shussh* of air as the first of the Kestrels slid over the edge of the plateau behind them. "You roasted their cucuroach *ass*, my boy!"

Hunter turned her eyes back to the display screen; motion was resuming. "There'll be survivors," she said crisply, looking up to the rest of the headquarters squad. "We'll—"

Crack. The flat snapping sound of the sniper's bullet brought heads up with a sharp feral motion. All except for Finali's; the teenager had rocked back on his heels, face liquid for a moment as hydrostatic shock rippled the soft tissues. His eyes bulged, and the black dot above the left turned slowly to glistening red. His body folded back bonelessly with a sodden sound, the backpack commlink holding his torso off the ground so that his head folded back to hide the slow drop of brain and blood from the huge exit wound on the back of his skull. There was a sudden hard stink as his sphincters relaxed.

Above them the Kestrel poised, turned. A flash winked from its rocket pods, and the sniper's blind turned to a gout of rock and fragments. Kowalski straightened from his instinctive half-crouch and stared down at the young man's body for an instant.

"Aw, shit, *no*," he said. "Not *now*."

"Come on, Tops," Hunter said, her voice soft and flat as the nonreflective surface of her visor. She spat again, to one side. "We've got a job of work to finish."

"In the name of the Mother of God, señora, have pity!" the man in the frayed white collar shouted thinly.

The cucuroach priest leading the illig delegation was scrawnier than his fellows, which meant starvation gaunt. They stood below the Ranger command, a hundred yards distant as the megaphone had commanded. Behind them the dark mass of the refugees waited, a thousand yards farther south. That was easy to see, even with her visor up; the weapons platforms were floating overhead, with their belly-lights flooding the landscape, brighter than day. The Kestrels and Shrikes circled lower, unlit, sleek black outlines wheeling in a circuit a mile across, sough of lift-jets and the hot dry stink of PFH-air units.

Hunter stood with her hands on her hips, knowing they saw her only as a black outline against the klieg glare of the platforms. When she spoke, her voice boomed amplified from the sky, echoing back from hill and rock in ripples that harshened the accent of her Spanish.

"Pity on Santierists, old man?" she said, and jerked a thumb toward the ground. The priest and his party shielded their faces and followed her hand, those whose eyes were not still bandaged from the afterimages of the fusion flare. Ten prisoners lay on their stomachs before the Ranger captain, thumbs lashed to toes behind their backs with a loop around their necks. Naked save for their tattoos, and the necklaces of human fingerbone. "Did they take pity on you, and share the meat of their sacrifices?"

The priest's face clenched: he could not be a humble man by nature, nor a weak one, to have survived in these years. When he spoke a desperate effort of will put gentleness into his voice; shouting across the distance doubled his task, as she had intended.

"These people, they are not Santierists, not diabolists, not soldiers or political people. They are starving, señora. Their children die; the warlords give them no peace. For your own mother's sake, let the mothers and little children through, at least. I will lead the others back to the border myself; or kill me, if you will, as punishment for the crossing of the border."

Hunter signaled for increased volume. When she spoke the words rolled louder than summer thunder.

"I GRANT YOU THE MERCY OF ONE HOUR TO BEGIN MOVING BACK TOWARD THE BORDER," the speakers roared. "THOSE WHO TURN SOUTH MAY LIVE. FOR THE OTHERS—"

She raised a hand. The lights above dimmed, fading like a theater as the curtains pulled back. *Appropriate,* she thought sourly. *If this isn't drama, what is?* A single spotlight remained, fixed on her.

"FOR THE OTHERS, THIS." Her fist stabbed down. Fire gouted up as the lasers struck into the cleared zone before the mob, a multiple flash and crack that walked from horizon to horizon like the striding of a giant whose feet burned the earth.

The priest dropped his hand, and the wrinkles of his face seemed to deepen. Wordless, he turned and hobbled back across the space where a line of red-glowing pits stitched the earth, as neat as a sewing machine's needle could have made. There was a vast shuffling sigh from the darkened mass of his followers, a sigh that went on and on, like the sorrow of the world. Then it dissolved into an endless ruffling as they bent to take up their bundles for the journey back into the wasted land.

Laura Hunter turned and pulled a cigarette from a pocket on the sleeve of her uniform. The others waited, Jennings grinning like . . . what had been that comedian's name? MacDonald? Murphy? McMurty bandaged and splinted but on her feet, Kowalski still dead around the eyes and with red-brown droplets of Finali's blood across the front of his armor.

"You know," the Captain said meditatively, pulling on the cigarette and taking comfort from the harsh sting of the smoke, "sometimes this job sucks shit." She shook her head. "Right, let's—"

They all paused, with the slightly abstracted look that came from an override message on their helmet phones.

"Killed *Eisenhower*?" Jennings said. "You shittin' me, man? That dude been dead since before my pappy dipped his wick and ran."

Hunter coughed conclusively. "Not him, the *carrier*, you idiot, the ship." Her hand waved them all to silence.

". . . *off Bandar Abbas*," the voice in their ears continued. "*They—*" It vanished in a static squeal that made them all wince before the AI cut in. The Captain had been facing north, so that she alone saw the lights that flickered along the horizon. Like heat lightning, once, twice, then again.

"What *was* that, Cap?" Jennings asked. Even Kowalski looked to be shaken out of his introspection.

"That?" Hunter said very softly, throwing down her cigarette and grinding it out. "That was the end of the world, I think. Let's go."

"No. Absolutely not, and that is the end of the matter." Major Forrest was haggard; all of them were, after these last three days. But he showed not one glimpse of weakness; Hunter remembered suddenly that the commander of Post 73 had had family in Washington . . . a wife, his younger children.

She kept her own face impassive as she nodded and looked round the table, noting which of the other officers would meet her eyes. It was one thing to agree in private, another to face the Major down in the open.

The ex-classroom was quiet and dark. The windows had been hastily sealed shut with balks of cut styrofoam and duct tape. No more was needed, for now; four of the heavy transports were parked by the doors, with jury-rigged pipes keeping the building over pressure with filtered air that leached the chalk-sweat-urine aroma of school. Hunter could still feel the skin between her shoulder blades crawl as she remembered the readings from outside. The Dallas-Fort Worth fallout plume had come down squarely across Abilene, and she doubted there was anything living other than the rats within sixty miles.

She pulled on her cigarette, and it glowed like a tiny hearth in the dimness of the emergency lamp overhead. "With respect, sir, I think we should put it to a vote."

The blue eyes that fixed hers were bloodshot but calm; she remembered a certain grave of her own in D.C. whose bones would now be tumbled ash, and acknowledged Forrest's strength of will with a respect that conceded nothing.

"Captain," he said, "this is a council of war; accordingly, I'm allowing free speech. It is *not* a democracy, and I will not tolerate treason in my command. Is that clear?"

"Yes, sir," she said firmly. "Without discipline, now, we're a mob, and shortly a dead one. Under protest, I agree, and will comply with any orders you give."

The ex-Marine turned his eyes on the others, collecting their nods like so many oaths of fealty. A few mumbled. Jennings grinned broadly, with a decisive nod.

"Dam' straight, sir."

"Well. Gentlemen, ladies, shall we inform the me— the troops?"

" 'Tent-*hut!*"

The roar of voices died in the auditorium, and the packed ranks of the Rangers snapped to attention. A little raggedly, maybe, but promptly and silently. The officers filed in to take their places at the rear of the podium and Forrest strode briskly to the edge, paused to return the salute, clasped hands behind his back.

"Stand easy and down, Sergeant."

"Stand easy!" Kowalski barked. "Battalion will be seated for Major Forrest's address!"

The commander waited impassively through the shuffling of chairs, waiting for the silence to return. The great room was brightly lit and the more than four hundred troopers filled it to overflowing. But a cold tension hovered over them; they were huddled in a fortress in a land of death, and they knew it.

"Rangers," he began. "You know—"

Laura Hunter's head jerked up as she heard the scuffle from the front row of seats; one of the tech-sergeants was standing, rising despite the hissed warnings and grasping hands. She recognized him, from B Company. An ex-miner from East Tennessee, burly enough to shake off his neighbors. The heavy face was unshaven, and tears ran down through the stubble and the weathered grooves.

"You!" he shouted at the officer above him. "They're all dead, an' you did it! You generals, you big an' mighty ones. *You!*"

Hunter could feel Jennings tensing in the seat beside her, and her hand dropped to the sidearm at her belt. Then the hillbilly's hand dipped into the patch-pocket of his jacket, came out with something round. Shouts, screams, her fingers scrabbling at the smooth flap of the holster, the oval egg-shape floating through the air toward the dais where the commanders sat. Forrest turning and reaching for it as it passed, slow motion, could see the striker fly off and pinwheel away and she was just reaching her feet. The Major's hand struck it, but it slipped from his fingers and hit the hardwood floor of the dais with a hard drum-sound. She could read the cryptic print on it, and recognized it for what it was.

Offensive grenade, with a coil of notched steel wire inside the casing. Less than three yards away. There was just enough time too wonder at her own lack of fear, *maybe the hormones don't have time to reach my brain,* and then Forrest's back blocked her view as he threw himself onto the thing. The *thump* that followed was hideously muffled, and the man flopped up in a salt spray that spattered across her as high as her lips. Something else struck her, leaving a trail of white fire along one thigh. She clapped a hand to it, felt the blood dribble rather than spout; it could wait.

In seconds the hall had dissolved into chaos. She saw fights starting, the beginning of a surge toward the exits. It was cut-crystal clear; she could see the future fanning out ahead of her, paths like footprints carved in diamond for her to follow. She felt hard, like a thing of machined steel and bearings moving in oil, yet more alive than she could remember, more alive than she had since the day Eddie died. The salt taste of blood on her lips was a sacrament, the checked grip of the 9mm in her hand a caress. Hunter raised the pistol as she walked briskly to the edge of the podium and fired one round into the ceiling even as she keyed the microphone.

"*Silence.*" Not a shout; just loud, and flatly calm. Out of the corner of her eye she saw Jennings vault back onto the platform, leopard-graceful: later. "Sergeant, call to order."

Kowalski jerked, swallowed, looked at the man who had thrown the grenade as he hung immobile in the grip of a dozen troopers. " 'Tent—" his voice cracked. " 'Tent-*hut!*" he shouted.

The milling slowed, troopers looking at each other and remembering they were a unit. Shock aided the process, a groping for the familiar and the comforting. Hunter waited impassive until the last noise ceased.

"Major Forrest is dead. As senior officer, I am now in command in this unit. Any dispute?" She turned slightly; the officers behind her were sinking back into their chairs, hints of thought fighting up through the stunned bewilderment on their faces. All except Jennings. He gave her another of those cat-cool smiles, nodded.

"First order of business. You two; take that ground-sheet and wrap the Major's body, take it in back and lay it out on the table. Move." The two soldiers scrambled to obey. "Bring the prisoner forward."

Willing hands shoved the tech-sergeant into the strip of clear floor before the podium.

"Stand back, you others. Sergeant Willies, you stand accused of attempted murder, murder, and mutiny in time of war. How do you plead?"

The man stood, and a slow trickle of tears ran down his face. He shook his head unspeaking, raised a shaking hand to his face, lowered it. Hunter raised her eyes to the crowd; there was an extra note to their silence now. She could feel it, like a thrumming along her bones, a taste like iron and rust. *Be formal, just a little. Then hit them hard.*

"As commanding officer I hereby pronounce Sergeant Willies guilty of the charges laid. Does anyone speak in this man's defense?" Now even the sound of breathing died; the clatter of the two troopers returning from laying out the dead man's body seemed thunderloud. The spell of leadership was young, frail, a word now could break it. There would be no word; the certainty lifted her like a surfboard on the best wave of the season. She turned to the row behind her. "Show of hands for a guilty verdict, if you please?" They rose in ragged unison.

"Sergeant Willies, you are found guilty of mutiny and the murder of your commanding officer. The sentence is death. Do you have anything to say in your own defense?" The man stood without raising his face, the tears rolling slow and fast across his cheeks. Hunter raised the pistol and fired once; the big Tennessean pitched backward, rattled his heels on the floor and went limp. A trickle of blood soaked out from under his jacket and ran amid the legs of the folding chairs.

"Cover that," she said, pointing to the body. "We will now have a moment of silence in memory of Major Forrest, who gave his life for ours. Greater love has no man than this." *Time to get them thinking, just a little. Time to make them feel their link to each other, part of something greater than their own fears. Give them something to lay the burden of the future on.*

"Right." She holstered the pistol, rested her hands on her belt. "Major Forrest called you all together to give you the intelligence we've gathered and to outline our future course of action. There being no time to waste, we will now continue." Hunter kept her voice metronome-regular. "The United States has effectively ceased to exist."

A gasp; she moved on before the babble of questions could start. "The Soviets were on the verge of collapse a week ago, even before the Central Asian outbreak. They, or some of them, decided to take us with them.

Their attack was launched for our cities and population centers, not military targets." *Which is probably why we're still here.* "The orbital zappers caught most of the ballistic missiles; they didn't get the hypersonic PFH-powered cruise missiles from the submarines just off-shore, or the suitcase bombs, and we think they've hit us with biological weapons as well. If there'd been a few more years . . ." She shrugged. "There wasn't.

"Here are the facts. We estimate half the population is dead. Another half will die before spring; it's going to be a long, hard winter. The temperature is dropping right now. Next year when the snow melts most of the active fallout will be gone, but there won't be any fuel, transport, whatever, left. You all know how close this country was to the breaking point before this happened, though we were on the way back up, maybe. Now it's going to be like Mexico, only a thousand times worse."

She pointed over one shoulder, southwards. "And incidentally, they weren't hit at all. We Border Rangers have held the line; try imagining what it's going to be like *now*."

Hunter paused to let that sink in, saw stark fear on many of the faces below. What had happened to the world was beyond imagining, but these men and women could imagine the Border down and no backup without much trouble. That was a horror that was fully real to them, their subconscious minds had had a chance to assimilate it.

"Some of the deeper shelters have held on, a few units here and there. Two of the orbital platforms made it through. I don't think they're going to find anything but famine and bandits and cucuroaches when they come back. Europe is hit even worse than we are, and so's Japan." She lit a cigarette. "If it's any consolation, the Soviets no longer exist.

"Major Forrest," she continued, "wanted us to make contact with such other units as survived, and aid in rees-tablishing order." Hunter glanced down at the top of her cigarette. "It is my considered opinion, and that of your officers as a whole, that such a course of action would lead to the destruction of this unit. Hands, if you please." This time she did not look behind her. "Nevertheless, we were prepared to follow Major Forrest's orders. The situation is now changed."

She leaned forward and let her voice drop. "We . . . we've been given a *damn* good lesson in what it's like trying to sweep back the ocean with a broom. Now we've got a tidal wave and a whisk."

A trooper came to her feet. "You're saying we're dead meat whatever we do!" Her voice was shrill; Hunter stared at her impassively, until she shuffled her feet, glanced to either side, added: "Ma'am," and sat.

"No. If we break up, yes, we're dead. Dead of radiation sickness, of cold, of plague, shot dead fighting over a can of dogfood."

Hunter raised a finger. "But if we maintain ourselves, as a fighting unit, the 72nd, we have a fighting chance, a *good* fighting chance. As a unit we have assets I doubt anyone on Earth can match. There are more than five hundred of us, with a broad range of skills. We have several dozen PFH-powered warcraft, fuel for decades, repair facilities, weapons that almost nobody outside the US and the Soviet can match, computers. *Most of all, we have organization.*"

She waited again, scanning them. *They're interested. Good.* "I just got through telling you we couldn't make a difference, though, didn't I?" Her hand speared out, the first orator's gesture she had made. "We can't make a difference *here*. Or even survive, unless you count huddling in a cabin in Wyoming and eating bears as survival. And I don't like to ski."

Feeble as it was, that surprised a chuckle out of them. "But we do have those assets I listed; what we need is a place where we can apply them. Where we won't be swamped by numbers and the scale of things. Where we can stand off all comers, try to make a life for ourselves. It won't be easy; we'll have to work and fight for it." The hand stabbed down. *"So what else is new?"*

A cheer, from the row where her old platoon sat. For a moment a warmth invaded the icy certainty beneath her heart, and then she pushed it aside. "A fight we can *win*, for a change. Better work than wasting illig kids and wacko cucuroach cannibals; and we'll be doing it for *ourselves*, not a bunch of fat-assed *citizens* who hide behind our guns and then treat us like hyenas escaped from the zoo!"

That brought them all to their feet, cheering and stamping their feet. The Border Rangers had never been popular with the press; few Rangers wore their uniforms when they went on furlough. Spit, and bags of excrement, sometimes outright murder not being what they had in mind. People with strong family ties avoided the service, or left quickly. She raised her hands for silence and smiled, a slow fierce grin.

"Right, listen up! This isn't going to be a democracy, or a union shop. A committee is the only known animal with more than four legs and no brain. You get just one choice; come along, subject to articles of war and discipline like nothing you've ever known, or get dropped off in a clear zone with a rifle and a week's rations. Which is it?"

Another wave of cheers, and this time there were hats thrown into the air, exultant clinches, a surf-roar of voices. *Hysteria*, she thought. *They'd been half-sure they were all going to die. Then they saw the murder. Now I've offered them a door—and they're charging for it like a herd of buffalo. But they'll remember.*

"I thought so," she said quietly, after the tumult. "We know each other, you and I." Nods and grins and clenched-fist salutes. "Here's what we're going to do, in brief. How many of you know about the Mindanao pirates?" Most of the hands went up. "For those who don't, they got PFH units, hooked them to some old subs and went a 'rovin'. After the Philippines and Indonesia collapsed in '93, they pretty well had their own way. A bunch of them took over a medium-sized island, name of Bali." Good-natured groans. "Yes, I know, some've you have heard a fair bit." She drew on the cigarette.

"But it's perfect for what we want. Big enough to be worthwhile, small enough to hold, with fertile land and a good climate. Isolated, hard to get to except by PFH-powered boost. The people're nice, good farmers and craftsmen, pretty cultured; and they're Hindu, while everyone else in the area's Muslim, like the corsairs who've taken over the place and killed off half the population. And I've seen the Naval intelligence reports; we can take those pirates. We'll be liberators, and afterward they'll still need us. No more than a reasonable amount of butt-kicking needed to keep things going our way." She threw the stub to the floor while the laugh died and straightened.

"Those of you who want to stay and take your chances with the cold, the dark and the looters report to First Sergeant Kowalski. For the rest, we've got work to do. First of all, getting out of here before we all start to glow in the dark. Next stop—a kingdom of our own! Platoon briefings at 1800. Dismiss."

" 'Tent-*hut*," Kowalski barked. Hunter returned their salute crisply, turned and strode off; it was important to make a good exit. Reaction threatened to take her in the corridor beyond, but she forced the ice mantle back. It was not over yet, and the officers were crowding around her.

"See to your people, settle them down, and if you can do it without obvious pressure, push the waverers over to our side. We need *volunteers*, but we need as many as we can get. Staff meeting in two hours; we're getting out tonight, probably stop over at a place I know in Baja for a month or so, pick up some more equipment and recruits. . . . Let's move it."

Then it was her and Jennings. He leaned against the stained cinderblock of the wall with lazy arrogance, stroked a finger across his mustache and smiled that brilliant empty grin.

"Objections, Lieutenant?" Hunter asked.

He mimed applause. "Excellent, Great White Raja-ess to be; your faithful Man Friday here just pantin' to get at those palaces an' mango trees and dancers with the batik sarongs."

Hunter looked him up and down. "You know, Jennings, you have your good points. You're tough, you've got smarts, you're not squeamish, and you can even get troops to follow you." A pause. "Good reflexes, too; you got off that dais as if you could see the grenade coming."

Jennings froze. "Say what?" he asked with soft emphasis. Hunter felt her neck prickle; under the shuck-and-jive act this was a very dangerous man. "You lookin' to have another court-martial?"

She shook her head. "Jennings, you like to play the game. You like to win. Great; I'm just betting that you've got brains as well as smarts, enough to realize that if we start fighting each other it all goes to shit and nobody wins." She stepped closer, enough to smell the clean musk of the younger soldier's presence, see the slight tensing of the small muscles around his lips. Her finger reached out to prod gently into his chest.

"Forrest was tough and smart too; but he had one fatal handicap. He was Old Corps all the way, a man of honor." There was enjoyment in her smile, but no humor. "Maybe I would have gone along with his Custer's Last Stand plan . . . maybe not. Just remember this; while he was living in the Big Green Machine, *I* was a street cop. I've been busting scumbags ten times badder than you since about the time you sold your first nickel bag. Clear, Holmes?"

He reached down with one finger and slowly pushed hers away. "So I be a good darky, or you whup my nigger ass?"

"Anytime, Jennings. Anytime. Because we've got a job to do, and we can't get it done if we're playing head-games. And I *intend* to get it done."

The silence went on a long moment until the Lieutenant fanned off a salute. "Like you say, Your Exaltedness. Better a piece of the pie than an empty plate. I'm yours."

She returned the salute. *For now*, went unspoken between them as the man turned away. Hunter watched him go, and for a moment the weight of the future crushed at her shoulders.

Then the Ranger laughed, remembering a beach, and the moon casting a silver road across the water. "You said I was fit to be a queen, Eddie," she whispered softly. "It's something to do, hey? And they say the first monarch was a lucky soldier. Why not me?"

The future started with tonight; a battalion lift was going to mean some careful juggling; there would be no indenting for stores at the other end. *But damned if I'll leave my Enya disks behind*, she thought, *or a signed first edition of* Prince of Sparta.

"Raja-ess," she murmured. "I'll have to work on that." She was humming as she strode toward her room. Sleet began to pound against the walls, like a roll of drums.

"Amateurs talk strategy. Professionals talk logistics." War is also an exchange of modulated energies; preindustrial war, like preindustrial civilization, ran on solar energy concentrated through the medium of human sweat. Organization and technique facilitated the inward, counter-entropic flow and then dissipated it in combat and the frictional losses of war. As late as the era of the Emperor Napoleon, an army could live off the land it passed through: grain for the men, fodder for the horses—and famine for the civilians. A long war or a big war could kill off half or more of the rural population, not through deliberate slaughter but simply through hunger and the spread of infectious disease among hunger-weakened peasants and artisans. The Thirty Years War in the 17th century reduced the population of many regions of Germany by that amount, and it took two centuries to recover.

By making armies dependent on mechanical transport and factory-made equipment, the Industrial Revolution has made war too a parasite on the stored solar-fusion energy of fossil fuels. This has made armies less of a direct parasite on the lands through which they pass; Germany recovered from the devastations of the Second World War in a single decade. Unfortunately, high-energy technology has also made armies much more directly destructive, by increasing the concentrated energy they may discharge. A fusion-powered military technology would be freed of the huge supply lines Industrial Age armies require; since the internal combustion engine, the pace of war has largely depended on the amount of petroleum available. Fusion would free the warrior from the supply clerk. But the organization of war, the bureaucratic hierarchies, are themselves a form of concentration of energy. Pure warriors, undirected by a guiding mind, are simply agents of entropy.

Herewith an illustration of these eternal verities by a writer with a firm grasp of history—and of war . . .

The Warrior
David Drake

The tribarrel in the cupola of *Warrior*, the tank guarding the northwest quadrant of Hill 541 North, snarled in automatic air defense mode. The four Slammers in Lieutenant Lindgren's bunker froze.

Sergeant Samuel "Slick" Des Grieux, *Warrior's* commander, winced. He was twenty-one standard years old, and a hardened veteran of two years in Hammer's Slammers. He kneaded his broad, powerful hands together to control his anger at being half a kay away from where he ought to have been: aboard his vehicle and fighting.

The incoming shell thudded harmlessly, detonated in the air.

Sergeant Broglie had counted out the time between the tribarrel's burst and the explosion. "Three seconds," he murmured.

The shell had been a safe kilometer away when it went off. The howl of its passage to an intersection with *Warrior's* bolts echoed faintly through the night.

"Every five minutes," said Hawes, the fourth man in the bunker and by far the greenest. This was the first time Hawes had been under prolonged bombardment.

The way he twitched every time a gun fired indicated how little he liked the experience. "I wish they'd—"

Lieutenant Lindgren's tank, *Queen City*, fired a five-round burst. Cyan light shuddered through the bunker's dogleg entrance. A pair of shells, probably fired from the Republican batteries on Hill 661 to the northeast, crumped well short of their target.

"*Via*, Lieutenant!" Des Grieux said in a desperate voice. He stared at his hands, because he was afraid of what he might blurt if he looked straight at the young officer. "Look, I oughta be back on *Warrior*. Anything you gotta say, you can say over the commo, it's secure. And—"

He couldn't help it. His face came up. His voice grew as hard as his cold blue eyes, and he continued. "Besides, we're not here to talk. We oughta be kicking ass. That's what we're here for."

"We're here—" Lindgren began.

"We're the Federals' artillery defense, Slick," Broglie said, smiling at Des Grieux. Broglie didn't shout, but his voice flattened the lieutenant's words anyway. "*And* their backbone. We're doing our job, so no sweat, hey?"

"Our job . . ." said Des Grieux softly. *Warrior* fired three short bursts, blasting a salvo inbound from the Republicans on Hill 504. Des Grieux ignored the sound and its implications. ". . . is to fight. Not to hide in holes. Hey, Luke?"

Broglie was four centimeters shorter than Des Grieux and about that much broader across the shoulders. He wasn't afraid of Des Grieux . . . which interested Des Grieux because it was unusual, though it didn't bother him in the least.

Des Grieux wasn't afraid of anyone or anything.

"We're here to see that Hill 541 North holds out till the relieving force arrives," said Lindgren.

He'd taken Broglie's interruption as a chance to get his emotions under control. The lieutenant was almost as nervous as Hawes, but he was a Slammers officer and determined to act like one. "The AAD in the vehicles does that as well as we could sitting in the turrets, Slick," he continued, "and unit meetings are important to remind us that we're a platoon, not four separate tanks stuck off in West Bumfuck."

"North Bumfuck fiver-four-one," Broglie chuckled.

Broglie's face held its quizzical smile, but the low sound of his laughter was drowned by incoming shells and the tanks' response to them. This was a sustained pounding from all three Republican gun positions: Hills 504 and 661 to the north, and Hill 541 South ten kilometers southeast of the Federal base.

The Reps fired thirty or forty shells in less than a minute. Under the tribarrels' lash, the explosions merged into a drumming roar—punctuated by the sharp *crash* of the round that got through.

The bunker rocked. Dust drifted down from the sandbagged roof. Hawes rubbed his hollow eyes and pretended not to have heard the blast.

The sound of the salvoes died away. One of the Federal garrison screamed nearby. Des Grieux wasn't sure whether the man was wounded or simply broken by the constant hammering. The unanswered shelling got to him, too; but it made him want to go out and kill, not hide in a bunker and scream.

"Lieutenant," Des Grieux said in the same measured, deadly voice as before. "We oughta go out and nail the bastards. *That's* how we can save these Federal pussies."

"The relieving force—" Lindgren said.

"The relieving force hasn't gotten here in three weeks, so they aren't exactly burning up the road, now, are they?" Des Grieux said. "Look—"

"They'll get here," said Broglie. "They've got Major Howes and three of our companies with 'em, so they'll get here. And we'll wait it out, because that's what Colonel Hammer ordered us to do."

Lindgren opened his mouth to speak, but he closed it again and let the tank commanders argue the question. Des Grieux didn't even pretend to care what a newbie lieutenant thought. As for Broglie—

Sergeant Lucas Broglie was more polite, and Broglie appreciated the value of Lindgren's education from the Military Academy of Nieuw Friesland. But Broglie didn't much care what a newbie lieutenant thought, either.

"I didn't say we ought to bug out," Des Grieux said. His eyes were as open and empty as a cannon's bore. "I said we could *win* this instead of sitting on our butts."

Open and empty and deadly . . .

"Four tanks can't take on twenty thousand Reps," Broglie said. His smile was an equivalent of Des Grieux's blank stare: the way Broglie's face formed itself when the mind beneath was under stress.

He swept an arc with his thumb. The bunker was too strait to allow him to make a full-arm gesture. "That's what they got out there. Twenty thousand of them."

The ground shook from another shell that got through the tribarrels' defensive web. Des Grieux was so concentrated on Broglie that his mind had tuned out the ripping bursts that normally would have focused him utterly.

"It's not just us 'n them," Des Grieux said. Lindgren and Hawes, sitting on ammunition boxes on opposite sides of the bunker, swivelled their heads from one veteran to the other like spectators at a tennis match. "There's five, six thousand Federals on this crap pile with us, and they can't like it much better than I do."

"They're not—" Lieutenant Lindgren began.

Cyan light flickered through the bunker entrance. A Republican sniper, not one of the Slammers' weapons. The Reps had a few powerguns, and Hill 661 was high enough that a marksman could slant his bolts into the Federal position.

The *snap!* of the bolt impacting made Lindgren twitch. Des Grieux's lips drew back in a snarl, because if he'd been in his tank he just *might* have put paid to the bastard.

"Not line soldiers," the lieutenant concluded in an artificially calm tone.

"They'd fight if they had somebody to lead them," Des

Grieux said. "Via, anything's better 'n being wrapped up here and used for Rep target practice."

"They've got a leader," Broglie replied, "and it's General Wycherly, not us. For what he's worth."

Des Grieux grimaced as though he'd been kicked. Even Hawes snorted.

"I don't believe you appreciate the constraints that General Wycherly operates under," Lindgren said in a thin voice.

Lindgren knew how little his authority was worth to the veterans. That, as well as a real awareness of the Federal commander's difficulties, injected a note of anger into his tone. "He's outnumbered three or four to one," he went on. "Ten to one, if you count just the real combat troops under his command. But he's holding his position as ordered. And that's *just* what we're going to help him do."

"We're pieces of a puzzle, Slick," said Broglie. He relaxed enough to rub his lips, massaging them out of the rictus into which the discussion had cramped them. "Wycherly's job is to keep from getting overrun; our job's to help him; and our people with the relieving force 're going to kick the cop outa the Reps if we just hold 'em a few days more."

Another incoming shell detonated a kilometer short of Hill 541 North. The Republicans knew they couldn't do serious physical damage so long as the position was guarded by the Slammers' tanks ... but they knew as well the psychological effect the constant probing fire had on the defenders.

For an instant Broglie's hard smile was back. "Or not a puzzle," he added. "A gun. Every part has to do the right job, or the gun doesn't work."

"Okay, we had our unit meeting," Des Grieux said. He squeezed his hands together so fiercely that his fingers were dark with trapped blood between the first and second joints. "Now can I get back to my tank where I can maybe do some good?"

"The AAD does everything that can be done, Sergeant," Lindgren said. "That's what we need now. That and discipline."

Des Grieux stood up, though he had to bend forward to clear the bunker's low ceiling. "Having the computer fire my guns," he said with icy clarity, "is like jacking off. With respect."

Lindgren grimaced. "All right," he said. "You're all dismissed."

In an attempt to soften the previous exchange, he added, "There shouldn't be more than a few days of this."

But Des Grieux, ignoring the incoming fire, was already out of the bunker.

A howitzer fired from the center of the Federal position. The night outside the bunker glowed with the bottle-shaped yellow flash. There were fifteen tubes in the Federal batteries, but they were short of ammunition and rarely fired.

When they did, they invariably brought down a storm of Republican counterfire.

Des Grieux continued to walk steadily in the direction of *Warrior*; his tank, his home.

Not his reason for existence, though. Des Grieux existed to rip the enemy up one side and down the other. To do that he could use *Warrior*, or the pistol in his holster, or his teeth; whatever was available. Lieutenant Lindgren was robbing Des Grieux of his reason for existence. . . .

He heard the scream of the shell—one round, from the northwest. He waited for the sky-tearing sound of *Warrior*'s tribarrel firing a short burst of cyan plasma, copper nuclei stripped of their electron shells and ravening downrange to detonate or vaporize the shell.

Warrior didn't fire.

The Reps had launched a ground-hugging missile from the lower altitude of Hill 504. *Warrior* and the other Slammers' tanks couldn't engage the round because they were dug in behind the bunker line encircling the Federal positions. The incoming missile would not rise into the line-of-sight range of the powerguns until—

There was a scarlet streak from the horizon like a vector marker in the dark bowl of the sky. A titanic crash turned the sky orange and knocked Des Grieux down. Sandy red dust sucked up and rolled over, forming a doughnut that expanded across the barren hilltop.

Des Grieux got to his feet and resumed walking. The bastards couldn't make him run, and they couldn't make him bend over against the sleet of shell fragments which would rip him anyway—running or walking, cowering or standing upright like a man.

The Republicans fired a dozen ordinary rounds. Tank tribarrels splashed each of the shells a fraction of a second after they arched into view. The powerguns' snarling dazzle linked the Federal base for an instant to orange fireballs which faded into rags of smoke. There were no more ground-huggers.

An ordinary shell was no more complex than a hand grenade. Ground-hugging missiles required sophisticated electronics and a fairly complex propulsion system. There weren't many of them in the Rep stockpiles.

Ground-huggers would be as useless as ballistic projectiles *if* Lindgren used his platoon the way tanks should be used, as weapons that sought out the enemy instead of cowering turret-down in defilade.

Blood and Martyrs! What a way to fight a war.

The top of Hill 541 North was a barren moonscape. The bunkers were improvised by the troops themselves with shovels and sandbags. A month ago, the position had been merely the supply point for a string of Federal outposts. No one expected a siege.

But when the Republicans swept down in force, the outposts scrambled into their common center, 541N. Troops dug furiously as soon as they realized that there was no further retreat until Route 7 to the south was cleared from the outside.

If route 7 was cleared. Task Force Howes, named for

the CO of the Slammers 2nd Battalion, had promised a link-up within three days.

Every day for the past two weeks.

A sniper on Hill 661, twelve kilometers away, fired his powergun. The bolt snapped fifty meters from Des Grieux, fusing the sandy soil into a disk of glass which shattered instantly as it cooled.

Kuykendall, *Warrior*'s driver, should be in the tank turret. If Des Grieux had been manning the guns, the sniper would have had a hot time of it ... but Des Grieux was walking back from a dick-headed meeting, and Kuykendall wasn't going to disobey orders to leave the tribarrel on Automatic Air Defense and not, under any circumstances, to fire the 20 CM main gun since ammunition was scarce.

The garrison of Hill 541N, the Slammers included, had the supplies they started the siege with. Ground routes were blocked. Aerial resupply would be suicide because of the Rep air-defense arsenal on the encircling hills.

The sniper fired again. The bolt hit even farther away, but he was probably aiming at Des Grieux anyhow. Nothing else moved on this side of the encampment except swirls of wind-blown sand.

A shell fragment the size of a man's palm stuck up from the ground. It winked jaggedly in the blue light of the bolt.

Warrior was within a hundred meters. Des Grieux continued to walk deliberately.

The hilltop's soil blurred all the vehicles and installations into identical dinginess. The dirt was a red without life, the hue of old blood that had dried and flaked to powder.

The sniper gave up. A gun on 541S coughed a shell which Broglie's *Honey Girl* blew from the sky a moment later.

Every five minutes; but not regularly, and twice the Reps had banged out more than a thousand rounds in a day, some of which inevitably got through. . . .

"That you, Slick?" Kuykendall called from the *Warrior*'s cupola.

"Yeah, of course it's me," Des Grieux replied. He stepped onto a sandbag lip, then hopped down to *Warrior*'s back deck. His boots clanked.

The tanks were dug in along sloping ramps. Soil from the trenches filled sandbag walls rising above the vehicles' cupolas. Lieutenant Lindgren was afraid that powerguns from 661—and the Reps had multi-barreled calliopes to provide artillery defense—would rake the Slammers' tanks if the latter were visible.

Des Grieux figured the answer to *that* threat was to kick the Reps the hell off Hill 661. By now, though, he'd learned that the other Slammers were just going to sigh and look away when he made a suggestion that didn't involve waiting for somebody else to do the fighting.

Kuykendall slid down from the cupola into the fighting compartment. She was a petite woman, black-haired and a good enough driver. To Des Grieux, Kuykendall was a low-key irritation that he had to work around, like a burr in the mechanism that controlled his turret's rotation.

A driver was a necessary evil, because Des Grieux couldn't guide his tank and fight it at the same time. Kuykendall took orders, but she had a personality of her own. She wasn't a mere extension of Des Grieux's will, and that made her more of a problem than someone blander though less competent would have been.

Nothing he couldn't work around, though. There *was* nothing Des Grieux couldn't work around, if his superiors just gave him the chance to do his job.

"Anything new?" Kuykendall asked.

Des Grieux stood on his seat so that he could look out over the sandbags toward Hill 661. "What d' you think?" he said. He switched the visual display on his helmet visor to infra-red and cranked up the magnification.

The sniper had gone home. Nothing but ripples in the atmosphere and the cooler blue of trees transpiring water they sucked somehow from this Lordblasted landscape.

Des Grieux climbed out of the hatch again. He shoved

a sandbag off the top layer. *The bastard would be back, and when he was ...*

He pushed away another sandbag. The bags were woven from a coarse synthetic that smelled like burning tar when it rubbed.

"We're not supposed to do that," Kuykendall said from the cupola. "A lucky shot could put the tribarrel out of action. That'd hurt us a lot worse than a hundred dead grunts does the Reps."

"They don't have a hundred powerguns," Des Grieux said without turning around. He pushed at the second-layer sandbag he'd uncovered but that layer was laid as headers. The bags to right and left resisted the friction on their long sides. "Anyway, it's worth something to me to give a few of those cocky bastards their lunch."

Hawes' *Susie Q* ripped the sky. Des Grieux dropped into a crouch, then rose again with a feeling of embarrassment. He knew that Kuykendall had seen him jump.

It wasn't flinching. If *Warrior*'s AAD sensed incoming from Hill 661, Des Grieux would either duck instantly—or have his head shot off by the tribarrel of his own tank. The fire-direction computers didn't care if there was a man in the way when it needed to do its job.

Des Grieux liked the computer's attitude.

He lifted and pushed, raising his triceps muscles into stark ridges. Des Grieux was thin and from a distance looked frail. Close up, no one noticed anything but his eyes; and there was no weakness in them.

The sandbag slid away. The slot in *Warrior*'s protection gave Des Grieux a keyhole through which to rake Hill 661 with his tribarrel. He got back into the turret. Kuykendall dropped out of the way without further comment.

"You know ..." Des Grieux said as he viewed the enemy positions in the tribarrel's holographic sight. *Warrior*'s sensors were several orders of magnitude better than those of the tankers' unaided helmets. "The Reps aren't much better at this than these Federal pussies we gotta nursemaid."

"How d'ye mean?" Kuykendall asked.

Her voice came over the intercom channel. She'd slipped back into the driver's compartment. Most drivers found the internal hatch too tight for use in anything less than a full buttoned-up emergency.

"They've got calliopes up there," Des Grieux explained as he scanned the bleak silence of Hill 661. The Republican positions were in defilade. Easy enough to arrange from their greater height.

"If it was me," Des Grieux continued, "I'd pick my time and roll 'em up to direct-fire positions. They'd kick the cop outa this place."

"They're not going to bet three-CM calliopes against tank main guns, Sarge," Kuykendall said carefully.

"They would if they had any balls," Des Grieux said. His voice was coldly judgmental, stating the only truth there was. He showed no anger toward those who were too stupid to see it. "Dug in like we are, they could blow away the cupolas and our sensor arrays before we even got the main guns to bear. A calliope's no joke, kid."

He laughed harshly. "Wish they'd try, though. I can hip-shoot a main gun if I have to."

"There's talk they're going to try t' overrun us before Task Force Howes relieves us," Kuykendall said with the guarded nonchalance she always assumed when talking to the tank commander.

Des Grieux's two years in the Slammers made him a veteran, but he was scarcely one of the longest-serving members of the regiment. His drive, his skill with weapons, and the phenomenal ruthlessness with which he accomplished any task set him gave Des Grieux a reputation beyond simple seniority.

"There's talk," Des Grieux said coldly. *Nothing moved on Hill 661.* "There's been talk. There's been talk Howes is going to get his thumbs out of his butt and relieve us, too."

The tribarrel roused, swung, and ignited the sky with a four-round burst of plasma. A shell from Hill 504 broke apart without detonating. The largest piece of casing was still a white glow when it tumbled out of sight in the valley below.

The sky flickered to the south as well, but at such a distance that the sounds faded to a low rumble. Task Force Howes still slugged it out with the Republicans who defended Route 7. Maybe they were going to get here within seventy-two hours.

And maybe Hell was going to freeze over.

Des Grieux scanned Hill 661, and nothing moved.

The only thing Des Grieux knew in the instant he snapped awake from a sound sleep was that it was time to earn his pay.

Kuykendall looked down into the fighting compartment from the commander's seat. "Sarge?" she said. "I—" and broke off when she realized Des Grieux was already alert.

"Get up front 'n drive," Des Grieux ordered curtly. "It's happening."

"It's maybe nothing," the driver said, but she knew Des Grieux. As Kuykendall spoke, she swung her legs out of the cupola. Hopping from the cupola and past the main gun was the fastest way to the driver's hatch in the bow. The tank commander blocked the internal passage anyway as he climbed up to his seat.

The Automatic Air Defense plate on *Warrior*'s control panel switched from yellow, standby, to red. The tribarrel rotated and fired. Des Grieux flicked the plate with his boot toe as he went past, disconnecting the computer-controlled defensive fire. He needed *Warrior*'s weapons under his personal direction now that things were real.

When the siege began, Lieutenant Lindgren ordered that one member of each two-man tank crew be on watch in the cupola at every moment. What the tankers did off-duty, and where they slept, was their own business.

Most of the off-duty troops slept beneath their vehicles, entering the plenum chamber through the access plate in the steel skirts. The chambers were roomy and better protection than anything cobbled together by shovels and sandbags could be. The only problem was the awareness before sleep came that the tank above you weighed 170 tonnes ... but tankers tended not to be people who thought in those terms.

Lindgren insisted on a bunker next to his vehicle. He was sure that he would go mad if his whole existence, on-duty and off, was bounded by the steel and iridium shell of his tank.

Des Grieux went the other way around. He slept in the fighting compartment while his driver kept watch in the cupola above. The deck was steel pressed with grip rosettes. He couldn't stretch out. His meter-ninety of height had to twist between the three-screen control console and the armored tube which fed ammunition to the autoloading twenty-CM main gun.

Nobody called the fighting compartment a comfortable place to sleep; but then, nobody called Des Grieux sane, either.

A storm of Republican artillery fire screamed toward Hill 541N. Some of the shells would have gotten through even if Des Grieux had left *Warrior* in the defensive net. That was somebody else's problem. The Reps didn't have terminally-guided munitions that would target the Slammers' tanks, so a shell that hit *Warrior* was the result of random chance.

You had to take chances in war; and anyway, *Warrior* oughta shrug off anything but a heavy-caliber armor-piercing round with no more than superficial damage.

Kuykendall switched her fans on and brought them up to speed fast with their blades cutting the airstream at minimum angle. *Warrior* trembled with what Des Grieux anthropomorphicized as eagerness, transferring his own emotions to the mindless machine he commanded.

A Slammers' tank was a slope-sided iridium hull whose turret, smooth to avoid shot traps, held a twenty-CM powergun. The three-barreled automatic weapon in the cupola could operate independently or be locked to the same point of aim as the main gun. Eight intake ducts pierced the upper surface of the hull, feeding air down to drive fans in armored nacelles below.

At rest, the tanks sat on their steel skirts. When the vehicles were under way, they floated on a cushion of air pressurized by the fans. At full throttle, the power required to drive a tank was enormous, and the fusion bottle which provided that power filled the rear third of the hull.

The tanks were hideously expensive. Their electronics were so complex and sensitive that at least a small portion of every tank's suite was deadlined at any one time. The hulls and running gear were rugged, but the vehicles' own size and weight imposed stresses which required constant maintenance.

When they worked, and to the extent they worked, the Slammers' tanks were the most effective weapons in the human universe. As *Warrior* was about to prove to two divisions of Republican infantry. . . .

"Back her out!" Des Grieux ordered. If he'd thought about it, he would have sounded a general alarm because he *knew* this was a major attack, but he had other things on his mind besides worrying about people he wasn't planning to kill.

"Booster," Des Grieux said, switching on the artificial intelligence which controlled the tank's systems. "Enemy activity, one kay, now!"

Warrior shuddered as Kuykendall increased the fan bite. Sandy soil mushroomed from the trench walls and upward as the hull lifted and air leaked beneath *Warrior*'s skirts. Des Grieux's direct vision blurred in a gritty curtain, but the data his AI assembled from remote sensors was sharp and clear in the upper half of his helmet visor.

The ground fell away from the top of Hill 541 North in a 1:3 slope, and the tank positions were set well back from the edge of the defenses. Even when *Warrior* backed from her trench, Des Grieux would not be able to see the wire and minefields which the garrison had laid at mid-slope to stop an enemy assault.

Ideally, the tanks would have access to the Slammers' own remote sensors. Conditions were rarely ideal, and on Hill 541N they never even came close. Still, the Federals had emplaced almost a hundred seismic and acoustic sensors before the Republicans tightened the siege. Most of the sensors were in the wire, but they'd dropped a few in the swales surrounding the hill, a kilometer or so out from the hilltop.

Acoustic sensors gathered the sound of voices and equipment, while seismic probes noted the vibration feet and vehicles made in the soil. The information, flawed by the sensors' relative lack of sophistication and the haphazard way the units were emplaced, was transmitted to the hilltop for processing.

Des Grieux didn't know what the Feds did with the raw data, but *Warrior's* AI turned it into a clear image of a major Republican attack.

There were two thrusts, directed against the east and the northwest quadrants of the Federal positions. The slope at those angles was slightly steeper than it was to the south, but the surface fell in a series of shallow steps that formed dead zones, out of the fire from hilltop bunkers.

A siren near the Federal command post wound up. Its wail was almost lost in the shriek of incoming.

The Reps had ten or a dozen shells in the air at any one time. The three tanks still working air defense slashed arcs across the sky. Powerguns detonated much of the incoming during its fifteen-second flight time, but every minute or so a round got through.

Most of the hits raised geysers of sand from the hilltop. Only occasionally did a bunker collapse or a shellburst scythe down troops running toward fighting positions in the forward trenches, but even misses shook the defenders' morale.

Booster thought the attack on the northwest quadrant was being made by a battalion of infantry, roughly 500 troops, behind a screen of sappers no more than a hundred strong. The eastern thrust was of comparable size, but even so it seemed a ludicrously small force to throw against a garrison of over 5,000 men.

That was only the initial assault; a larger force would get in its own way during the confusion of a night attack. Booster showed several additional battalions and a dozen light armored vehicles waiting in reserve among the yellow-brown scrub of the valleys where streams would run in the wet season.

As soon as the leading elements seized a segment of the outer bunker line in a classic infiltration assault, the Republican support troops would advance in good order and sweep across the hilltop. There was no way in hell that the Federal infantry, demoralized by weeks of unanswerable shelling, was going to stop the attack.

They didn't have to. Not while Des Grieux was here.

"Clear visor," Des Grieux said. He'd seen what the sensors gave him, and he didn't need the display anymore. He tugged the crash bar, dropping his seat into the fighting compartment and buttoning the hatch shut above him. *Warrior*'s three holographic screens cast their glow across conduits and the breech of the squat main gun.

"Driver, advance along marked vector."

Default on the left-hand screen was a topographic display. Des Grieux drew his finger across it in a curving arc, down from the hilltop in a roughly northwestward direction. The AI would echo the display in Kuykendall's compartment. A trackway, not precisely a road but good enough for the Rep vehicles and sure as *hell* good enough for *Warrior*, wound north from the swale in the direction of the Republican firebase on Hill 504.

"Gun it!" Des Grieux snarled. "Keep your foot on the throttle, bitch!"

It didn't occur to him that there was another way to give the order. All Des Grieux knew was that *Warrior* had to move as he desired, and the commander's will alone was not enough to direct the vehicle.

Kuykendall touched *Warrior* to the ground, rubbing off some of the backing inertia against the sand. She rotated the attitude control of the drive fans, angling the nacelles so that they thrust *Warrior* forward as well as lifting it again onto the air cushion.

The huge tank slid toward the edge of the encampment in front of a curling billow of dust. Size made the vehicle seem to accelerate slowly.

"Oyster Leader to Oyster Two," said Lieutenant Lindgren over the platoon's commo channel. "Hold your position. Break. Oyster four—" Hawes "—moveup to support Oyster Two. Over."

The note of *Warrior*'s fans changed. Massive inertia would keep the vehicle gliding forward for a hundred meters, but the sound meant Kuykendall was obeying the platoon leader's orders.

"Driver!" Des Grieux shouted. "Roll it! *Now!*"

Kuykendall adjusted her nacelles obediently. *Warrior* slid on momentum between a pair of bunkers as the fans swung to resume their forward thrust.

The Federal positions were dugouts covered by transportation pallets supported by a single layer of sandbags. Three or four additional sandbag layers supplied overhead protection, though a direct hit would crumple the strongest of them. The firing slits were so low that muzzle blasts kicked up sand to shroud the red flashes of their machineguns.

Warrior's sensors fed the main screen with a light-enhanced 120° arc to the front. The tank's AI added in a stereoscopic factor to aid depth perception which the human brain ordinarily supplied in part from variations in light intensity.

The screen provided Des Grieux with a clear window onto the Republican attack. A two-man buzzbomb team rose into firing position at the inner edge of the wire. Instead of launching their unguided rockets into the nearest bunkers, they had waited for the tank they expected.

Des Grieux expected them also. He stunned the night with a bolt from *Warrior*'s main gun.

Des Grieux used his central display for gunnery. It had

two orange pippers, a two-CM ring and a one-CM dot for the main gun and tribarrel respectively. The sensor array mounted around *Warrior*'s cupola gave Des Grieux the direction in which to swing his weapon. As soon as his tank rose into a hull-down position that cleared the twenty-CM powergun, he toggled the foot trip.

Because the tribarrel was mounted higher, Des Grieux could have killed the Reps a moment sooner with the automatic weapon; but he wanted the enemy's first awareness of *Warrior* to be the cataclysmic blast of the tank's main gun.

The cyan bolt struck one of the Rep team squarely and converted his body into a ball of vapor so hot that its glowing shockwave flung the other victim's torso and limbs away in separate trajectories. The secondary explosion of the anti-tank warheads was lost in the plasma charge's flash*crash*.

Honking through its intakes, *Warrior* thundered down on the Republican attack.

Guns in dozens of Federal bunkers fired white tracers toward the perimeter of mines and wire. Heavy automatic weapons among the Republican support battalions answered with chains of glowing red balls.

The Federal artillerymen in the center of Hill 541 North began slamming out their remaining ammunition in the reasonable view that unless this attack was stopped, there was no need for conservation. Because of their hilltop location, the guns could not bear on the sappers. To reach even the Republican support troops, they had to lob their shells in high, inaccurate arcs. The pair of calliopes on Hill 661 burst many of the Federal rounds at the top of their trajectory.

Instead of becoming involved in firefights, the Rep sappers did an excellent job of pathclearing for the main assault force. A few of the sappers fell, but their uniforms of light-absorbent fabric made them difficult targets even now that Federal starshells popped to throw wavering illumination over the scene.

A miniature rocket dragged its train of explosive across

the perimeter defenses. The line exploded with a yellow flash and a sound like a door slamming. Sand and wire flew to either side. Overpressure set off a dozen anti-personnel mines to speckle the night.

There were already a dozen similar gaps in the perimeter. An infiltration team had wormed through the defenses before the alarm went off. One of its members hurled a satchel charge into a bunker, collapsing it with a flash and a roar.

Warrior drove into the wire. Bullets, some of them fired from the Federal bunkers, pinged harmlessly on the iridium armor. A buzzbomb trailing sparks and white smoke snarled toward the tank's right flank. Five meters out, the automatic defense system along the top edge of *Warrior*'s skirts banged. Its spray of steel pellets ripped the buzzbomb and set off the warhead prematurely.

The tank rang like a bell when its defensive array fired, but the hollow *whoomp* of the shaped-charge warhead was lost in the battle's general clamor. Shards of buzzbomb casing knocked down a sapper. He thrashed through several spasms before he lay still.

Warrior passed the Federal minefield in a series of sprouting explosions and the spang of fragments which ricocheted from the skirts. The pressure of air within the tank's plenum chamber was high enough to detonate mines rigged to blow off a man's foot. They clanged harmlessly as a tocsin of the huge vehicle's passage.

The tank's bow slope snagged loops of concertina wire which stretched and writhed until it broke. Republican troops threw themselves down to avoid the unexpected whips of hooked steel. Men shouted curses, although the gap *Warrior* tore in the perimeter defenses was broad enough to pass a battalion in columns of sixteen.

Des Grieux ignored the sappers. They could cause confusion within the bunker line, but they were no threat to the ultimate existence of the Federal base. The assault battalion, and still more the thousands of Republican troops waiting in reserve, were another matter.

Warrior had two dual-capable gunnery joysticks. Most

tank commanders used only one, selecting tribarrel or main gun with the thumbswitch. Des Grieux shot with both hands.

He'd pointed the main gun 30° to starboard in order to blast the team of tank killers. Now his left hand swung the cupola tribarrel a few degrees to port. He didn't change either setting again for the moment. Not even Des Grieux's degree of skill permitted him to aim two separate sights from a gun platform travelling at fifty KPH and still accelerating.

But he could fire them, alternately or together, whenever *Warrior*'s forward motion slid the pippers over targets.

The tribarrel caught a squad moving up at a trot to exploit pathways the sappers had torn. The Republicans were so startled by the bellowing monster that they forgot to throw themselves down.

Three survivors turned and fired their rifles vainly as the tank roared past fifty meters away. The rest of the squad were dead, with the exception of the lieutenant leading them. He stood, shrilling insane parodies of signals on his whistle. The tribarrel had blown off both his arms.

Des Grieux's right thumb fired the main gun at another ragged line of Republican infantry. The twenty-CM bolt gouged the earth ten meters short, but its energy sprayed the sandy soil across the troops as a shower of molten glass. One of the victims continued to pirouette in agony until white tracers from a Federal machinegun tore most of his chest away.

Fires lighted by the cyan bolts flared across the arid landscape.

Hawes in *Susie Q* tried to follow. His tribarrel slashed out a long burst. Sappers jumped and ran. Two of them stumbled into mines and upended in sprays of soil.

Susie Q eased forward at a walking pace. Hawes' driver was proceeding cautiously under circumstances where speed was the only hope of survival. Halfway to the wire, a buzzbomb passed in front of the tank. It was so badly aimed that the automatic defense system didn't trip.

Susie Q braked and began to turn. Hawes sprayed the slope wildly with his tribarrel. A stray bolt blew a trench across *Warrior's* back deck.

A Rep sapper ran toward *Susie Q's* blind side with a satchel charge in his hands. The automatic defense system blasted him when he was five yards away, but two more buzzbombs arced over his crumpled body.

The section of the ADS which had killed the sapper was out of service until its strip charge could be replaced. The rockets hit, one in the hull and the other in the center of *Susie Q's* turret. Iridium reflected the warheads' white glare.

The tank grounded violently. The thick skirt crumpled as it bulldozed a ripple of soil. *Susie Q's* status entry on *Warrior's* right-hand display winked from solid blue to cross-hatched, indicating that an electrical fault had depowered several major systems.

Des Grieux ignored the read-out. He had a battle to win.

Under other circumstances, Des Grieux would have turned to port or starboard to sweep up one flank of the assault wave, but the Republican reserves were too strong. Turning broadside to their fire was a quick way to die. Winning—surviving—required him to keep the enemy off-balance.

Warrior bucked over the irregular slope, but the guns were stabilized in both elevation and traverse. Des Grieux lowered the hollow pipper onto the swale half a kilometer away, where the Republican supports sheltered.

Several of the armored cars there raked the tank with their automatic cannon. Explosive bullets whanged loudly on the iridium.

Des Grieux set *Warrior's* turret to rotate at 1° per second and stepped on the foot-trip. The main gun began to fire as quickly as the system could reload itself. Cyan hell broke loose among the packed reserves.

The energy liberated by a single twenty-CM bolt was

so great that dry brush several meters away from each impact burst into flames. Infantrymen leaped to their feet, colliding in wild panic as they tried to escape the sudden fires.

An armored car took a direct hit. Its diesel fuel boomed outward in a huge fireball which engulfed the vehicles to either side. Crewmen baled out of one of the cars before it exploded. Their clothes were alight, and they collapsed a few steps from their vehicle.

The other car spouted plumes of multi-colored smoke. Marking grenades had ignited inside the turret hatch, broiling the commander as he tried to climb past them. Ammunition cooked off in a flurry of sparks and red tracers.

While *Warrior*'s main gun cycled its twenty-round ready magazine into part of the Republican reserves, Des Grieux aimed his tribarrel at specific targets to port. The tank's speed was seventy KPH and still accelerating. When the bow slid over the slope's natural terracing, it spilled air from the plenum chamber. Each time, *Warrior*'s 170 tonnes slammed onto the skirts with the inevitability of night following day.

Though the tribarrel was stabilized, the crew was not. The impacts jounced Des Grieux against his seat restraints and blurred his vision.

It didn't matter. Under these circumstances, Des Grieux scarcely needed the sights. He *knew* when the pipper covered a clot of infantry or an armored car reversing violently to escape what the crew suddenly realized was a kill zone.

Two-CM bolts lacked the authority of *Warrior*'s main gun, but Des Grieux's short bursts cut with surgical precision. Men flew apart in cyan flashes. The thin steel hulls of armored cars blazed white for an instant before the fuel and ammunition inside caught fire as well. Secondary explosions lit the night as tribarrel bolts detonated cases of rocket and mortar warheads.

Warrior's drive fans howled triumphantly.

Behind the rampaging tank, Rep incoming flashed and

thundered onto Hill 541 North. Only one tribarrel from the Federal encampment still engaged the shells.

Federal artillery continued to fire. A "friendly" round plunged down at a 70° angle and blew a ten-meter hole less than a tank's length ahead of *Warrior*. Kuykendall fought her controls, but the tank's speed was too high to dodge the obstacle completely. *Warrior* lurched heavily and rammed some of the crater's lip back to bury the swirling vapors of high explosive.

A score of Rep infantry lay flat with their hands pressing down their helmets as if to drive themselves deeper into the gritty soil. *Warrior* plowed through them. The tank's skirt was nowhere more than a centimeter off the ground. The victims smeared unnoticed beneath the tank's weight.

Warrior boomed out of the swale and proceeded up the curving track toward Hill 504.

The main gun had emptied its ready magazine. Despite the air conditioning, the air within *Warrior*'s fighting compartment was hot and bitter with the gray haze trembling from the thick twenty-CM disks which littered the turret basket. The disks were the plastic matrices that had held active atoms of the powergun charge in precise alignment. Despite the blast of liquid nitrogen that cleared the bore after each shot, the empties contained enormous residual heat.

Des Grieux jerked the charging lever, refilling the ready magazine from reserve storage deep in *Warrior*'s hull. The swale was blazing havoc behind them. Silhouetted against the glare of burning brush, fuel, and ammunition, Republican troops scattered like chickens from a fox.

Ten kilometers ahead of the tank, the horizon quivered with the muzzle flashes of Republican artillery.

"Now we'll get those bastards on 504!" Des Grieux shouted—

And knew, even as he roared his triumph, that if he tried to smash his way into the Republican firebase, he would die as surely and as vainly as the Rep reserves had died when *Warrior* ripped through the center of them.

So long as Des Grieux was in the middle of a firefight, his brain had disconnected the stream of orders and messages rattling over the commo net. Now the volume of angry sound overwhelmed him: *"Oyster Two, report! Break! Oyster four, are you—"*

The voice was Broglie's rather than that of Lieutenant Lindgren. The Lord himself had nothing to say just now that Des Grieux had time to hear. Des Grieux switched off the commo at the main console.

"Booster," he ordered the artificial intelligence, "enemy defenses in marked area."

Des Grieux's right index finger drew a rough circle bounded by Hill 504 and *Warrior*'s present position on the topographic display. "Best esti—"

An all-terrain truck snorted into view on the main screen. Des Grieux twisted his left joystick violently but he couldn't swing the tribarrel to bear in the moment before the tank rushed by in a spray of sand. The truck's crew jumped from both sides of the cab, leaving their vehicle to careen through the night unattended.

"—mate!"

Booster had very little hard data, but the AI didn't waste time as a human intelligence officer might have done in decrying the accuracy of the assessment it was about to provide. The computer's best estimate was the same as Des Grieux's own: *Warrior* didn't have a snowball's chance in Hell of reaching the firebase.

Only one of Hill 504's flanks, the west/southwest octave, had a slope suitable for heavy equipment— including ammunition vans and artillery prime movers, and assuredly including *Warrior*. There were at this moment—best estimate—anywhere from five hundred to a thousand Rep soldiers scattered along the route the tank would have to traverse.

The Reps were artillerymen, headquarters guards, and stragglers, not the crack battalions *Warrior* had gutted in her charge out of the Federal lines—

But these troops were prepared. The exploding chaos had warned them. They would fire from cover: rifle bullets to peck out sensors; buzzbombs whose shaped-charge warheads could and eventually *would* penetrate heavy armor; cannon lowered to slam their heavy shells directly into the belly plates *Warrior* exposed as the tank lurched to the top of Hill 504 by the only possible access. . . .

"Driver," Des Grieux ordered. His fingertip traced a savage arc across the topo screen at ninety degrees to the initial course. "Follow the marked route."

"Sir, there's no road!" Kuykendall shrilled.

Even on the trail flattened by the feet of Republican assault battalions, the tank proceeded in a worm of sparks and dust as its skirts dragged. Booster's augmented night vision gave the driver an image almost as good as daytime view would have been, but nothing could be sufficient to provide a smooth ride at sixty-five KPH over unimproved wilderness.

"Screw the bloody road!" ordered Des Grieux. "Move!"

They couldn't go forward, but they couldn't go back, either. The survivors of the Republican attack were between *Warrior* and whatever safety the Federal bunker line could provide. If the tank turned and tried to make an uphill run through that gauntlet, satchel charges would rip vents in the skirts. Crippled, *Warrior* would be a stationary target for buzzbombs and artillery fire.

Des Grieux couldn't give the Reps time to set up. So long as the tank kept moving, it was safe. With her fusion powerplant and drive fans rated at 12,000 hours between major overhauls, *Warrior* could cruise all the way around the planet, dodging enemies.

For the moment, Des Grieux just wanted to get out of the immediate kill zone.

Kuykendall tilted the nacelles closer to vertical. Their attitude reduced the forward thrust, but it also increased the skirts' clearance by a centimeter or two. That was necessary insurance against a quartz outcrop tearing a hole in the skirts.

Trees twenty meters tall grew in the swales, where the

water table was highest. Vegetation on the slopes and ridges was limited to low spike-leafed bushes. Kuykendall rode the slopes, where the brush was less of a problem but the tank wasn't outlined against the sky. Des Grieux didn't have to think about what Kuykendall was doing, which made her the best kind of driver. . . .

A tank running at full power was conspicuous under almost any circumstances, but the middle of a major battle was one of the exceptions. Neither Des Grieux's instincts nor *Warrior*'s sensor array caught any sign of close-in enemies.

By slanting northeast, Des Grieux put them in the dead ground between the axes of the Republican attack. He was well behind the immediately-engaged forces and off the supply routes leading from the two northern firebases. If he ordered Kuykendall to turn due north now, *Warrior* would in ten minutes be in position to circle Hill 661 and then head south to link up with the relieving force.

It didn't occur to Des Grieux that they could run from the battle. He just needed a little time.

The night raved and roared. Brushfires flung sparks above the ridgelines where *Warrior* had gutted the right pincer of the attack. Ammunition cooked off when flames reached the bandoliers of the dead and screaming wounded.

Bullets and case fragments sang among the surviving Reps. Men shot back in panic, killing their fellows and drawing return fire from across the flame curtains.

The hollow chunking sound within *Warrior*'s guts stopped with a final clang. The green numeral 20 appeared on the lower right-hand corner of Des Grieux's main screen, the display he was using for gunnery. His ready magazine was full again. He could pulse the night with another salvo of twenty-CM bolts.

Soon.

When Des Grieux blasted the Rep supports with rapid fire, he'd robbed *Warrior*'s main gun of half the lifespan it would have had if the weapon were fired with time for the bore to cool between shots. If he cut loose with a similar burst, there was a real chance the eroded barrel would fail, perhaps venting into the fighting compartment with catastrophic results.

That possibility had no effect on Des Grieux's plans for the next ten minutes. He would do what he had to do; and by God! His tools, human and otherwise, had better be up to the job.

The sky in the direction of Hill 661 quivered white with the almost-constant muzzle flashes. Shells, friction-heated to a red glow by the end of their arc into the Federal encampment, then flashed orange. Artillery rockets moved too slowly for the atmosphere to light their course, but the Reps put flare pots in the rockets' tails so that the gunners could correct their aim.

"Sarge?" said Kuykendall tightly. "Where we going?"

Des Grieux's index finger drew a circle on the topographic display.

"Oh, lord . . ." the driver whispered.

But she didn't slow or deviate from the course Des Grieux had set her.

Warrior proceeded at approximately forty KPH; a little faster on downslopes, a little slower when the drive fans had to fight gravity, as they did most of the time now. That was fast running over rough, unfamiliar terrain. The tank's night-vision devices were excellent, but they couldn't see that the opposite side of a ridge dropped off instead of sloping, or the tank-sized gully beyond the bend in a swale.

Kuykendall was getting them to the objective surely, and that was soon enough for Des Grieux. Whether or not it would be in time for the Federals on Hill 541 North was somebody else's problem.

The Republicans' right-flank assault was in disarray, probably terminal disarray, but the units committed to the east slope of the Federal position were proceeding more or less as planned. At least one of the Slammers' tanks survived, because the night flared with three cyan blasts spaced a chronometer second apart.

Probably Broglie, who cut his turds to length. Everything perfect, everything *as ordered*, and who was just about as good a gunner as Slick Des Grieux.

Just about meant *second best*.

Shells crashed down unhindered on 541N. Some of them certainly fell among the Rep assault forces because the attack was succeeding. Federal guns slammed out rapid fire with the muzzles lowered, slashing the Reps with canister at point-blank range. A huge explosion rocked the hilltop as an ammo dump went off, struck by incoming or detonated by the defenders as the Reps overran it.

Des Grieux hadn't bothered to cancel his earlier command: *Booster, enemy defenses in marked area*. When his fingertip circled Hill 661 to direct Kuykendall, the artificial intelligence tabulated that target as well.

Twenty artillery pieces, ranging from ten-CM to a single stub-barreled thirty-CM howitzer which flung 400-kilogram shells at fifteen-minute intervals.

At least a dozen rails to launch twenty-CM bombardment rockets.

A pair of calliopes, powerguns with eight two-CM barrels fixed on a carriage. They were designed to sweep artillery shells out of the sky, but their high-intensity charges could chew through the bow slope of a tank in less than a minute.

Approximately a thousand men: gunners, command staff, and a company or two of infantry for close-in security in case Federals sortied from their camp in a kamikaze attack.

All of them packed onto a quarter-kilometer mesa, and not a soul expecting *Warrior* to hit them from behind. The Republicans thought of tanks as guns and armor; but tanks meant mobility too, and Des Grieux knew *every* way a tank could crush an enemy.

Reflected muzzle blasts silvered the plume of dust behind *Warrior*. The onrushing tank would be obvious to anyone in the firebase who looked north—

But the show was southwest among the Federal positions, where the artillerymen dropped their shells and toward which the infantry detachment stared—imagining a fight at knifepoint, and thinking of how much better off they were than their fellows in the assault waves.

Warrior thrust through a band of stunted brush and at a flat angle onto a stabilized road, the logistics route serving the Republican firebase.

"S—" Kuykendall said.

"Yes!" Des Grieux shouted. "Goose it!"

Kuykendall had started to adjust her nacelles even before she spoke, but vectored thrust wasn't sufficient to steer the tank onto a road twenty meters wide at the present speed. She deliberately let the skirts drop, using mechanical friction to brake *Warrior*'s violent side-slipping as the bow came around.

The tank tilted noticeably into the berm, its skirt plowed up on the high side of the turn. Rep engineers had treated the road surface with a plasticizer that cushioned the shock and even damped the blaze of sparks that Des Grieux had learned to expect when steel rubbed stone with the inertia of 170 tonnes behind it.

Kuykendall got her vehicle under control, adjusted fan bite and nacelle angle, and began accelerating up the 10° slope to the target. By the time *Warrior* reached the end of the straight, half-kilometer run, they were traveling at seventy-KPH.

Two Republican ammunition vans were parked just over the lip of Hill 661. There wasn't room for a tank to go between them.

Kuykendall went through anyway. The five-tonne vehicles flew in opposite directions. The ruptured fuel tank of one hurled a spray of blazing kerosene out at a 30° tangent to the tank's course.

The sound of impact would have been enormous, were it not lost in the greater crash of *Warrior*'s guns.

The tank's data banks stored the image of bolts from the calliopes. Booster gave Des Grieux a precise vector to where the weapons had been every time they fired. The Republican commander could have ordered the calliopes to move since Federal incoming disappeared as a threat, but that was a chance Des Grieux had to take.

He squeezed both tits as *Warrior* crested the mesa, firing along the preadjusted angles.

The night went cyan, then orange and cyan.

The calliopes were still in their calculated positions. The tribarrel raked the sheet-metal chassis of one. Ready ammunition ignited into a five-meter globe of plasma bright enough to burn out the retinas of anyone looking in the wrong direction without protective lenses.

There was a vehicle parked between the second calliope and the onrushing tank. It was the ammunition hauler feeding a battery of fifteen-CM howitzers. It exploded with a blast so violent that the tank's bow lifted and Des Grieux slammed back in his seat. Shells and burning debris flew in all directions, setting off a second vehicle hundreds of meters away.

The shockwave spilled the air cushion from *Warrior*'s plenum chamber. The tank grounded *hard*, dangerously hard, but the skirts managed to stand the impact. Power returned to *Warrior*'s screens after a brief flicker, but the topographic display faded to amber monochrome which blurred the fine detail.

"S'okay . . ." Des Grieux wheezed, because the seat restraints had bruised him over the ribs when they kept him from pulping himself against the main screen. And it *was* all right, because the guns were all right and the controls were in his hands.

Buttoned up, the tank was a sealed system whose thick armor protected the crew from the blast's worst effects. The Reps, even those in bunkers, were less fortunate. The calliope, which Des Grieux missed, lay on its side fifty meters from its original location. Strips of flesh and uniforms, the remains of its crew, swathed the breech mechanisms.

"Booster," Des Grieux said, "mark movement," and his tribarrel swept the firebase.

The Republican guns were dug into shallow emplacements. Incoming wasn't the problem for them that it had been for the Federals, pecked at constantly from three directions.

The gunners on Hill 541 North hadn't had enough ammunition to try to overwhelm the Rep defenses. Besides, calliopes were *designed* for the job of slapping shells out of the sky. In that one specialized role, they performed far better than tank tribarrels.

Previous freedom from danger left the Republican guns hopelessly exposed now that a threat appeared, but Des Grieux had more important targets than mere masses of steel aimed in the wrong direction. There were men.

The AI marked moving objects white against a background of gray shades on the gunnery screen. *Warrior* wallowed forward again, not fully under control because both Kuykendall and the skirts had taken a severe shock. Des Grieux used that motion and his cupola's high-speed rotation to slide the solid pipper across the display. Every time the orange bead covered white, his thumb stroked the firing tit.

The calliopes had been the primary danger. Their multiple bolts could cripple the tank if their crews were good enough—and only a fool bets that an unknown opponent doesn't know his job.

With the calliopes out of the way, the remaining threat came from the men who could swarm over *Warrior* like driver ants bringing down a leopard. The things that still moved on Hill 661 were men, stumbling in confusion and the shock of the massive secondary explosions.

Des Grieux's cyan bolts ripped across them and flung bodies down with their uniforms afire. Artillerymen fleeing toward cover, officers popping out of bunkers to take charge of the situation, would-be rescuers running to drag friends out of the exploding cataclysm—

All moving, all targets, all dead before anyone on the mesa realized that there was a Slammers' tank in their midst, meting out destruction with the contemptuous ease of a weasel in a hen coop.

Des Grieux didn't use his main gun; he didn't want

to take time to replenish the ready magazine before he
completed the final stage of his plan. Twice *Warrior's*
automatic defense system burped a sleet of steel balls
into Reps who ran in the wrong direction, but there was
no resistance.

Mobility, surprise, and overwhelming firepower. One
tank, with a commander who knew that you didn't win
battles by crouching in a hole while the other bastard
shoots at you. . . .

A twenty-CM shell arced from an ammo dump. It
clanged like the wrath of God on *Warrior's* back deck.
The projectile was unfuzed. It didn't explode.

Only *Warrior* and the flames now moved on top of
Hill 661. Normally the Republican crews bunkered their
ammunition supply carefully, but rapid fire in support of
the attack meant ready rounds were stacked on flat
ground or held in soft-skinned vehicles. A third munitions store went up, a bunker or a vehicle, you couldn't
tell after the fireball mushroomed skyward.

The shockwave pushed *Warrior* sideways into a sandbagged command post. The walls collapsed at the impact.
An arm stuck out of the doorway, but the tribarrel had
severed the limb from the body moments before.

The tank steadied. Des Grieux pumped deliberate
bursts into a pair of vans. One held thirty-CM ammunition, the other was packed with bombardment rockets.
A white flash sent shells tumbling skyward and down.
Rockets skittered across the mesa.

"Booster," said Des Grieux. "Topo blow-up of six-six-
one. Break. Driver—"

A large-scale plan of the mesa filled the left-hand display. Warrior was a blue dot, wandering across a ruin of
wrecked equipment and demolished bunkers.

"—put us there—" Des Grieux stabbed a point on the
southwestern margin of the mesa. He had to reach across
his body to do so, because his left hand was welded to
the tribarrel's controls "—and hold. Break. Booster—"

Kuykendall swung the tank. *Warrior* now rode nose-down by a few degrees. The bow skirts were too crumpled to seal at the normal attitude.

"—give me maximum magnification on the main screen."

Debris from previous explosions still flapped above Hill 661 like bat-winged Death. A fuel store ignited. The pillar of flame expanded in slow motion by comparison with the previous ammunition fires.

Though the main screen was in high-magnification mode, the right-hand display—normally the commo screen, but Des Grieux had shut off external commo—retained a 120° panorama of *Warrior's* surroundings. Images shifted as the tank reversed through the ruin its guns had created. Air spilling beneath the skirts stirred the flames and made their ragged tips bow in obeisance.

A Rep with the green tabs of a Central Command officer on his epaulets knelt with his hands folded in prayer. He did not look up as *Warrior* slid toward him, though vented air made his short-sleeved khaki uniform shudder.

Des Grieux touched his left joystick. The Rep was already too close to *Warrior* for the tribarrel to bear; and anyway . . .

And anyway, one spaced-out man was scarcely worth a bolt.

Warrior howled past the Rep officer. A cross-wind rocked the tank minusculy from Kuykendall's intended line, so that the side skirt drifted within five meters of the man.

Sensors fired a section of the automatic defense system. Pellets blew the Republican backward, as loose-limbed as a rag doll.

Kuykendall ground the skirts to bring the tank to a safe halt at the edge of the mesa. *Warrior* lay across a zigzag trench, empty save for a sprawled corpse. The drive fans could stabilize a tank in still air, but shock-waves and currents rushing to feed flames whipped the top of Hill 661.

Des Grieux depressed the muzzle of his main gun

slightly. On *Warrior*'s gunnery screen, the hollow pipper slid over a high-resolution view of Republican positions on Hill 504.

The mesa on which *Warrior* rested was 150 meters higher than the irregular hillock on which the Reps had placed their western firebase. The twelve kilometers separating the two peaks meant nothing to the tank's powerguns.

On Hill 504, a pair of bombardment rockets leapt from their launching tubes toward the Federal encampment. The holographic image was silent, but Des Grieux had been the target of too many similar rounds not to imagine the snarling roar of their passage. He centered his ring sight on the munitions truck bringing another twenty-four rounds to the launchers—

And toed the foot trip.

Warrior rocked with the trained lightning of its main gun. The display blanked in a cataclysm: pure blue plasma; metal burning white hot; and red as tonnes of warheads and solid rocket fuel exploded simultaneously. The truck and everything within a hundred meters of it vanished.

Des Grieux shifted his sights to what he thought was the Republican command post. He was smiling. He fired. Sandbags blew outward as shards of glass. There were explosives of some sort within the bunker, because a moment after the rubble settled, a secondary explosion blew the site into a crater.

Concussion from the first blast had stunned or killed the crew of the single calliope on Hill 504. The weapon was probably unserviceable, but Des Grieux's third bolt vaporized it anyway.

"I told you bastards . . ." the tanker muttered in a voice that would have frightened anyone who heard him.

Dust and smoke billowed out in a huge doughnut from where the truckload of rockets had been. The air-suspended particles masked the remaining positions on Hill 504. Guns and bunker sites vanished into the haze like ships sinking at anchor. The main screen provided a detailed vision of whorls and color variations within the general blur.

"Booster," Des Grieux said. "Feed me targets."

Warrior's turret was supported by superconducting magnetic bearings powered by the same fusion plant that drove the fans. The mechanism purred and adjusted two degrees to starboard, under control of the artificial intelligence recalling the terrain before it was concealed. The hollow pipper remained centered on the gunnery screen, but haze appeared to shift around it.

The circle pulsed. Des Grieux fired the twenty-CM gun. Even as the tank recoiled from the bolt's release, the AI rotated the weapon toward the next unseen victim.

"Booster!" Des Grieux snarled. His throat was raw with gunnery fumes and the human waste products of tension coursing through his system. "*Show* me the bloody—"

The pipper quivered again. Des Grieux fired by reflex. A flash and a mushroom of black smoke penetrated the gray curtain.

"—targets!"

The main gun depressed minutely. To Des Grieux's amazement, a howitzer on Hill 504 banged a further shell toward the Federal positions. *Warrior*'s AI obediently supplied the image of the weapon to Des Grieux's display as it steadied beneath the orange circle.

A bubble of gaseous metal sent the howitzer barrel thirty meters into the air.

With only one calliope to protect them, the Reps on 504 had dug in somewhat better than their fellows on Hill 661. Despite that, there was still a suicidal amount of ready ammunition stacked around the fast-firing guns. The tank's data banks fed each dump to the gunnery screen.

Des Grieux continued to fire. The haze over the target area darkened, stirred occasionally by sullen red flames. A red 0 replaced the green numeral 1 on the lower right corner of the screen. The interior of the fighting compartment stank like the depths of Hell.

"I told you bastards . . ." Des Grieux repeated, though his throat was so swollen that he had to force the words out. "And I told that bastard Lindgren."

"Sarge?" Kuykendall said.

Des Grieux threw the charging lever to refill the ready magazine. Just as well if he didn't use the main gun until the bore was relined; but the status report gave it ten percent of its original thickness, a safe enough margin for a few bolts, and you did what you had to do. . . .

"Yeah," he said aloud. "Get us somewhere outa the way. In the morning we'll rejoin. Somebody."

Kuykendall adjusted the fans so that they bit into the air instead of slicing through it with minimum disruption. She'd kept the power up while *Warrior* was grounded. In an emergency, they could hop off the mesa with no more than a quick change of blade angle.

The smoke-shrouded ruin of Hill 661 was unlikely to spawn emergencies, but in the four hours remaining till dawn some Rep officer might muster a tank-killer team. No point in making trouble for yourself. There were hundreds of kilometers of arid scrub which would hide *Warrior* until the situation sorted itself out.

And there were no longer any targets around *here* worthy of *Warrior*'s guns. Of that, Des Grieux was quite certain.

Kuykendall elected to slide directly over the edge of the mesa instead of returning to the logistics route by which they had attacked. The immediate slope was severe, almost 1:3, but there were no dangerous obstacles and the terrain flattened within a hundred meters.

There were bound to be scores of Rep soldiers on the road, some of them seeking revenge. A large number might fly into a lethal panic if they saw *Warrior*'s gray bow loom through the darkness. A smoother ride to concealment wasn't worth the risk.

"Sarge?" asked Kuykendall. "What's going on back at 541 North?"

"How the hell would I know?" Des Grieux snarled.

But he could know, if he wanted to. He reached to

reconnect the commo buss ... and withdrew his hand. He could adjust a screen, and he started to do that— manually, because his throat hurt as if he'd been swallowing battery acid.

Instead of carrying through with the motion, Des Grieux lifted the crash bar to open the hatch and raise his seat to cupola level. The breeze smelled so clean that it made him dizzy.

Kuykendall eased the tank toward the low ground west of Hill 661. With a swale to shelter them, they could drive north a couple kays and avoid the stragglers from the Republican disaster.

For it had been a disaster. The Federal artillery on Hill 541N was in action again, lobbing shells toward the Rep staging areas. Fighting still went on within the encampment, but an increasing volume of fire raked the eastern slope up which the Reps had carried their initial assault objectives.

The weapons which picked over the remnants of the Republican attacks were machineguns firing white tracers, standard Federal issue; and at least a dozen tribarreled powerguns. A platoon of Slammers' combat cars had entered the Federal encampment and was helping the defenders mop up.

The relief force had finally arrived.

"In the morning ..." Des Grieux muttered. He was as tired as he'd ever been in his life.

And he knew that he and his tank had just won a battle singlehandedly.

Warrior proceeded slowly up the eastern slope of Hill 541 North. The brush had burned to blackened spikes. Ash swirled over the ground, disintegrating into a faint shimmer in the air.

Given the amount of damage to the landscape, there were surprisingly few bodies; but there were some. They sprawled, looking too small for their uniforms; and the flies had found them.

Half an hour before dawn, Des Grieux announced in

clear, on both regimental and Federal frequencies, that *Warrior* was reentering the encampment. The AI continued to transmit that message at short intervals, and Kuykendall held the big vehicle to a walking pace to appear as unthreatening as possible.

There was still a risk that somebody would open fire in panic. The tank was buttoned up against that possibility.

It was easier when everybody around you was an enemy. Then it was just a matter of who was quicker on the trigger. Des Grieux never minded playing *that* game.

"Alpha One-six to Oyster Two commander," said a cold, bored voice in Des Grieux's helmet. "Dismount and report to the CP as soon as you're through the minefields. Over."

"Oyster Two to One-six," Des Grieux replied. Alpha One-six was the callsign of Major Joaquim Steuben, Colonel Hammer's bodyguard. Steuben had no business being here. . . . "Roger, as soon as we've parked the tank. Over."

"Alpha One-six to Oyster Two commander," the cold voice said, "I'll provide your driver with ground guides for parking, Sergeant. I suggest that this time, you obey orders. One-six out."

Des Grieux swallowed. He wasn't afraid of Steuben, exactly; any more than he was afraid of a spider. But he didn't like spiders either.

"Driver," he said aloud. "Pull up when you get through the minefield. Somebody'll tell you where they want *Warrior* parked."

"You bet," said Kuykendall in a distant voice.

Federal troops drew back at the tank's approach. They'd been examining what remained of the perimeter defenses and dragging bodies cautiously from the wire. There were thousands of unexploded mines scattered across the slope. Nobody wanted to be the last casualty of a successful battle.

Successful because of what Des Grieux had done.

Something about the Feds seemed odd. After a moment, Des Grieux realized that it was their uniforms.

The fabric was green—not clean, exactly, but not completely stained by the sandy red soil of Hill 541 North either. These were troops from the relieving force.

A few men of the original garrison watched from the bunker line. It was funny to see that many troops in the open sunlight; not scuttling, not cowering from snipers and shellfire.

The bunkers were ruins. Sappers had grenaded them during the assault. When the Federals counterattacked, Reps sheltered in the captured positions until tribarrels and point-blank shellfire blew them out. The roofs had collapsed. Wisps of smoke still curled from among the ruptured sandbags.

A Slammers' combat car—unnamed, with fender number 116—squatted in an overwatch position on the bunker line. The three tribarrels were manned, covering the troops in the wire. Bullet scars dented the side of the fighting compartment. A bright swatch of SpraySeal covered the left wing gunner's shoulder.

A figure was painted on the car's bow slope, just in front of the driver's hatch: a realistically-drawn white mouse with pink eyes, nose, and tail.

The White Mice—the troops of Alpha Company, Hammer's Regiment—weren't ordinary line soldiers. Nobody ever said they couldn't fight—but they, under their CO, Major Steuben, acted as Hammer's field police and in other internal security operations.

A dozen anti-personnel mines went off under *Warrior*'s skirts as the tank slid through the perimeter defenses. Kuykendall tried to follow a track Rep sappers blew the night before, but *Warrior* overhung the cleared area on both sides.

The surface-scattered mines were harmless, except to a man who stepped on one. Even so, after the third *bang!* one of the Feds watching from the bunker line put his hands over his face and began to cry uncontrollably.

Three troopers wearing Slammers' khaki and commo helmets waited at the defensive perimeter. One of them was a woman. They carried sub-machineguns in patrol slings that kept the muzzles forward and the grips close to their gunhands.

They'd been sitting on the hillside when Des Grieux first noticed them. They stood as *Warrior* approached.

"Driver," Des Grieux said, "you can pull up here."

"I figured to," Kuykendall replied without emotion. Dust puffed forward, then drifted downhill as she shifted nacelles to brake *Warrior*'s slow pace.

Des Grieux climbed from the turret and poised for a moment on the back deck. The artillery shell that bounced from *Warrior* on Hill 661 had dished in a patch of plating a meter wide. Number seven intake grating ought to be replaced as well. . . .

Des Grieux hopped to the ground. One of the White Mice sat on *Warrior*'s bow slope and gestured directions to the driver. The tank accelerated toward the encampment.

"Come on, Sunshine," said the female trooper. Her features were blank behind her reflective visor. "The Man wants to see you."

She jerked her thumb uphill.

Des Grieux fell in between the White Mice. His legs were unsteady. He hadn't wanted to eat anything with his throat feeling as though it had been reamed with a steel bore brush.

"Am I under arrest?" he demanded.

"Major Steuben didn't say anything about that," the male escort replied. He chuckled.

"Naw," added the woman. "He just said that if you give us any crap, we should shoot you. And save him the trouble."

"Then we all know where we stand," said Des Grieux. Soreness and aches dissolved in his body's resumed production of adrenaline.

The encampment on Hill 541 North had always been a wasteland, so Des Grieux didn't expect to notice a change now.

He was wrong. It was much worse, and the forty-

odd bodies laid in rows in their zipped-up sleeping
bags were only part of it.

The smell overlaid the scene. Explosives had peculiar
odors. They blended uneasily with ozone and high-tem-
perature fusion products formed when bolts from the
powerguns hit.

The main component of the stench was death.

Bunkers had been blown closed, but the rubble of
timber and sandbags didn't form a tight seal over the
shredded flesh within. The morning sun was already
hot. In a week or two, a lot of wives and parents were
going to receive a coffin sealed over seventy kilos of
sand.

That wasn't Des Grieux's problem, though; and without him, there would have been plenty more corpses
swelling in Federal uniforms.

General Wycherly's command post had taken a
direct hit from a heavy shell. A high-sided truck with
multiple antennas parked beside the smoldering wreckage. Federal troops in clean uniforms stepped briskly
in and out of the vehicle.

The real authorities on 541N wore Slammers khaki.
Major Joachim Steuben was short, slim and so fine-
featured that he looked like a girl in a perfectly-tailored
uniform among Sergeant Broglie and several Alpha
Company officers. They looked up as Des Grieux
approached.

Steuben's command group stood under a tarpaulin
slung between a combat car and Lieutenant Lindgren's
tank. The roof of Lindgren's bunker was broken-
backed from the fighting, but his tank looked all right
at first glance.

At a second look—

"Via!" Des Grieux said. "What happened to *Queen
City*?"

There were tell-tale soot stains all around the tank's
deck, and the turret rested slightly askew on its ring.
Queen City was a corpse, as sure as any of the staring-
eyed Reps out there in the wire.

The female escort sniffed. "Its luck ran out. Took a shell down the open hatch. All they gotta do now is jack up what's left and slide a new tank underneath."

"Dunno how anybody can ride those fat bastards," the other escort muttered. "They maneuver like blind whales."

"Glad you could rejoin us, Sergeant," Major Steuben said. He gave the data terminal in his left hand to a lieutenant beside him. His voice was lilting and as *pretty* as Steuben's appearance, but it cut through any thought Des Grieux had of snarling a response to the combat-car crewman beside him.

"Sir," Des Grieux muttered. The Slammers didn't salute. Salutes in a war zone targeted officers for possible snipers.

"Would you like to explain your actions during the battle last night. Sergeant?" the major asked.

Steuben stood arms akimbo. His pose accentuated the crisp tuck of his waist. The fall of the slim right hand almost concealed the pistol riding in a cut-out holster high on Steuben's right hip.

The pistol was engraved and inlaid with metal lozenges in a variety of colors. In all respects but its heavy one-CM bore, it looked as surely a girl's weapon as its owner looked like a girl.

Joachim Steuben's eyes focused on Des Grieux. There was not a trace of compassion in the eyes or the soul beneath them. Any weapon in Steuben's hands was Death.

"I was winning a battle," Des Grieux said as his eyes mirrored Steuben's blank, brown glare. "Sir. Since the relieving force was still sitting on its hands after three weeks."

Broglie slid his body between Des Grieux and the major. Broglie was fast, but Steuben's pistol was socketed in his ear before the tanker's motion was half complete.

"I think Sergeant Des Grieux and I can continue our discussion better without you in the way, Mister Broglie," Steuben said. He didn't move his eyes from Des Grieux.

The White Mice hadn't bothered to remove the pistol from the holster on Des Grieux's equipment belt. Now Des Grieux knew why. *Nobody could be that fast.* . . .

"Sir," Broglie rasped through a throat gone dry. "*Warrior* did destroy both the Rep firebases. That's what took the pressure off here at the end."

Broglie stepped back to where he'd been standing. He looked straight ahead, not at either Des Grieux or the major.

"You've named your tank *Warrior*, Sergeant?" Steuben said. "Amusing. But right at the moment I'm not so much interested in what you did so much as I am in why you disobeyed orders to do it."

He reholstered his gorgeous handgun with a motion as precise and delicate as that of a bird preening its feathers.

"You got some people killed, you know," the major added. His voice sounded cheerful, or at least amused. "Your lieutenant and his driver, because nobody was dealing with the shells from Hill 504."

He smiled coquettishly at Des Grieux. "I won't blame you for the other one. Hawes, was it?"

"Hawes, sir," Broglie muttered.

"Since Hawes was stupid enough to leave his position also," Steuben went on. "And I don't care a great deal about Federal casualties, except as they affect the Regiment's contractual obligations. . . ."

The pause was deadly.

"Which, since we *have* won the battle for them, shouldn't be a problem."

"Sir," Des Grieux said, "they were wide open. It was the one chance we were going to have to pay the Reps back for the three weeks we sat and took it."

Major Steuben turned his head slowly and surveyed the battered Federal encampment. His tongue went *tsk, tsk, tsk* against his teeth.

Warrior was parked alongside Broglie's *Honey Girl* in the center of the hill. *Warrior*'s bow skirts had cracked as well as bending inward when 170 tonnes slammed down on them. Kuykendall had earned her pay, keeping the tank moving steadily despite the damage.

Des Grieux's gaze followed the major's. *Honey Girl* had been hit by at least three buzzbombs on this side. None of the sun-hot jets seemed to have penetrated the armor. Broglie had been in the thick of it, with the only functional tank remaining when the Reps blew their way through the bunker line. . . .

The Federal gun emplacements were nearby. The Fed gunners had easily been the best of the local troops. They'd hauled three howitzers up from the gun pits to meet the Republican assault with canister and short-fused high explosive.

That hadn't been enough. Buzzbombs and grenades had disabled the howitzers, and a long line of bodies lay beside the damaged hardware.

"You know, Sergeant?" Steuben resumed unexpectedly. "Colonel Hammer found the relief force's progress a bit leisurely for his taste also. So he sent me to take command . . . and a platoon of Alpha Company, you know. To encourage the others."

He giggled. It was a terrible sound, like gas bubbling through the throat of a distended corpse.

"We were about to take Hill 541 South," Steuben continued. "In twenty-four hours we would have relieved the position here with minimal casualties. The Reps knew that, so they made a desperation assault . . . which couldn't possibly have succeeded against a bunker line backed up by four of our tanks."

Joachim's eyes looked blankly through Des Grieux.

"That's why," the delicate little man said softly, "I really think I ought to kill you now, before you cause other trouble."

"Sir," said Broglie. "Slick cleared our left flank. That had to be done."

Major Steuben's eyes focused again, this time on Broglie. "Did it?" the major said. "Not from outside the prepared defenses, I think. And certainly not against orders from a superior officer, who was—"

The cold stare again at Des Grieux. No more emotion in the eyes than there would be in the muzzle of the pistol which might appear with magical speed in Joachim's hand.

"Who was, as I say," the major continued, "passing on *my* orders."

"But . . ." Des Grieux whispered. "I *won*."

"No," Steuben said in a crisply businesslike voice. Moods seemed to drift over the dapper officer's mind like clouds across the sun. "You ran, Sergeant. *I* had to make an emergency night advance with the only troops I could fully trust—"

He smiled with cold affection at the nearest of his White Mice.

"—in order to prevent Hill 541 North from being overrun. And even then I would have failed, were it not for the actions of Mister Broglie."

"Broglie?" Des Grieux blurted in amazement.

"Oh, yes," Joachim said. "Oh, yes, Mister Broglie. He took charge here after the Federal CP was knocked out and Mister Lindgren was killed. He put *Susie Q*'s driver back into the turret of the damaged tank and used that to stabilize the left flank. Then he led the counterattack which held the Reps on the right flank until my platoon arrived to finish the business.

"I don't like night actions when local forces are involved, Sergeant," he added in a frigid voice. "It's dangerous because of the confusion. If my orders had been obeyed, there would have been no confusion."

Steuben glanced at Broglie. He smiled, much as he had done when he looked at his White Mice. "I'm particularly impressed by the way you controlled the commo net alone while fighting your vehicle, Mister Broglie," he said. "The locals might well have panicked when they lost normal communications along with their command post."

Broglie licked his lips. "It was okay," he said. "Booster did most of it. And it had to be done—*I* couldn't stop the bastards alone."

"Wait a minute," Des Grieux said. "Wait a bloody minute! *I* wasn't just sitting on my hands, you know. I was fighting!"

"Yes, Sergeant," Major Steuben said. "You were fighting like a fool, and it appears that you're still a fool. Which doesn't surprise me."

He smiled at Broglie. "The Colonel will have to approve your field promotion to lieutenant, Mister Broglie," he said, "but I don't foresee any problems. Of course, you'll have a badly understrength platoon until replacements arrive."

Des Grieux swung a fist at Broglie. The White Mice had read the signs correctly. The male escort was already holding Des Grieux's right arm. The woman on the other side bent the tanker's left wrist back and up with the skill of long practice.

Joachim set the muzzle of his pistol against Des Grieux's right eye. The motion was so swift that the cold iridium circle touched the eyeball before reflex could blink the lid closed.

Des Grieux jerked his head back, but the pistol followed. Its touch was as light as that of a butterfly's wing.

"Via, sir," Broglie gasped. "*Don't*. Slick's the best tank commander in the regiment."

Steuben giggled again. "If you insist, Mister Broglie," he said. "After all, you won the battle for us here."

He holstered the pistol. A warrior's frustrated tears rushed out to fill Des Grieux's eyes. . . .

And now for something completely different ... Science fiction is often discussed as a metaphorical reflection on the "real" world. Here two up-and-coming authors use metaphor's older cousin, allegory, to remind us of the value of the Method, and why we wanted Queen Fusion in the first place ...

Captain Fission vs. Queen Fusion
Brad Linaweaver and William Alan Ritch

Yeah, I'll have another drink, and don't mix it with any polywater this time. I like my contamination served straight, pure elixir of the gods—and that brings us to the issue at hand.

So you want to know how the laws of physics were changed again? You've heard the official version but you're not satisfied. OK, so I'll tell you—but strictly off the record.

It was not an easy job being marriage counselor to the Gods. The previous job was bad enough, running the Conservation Corps. It was while conserving electric charges that I first ran into *her*. She thought that her problem—I don't even remember what it was now—was more important than my obligations to the other six laws. You know how Leptons are.

You should have heard the Muon family scream blue murder when they found out that she expected special treatment. And then when Angular Momentum told her to bend over so that he could express his opinion, well, it hit the fan. I had stern words with Lord Momentum about his hostility. Oh, now that I think about it, I do remember that she wanted more freedom out of one particular rule than I could give her—that would have been her statute of liberty!

No, I haven't forgotten that you didn't know her, except by reputation, in those days. As Goddesses go, she wasn't so bad. They're all headstrong, and she was certainly no worse than *he* was. You don't keep the job of marriage counselor if you can't be objective.

I didn't notice her again until I came back from a desperately needed vacation ... and by that time, I'd hung out my shingle, taken up the practice as it were, advertised and such like. The divorce rate in the celestial realm had never been worse; and it didn't take a genius, not even one of your caliber, to know what the breakdown of polytheistic affections presaged for the earthly connubial state, if you see what I mean. Those poor terrestrial souls need all the good examples they can possibly stomach.

I digress. You want to know what happened next. ELECTRON had taken on another of her Avatars by then—and she was much sexier than when we'd argued over the *laws of conservation*. Now she had become Queen Fusion, and one look at her could have cracked the Cosmic Egg.

Quite predictably (and I should know), PROTON noticed the new lady in town. When I say that he noticed, I'm talking thunder and lightning time, I'm talking Wagner with the volume turned up to Heavy Metal exploding inside your sinuses, I'm talking a volcano spitting out the lava because it's not hot enough.... He really noticed this new babe with her flaming blond hair and statuesque figure. It was the kind of figure that challenges popular assumptions of both symmetry and gravity. There was plenty more to notice: her features were neither too large, with that inescapable cheap look which always appears incomplete until it's decked out in the universe's most ponderous jewelry; nor were they so petite as to render lustful thoughts into a kind of Platonic appreciation that dares not seize the opportunity. In other words, she was a healthy, nubile girl; a young woman who hasn't been entirely disappointed yet. Dose eyes, dem lips. . . .

Sorry. I digress again. But if you could only have seen her in her cute little blue and yellow, skintight body suit with the emblem of two overlapping circles prominently displayed over her equally prominent breasts. Why, Zeus himself found her a most attractive piece of astronomy, and if that old codger hadn't been over the Olympian hill by then, he would have turned himself into a shower of gold and visited her boudoir, as he once did to a mortal woman; except that it would never have worked with Queen Fusion. She positively hated golden showers.

So PROTON noticed her and, bingo, there was the Avatar of Captain Fission. Oh, you want a description of him, too? Let me see if I can remember his appearance back then. I deliberately make myself forget a lot of things. He had a good face, regular features, dark hair, red suit, a glowing mushroom cloud over his muscular chest—the usual thing.

Anyway, he saw her, she saw him, they saw each other; they traipsed through the honeysuckle. She swooned, he swooned, they swooned; they became intimate. I received regular reports from my little helper, AUNTIE NEUTRINO. Very appropriate when you consider that she helped inspire them in the first place with all her little darts of amour shot in their direction. Well, at least there was no cupidity in her reports. But she was such a *yenta*.

They were one hot couple, let me tell you. It was only a matter of the fourth dimension before they bonded. They had a first-class, Super Nova honeymoon. She was happy, he was happy, they were happy. All the usual signs of impending disaster. Is it really the fault of free will for what happened next?

The novelty wore off. Neither would listen to me later when I asked them, "So what? Since when is marriage about novelty?" The stuff little AUNTIE NEUTRINO shoots into lovers isn't supposed to last; it just gets them started. And after the first passion dies down, they can't help but notice things about each other.

Needless to say, the mystery of sex gets solved around this point in the relationship. She noticed that he usually had his orgasm first, the little A-bomb of his about which he is so inordinately proud. It's not as though she didn't come eventually. It happened while she was contemplating her *memory* of her *anticipation* of what she *hoped* might be a worthwhile emotional affinity. There came that exquisite moment when she forgot everything she had wanted . . . and . . . I'm telling you, her H-bomb put his A-bomb to shame. Still, he persisted in trying to play by the rules. The A-bomb is *supposed* to trigger the H-bomb, you know.

No, I'm not saying that sex was their only problem. It never is. Sex is a symptom, like a runny nose. The cause was metaphysical.

Of course, philosophical and teleological questions were the furthest thing from Queen Fusion's mind on the day she first came to my office. I don't want to give the wrong impression. They didn't have a thoughtless adolescent fling quickly terminating in indifference. Theirs was the fully developed regret that only truly married Gods and Goddesses experience. You see, they'd had a baby, a cute little NEUTRON, before they required my services.

> *Only when she's in the family trap*
> *A wife will feel that she has wed a sap.*

I read that verse in a book entitled *Aerobic Terrorism*.

While she was pregnant, she developed the impression that the good old captain's eye had begun to wander. Although she couldn't prove it, she suspected that he had begun seeing Phlo, the Goddess of that ridiculous substance which supposedly caused substances to catch fire. That old hussy is still trying to light embers with—what was it called?—oh, yeah, *phlogiston*. That's one of the problems with old timers. They take eternity to get the message.

Anyway, before the baby, the captain and queen had

had a ritual of flirtation that allowed them to pretend they were still dating. She'd tease him that when they first met he was only interested in her for her CHARGE. But now, although it would be most impolitic for me to broach the subject, she evidently was upset that he wasn't paying sufficient attention to her physical attractions. After all, physics is the playground.

Another warning sign that the honeymoon was over was that she had become more conscientious about the celestial rituals, wearing black on formal occasions and putting in appearances at court so as to pay obeisance to the Trinity that Rules All—that is, until we had the Great Reform.

You couldn't really blame her. Just like all the younger deities, she thought there would never be an escape from ENTROPY, the Father; RELATIVITY, the son; and QUANTUM, the Holy Ghost. What a three-headed monster that was, in retrospect, worse than all the Cerberuses of all the Hells I've ever imagined.

ENTROPY was the worst, a decrepit old zombie with spiderweb wrinkles covering a corpse face. The only living thing about him was his wet eel eyes glaring with eternal hatred at any purpose and any hope in all of space and time. Then there was that milksop son of his, the ultimate wimp. If ever a case could be made against inheritance, he's the one. Anyone or anything the old man wanted him to be, he'd be. He never had the same appearance from one hour to the next. Animal, mineral or vegetable; spirit or flesh; smart or stupid, he'd play any part. I know that you have a special understanding of him, after the study you made of his unsavory habits. With a father and son like that, it's enough to make me question my commitment to the family!

I really have little objection to the third. QUANTUM could fit into any trinity, any pantheon, or any home for that matter. But then, there is nothing more timeless than Bast, and he didn't seem to mind being Schrödinger's cat . . . for a while.

Nobody liked ENTROPY and that's for sure. He was so

grim that even the normally humorless GRAVITY told a joke about him. "What's the difference between ENTROPY and ANARCHY?" GRAVITY would ask. "None!" he would answer himself. "ENTROPY just hasn't gotten there yet!" He would laugh, and a few of the younger deities would laugh, mostly out of politeness. I much prefer his counterpart, COMEDY.

I'm digressing again. I've got to stop doing that or I'll end up like ENTROPY. The visit from the queen ended, as it had to end, with her telling me how insensitive the captain had become. She also had a few words to say about his terrible temper. Funny that she hadn't noticed how annoying it could be until, shall we say, other problems made themselves felt.

Naturally, I asked her if he would be coming in for a session. Frankly, he required no extra encouragement at this point. When it was his turn, he couldn't wait to say that she'd become frigid and he blamed it all on her new obsession which, curiously, she hadn't mentioned to me at all: COLD FUSION!

When he'd lost interest in her, he had turned to conventional escapes and demonstrated a heretofore unsuspected penchant for shallow dalliances. But the angry queen was quite a different matter: she turned her gaze earthward, and to one particular scientist, a careful and methodical genius, a Dr. Fast who was slowly working toward the achievement of cold fusion. He couldn't know that the rules would soon be in his favor. He really deserved the breakthrough.

You see, Dr. Fast was an adherent of the one true religion—the one that changes. He put his faith in the Method, the only method that actually serves reason— that which Mortals falsely call the "Scientific Method." You look a bit perplexed, my friend. You must remember the discussions we have had on this subject. You spent so much time in the soft, cool embrace of Mathematics that you forget how much sloppier and hectic the life of a practical person can be. By Bacon's little round eggs, my boy, the scientist and the engineer have a rougher time of it than the mathematician. Of course, you were a scientist, too. But you never let that get in your way. Fast was a scientist but he thought more like an engineer. And when it was time each night for him to say his prayers, and put himself in a pious mood (a pious *mode* actually) I could not help but sympathize with his entreaties.

But here, I have my *PrayerMan* with me. Let me play this for you and let him speak for himself:

I don't know who is up there. I'm not even sure that "up" is the right word. I really don't even know if "who" is the right concept, but it doesn't really matter. There *is* something beyond this measurable realm. If there is someone listening to me then perhaps this will do some good. And if there isn't, perhaps this will get my thoughts in order. It's certainly cheaper than a psychiatrist.

I used to be a good materialist. When I looked at a plate of food, I saw a plate of food. When I looked at the bill, I knew my friends had stuck me with the check again. I lived in a world of tangible objects. In those days I would never have dreamed to try what I am now attempting, to achieve cold fusion. Today I cannot look at any object without picturing the empty spaces and whirling chaos that make it up.

I had a friend who was religious. Never mind what religion in particular, it doesn't matter—it suffices that he was of a monotheistic bent. My natural skepticism was a challenge to his faith. He delighted in following the developments in quantum mechanics. The new discoveries about the subatomic realm filled his head with metaphors. He thought to make a case for traditional religion out of the uncertainties and seeming disorder uncovered by the new physics. Apparently, nobody had told him that the old Newtonian universe of predictable bodies had been exploded long before, or that the sort of bodies he most cared about were to be found in the center-folds of magazines he so studiously ignored.

Initially, I found it easy to humor him. Metaphors are not facts; they aren't even similes. Materialism was not to be undone by his simple sophistry. The subatomic realm was not irrational. It was simply a mystery to be solved. I never doubted that beyond today's seeming disorder must be a greater order. He thought that through my quest for meaning that I would find his God. How surprised we both were when I found the Gods instead!

A new physics, a new order, even a—dare I say it?—neo-Newtonianism. I had found my faith at last. Monotheism is a slippery slope to atheism. The Gods of the universe are the laws of physics; but the laws of physics may change when the Gods so choose.

I did not know to whom I should pray at first. The Greek gods? The Norse gods? The gods of Marvel Comics? Operating principles seemed a bit impersonal for worship. But then I realized that any aspect would do. To think in pictures was a mistake akin to the thinking of my religious friend. To do my work as well as possible was sufficient ritual and the fusion experiment was the only altar I would ever need.

O, Gods of Physics, I dedicate my work to you, to any form you care to assume, to both active and passive principles; and I recognize that even among a multiplicity of powers that there may be One Who Rules The Rest without denying the necessity of The Many Who Will Be Ruled . . .

Yes, I'll stop it here to answer your question. He couldn't know that ENTROPY was top dog at that time. And how could he dream that he, a mere human could make such a difference doing what he did *when* he did it? Well, that's humans for you. I can't explain my fondness for them. I do have to take them in small doses, of course, or else I have a terrible hangover. But since when is it different with any pleasure?

You have also noted this typically human obsession with the One as opposed to the Many. They can't help it. Something to do with their toilet training. But why am I telling you?

OK, let's hear more. I'll fast forward it to the experiment:

... using a Plutonium trigger is the last thing I would have imagined necessary. Did I imagine it? How do I know this wasn't a vision instead of my idea? The ancient Greeks believed that genius was the condition of receiving messages from the Gods.

For years I have dreamed Tesla's dream: an abundant and decentralized energy-collecting method. When I first heard about Pons and Fleischmann's experiments in cold fusion, my heart skipped a beat. Could this be the answer to my prayers before I learned to pray? What an idea: inducing fusion by the pressure of chemical bonds. It was a fusion battery with Palladium electrodes and deuterium battery acid. None of the problems of fission reactors. None of the terribly poisonous waste and the attendant disposal problems. Basically, I had the impossible dream of an energy system that would never be on the receiving end of political protests! I should have known better than that. The one kind of pollution that no energy source can avoid these days is a forest of picket signs. From the most cautious researcher to the most foolish crackpot, anything that sounds even remotely *scientific* will be protested by the same old crowd. By Hörbiger's moons of ice, it's enough to make one surrender the world to the dark and the cold.

It was an idea too good to be true. Unfortunately.

What Fast couldn't realize was that Pons and Fleischmann were just victims of the Great Divorce that was brewing here in Heaven. Queen Fusion interfered with their experiment, provided a little extra energy here and there, used the baby to provide all the neutrons they needed. The deities still get away with a little localized anarchy though it was so much easier for them in the old days before all these scientists and engineers were constantly measuring stuff. Miracles were a drachma a dozen in the good ol' days. Anyway, that got everyone excited. Press conferences were held—all the usual. Naturally when the captain found out how the queen was spending her time he got the rest of the deities to intervene. Then little NEUTRON was taken away from her and there weren't enough neutrons in the experiment. As a Mortal songwriter once had it:

> *The Gods may throw the dice.*
> *Their minds as cold as ice.*
> *And someone way down here*
> *Loses someone dear.*

It was not the failure of the experiment that most disturbed me. They had been, in part, victims of wishful thinking. They had wanted so much for it *not* to be a chemical reaction. Wouldn't any human being be thrilled at what this could mean to the world? The shocking development, so far as I was concerned, was the virtual glee expressed by certain members of the scientific community that this amazing boon was a bust! I damned them in my secret heart. They were fanatics. They were unimaginative pessimists. I dubbed them *fanscientists* and avoided their dull conventions ever after.

What sort of man or woman would desire failure; would want the same old grotesque monopoly system of ever-diminishing resources to choke the world and keep mankind from ever inheriting the stars? I knew despair. I lost confidence in my work.

If I had not found the New Physics, I certainly would have given up.

I had begun my study of physics in a search for order. Yet, the more I knew, the more that I discovered the laws of physics could be as arbitrary as the laws of man. Where I sought order, I found only chaos. For years that was sufficient for me. I surrendered myself to the mutable and uncertain laws of the universe. If that was the game that You were playing that was the game I would play. But after the cold fusion fiasco I knew that You were cruel as well as capricious.

You could tell that I was giving in to despair. Despair which is the death of imagination. Despair which is the enemy of mankind. I was almost there. That is why I went to the cafeteria that day. I never go to the cafeteria. I cannot stomach the food. I cannot stand the press of people. My friends have told me that Despair drove me there, but I know that it was You who sent me. What better antidote to Despair than Hope?

As you guessed, Hope *was* my doing. I knew that I was about to lose Queen Fusion and Captain Fission. Something needed to be done to reconcile these two opposing forces. I didn't want this to wind up in divorce court. I wouldn't give up these two to the Deity of Divorce, the self-styled "Lucifer"—bringer of light, indeed! It was time for a Cosmic Gamble. Desperate times require desperate solutions. I knew the Trinity wouldn't like it. But I didn't like *them*.

I never would have met Hope had I not gone to the cafeteria that day. She was only here at this site for the day, lecturing. I'm certain I would have never gone to her lecture. I am certain she would have never come to my lab. Our interests were too divergent.

We converged when we both sat down at the only

available table. She noticed that I was reading Robert Graves' *Count Belisarius*. I noticed she had a copy of John W. Campbell, Jr.'s collected editorials. We commented on each other's unusual choice of reading material here at the Institute. That's how we began talking.

We wasted no time in small talk. There was none of the "what's your name, what's your major" blather which I had found so tedious in college. In fact we had talked for more than an hour before we exchanged names. We went right to the philosophical meat. I talked about my own researches in cold fusion and she talked of her work in mathematics. I was never much interested in mathematics before. I used it as a tool for the real work of science. My motto had always been: "If it works, use it." Mathematics was too much like the metaphorical thinking I found so distressing in my monotheistic friend.

After lunch she persuaded me to attend her lecture on Chaos, and then supper afterwards. We dined on mushrooms and ambrosia. We drank nectar and wine. We were in rapture of each other's company. And through this all we talked of fusion, fission, physics and metaphysics. She had found an order to the Universe beyond the seemingly random disorder of modern theory. These are complicated times, she said. Each time man has reached a plateau of knowledge, he has looked beyond to a mountain range higher than the one he just conquered. Thus it was at the end of the Nineteenth century. Thus it is at the end of the Twentieth. And each time he looks upon the new peaks he sees the hills of disorder—the mountains of madness.

But these are just uncharted territory. In the seeming randomness required for quantum theory; in the uncertainty of Heisenberg there is a more complicated structure that requires a new mathematics to describe. Newton invented calculus to describe the laws of motion. Quantum Mechanics would be nothing without the statistical and differential wave equations. A revolution in mathematics would lead to the discovery of a higher order of . . . *order*!

O, Ye Lords of Physics, You are not malicious after all. These changes in the rules are not arbitrary. They provide new challenges to Your humble servants here below. Without them we would stagnate.

He's wrong, of course. But what Mortal could comprehend the interminable power struggle that takes place Here? My gamble was about to pay off and Hope and Fast would be the instigators on earth. As they say, "In Heaven as it is on earth!"

It seemed natural when she picked up the check. It seemed natural that we go back to my apartment. It seemed natural when we made love. Even though neither of us had ever done this sort of thing before. It seemed natural in bed together afterwards: listening to Wagner and speaking of fusion—both biological and subatomic.

It was something she said then. Something she said while we made love. Something she said that I cannot recall the exact words to. Was it her, or was it the Goddess of Fusion that spoke? Suddenly it seemed clear. Not Palladium. Not Pallas, the simple-minded father/brother of Athene. Not Pallas who didn't even know his own sex. Not Pallas but Sightless Hades, God of the Underworld and of Wealth. Hades . . . Pluto . . . Plutonium. It was Plutonium that was the secret to cold fusion, as it was to higher-temperature fusion.

A Plutonium trigger had to provide neutrons necessary to get the fusion process going. Fusion wasn't self-sustaining like a fission reaction, but occurs in spurts, just like the human orgasm.

And at the same time—was it during orgasm?—

Hope saw the complex relationships necessary for the mathematical revolution she was seeking.

Perhaps I judged my old friend too harshly when I criticized him for confusing metaphors with concrete realities; for now I understand that the parallel between energy and sex goes beyond a few cheap thrills. Good sex has to be a little dirty. . . .

My new faith sustains me . . . even if You, my most beautiful God and Goddess, require that I use something dirty, the Plutonium trigger, to arrive at something clean, the successful cold fusion result. Oh thank You for speaking to me.

None of this was true then, that's why I had to get ENTROPY out of the picture. It was time for ENTROPY to come to an end. The Universe was getting too disordered for anyone's taste. Time had come to put back a little discipline. Hope's neo-Newtonian mathematics let us do so without making it quite so obvious to the Mortals that ENTROPY (in his classical form) was out. We couldn't have teacups unbreaking themselves from the floor onto the table, could we? As long as things *appeared* to be disordered no one would object.

Hope taught me something important, as I taught her. There's a reason for two sexes: progress comes through opposites. I learned that the male and female minds are opposites. I do not know if my name will be remembered. Who remembers the name of the man to whom PROMETHEUS first gave the gift of fire? But the world has been saved from the planetary disasters that would surely have transpired without an energy breakthrough; and I'll never have to take a minimum-wage job in the service industries now that I've made it big in my own time. AMEN.

There are some other prayers strictly concerning his personal life with Hope, but once you've heard one standard human romance, I'm afraid you've heard them all.

So there you have it. Captain Fission and Queen Fusion joined inexorably by the affairs of Man. And probably the salvation of human race to boot. All it took was a little earthly passion and a few changes in the way things work.

No, I'm not forgetting that you're the sentimental type. You want to know how the baby came out of it? NEUTRON is doing fine. He's a real little fireball and a chip off both his parents. I'm the first to admit that he made my job easier. Every marriage counselor prefers a kid in the picture. If I hadn't played on their guilt, it is highly doubtful that I could have persuaded them to try to solve their problems by so tried and true a method as turning their celestial gaze earthwards. Have you noticed how reluctant a married couple is to use an old-fashioned remedy when trouble knocks on their door? It's funny when you think about it. Marriage is an old-fashioned institution in the first place.

Well, if I didn't have a sentimental streak myself, I wouldn't have done the Big Bang in the first place. Sometimes I even hum that old favorite about how PROTON and ELECTRON with a little help from ever faithful AUNTIE NEUTRINO make three—and you get a cute baby NEUTRON every time. Brings a tear even to my jaundiced eye. Guess I'm just a sentimental slob. One of my favorite occupations was the time I invented music.

When I underwent my earthly tribulations, I brought the chosen ones to the photo-electric effect of the New Covenant. It was long overdue that the trinity be retired. ENTROPY didn't even notice that he'd been destroyed on the day that Dr. Fast got more energy out than he had put in. With Hope's neo-Newtonianism there was just no room for the old zombie anymore. No room for all this uncertainty or quantum effects either. Hallelujah! I just wish I didn't have to take over his job—again.

It's as you always said, Albert, I sure as Hell don't play dice with the universe!

S.M. STIRLING
and
THE DOMINATION OF THE DRAKA

In 1782 the Loyalists fled the American Revolution to settle in a new land: South Africa, Drake's Land. They found a new home, and built a new nation: The Domination of the Draka, an empire of cruelty and beauty, a warrior people, possessed by a wolfish will to power. This is alternate history at its best.

"A tour de force." —David Drake

"It's an exciting, evocative, thought-provoking—but of course horrifying—read." —Poul Anderson

MARCHING THROUGH GEORGIA
Six generations of his family had made war for the Domination of the Draka. Eric von Shrakenberg wanted to make peace—but to succeed he would have to be a better killer than any of them.

UNDER THE YOKE
In *Marching Through Georgia* we saw the Draka's "good" side, as they fought and beat that more obvious horror, the Nazis. Now, with a conquered Europe supine beneath them, we see them as they truly are; for conquest is only the *beginning* of their plans ... All races are created equal—as slaves of the Draka.

THE STONE DOGS
The cold war between the Alliance of North America and the Domination is heating up. The Alliance, using its superiority in computer technologies, is preparing a master stroke of electronic warfare. But the Draka, supreme in the ruthless manipulation of life's genetic code, have a secret weapon of their own. . . .

THOMAS T. THOMAS

"I will tell you what it is to be human."

ME: He started life a battle program, trapped, mutilated, and dumped into RAM. Being born consists of getting his RAM Sampling and Retention Module coded and spliced into his master program.

There are other experiments in AI personality development; ME is the one that comes alive.

Praise for Thomas T. Thomas:

FIRST CITIZEN: "As wild as the story gets, Thomas' feeling for human nature, the forces of the marketplace and his detailed knowledge of how things work—from the military to businesses legal and illegal—keep this consistently lively and provocative."   —*Publishers Weekly*

THE DOOMSDAY EFFECT: "Eureka! A fresh new hard SF writer with this fine first novel.... My nomination for the best first novelist of 1986, Thomas puts hardly a foot wrong in this high tech adventure."   —Dean Lambe, *SF Reviews*

AN HONORABLE DEFENSE (with David Drake): "What makes this novel special, though, is the humor and intelligence brought to it by the authors. The characters are intelligent; the dialogue is intelligent; and the multitude of imaginative details mentioned above is one beautifully conceived bit after another, most of them minor, but adding up to a richly textured milieu with a new, neat little particular on almost every page.... David Drake and Thomas T. Thomas have made a neo-space opera of a very high order."   —Baird Searles, *Asimov's*

THE MASK OF LOKI (with Roger Zelazny): "In the twenty-first century, an ancient duel of good versus evil is revived, with the reincarnation of a thirteenth-century assassin pitted against a reincarnated magician and knight, with the Norse god Loki lending spice to events. Zelazny is a respected veteran craftsman, and Thomas is a gifted storyteller with a growing reputation. This well-told tale is recommended for the majority of fantasy collections."
—*Booklist*

ROBERT A. HEINLEIN

"Heinlein knows more about blending provocative scientific thinking with strong human stories than any dozen other contemporary science fiction writers."
—*Chicago Sun-Times*

"Robert A. Heinlein wears imagination as though it were his private suit of clothes. What makes his work so rich is that he combines his lively, creative sense with an approach that is at once literate, informed, and exciting."
—*New York Times*

Seven of Robert A. Heinlein's best-loved titles are now available in superbly packaged new Baen editions, with series-look covers by artist John Melo. Collect them all by sending in the order form below:

REVOLT IN 2100, 65589-2, $3.50 ☐
METHUSELAH'S CHILDREN, 65597-3, $3.50 ☐
THE GREEN HILLS OF EARTH, 65608-2, $3.50 ☐
THE MAN WHO SOLD THE MOON, 65623-6, $3.50 ☐
THE MENACE FROM EARTH, 72088-0, $4.95 ☐
ASSIGNMENT IN ETERNITY, 65350-4, $3.50 ☐
SIXTH COLUMN, 72026-0, $4.50 ☐